A MAN

Doc saw the creature before he heard the gurgling, purring snarl. *Smilodon californicus*—Sabertooth Tiger! It stepped from shadow into moonlight, pausing to consider the scent of two prospective victims.

Epworth heard the gurgling, throaty snarl, and he saw the gleaming coat ripple as the muscles played. He stood paralyzed, but Doc bounded, gripping the bamboo spear. Having started before the tiger, he was in place when the animal picked his quarry.

The glass-hard, curved-chisel edge caught the white furred belly and sank deep, driven home by the force of the charge. Doc was yanked from his knees before he could let go of his pike, when a small man pounced from darkness. An axe flashed . . .

OPERATION LONGLIFE

E. Hoffmann Price

A Del Rey Book

BALLANTINE BOOKS • NEW YORK

A Del Rey Book
Published by Ballantine Books

Library of Congress Catalog Card Number: 82-90448

ISBN 0-345-30715-1

Manufactured in the United States of America

First Edition: January 1983

Cover art by Darrell K. Sweet

In memory of
Edmond & Leigh Brackett Hamilton:
The happy days I shared with them;
&
with all the other Hamiltons
since 1930.

Chapter 1

That his one hundred eighty-sixth birthday stared Avery Jarvis—"Doc"—Brandon in the face had a good deal to do with engaging a technical and administrative assistant to give him a hand with the genetic engineering foundation and Nameless Island's experimental teak forest. During his first year on the job, Oswald Fenton—Sc.D., Ph.D., and a Master's in Business Administration—had done well indeed. However, Nameless Island was a vortex of emotional problems, actual and prospective, which threatened to complicate a situation not as simple as it appeared,

Oswald Fenton was 158 years younger than Brandon; Mona, six years younger than Oswald, did all the office work when not too busy being the Old Man's dream girl. The young persons had emotions, and so did Doc, but his had created a problem which they did not have and would never live to have.

Doc and his assistant sat in the lounge of the Brandon Genetic Engineering Foundations's guest house, which was perched on a headland overlooking the Atlantic Ocean. Isaiah Winthrop, Litt.D., the Black steward, brought rye and soda, which was not Doc's drink. The younger man would have been ill at ease, might even have felt inferior, watching the Old Man tackling absinthe drips, snorts of 151-proof Demerara rum, unblended Islay Scotch whiskey, or other goodies favored by Men of Iron.

Oswald Fenton's rangy frame slouched comfortably into

1

a rattan chair: a good-looking youngster, in a rugged way, and sunblasted more than one of darker pigmentation would have been. That bitch of an earthquake of 2052 had neither raised Atlantis nor any remains thereof but it had caused a shift of the Gulf Stream, so that Nameless Island, no great way south of Savannah, became tropical.

Oswald brushed back his perfectly pomaded sandy-blond hair, a nervous habit which mildly irritated Doc Brandon. The older he became, the more irritable: And since he appeared to be in his middle thirties, irritability would be unseemly.

"Your work has been good, Oswald. Your thinking is good." Doc swirled his rye and mineral water. *"God-damn swill! These young punks can't outgrow the soda pop they were raised on."* Then, audibly, "You look thirsty. Drink up, man, drink up."

Oswald did a neat bottoms-up. Doc resumed, "You are dedicated. You have an ingredient which I did not mention in the job specs. Something so scarce that no realist would be so unchristly stupid as to ask for."

"May *I* be so stupid as to ask what that is?"

Doc chuckled, wagged his head appreciatively. "Since you have already asked, I'll answer. Vision. Imagination. Before you sign a long-term contract, you'd better be sure about a number of trifles. Such as, it's twenty kilometers to the mainland, and you know the hinterland, that jungle of Alleluia Stompers feuding with the Testifiers as to which is saved?"

Oswald smiled, recalling the country through which he had passed to meet Doc for the initial interview. "They were quite plentiful around Jump Off and Fiery Gizzard."

"Then you don't need reminding that Megapolitan life would be a long way off, no matter how long you worked here. Meanwhile, however well qualified you are, you've not had time to decide whether this isolated spot would have a long-term appeal. If you got fed up and resigned, I'd regret it, though it'd be no disaster for me. But at your age, time is significant."

"Dr. Brandon, this is an opportunity many have been wanting. It's the first time you've invited anyone to work with you."

"I'm glad to hear that from you. Mmmm . . ." Doc eyed the young man, looking through him, until without warning he blasted him with a question: "How are you and Amina getting along?"

Fenton blinked, gulped. "Ah—uh—um—she's most congenial."

"You don't sound too God-damned enthusiastic!"

"Sir—uh—that was an unusual and sudden question."

Doc smiled, nodded. "An invasion of privacy, but it is relevant. The Malays, male or female, they're amazing people, natural aristocrats, proud and touchy. Reason I ask is that it takes more than social theories and democratic propaganda to bridge what are called cultural gaps. We are not 'all the same.' There is more than a difference in complexion. The idea that environment makes the culture is nonsense. It's the innate qualities which shape the culture! Forget democratic hogwash! The psyche is born different."

Doc paused for breath. Oswald said, "Ah—uh—um—"

"What I mean is, are you sure you and Amina are compatible? If you're not, there are some charming unattached Burmese girls in the village and a few elegant Eurasians.

"You may have attachments, memories of back home? An Occidental girl, one of your own people? How long could she be happy here after the honeymoon is over?" Doc snapped to his feet. "I've got to make a phone call. You relax and do a bit of cogitating. Be back presently."

Doc said to the steward, "Isaiah, drip me one of the usual."

He needed a few minutes to integrate past and present. The Malay, the Burmese, the other exotica he had not mentioned to Oswald were not harassed by the kinks and quirks of his own people. That he had questioned Oswald regarding the arrangement with Amina indicated to Doc that he had had his own wonderings.

More than that, the master of Nameless Island had a problem which had grown out of his experiment in anthropology some twenty-two years ago. Brandon had found a home for Mona, then an infant, in the heartland colony of the Alleluia Stompers, fine old Anglo-Saxon fundamentalists, a significant minority dedicated to guarding the morals and saving the damned, that is, most other citizens of the

Parliamentary Republic of North America. Doc knew all about Mona's heredity. As a genetic engineer, he had undertaken to learn what effect her puritanical childhood environment would have on her expressing herself as an adult. As she had quit the Alleluia Stompers in her late teens, the investigation, Phase One, was complete.

It was Phase Two and the emotional complications which were giving Doc Brandon a package of serious pains.

More than a century and a half previous, Doc and Iris started with happy years which became miseries when her fifties, sixties, seventies became a losing fight to continue looking and living as did her spouse, an apparently perpetual middle-thirties athlete and Man of Iron.

Iris died fighting. Doc lived, grieving. And now, after five years with Doc, Mona had become a problem. The only fair deal was to let Mona undertake Phase Two, quitting Nameless Island, to meet life in the Parliamentary Republic. That would not only be in the furtherance of science. It would also be saving himself and Mona from what he and Iris had endured.

There was only one obstacle. Each had become quite too fond of the other.

Returning to the lounge, Doc picked up where he had left off. "I was about to say, any time you and Amina have problems, there are unattached Burmese girls in the village and several quite attractive Eurasians—a perfectly fabulous aesthetic appeal, the Eurasian woman, and a liberal education.

"Oh, hell! I'm digressing again. What I've been getting at is that you've had my secretary on the brain ever since you got your first look. Sit down, Oswald, sit down! I don't blame you one God-damn tiny little bit! It's only the way you look at Mona, especially when that backside is toward you. And the front view does things to you. Your height and her see-more *piña*-fiber blouses—you'd have to have marbles and buttons missing, not to go pop-eyed and blinking."

Oswald gulped and chewed air.

"Your girl-watcher expression is a dead giveaway. You

look as though you'd chew her girdle on the courthouse steps at high noon."

"Sir—Dr. Brandon! I give you my word—"

"Of course you've not got out of line! If you'd got anywhere at all, you'd not have that expression, that drooling look, whenever Mona's within smelling distance. I told you, I don't blame you a bit. Without the appreciation of women, good liquor, and good books, life would be too dreary to be lived."

Good fellowship and understanding reassured Oswald. "I never realized that I was so obvious about it."

"Before you sign the contract, take time off. Go back to your hometown, make the rounds of Megapolis Alpha, and try Beta if you're in the mood. All expenses are on the Foundation—'Personnel Recruitment' or something equally ponderous.

"See how special girls look and sound now, after you've been away for a year. Whatever you said in your leavetakings is history. What counts is how you feel about them and how you look to them. You may have a girl back there who would love a spot like this. Amina has no claim on you. I made that clear to her from the beginning.

"Getting back to your work: When you insisted on lowering the pressure in the ionization chamber to sterilize air that'd eventually leak out of the laboratory, the Board of Visitors was crusading, raising hell on that very point, all up and down the country. We got good marks. And you got full credit.

"With your record here, there are plenty of spots on the mainland that'd be yours for the taking." He thrust out his hand. "Good luck, whatever you do."

With Oswald Fenton on his way, Doc Brandon remained to cope with a problem not so readily solved.

Although he had never told her, Mona was a product of genetic engineering, one of the sixth generation of Simianoids who kept the country going. Thanks to gene splicing and cloning, this happy blend of chimpanzee and human permitted the standard citizens of the Parliamentary Republic, coddled and thought controlled, to lead the Magnificent Life. Neither Doc nor his late father had anticipated the extremes to which Gracious Living would go. The elder

Brandon, not endowed with life everlasting, had left his son to cope with what science had achieved. As far as women had been concerned, the coping had been varied and congenial.

Whether Asiatic or Occidental, each had gone her way, half sadly quitting a cozy relationship and quite happily returning to her own world, her own generation, with an endowment which neither lovers nor husbands could touch. She could assign neither capital nor income deriving from the Brandon Foundation. Some became Pleasure, Vice, & Recreation girls, others, career women in less interesting fields, and quite a few married happily, with beautiful children to increase the congestion of the overpopulated Parliamentary Republic.

With Mona it had been different. Despite rigorously puritanical indoctrination, her hereditary skepticism kept her from being tainted by environment. She was the perfect yes-girl, agreeing with the overwhelming majority and resolutely looking forward to doing as she damn well pleased. The Alleluia Stompers never suspected that they had failed to instill in Mona the standard American sense of guilt—instinct told her that Adam had been very lucky when Eve tempted him with something without which the Garden of Eden would have been a hellish spot.

Without suspecting that there might be an arrangement in her future, Mona responded to her feeling that she was old enough and big enough: a spontaneous combustion so prolonged that negotiation would have been a ridiculous anticlimax. The longer the delay, the greater the difficulty in suggesting that some day she would be a bundle of aches and pains.

When, after her first experience, she stepped from the shower, Mona did not say, *"And I don't feel a bit guilty . . ."* As nearly as Doc could remember, what she said was, "Oooh . . . that was fun."

Chapter 2

Doc Brandon enjoyed freedom from the benefits and the masquerades of the Thought Controlled, the Plastic Society, and the Megapoli which were its heart. Nameless Island gave him a comfortable feeling like that of the many whites and Blacks who had rejected great cities in favor of farming, fishing, hunting, and getting along with their neighbors. With no socially conscious intellectuals to remind them of their rights, the rural folk had nothing to wrangle about except matters such as the sixteen-gauge versus the twelve-gauge shotgun, or whether the changing phases of the moon could be offset by changing fishing bait to accord.

"If scientists had a spot like my island," Doc summed up, "they'd not have gone mad as often as they did in the fiction written during the early nineteen hundreds. Longer I look around me, the more I quit wondering why nobody ever wrote about a *sane* scientist. If I ever hear of one, I'll write a book."

Barefooted, Doc sat in a rattan chair which was horribly out of place in Mona's bedroom-sitting-room-and-kitchenette suite adjoining the office of the Brandon Foundation. Four empty glasses stood shoulder to shoulder on the nighttable. Each was cloudy with the dregs of an absinthe drip, genuine absinthe which Doc had made according to the ancient and illegal formula.

The fifth glass, a broad shallow goblet, was full of

7

shaved ice. A saucerlike device with bottom fitting into the goblet pressed down into the ice. The saucer thing contained a pool of greenish liqueur which was dripping through a pinhole in the center. As each drop was diluted by melting ice, it became milky; and when the final one joined its comrades, Doc's aperitif would be ready.

Doc had decided, a century and a half ago, that eating on an empty stomach was bad for the digestion. His glance shifted to the sea-green sleeping gown Mona had flipped to the bed. Next he regarded the frail *piña*-cloth robe she'd eventually be wearing. He cocked his head, brushed back a shock of sandy-to-neutral hair, and listened to the shower. Though blasted by sun and wind, his face was devoid of lines except for a few at the corners of a stubborn mouth. However, at the moment his usual expression of eager anticipation prevailed. Despite his age, something or someone fascinating was always at hand or around the corner. And that inner glow, though centering in eyes deceptively wide open and innocent, contrived to harmonize facial features which would otherwise have been a haphazard assortment of spare parts, nothing bad and nothing matching anything else.

Doc lifted the dripper and set it on one of the emptied glasses, then tasted his timekiller-appetizer. If Mona did not rate her interminable showers, Brandon did not know who in the Parliamentary Republic did. At sunrise, August twenty-seventh, 2086 A.D., the thermometer read 43° Celsius, with humidity ninety-eight sweltering percent. It was ten o'clock and getting no cooler.

Ten o'clock was a reminder. Brandon switched on the Three Dee lookee-squawkee for an aesthetic aperitif: North America's supreme detergent opera. Between Mona and genetic engineering, he had been distracted from the program which for six years had kept him cogitating, speculating, wondering.

"Mutate the Immutable; solve the Insoluble; screw the Inscrutable." Brandon's code, the spirit of science.

Flora, widow of that troublemaker, Roderick David Garvin, who had been reported lost with all hands when something happened to the *Saturnienne* after making the first manned flight around Saturn: Flora Garvin, Queen of

Space Widows, and there she was, radiant, glowing.

And that voice! If she were to sing the Greek alphabet, women the world over would perish of frustration, men would fall in love with her—and before she trilled her way past *theta.* Her theme song had made one and one-half hemispheres detergent-conscious.

For each appearance, an exotic new gown was worn, one which she herself had designed. And the morning of August 27, 2086, Flora wore tight silver lamé. The table behind which she stood with her basin of *Sudzo* was of a height precisely calculated to present her hips in slender-sensuous curvature which seconded breadth of breast and shoulder, an enchanting paradox: slenderness, yet spaciousness; luxury where it meant the most; restrained and understated opulence.

Like pagoda eaves, the tunic's shoulder trim reached up in points almost to the level of ears from which hung long pendants. A tall ornate miter towered from shimmering black hair. Hands elongated by artificial nails made blue panties ripple and flaunt what had become traditional, a triangular group of rosebuds where they would be most meaningful.

And that lyric, a spell which ensorceled every continent:

"... *Sudzo for your frilly dudzo* ..."

As she sang, the dark-eyed enchantress swished the silky bits in the detergent: a triple swish, a glimpse of dripping garment that would find a place between Flora's recreation area and whatever costume she wore for the following show. And what could come after the silver lamé tunic of a Burmese festival dancer, only the next program could tell. She herself would not know until she had designed it.

Swirling mists concealed Flora. They became tantalizingly dense as slender arms reached through. She held the silver tunic, rippled it, dipped the twinkling fabric into the foam and for a moment displayed it, then drew it back into the mist which concealed her.

"*Sudzo for your clothzo-o-o* ..." Thinning mist revealed Flora, full length now, and again in her exotic dress. Like each of many recent appearances, this was a playback of a tape filmed several years ago. None of the

Plastic Society had sufficient memory or attention span to be aware of the repetition. Doc Brandon was an exception, and more than girl watching sustained his interest in the darling among space widows and the beauty of her lyrics.

Flora called to mind a late broadcast, back in the early 2080s. Mars, with its thin air, was ideal for astronomical observatories. One of them had radioed news of a nova. When Doc got in touch with the broadcasting source, he was informed that no such report had been made and that there never would be any report of a nova in the asteroid belt.

That the broadcast had been cut off abruptly aroused Doc's suspicion, and the denial that there ever had been such a report redoubled his skepticism. Something must have occurred, such as the detonation of a considerable mass of fissionable mineral. He had heard gossip about prospecting in the asteroid belt by bombing planetoids with nuclear projectiles and making spectroscopic analyses of the flash.

For a century or more, Doc Brandon had been unable to decide which released the greater number of false reports, the government bureaucracy or the news media. To decide what percentage of such yarns was deliberate falsification and what portion derived from bungling incompetence was beyond even his reckoning.

It was not until Floyd's reported the loss of the *Saturnienne* and her crew, somewhere between Mars and the asteroid on which she had landed to make routine repairs, that Doc resolved to learn more about the nova which certainly was not a nova.

Doc snapped the switch, reached for the absinthe drip. Next time he was in Megapolis Alpha he would have a talk with Alexander Heflin, Chairman of the Consortium, that unofficial group which struggled to check Parliament's ever more successful efforts to drive the Republic down the cesspool of history.

Flora Garvin was a fifth cousin of Alexander Heflin.

Brandon's contentment with a day well started fell apart when he heard the *clump-clump-clump* of a helicopter. He disliked the intrusion. The Burmese villagers who worked in the teak forest and attended to the nursery which supplied infants for an under-the-counter adoption society would riot if the flyer or propwash knocked the *hti* from the gilded pagoda.

"That son of a bitch sounds low enough to be picking papayas!" Doc grumbled.

His cursing was punctuated by the *whack-whack-whack* of a 5.56-millimeter assault carbine. At least one villager had decided to demonstrate. Then came the reverbrant *boooom* of the double-barrel .600 Jeffries which old U Po Mya had stolen from one of the last of the English gentlemen come to the Malay States to hunt seladang and tigers. A sixty-gram slug would play hell with a chopper blade. U Po Mya's zeal was commendable, but householder's liability insurance on a Burmese village was already extortionately high.

The intercom lookce-squawkee came to life. The face on the screen was wrinkled and pock-marked. White hair twisted into a bun crowned the village headman. He clutched the antique double-barrel gun which in the first quarter of the twentieth century had cost eight hundred pounds sterling, when Great Britain and the United States issued a respected currency.

Aside from the villagers, Doc was probably the only man within a radius of two thousand kilometers who could speak Burmese.

"*Payaaa,*" the old man led off.

"God-damn it, I've been telling you these past twenty years not to call me 'divinity'!"

"Yes, *payaaa*! I put my head beneath your Golden Feet. Those mother-fornicators in the whirly bird flew over and around the nursery and the brats woke up and howled, and Maung Gauk fired his pipsqueak of a carbine and the nurses screamed rape-murder-and-arson, so I took a man's gun. We missed the whirly-thing but chunks flew from the basket-thing."

"Builder of pagodas," Doc implored, "get off the air, stay off till I call you back."

"*Payaaa,* I have never built a pagoda! I hear with fear and trembling."

U Po Mya cut the switch. And then Mona stepped from the shower. Doc said, "Get dressed as quick as you can.

This is not our day for fun and games. We may have time for breakfast, maybe."

Mona snatched an acre of towel and set to work as Doc explained, "This sneaking up is political!" He got into checkered green pajamas. "You answer the next call. When those bastards land, I know there's going to be an inspection. Say I always sleep late. Have Isaiah take them to the guest house. Give them the limit in hospitality. And be sure to pull the fuses from the air conditioning."

As the briefing progressed, Mona fitted herself with lace panties, pink, with a cluster of forget-me-nots arranged Flora Garvin style, and got her bra secured. It was a queen size, for a princess-shaped girl. Although Doc referred to her as "long-legged redhead," he was somewhat in error. However elegant her legs, Mona's hair was tawny-bronze, with ruddy glints when the sun was quite low.

"Kill air conditioning?" A happy twinkle animated her gray-green eyes with hazel lights. "Think they might die of heat stroke or suffocation?"

"I'm afraid they're going to live. Tell them I am stinking drunk if they are official, which I'm afraid they are. Let them have a good look. Those glasses . . ." He chuckled, sniffed the air. "Delicious reek—your perfume, absinthe, Calvados, and—"

"It was Marc de Bourgogne," she corrected, and found a skirt.

Doc drained his glass and pulled the switch of the lookee-squawkee. "You stand by in the office. If you want to make this a good horror story, go virginal and say I was sleeping with a Burmese girl. They're frightful alcoholics, you know."

He took a dive for the rumpled bed and inhaled essence of Mona from the pillow. He had almost composed himself to the verge of Taoist trance when he heard the code call of Nameless Island. A man demanded Dr. Brandon. Mona answered, "I'm frightfully sorry . . . if all they did was shoot a few chunks from the cabin, you're awfully lucky."

"I'm Dr. Wilson Epworth, and I want to speak to Dr. Brandon at once!"

Mona raised her voice to an agonized screech. "The Board of Visitors? Oh, land at once! You can't speak to Dr. Brandon. He is sleeping."

Things began to be coherent.

"Wake him up."

"Dr. Epworth, you might as well land. I'll send the station wagon to pick you up and take you to the guest house."

"You dizzy bitch, I want to speak to Brandon at once!"

"Come on over and see if you can wake him. He *never* gets up before three."

"I told you I am Wilson Epworth! I'll have you fired."

"You'll defecate, too, unless you are constipated," she retorted sweetly. "I am not in the civil service."

She pulled the switch, then called Isaiah, the steward, and gave him instructions. That done, she heard Doc's closing directions:

"This is a sneak attack! Those bastards have always given me three days' notice. Tell U Po Mya and Maung Gauk that everything is under control. You take over and run things. I'm not a full-blown *tao shih*; I can't fake drunken stupor instantly."

Chapter 3

Simianoids had no conscientious scruples against work or military service, nor were they handicapped by ideals or by a passion for causes or crusades. Their realistic minds were not susceptible to suggestion as was the mass mind of the thought-controlled populace of the Parliamentary Republic. Skillful gene splicing had modified the simian palate and changed the facial structure from prognathous to orthognathous, allowing the Simianoids to vocalize and—thanks to minor cosmetic changes—look like standard humans. In view of his many years of observing the norm of the Republic, Doc had made few changes in the chimpanzee mental workings.

Because of his isolation on an island two thousand kilometers from Megapolis Alpha, Brandon had survived the organized opposition which had driven most of his colleagues into socially approved sciences. Religionists, many intellectuals, and quite a few scientists had spearheaded opposition to gene splicing.

In addition to teak forestry, his menagerie reinforced the protective front which unorthodoxy required; and his work in combatting sickle-cell anemia and hepatitis contributed.

When Doc regained normal consciousness, the temperature was comfortable. After a shower, he put on a *camisa de chino* of undyed Shantung silk and floppy trousers of white duck. Peeping into the office, he saw Mona at her desk, sleeping lightly.

14

She blinked, got her satin slippers to the floor, and sat up, hazel eyes all alert and sparkling.

"They demanded a look and they got it. Anyone who could sleep through that horrible heat had to be paralyzed drunk. And Isaiah called a little while ago, and said that when the wind shifted, the Board of Visitors figured it'd be cooler outside. One of them said something about getting out of that suffocating guest house and having a look at the menagerie."

After finding his shoes, Doc decided that he'd go to tell his guests that he was reasonably sober. But first he would stop at the guest house, which was a hundred meters short of the stunted conifers that protected it from the winds which often lashed the headland.

When Doc stepped into the vestibule, Isaiah Winthrop emerged from the interior. The white-haired steward said, "When I called, I couldn't tell you how indignant they were because the villagers had fired at them while they circled over the settlement. They had been taking pictures." As Doc's eyebrows rose, Isaiah explained, "That's the way of the Magapolitan people. They are convinced that Blacks are unable to understand English.

"They never suspected that I couldn't qualify for my Master's until I had taken two semesters of Afro-English.

"Dr. Epworth took the pictures. They were looking at them. They'd used Insta-Kolor. They were so interested they paid little attention to me. Apparently the nursery was important."

"See the color stuff after they left?"

"I saw but did not touch. I left nothing but eye-prints."

"Did you speak Afro-English to our guests?"

"I was sorely tempted to say, '*Y'all white gennel men done et?*' but I settled for a southern drawl."

"Just right." Brandon nodded. "Tell the chef that late nineteenth-century New Orleans cuisine will be in order for dinner. Pick five waitresses and waiters to match and see if you can persuade Habeeb to supervise the service. Now I'm going to greet the guests.

"When you've given your orders, come on out and stand by until I hail you."

Despite the crunch of gravel under his feet, Doc's visitors were unaware of his approach. They stood bellied up against the heavy wire mesh of an aviary.

"That freak is actually eating," one of the Board grumbled, and another, stocky and short-necked, remarked, "Plastic surgery assembled that impossible thing."

"Dr. Epworth, you might at least compliment a slick surgeon," Brandon cut in.

The Board of Visitors faced about. Being confronted by the master of Nameless Island, articulate and standing on his own feet, disconcerted them. Though not so tall as to be stately, his posture, upright and arms folded, lent him presence which his 180 centimeters would otherwise have denied.

"Gentlemen, take a look." He thrust out his right foot. "So busy finding fault with the incomprehensible that you didn't hear me crunching gravel."

Doc's glance moved along the row of sweaty faces: Gridley, the long-nosed paleontologist, then Finley Benson, who professed ornithology. Brandon's eyes skipped his favorite enemy, Wilson Epworth, a stocky, square-rigged person with a stubborn face, and centered on Whitby Foster, an outstanding gene splicer who was fingering drooping straw-colored moustaches. Doc could not place the fifth visitor, a ruddy, squint-eyed character whose skin was none the better for its overdose of sun.

"I've never had the pleasure of meeting you." Doc smiled engagingly. "We've not had time to become enemies. That's customary but actually, it's optional."

"I'm Bernard Wilkins."

"Now I remember! And I'm sure we'll not wrangle. You specialize in safeguarding laboratories—preventing accidental escape of untested bacterial strains. Sorry my assistant, Oswald Fenton, isn't here to meet you. He's done some good work in that line." And then Doc addressed the group. "Welcome aboard! Sorry I kept you waiting, but I do have to have my sleep."

Foster, the gene splitter, filled the pause. "Animated cartoons; feathered reptiles, and birds without feathers would give as good a picture of Jurassic life. I admire your expertise so much so that I deplore your wasting it!"

"Thank you for applause, and I'll not deplore your deplorings! I'm not financed by government grants. Anyone present who can say as much?" After a pause: "I thought so! Now if you'll humor me a few minutes more, I'll show you one of my improvements on nature. If you call it an animated cartoon, I'll buy drinks for the house."

He beckoned for the Board to follow. There was scarcely an exclamation to indicate interest in a small but striking *Rhamphorhynchus*. They did pause for a glimpse of the *Ichthyornis*. Doc was not amazed that they ignored the kiwi with sufficient wing spread for a ten-meter flight to perch on the limb of a tree. But when Doc halted, the visitors closed in.

They saw, and the silence was unbroken except for the soft voice of the creature behind heavy bars. The saber-toothed tiger made a sound neither purring nor snarling: the greeting of the death giver who loves his work. Whether sated or famished, whether he died or lived, as long as he could move he was the perfect slayer.

Brandon shivered when he heard the voice. His guests could scarcely react as he did. They did not know that while still a cub, this miniature *Machaerodus* had purred affectionately, capered and gamboled like a kitten, *Felis domestica*, whenever U Po Mya came within sight or scent. The Burmese village headman had bottle fed the infant tiger.

Doc turned abruptly. The guests started, composed themselves, relaxed. He knew then that *Machaerodus* had fascinated them.

"Who cares whether this is an example of genetic engineering, of plastic surgery, or a mutant wrought by nature, cosmic rays, or man-made radiation? Skip the quibbling and admire a beautiful animal."

The tiger welcomed his audience: topaz eyes shifted from visitor to visitor, appraising each in turn. The throaty purring-snarling was like distant Mongol drums. Benson brightened. "Elegant! And a miniature. Just as I'd visualized when I saw the assembled bones of the *Machaerodontinae* at La Brea asphalt pits. Superb, however you faked it!"

That final quip, good humored, was applause.

"Has any of you ever seen a seladang?"

"You mean the wild bull from the Malay States, nearly as nasty as the South African buffalo?"

"Perfect summing up. My miniature tiger doesn't weigh more than forty–fifty kilos, but he tackled and killed a seladang I'd imported at enormous expense."

Seeing Isaiah lurking among the towering bamboo stalks, Doc beckoned. "It's time for tall drinks to give us an appetite for early dinner. The steward is probably here to tell us that the air conditioner is working."

Isaiah approached and announced, "Dr. Brandon, cocktails will be served at the guest house."

Four of the Board followed Isaiah. Wilson Epworth lingered until his colleagues had gained half a dozen yards. Then he said, "Doc, you and I have clashed from time to time. To show you that there's no resentment on my side, I'll level with you. This visit is a front. We'll rephrase a former report and submit it instead of wasting time. What I want to talk about is your unusual longevity."

Doc sighed, pulled a long face. He wondered how color pictures of a Burmese village related to his unusual age. "Wilson, there is quite too much speculation about it. After I wrote a paper on the *apparent* immortality of Chinese adepts, Taoist masters, the mutterings became noisy, and the mutterers became nosy. It's become a God-damn pest!"

Epworth nodded. "I can imagine it would. I am sure that you realize why there is so much interest in a scientific approach to a . . . well . . . underlying truth, masked by Chinese superstition, Oriental nonsense, and fraud."

"Your approach has been straightforward," Doc conceded guardedly. "I don't know how far I can go with you. Writing a paper on Taoist psychic practices and citing passages from Ko Hung's classic work! You folks as good as called me a charlatan half an hour ago, when you saw living exhibits! Off the record, and no tape recording, I might tell enough for you to know that I cannot be certain whether I am a natural mutant, a freak, or whether my life style has something to do with my longevity. Maybe I *am* an undocumented example of my late father's genetic engineering. Bluntly, your colleagues do a lot to make me hesitate."

Epworth frowned. "That's a bit obscure!"

"The hell it is! I'll clarify. Five of you, each getting his own notions of what I really mean."

Epworth's heavy face was far from revealing, yet his expression gave Doc the idea that a decision was being shaped. The pause ended when the chairman of the Board said, "Off the record, Doc, it is this way. They are keenly interested but they came along mainly for fun and the expense account. Your hospitality is famous."

Doc's well-feigned expression of frowning consideration brightened into a glow of total comprehension. "Suppose your colleagues got themselves sufficiently drunk, and you and I remained quite sober?"

"You and I could have an off-the-record talk?"

"Don't know how far it'd go, but it would be a start. Have a cocktail or two, respond to a toast if in order, and tell your waiter and waitress to serve you tonic without gin and carbonated Normandy cider instead of champagne. Me, I'll do my damndest to stay coherently sober."

Epworth chuckled. "When I saw you about eleven this morning, you were an exemplary case of catatonia. How the hell you ever became ambulant in five hours! Two–three days would have been amazing."

Chapter 4

Five dreary dragging years passed before Flora Garvin yielded to the nagging conviction that she was not a widow. Only one person in the Parliamentary Republic could help her learn what had happened to Captain Roderick David Garvin: her fifth cousin, Alexander Heflin, Chairman of the Consortium which, with ever-diminishing success, kept the Republic from self-destruction.

Although he did not suspect it, Flora hated Alexander as a duty. Also, he had always fascinated her; and he had sensed it before she married that troublemaker, Rod Garvin. As in most matters, Heflin's sensings were realistic and accurate. His appraisal of women had been such that to let marriage interfere with matters of state would have been nonsense.

Before setting out to deal with Alexander, Flora surveyed the costumes she had designed for her Sudzo programs. She had almost selected a favorite when she remembered something. She reached for the gown which she had worn at the cocktail party, Martian Space Port, the eve of Rod's take-off for Saturn. Then, dressed for peak performance, Flora set out to keep her appointment with the master of the show.

Megapolis Alpha, capital of the Republic, had so long been a masquerade that Flora's space-theme gown, modified for the street, evoked only admiration. In that vortex of costumes ranging from Grecian classic to French Third

Empire, and geographically bounded by Orient and Occident, the few who wore traditional one-sex jacket and trousers were conspicuous. Most such eccentrics were the Coolies who had not yet made a career of being someone and something else. And the remainder was largely the scattering of Simianoids employed in the capital. Their simian component kept them from craving to be other than what they were.

These Simianoids, diverse in build and facial structure, were by no means uniform, despite their common origin as clones of six foundation types. Diversification had been introduced through half a dozen generations of polyandry. One female for each quartet of males offered a variety which offset the monotony of domestic life; it prevented overpopulation; and the arrangement made for an interesting range of complexions, hair colors, bodily and facial structures. In addition to avoiding a monotonous typing of offspring, the polyandrous female could rarely be accused of resorting to escapades far from home.

The only Simianoid abnormality was one which they shared with the Coolie class: They did not hate work. Despite their labor's supporting eighty percent of the population, neither Simianoid nor Coolie could endure the four-hour work week and the resulting ferocious pursuit of gracious living, recreation, cultural expression. And best of all, they felt no obligation to riot, protest, demonstrate in juvenile ignorance of what they were protesting. Only students had that obligation.

Because of her transhemispherical fame, Flora wore a mask which accorded with her bone structure yet disguised by harmonious changes in mask thickness at cheekbones, superciliary ridges, and frontal eminences. It made her a very good-looking someone else, and permitted total outward response to inward changes of expression. Since the film breathed, it was relatively comfortable. For the criminal and for the famous, such masks afforded privacy.

At her destination, some twenty kilometers beyond the corporate limits of Megapolis Alpha, Flora asked the driver for his card, so that she could call him for pickup, just in case. He said, "Mrs. Garvin. I'm sure you are Mrs. Garvin; your voice, you know. For a small surcharge, I'd wait up to

an hour. By that time you are likely to know whether and
when you'd be leaving."

"It's flattering to be recognized by voice," she answered
graciously, though her unspoken thought was "Someone
should sell voice distorters."

Although Flora always expected Alexander to wear toga
and laurel wreath, he never did so. Heflin himself, being
Heflin, was more effective than any masquerade. The angular features, the lordly nose, the patrician carriage of his
lean, tall frame contributed, but his presence derived from
the power which he radiated. It was the essence of those he
had outfought in the wars of his youth and those he had
outpointed in later years. But what made it difficult to
hate the man was his good fellowship, charm backed by
power.

Flora was tiptoe before he could bend to kiss her. Then,
holding her at arm's length, he took a moment for appraisal. "Beautiful as ever! You'll always be the country's
darling!"

"The Sudzo world doesn't know it sees reruns of tapes!
What they see is themselves wearing my outfits."

"And I see the original every couple of years, when I'm
lucky. Well, maybe I'm psychic instead of lucky." He pan-
tomimed gazing into a crystal ball, made a few passes.
". . . Now it clears . . . I see a woman, dark and fascinating . . . she perishes of thirst . . . nothing can save her
but an Amer Picon with a brandy float."

"You do remember!"

Heflin stepped to the bar. "Out in the country automation is banned. At the Alpha Beta Club, it was bad enough,
making martinis with dark Haitian rum, but when the vo-
calizer sounded off, *'This round of Old Fashioneds is on
the house. We're leaving out the fruit because—'* before the
explanation could follow, half a dozen gays walked out in
high dudgeon."

"Filed a suit, violation of civil rights?"

"There really was a shortage of fruit," he added, as he
poured Picon bitters, grenadine, wiped a zest of lemon
around the rim of the glass, then a splash of soda, a float
of cognac. For himself, a Palomino y Vergara sherry.

Glasses on a tray, tray poised on fingertips, he followed Flora to sofa and cocktail table.

"Still swamped with fan mail?"

She nodded, tasted the picon punch.

Alexander regarded her intently. "You never *look* tired, but there's something in your voice."

"This devil can get more solicitude going than all the do-gooders in the country, singing in chorus!" She said, "I am so mortally weary! All those social projects using me for bait."

"Griefs do carry on, and keeping busy is the best way. So I was surprised by your wearing the dress you wore that afternoon in Maritania."

Flora's eyes widened, dark, deep, sad. "That day, well, we forgot all our standard misunderstandings." She sighed, breathing resignation. "If he'd come back, we'd have got back into the wrangling groove."

"A vacation is what you need! It's in your voice. I can arrange the sort of thing that costs nothing whatever. But not one in millions can get a ticket."

Flora's brows reached their apex.

"World Spaceways stages an international golf tournament in Khatmandu every year. Chiefs of national air forces go. Chiefs of staff, and the unclassified ones who run governments from behind the scenes. Heads of state are too important to accept invitations. Nobody else is important enough to be invited."

What made the offer so tempting was Flora's feeling that she was not a widow. During that night of truth, just before his take-off for Saturn, Rod had told her that the crew of the *Saturnienne* was bin scrapings primed for a mutiny which they thought would force him to abort the mission and confess failure. Rod guessed that their attempts at sabotage were much more likely to destroy cruiser and crew. Either way, Garvin the nuisance would be silenced. But Rod had outwitted the mutineers and made it homeward as far as an uncharted asteroid populated by people whose language was much like that of the Gooks, the Martian aborigines.

The asteroidal girl who acted as interpreter, with Garvin's Martian girl relaying the message in English to Terra, was quite attractive. Flora had begun to suspect that instead of being a widow, she was still a wife with a lot of competition.

"Space Marshals," Alexander resumed, after a just-right pause, "and a few outstanding guests who are not allies, but important. And their wives, mistresses, concubines, playmates. I know you loathe golf, don't go for tatting or bridge, but some of the smartest shops in the world are in Khatmandu."

"Khatmandu? I'd always heard—"

"What you used to hear was true. But after Rod's caper—the time he was all set to abscond and set up housekeeping there—made Khatmandu fashionable. And the costuming—it'd start you out with some new basics."

"I'd love that!"

Alexander Heflin sensed that he had almost made a deal; and he realized that he was within a micromillimeter of being hooked. He'd never seen Flora as magnificent, as alluring as she had become since arrival.

"There'd be some who aren't terrestrian or spacers?"

"Bound to be."

Flora recalled the wife of Dmitri Barzan, an eccentric wench dedicated to wheedling and browbeating masters and mistresses of haute couture into concentrating their skills on the traditional dress of her background, at least for one season.

"Dmitri Barzan is retired," Flora resumed. "But he'd rate an invitation, and he'd just about have to bring his wife?"

Alexander shrugged, swirled his glass. " '*Si les cons peuvent voler, ce cochon-la serait chef d'escadrille!*' Darling lady, he'll not be there."

Several years in a girls' school in France had fitted Flora with colloquialisms not included in the North American curricula. Gallic whimsy and American vernacular misrendered into English set her laughing. " '*If cons could fly, that slob would be chief of the air force.*' What a picture!"

"It'd confuse science fiction fans and prison wardens," he solemnly conceded. "Especially with the way you pronounce *con*."

"Rod would have loved that one!" She sighed but the

eyes were no longer somber: They still had their sparkle, the carryover from the play of whimsy. "Khatmandu is alluring, Alex, but what I'd love above all else would be a few weeks in Maritania. I'd pay my way, of course, on a space-available basis."

Alexander's face tightened. His eyes became lanceheads at frosty dawn. "No can do. Sorry, but that's become critical territory. Flora, of all places, what's the attraction?"

"I want to talk to Rod's girl, Azadeh. He told me all about her that night. If I'd not come to Maritania, he'd have spent take-off eve with her." Alexander looked surprised, and for him, that was news. Flora drove home: "I saw playbacks of stuff that never got on the air. Azadeh was pregnant. She had that smug superior look, that I-know-something-you-don't-know expression, blended with a happy glow. And she didn't look the way I felt when Floyd's declared the *Saturnienne* lost in space."

Heflin was now unimperial. Flora had never seen him so convincingly human and busy absorbing thoughts new and impressive. "I begin to see what you mean. Something that never occurred to me. But I can't understand how talking to Azadeh could help you."

"She knows things we do not know. She must have reasons for knowing she is not a Number Two Widow."

"Where would he be?"

"Marooned on that asteroid. There were only routine problems when he radioed Mars. He set the *Saturnienne* down only because the asteroid had unusual density, atmosphere, vegetation."

"A meteor too big for the deflection screening could have totaled the cruiser after she took off from the asteroid."

"Azadeh knows something we do not know. She and Rod's asteroid girl were speaking a language that no proud American would ever bother to learn. Azadeh was Rod's sleeping dictionary. Azadeh released exactly the news she wanted to get to Terra, and nothing more. I want to get to Gook Town and talk her out of what she knows."

"No matter what you might learn about that asteroid and Azadeh's holdings out, we could not cruise the asteroid belt. We are in tough shape, and the knotheads in Parliament won't believe a fact when it hits them!"

Alexander paused, waiting for her to digest what he had said. Then he drew a deep breath and continued, "We are not down the cesspool of history, but we have too good a start. The country stinks with 'idealists,' pacificists, and quite a few religionists going Marxist.

"No more than five percent of the population is capable of being educated. Education, 'the educing, leading out, drawing out the latent powers of an individual.' Ninety-five percent have nothing to be 'drawn out' or developed. Imbeciles, cretins, morons get Master's degrees, or the school industry would shut down."

Heflin, going full bore, had the force of a double-bitted axe. The best Flora could do was to protest. "Alex, what does this have to do with sending one cruiser to explore the asteroid belt?"

"Hear me out! Yes, I was digressing. The five percent of students who have intelligence notably higher than a chimpanzee's are devoid of experience. The most dangerous substance on earth is intellect devoid of experience. Genghis Khan set out at age fourteen to become emperor of all mankind, and damn nearly made it, but he'd not had a babysitter to change his diapers until he reached the age of thirty.

"Our sixteen-year-old punks are voters, and the few talented ones are sold on their infinite wisdom and idealism. Their protest and disarmament drivel is inviting a war we are not ready to fight. If I persuaded Government to send a cruiser to explore the asteroid belt, there'd be demonstrations and rioting, the sort of thing that invites realistic people to take us over. As that grand old cavalry commander Nathan Bedford Forest used to say, couple of centuries ago, '*I told you twict, God damn it, NO!*' "

Seducing Alexander Heflin would be a tougher project than Flora had anticipated. Hoping he would believe she was beaten, she raced to the vestibule and to the driveway where her taxi was waiting. Flora did not even bother to put on her mask.

Chapter 5

When Doc Brandon stepped into the coolness of the guest house, he found the Board of Visitors comfortable in lounging chairs, sitting in a cozy group near the billiard alcove. The bouquet of Creole cookery scented the air. Doc turned to Isaiah.

"How many rounds have you served?"

"Only two, but it's time for the next."

When the Board was aware of his presence, he announced, "This is your home." And then, "Isaiah, bring me two absinthe drips to catch up with our guests, and one for keeping even."

"Sir, two are waiting in the freezer, and one is dripping."

Five Simianoid waiters filed in. Doc pulled up a chair and watched them serve Scotch and soda, which was in, since it was Love Britain Week. The sixth arrived in with three drips and three brandy chasers.

Doc rose and raised the first. "Good health, gentlemen, and happy hours. I've noticed anxious glancings about. Possibly wondering where the waitresses are? Look over yonder where the steward is standing."

Isaiah had moved to the wall which faced the entrance. At Doc's gesture, he slid a door aside, revealing a dining room and table set for six. Five Simianoid girls stood in line. Each wore white cap, white blouse, black skirt. They were of complexion, facial structure, and figure as diverse as their male counterparts: from a pint-size brunette to an

27

opulent blonde as tall as Mona, they covered the field, chromatically and dimensionally.

Somber-eyed, majestic and bearded, Habeeb towered ceilingward. He wore a blue Mogul kaftan and a massive turban. He was normally Nameless Island's elephant driver. Doc was making a study to ascertain the comparative merits of tractor versus pachyderm for snaking teak logs from rocky slopes to an imaginary river at sealevel. On special occasions, Habeeb doubled as captain of waiters.

When applause subsided, Doc resumed, "Each girl's card matches one in the basket. To keep me from accidentally being an object of envy, I'll have no girl wait on me. Isaiah, please carry on!"

Doc sat down to take care of his drinks and chasers.

The steward went from visitor to visitor, offering a lacquer basket. When the girls displayed their cards, the final shred of formality blinked out. Each took her station behind the visitor she was to serve. Once the guests were at the table, Doc turned on the volume to make himself heard. "A few of tonight's offerings and options may leave you perplexed. Your girls will be happy to offer suggestions. *Gung ho, fat choy!* Which reminds me. Isaiah, I forgot to tell you about the Lucky Money."

Habeeb's staff filed into the kitchen and straightway returned in stately procession. Each took his post behind a diner and conveniently apart from his waitress. Each girl took from her waiter a miniature tureen of green turtle soup and emptied it into a bowl beside which she set a glass of *fino* sherry, very dry.

Doc would get points for complying so zealously with the Parliament's More Employment Mandate. Since the Board of Psychology and Sociology's study, which had cost five hundred million *pazors*, had decided that every citizen should feel needed, wanted, necessary, the three-hour work week would be abolished and the four-hour week restored. Although there had been demonstrations and several five billion *pazor* class actions filed, thus far, no rioting.

Presently the second course, and Doc recommended *escargots bourguignons*. He enjoyed watching the faces as the girls recited the ingredients. Four, betraying horror, demanded coquille Saint Jacques. Doc addressed Wilson Epworth and raised his glass.

"Mr. Chairman, your health! I'd feel awkward being the only diner who enjoys snails."

The drinks selected ranged from California port to champagne. Wilson Epworth stuck to gin and tonic minus gin.

Pompano en Papillote: a filet of pompano, slowly simmered, then tucked into a parchment bag, along with a sauce containing mushrooms, truffles, herbs, and esoteric spiceries. After being sealed, the bag was put into the oven for a quarter hour.

"What the hell? How do I tackle this?"

Each waitress dipped small scissors from her apron pocket and snipped the parchment. Becoming ever more jovial, Doc ceased shuddering when visitors took Bourbon and Seven, or Oranjola and rye with each course. By the time *Faisan Souvaroff* was served, the hostesses no longer had to advise their guests.

Lamb Brains, Remoulade ... Braised Beef with Rum ...

Wilson Epworth remained amiably sober: His girl, who could charm a tiger away from a quarter of beef, was not being felt up.

Omelette Historiée à la Jules César, miniature loaf of egg white, a dash of rum, a dash of vanilla, all whipped to a rigid froth and baked perhaps thirty seconds. Each loaf was inscribed with the guest's name, in pink icing, by an adept who must have won a doctorate in Cake Icing.

Ultimate skill was demonstrated by the turtle doves on the ridge of each loaf. They were engaged in activities which would suggest ideas—whether to waitress or guest, Doc had never decided.

After fruit and cheese, Habeeb came in, stately as a war elephant in full regalia. With measured stride, he advanced holding a big silver bowl. From it, blue flame rose almost to the ceiling. This was *Café Diabolique*, though some persisted in calling it *Café Brûlot*: the blackest of New Orleans coffee, with cloves, cinnamon sticks, zest of orange and lemon. Floating cognac fueled the blaze.

Six waiters followed Habeeb. The hostesses made way.

At each place, Habeeb paused. A waiter dipped into the dark sea from which blue flame no longer rose and ladled the drink into a tall and slender porcelain cup. This was set on the table and with it, a small red envelope on which were Chinese ideograms in gilt.

Doc got to his feet. "Old custom! To thank a guest for attending, and to wish him luck." He swayed, steadied himself. It's uh—pro-to-col—a copper c-cash is enough."

Nicely timed. The fifth visitor had been served. Doc's cup was at hand, and with it, his envelope. A quick-witted guest laboriously got to his feet.

"Doc, how come? You don't rate lucky money. You're just throwing the party. You're too lucky already."

The objector sank but his girl shifted his chair and he plopped neatly into it.

Doc raised his *Café Diabolique*. "*Gung ho*, and so forth!" He waggled his red envelope, fumbled it, finally tore it apart. He flourished the thousand-*pazor* note it had contained. "Lucky money! You can keep it, or give it to your girl." He beamed, lecherous and happy. "Even if you don't lay her."

This sway-lurch was a good one. Doc missed the table, caught the cloth, dragged it with him to the floor. Fruit and cheese, china and silver followed him. He clawed the floor.

"I told you to take it easy!" a woman screamed.

Mona raced from the alcove in which she had been lurking. She knelt beside Doc. One of the waiters pounced to give her a hand. She brushed him aside and did the same to Isaiah.

"Doc, darling, you're too old to drink this way," she wailed.

Muttering and mumbling, Doc got to his feet. "Bring me another drink." Mona stood, long hands clawed like those of a witch. She dared not risk taking his arm. He swayed. He caught her shoulder. Nearly as tall as Brandon, she had the weight and balance to keep him on his feet. On their way out, the weaving couple knocked over a stand of samurai armor.

Isaiah announced, serene and in command, "Dr. Brandon begs leave to be excused. Coffee, cigars, liqueurs will be served presently."

Once clear of the guest house, Doc stumbled, clawed gravel, but without further difficulty wove his way through headquarters office and into Mona's apartment.

Finally under cover, Doc straightened up. "You did a marvelous job! Doll, that was a wonderful bit of almost hysterics!"

"You old son of a bitch!" She clung to him, sobbing. "I wasn't faking! You had me worried sick. I knew you were really drunk."

"If I fooled you, I convinced them. But it still is a guessing game."

Mona switched on the intercom lookee-squawkee. When the screen lighted up, party sounds came in.

"You're expecting someone to prowl," Mona said, minutes later. "You made hardly anything really clear. I know you were busy as a cat on a slate roof."

"Cat would at least know what he's trying to do, which is more than I know. You better get some rest while I consult the *I Ching*. Or the *Pao P'o Tzu*."

Mona frowned. "That's Chinese magic, isn't it?"

"Nothing's better, when science hits a dead end."

Chapter 6

Rod Garvin had not aged noticeably during his five or six years of self-imposed exile on an asteroid which Terrestrian astronomers had not yet spotted: Its albedo was quite too low. Despite what they considered to be enormous advances since their ancestors had left caves and forests, the world of the 2080s had not yet caught up with what the prehistoric folk once had enjoyed, and destroyed.

After making allowance for Asteroidan legend and tradition comparable to Terrestrian tribal legends and the Scriptures, Garvin was convinced that the inferences he had drawn were valid. Whether starfarers from a planet of an Alpha Centauri system, Martian aborigines, or prehistoric natives of Terra, the origin of the people was not relevant.

Regardless of origin, in almost eliminating infant mortality and lengthening the life span of the elderly science had brought disaster. Proud of their phenomenal skill in medicine, they had prolonged beyond all reason the lives of many who would happily have died as well as the existence of quasi-vegetables and the many who, professing belief in a life everlasting, lived in horror of death. Instead of making agonizing illnesses comfortable, narcotics became a recreation for those bored with living. Meanwhile, breeding like flies in a manure heap, humanity overcrowded the Earth.

Scientific warfare, however, and the happy coincidence of a cataclysm of Nature resolved the problem. Of the handful of survivors, a genius rediscovered fire, and another, the stone axe. History began anew.

The asteroid was ruled by self-made khans, each the head of a group of farmers, herdsmen, artisans, and others. The groups were retainers—vassals, but not serfs. No khan ventured to be an oppressor. With no democratic tradition to go to insane extremes and thus protect the intolerable, revolt or assassination disposed of the ruler who got out of line. Since the sword was the ultimate judgment, it was almost indecent for a man to appear in public unarmed. That made for a courteous and considerate society.

Garvin's contemplative assimilation of sociology was interrupted when a courier crossed to his flat-roofed house, catercorner from the palace of Alub Arslan, the Gur Khan. Garvin grabbed his curved sword, flipped the baldric over his shoulder, and happily honored the summons.

Garvin found Alub Arslan, the "Valiant Lion," in his private quarters: a black-bearded, stately man, little older than his guest. Instead of court dress, he wore sheepskin jacket, herdsman's boots, homespun woolen trousers, and a sheepskin cap.

"Rod, let's take a walk to the Lady's temple." He dug into a jacket pocket, took out a small ingot of gold which he handed to his visitor. On the rammed-earth bench, near the fireplace, were two small baskets. The Gur Khan took one and handed the other to Rod. "Here's the rest of your temple offering."

The openhandedness which tradition demanded of a khan made his position close to nonprofit. His wives did not complain: If he was niggardly toward his vassals, the ladies would either be barefooted ex-princesses or widows looking for a home. It was a good life for those who knew how to live it.

As an expression of proper humility in approaching the temple, Alub Arslan walked: no palanquin, no crew of bearers, no lancers, no octet of swordsmen; he went without drummers and without his three-tiered gold-overlaid parasol. The carpet spreaders, the refreshment servers, the musicians, and even the astrologer did not turn out.

Garvin, wiry, sun blasted, and in his mid-thirties, moved with the ease and grace of a panther. His restless eyes, sometimes gray, sometimes hazel, had unusual peripheral vision. Since their field was broader than careless observers suspected, three Terrestrial continents bore the graves of men who had not realized that Garvin could almost look behind him without turning his head.

The farther they walked from the palace, the more Garvin tasted trouble. The Gur Khan's frown, his drooping shoulders, suggested that something had gone sadly sour. Since a prince had little privacy in his palace, the temple of the Star Faring Lady was the only spot where they could risk talking.

They strode through the marketplace just beyond the city wall, where fruit, meat, vegetables, prepared food, textiles, and pottery were offered. Coppersmiths and ironmongers hammered away. Customers and shopkeepers courteously pretended to be unaware of the Gur Khan's approach. That neither trumpets nor drums sounded off meant that the prince was not present. It also meant *"Do not disturb me with petitions. I am busy."*

Garvin was worried because of Aljai, the ward of a neighboring khan, who had sent her to Alub Arslan as a gift of goodwill. Since neither had found the other congenial, the Gur Khan had given her to Garvin. Meanwhile, since Aljai was not one of Alub Arslan's wives, her guardian might have arranged an advantageous marriage for her. Naturally, that guardian would be so courteous as to send a replacement, or else Alub Arslan would do so.

"God damn it, they can't do that."

Garvin however had learned that whereas he had outwitted every idiotic twist of the Terrestrian social order, the easygoing and apparently purposeless asteroidal life style did with him as it pleased, and in a way which thus far had won his happy acceptance. Year after year, Aljai looked better and better, morning after morning, even before she put on her formal makeup. Garvin was worried. Alub Arslan's dark mood was so unusual as to be ominous.

The white masonry base of the temple was three meters high. The domed shrine, austere and unsculptured, rose from that platform. When they came to the stairs, the Gur Khan and Garvin ascended shoulder to shoulder. No man preceded another when approaching the Lady of Star Faring.

She sat in her shrine, sculptured in white marble: high cheekbones, wide-spaced eyes, not quite oblique. Her nose, though not as long as that of the standard Occidental, was slightly aquiline, elegant as the bone structure of that aristocratic face.

Each held his gift of gold with both hands. After bowing thrice, they laid on the altar the ingots and the nectarines, apricots, and tangerines they had brought in baskets. This done, they retreated, skirted the throne, and went to the back room, where the guardian stored archives, ingots of precious metals, and rubies. The guardian, the priest, and the astrologers would not return until the Gur Khan quit the temple.

They sat in silence, during which Garvin felt as though red ants were crawling all over him.

Finally Alub Arslan said, "Rod, I am in a nasty fix. Lani is pregnant."

Garvin got to his feet, thrust out his hand. "Congratulations. You had me worried. I was wondering whether the head to be chopped off was going to be mine."

The Gur Khan stood, gaping. Belatedly, he realized that not accepting Garvin's hand had been a gaffe. He corrected his social error. He was as bemuddled as Garvin.

"The astrologers predicted a son. Those bastards never miss."

Garvin began to feel lost in space. "Uh, what's wrong with that?"

The prince smiled bleakly. "Sit down, Rod. You have a wife back in your home world. A sort of wife and a son on Mars. And Aljai, a facsimile of a wife, right here in town. My wives are all in one cramped palace! Splendid women. Sweet and loving. Also, thoroughly jealous bitches because that red-headed Terrestrian junior wife is pregnant with a son. Not one of them has produced anything but daughters." He sighed. "Look at the prestige they are going to lose when Lani bears a son! I don't believe they'd go so far as to suffocate or drown an infant, though you can't ever tell what a humiliated woman will do."

He sighed, shook his head. "If it only turns out to be a girl, I'd feel as if I owned this whole world of ours! And the other wives would love them, Lani and daughter. They'd be so happy about my not getting a son, not even with an imported foreign wife. My fault, not theirs, that there's not a son in the house."

"Extravagant Lion, what the God damn hell, you lead the most complicated life."

"There's more to it than you realize."

"There is a waiting line of the younger khans who'd like to be my sons-in-law. That would be a great advantage. Give me an edge on—not mentioning names, a couple of arrogant bastards who make too much of a point about their rating the rank of *gur khan*. I've been telling my wives that daughters are a real blessing.

"If you don't know by now that it's impossible to talk three women out of one fixed opinion, there is nothing I can tell you."

"Sir, one woman is a full-time chore!"

"Lani's the widow of a foreigner, and she's a foreigner. I'm afraid Lani's never going to give birth."

"Uh, mmm, feed her an abortion drug?"

"Our women are purposeful. Fixed opinions. They'd not bother with slow poisons. Plenty of quick ones, you know. My life's become a three-phase nightmare! What are your ideas?"

"I'm just a space tramp."

"You're starfaring. I and my people, we're the descendants of farmers, sheepherders, miners, maybe a priest or two in my family, and one damned astrologer! If only he and the rest of them had died out centuries ago! No place Lani could hide in our little world. You have to get one of those grounded cruisers reconditioned. Fly Lani to Mars."

"That cruiser is eaten up by fumarole gases."

"There are several others that were grounded a hundred thousand years ago when war and cataclysms depopulated your world. We do not have any space captains. They were all lost in fighting. Some of the Earth continents sank. Some of our people escaped and made a home on Mars."

"Azadeh told me that my people and their enemies are going to exterminate each other."

"That's why I want Lani to go to Mars; it is not worth bombing."

"Flying a cruiser that's been sitting idle a hundred thousand years: You have been a friend, but that would be suicide."

"Rod, listen to this, study things out! Imagine going to Mars and seeing Azadeh and your son, seeing your Number One Wife." The Gur Khan sensed that Garvin was weakening. He hammered home with persuasion. "Lani won't ever be able to return. She told me how you were a loyal friend. She killed that fellow who tried to rape her. You helped her escape. Now you can save her again."

He paused, took a deep breath. He laid a hand on Garvin's shoulder. "Rod, she has always admired you—a hero in her life. Fly her to Mars, and she is yours. Forever!"

Garvin, whose blowing up the *Saturnienne* had made him a benefactor rating a single-tier golden parasol with golden pendants, had his limits. *"Alub Arslan is a prince in every sense of the word. It is not every son of a bitch who offers me twenty-five percent of his wives to do a job of spacing—after giving me five or six years with Aljai."* As the thought took shape, Garvin thrust out his hand. "Alub Arslan, you're not a small-scale thinker. I am not promising anything. Except this: I'll bust my arse trying, and if I can get a cruiser off the ground, I'll orbit your world. If there is a reasonable chance, I'll fly her to Mars."

He raised his hand before the Gur Khan could speak. "Just one more thing, Valiant Lion. If none of these cruisers are fit to take off and we have to stay here, I have an answer."

The Gur Khan licked his lips. He fingered his crisp and wavy black beard, the best-shaped Van Dyke type on the asteroid. "Let me hear the answer."

"No problem at all. Give me Lani, as she stands, and the calf goes with the cow. And any son of a bitch—or the sister of such—who tries to make trouble for my woman or your son will wish he or she had been blown up with the *Saturnienne*. Talk that over with Lani, while I go home and see if I can persuade Aljai."

Chapter 7

When the full moon rose, the pagoda bell sounded. Skilled hands timed each stroke so that the brazen voice swelled, subsided, surged again and softened until whispering, when the succeeding stroke brought it to full volume.

Sitting with Mona in darkness, Doc straightened up. "That'll start something."

She let go his hand. "If anyone is short of paralyzed drunk, he's awake now. Suppose Epworth did stay sober, how would he figure the full-moon ceremony means he can sneak and snoop?"

"Here's my reckoning. Flying over the village by broad daylight wasn't blundering, not with a pagoda reaching well over the trees. You can bet Epworth researched Burmese customs at full moon: everybody assembling to chant and burn incense to be nice to the seven hundred million jungle spirits that screw things up."

Flutes wailed. Brass whanged, and then came the mellow-golden sound of xylophones, the whine of fiddles, weaving ever-new spells from the same skein of sound.

Doc pictured dancers, girls dressed as Flora Garvin had been in the morning broadcast, tightly jacketed in silver lamé, with shoulder pieces perking up like pagoda eaves. They'd be pacing, stately and poised, doing impossible tricks with flexible hands and double-jointed fingers.

"The *nats* in Tawadeintha, all seven hundred million of them, they're bound to enjoy the show. I would, if I could watch."

"It's the music, Doc. That *pling-plannng-plonnnnngggg*, over and over and over, except when the *plong* goes short and the *plinnng* stretches out. It's always different. It does something to you if you hear it long enough."

"Mona, for you, *Onward Christian Soldiers* would stir up a mood."

"Coming from you, that's a laugh, you nice old lecher."

"Don't remind me I'll soon be two hundred years old, or I'll start looking for grown-up, mature women."

"Doc, I am not a nymphomaniac. Though sometimes I do think I might be wired up for polyandry like they say the Simianoid girls are."

"So that's it? I'm supposed to be equal to four Simianoid husbands?"

"Doc, darling, you are!"

"Whenever science or politics keep me from the important things of life, you and Oswald have a clear block. Just before he went north on vacation, I made it plain to him that I'm too old to be possessive. It'd be a sad business if he talked some schoolmate into moving in with him, I mean, marrying him, and then learned she simply could not endure being away from a nice social life."

"Oh, Oswald's nice enough, but he is so *dull*. Sometimes I think you've been seeing too much of the Sudzo broad."

"Speaking of broads, as soon as I get Wilson Epworth whittled down to size, you and I are going to have a honeymoon in New Orleans, and I'll buy you that broadtail jacket I've been promising you."

"How much longer is that music going to carry on?"

"While you're mixing us a drink, I'll feed data to the computer and get an estimate."

Mona set to work making a Ramos Fizz for two—three—four drinkers.

Before they had drunk more than half their ration, the lookee-squawkee intercom fired up. Isaiah's face filled the screen. "They dismissed the staff a little while after you left. I have not heard any ladies' voices. They stopped suddenly as though they had been doped or were drinking something too strong. All but one of the Board is petrified. He seems to be going for a moonlight walk."

"Just what I've been waiting to hear. You did a beautiful job at the banquet. Over, and out."

Brandon got into a black jacket, black trousers, and black felt-soled Chinese shoes.

Mona's environment had not squelched her heredity, Doc reflected, as he left by the back door of the headquarters complex. And, picking his way toward the village of teak foresters, he wondered whether six generations of Simianoids were sufficient to offset the pacifists, intellectuals, idealists whose antics were sure to convince the Marxist Federation that the Parliamentary Republic could easily be taken over.

Thought Control had kicked back. The Plastic Society had become so suggestible that it accepted whatever was offered, regardless of source. Most disastrous of all was that the elected representatives in Parliament were as other-directed as the electorate. The only qualification for office was the charm required to get votes. Social programs and theories, political so-called science, utopian economics were of a sort which if accepted by a chimpanzee would win him a spot in a simian booby-hatch. It was ponderings such as these which had given Mona the idea that Doc was overimpressed with Flora Garvin.

Stealthily, Doc picked his way along narrow paths which wriggled among bamboo and tropical vines. Bats flitted through the shadows. Small stirrings could be heard in the growth along the path. Birds chirped drowsily. The night was alive, yet without disturbing the stillness, any more than did the music. The jungle was talking in its sleep. For moments at a stretch, Doc forgot that he was stalking an enemy.

Startled by awareness that his attention was wavering, Doc regained control. Presently he sensed something which he had not yet heard or smelled. Halting, he closed his eyes so that other perceptions would have a better chance.

Somewhere to his right, that is, along the way leading from the village, barely perceptible cracklings sounded. Someone was moving toward the menagerie and toward headquarters. As the sound became louder, he recognized it: This was the season of falling teak leaves, long leaves which dropped and dried. Brittle, they crackled so readily that no human and few animals could move noiselessly among them. The distant sound became ever more faint and, shortly, was inaudible. Doc knew then that the prowler had cleared the short stretch of road which skirted a corner of the forest. He knew now where the prowler had been.

Brandon backtracked to intercept the man. Doc had two advantages: first, an inner line of approach, and second, a by-path which led close to the menagerie and to the surrounding clusters of bamboo. Their rustling would mask his approach.

Doc began to enjoy stalking the hunter of who-knew-what. And when he got the first whiff of menagerie scent, he knew that he had cut in well ahead of whoever was on the prowl. Soon he was worming his way among the bamboo which grew in clusters between the menagerie enclosures. As he neared the narrow road, he caught the odor of a cigar: not the smell of a Burmese cheroot, but the bouquet of good Havana exhaled by the garments of the prowler.

The breeze subsided and with it, the rustle of bamboo. Brandon fancied that he heard something stirring somewhat to his right, and then, a crisp click. It could have been the cocking of a pistol. It had not occurred to him that a snooper might be armed as insurance against having his departure disputed by villagers. And then he heard the crunch of footsteps. Someone wearing hard-soled shoes was moving toward him.

Still among bamboos, Brandon was now within sight of the dirt road, deeply rutted by Burmese cart wheels. Moonbeams dappled the track with light and shadow. The French had a word for it: *tigré*, irregularly striped, as a tiger, a zebra, or this cartway winding through jungle blackness and light.

From shadow-mass, a man emerged to cross a moon patch: a white man, almost certainly Wilson Epworth. He cuddled a small parcel in the crook of an arm. He took his time, trying to distinguish between shadow blobs and deep ruts.

Doc now knew where the man was, and within a meter, more or less. Groping in the darkness, he learned that he was on the fringe of a small circle cleared when a villager had chopped stalks of bamboo to build a thatched shack. Nga Than it was, always proud of his skill with the *kukri*: clean diagonal cuts, a single stroke to each stalk. Whether squaring the pieces or splitting them, his pride demanded that each length prove his expertise with sharp steel. A piece short of perfect: He'd not take it with him.

Brandon was not fussy. The first discard that came to hand suited his purpose. It was somewhat longer than three meters, and its silica-laden sap had long since dried, making the stalk hard and the slanting chisel edge glassy sharp. Doc shaped a prayer to the *nats*, all seven hundred million of them.

And then Doc understood that *click* which had sounded like the cocking of a pistol. He saw the creature before he heard the gurgling, purring, rasping-throaty snarl. The miniature *Machaerodus*, genus *Smilodon californicus*, had made that metallic sound in leaving his cage. He stepped from shadow into moonlight, pausing as he considered the scent of two prospective victims.

When Doc saw how prayer to the *nats* was to be answered, he knew that he could never convince a Parliamentary Commission that he had not planned the fatal caper. Doc's thinking was faster than the movement of any creature.

Epworth heard the gurgling throaty snarl, and he saw the gleaming coat ripple as the muscles played. He stood paralyzed—but his inability to move could not affect the outcome.

Thought being only a little slower than light, Doc had time to realize that *nats* had opened the locked cage. Gripping the bamboo, Doc bounded. Having started before the tiger, he was in place when the animal picked his quarry. The butt of the bamboo, firmly grounded, endured the shock when the slayer pounced. The bamboo shaft of a cavalry lance could survive a heavier impact, flex, recover, and be ready for the next enemy.

The glass-hard, curved chisel caught the white-furred belly and sank deep, driven home by the force of the charge. Doc was yanked from his knees before he could let go his pike. He was still rolling with the impaled tiger when a small man pounced from darkness. An axe flashed. Whether necessary or not, U Po Mya's chop settled the question.

Meanwhile, Brandon was directing action in the pattern planned before the tiger struck. He lunged, knocking Epworth off balance while the man still sought to do something, anything, fumbling while half paralyzed by panic. A *kung fu* chop as though struck by lightning.

Still moving as he had programed himself, Doc snatched the parcel which Epworth had dropped. U Po Mya helped Doc to his feet.

"*Payaaa!* That mother-fornicating brother of corpse-eating pigs—"

"Builder of pagodas," Brandon cut in, checking a new high in Burmese obscenities, "that man is not dead. He will come to his senses. Be so kind as not to kill him."

By the light of a high moon, Brandon and the village headman regarded each other. Between them was man-to-man understanding. U Po Mya waited for Divinity to speak, and Brandon knew what he had to say: "The *nats* from Tawadeintha unlocked the cage and cost me the life of a beautiful tiger."

U Po Mya pondered as propriety demanded before he said, "I grieve with you. I fed him when he was a kitten. I put my head beneath your golden feet. It would have offended the Lord Buddha if I had killed that dung-eater, but for a tiger, it would have been no sin at all, since killing is the *dharma* of tigers."

After considering Burmese logic, Doc said, "Without doubt the *nats* who unlocked the cage were agents of *karma*, and they did what they were required to do."

Two incomprehensibles faced each other. Each knew that between them was peace and goodwill: to demand understanding was for fools, not for grown men. Then Doc descended to reality.

"Builder of pagodas, perhaps you could persuade villagers to carry my guest to the guest house and ask the steward to take care of him. Then let them carry our tiger to the freezing place to be kept until I do some thinking.

"If everyone moves fast enough, this could be done before Dr. Epworth regains consciousness. If he recovers sooner, it cannot be helped. The beautiful tiger will not become a floor mat. He will be mounted, to look as alive."

Doc Brandon made for the headquarters complex and U Po Mya raced to the village to rout out a labor crew. Each in due course would burn incense to thank the *nats* who had unlocked the cage.

Chapter 8

When sleep and Isaiah's hangover antidotes had done their work, Doc Brandon went to the guest house for midday breakfast, made famous in New Orleans by Madame Bégué, more than two centuries ago. Stepping into the dining room, he caught the bouquet of crayfish bisque which a waiter was bringing from the kitchen.

"Good morning, gentlemen!" Doc turned on his sunrise glow. "Isaiah's prescription. Anyone wanting eggs, hash browns, toast and jelly, have at it. Grits and sowbelly optional."

The guests and especially Brandon's cherished enemy responded with more spontaneity than he had anticipated. "Revives the dead, the drunk, the drugged," he continued as he seated himself. "Parsley, thyme, bay leaves, minced green peppers, a dash of cayenne—those shrimpish looking things along the perimeter of your bowl, they are crayfish, shells stuffed with pounded crayfish. And just before serving, *filé*, pulverized sassafras leaves, go into the spicy lake of soup and happy crayfish.

"C-R-A-Y is the spelling, but C-R-A-W is how you say it."

One of the kitchen crew followed with a serving cart loaded with chilled glasses, bottles peeping from ice, and smaller bottles which should not be chilled. "Champagne?" Isaiah suggested. "The *Blanc des Blancs* is quite compatible, though many would prefer stout, half-and-half, or Black Velvet."

"I've heard that before. You're referring to porter and champagne?" Epworth said.

"Yes, sir, the classic you have in mind, not spirits."

Breakfast chit-chat was convincingly casual. Although the steward's therapies might have made the guests feel good as new, Doc got the impression that they were somewhat too pleased with themselves and the world. After stuffed crayfish in lakes of spicy soup had made way for oyster omelette, followed by halves of guinea hen, broiled, came strawberries in a rather dark Madeira wine. Doc, convinced that amiability was genuine, anticipated a showdown, with the Board of Visitors all relaxed and expecting victory. He was glad when coffee and cigars arrived, with brandy and *oloroso* sherry.

"Now that you've been welcomed," Doc led off, "let me stipulate that gene splicing is dangerous—that if *Bacillus e. Coli* combined, accidentally, with a hypothetical *Bacillus gubja*, it might produce something dangerous, something which could not be controlled by any known antibiotic. There might be a new cholera, or a quasi-bubonic plague which could wipe out ninety per centum of humanity. Right?"

"Right," Epworth echoed.

Brandon continued, "Many religionists are against modifying human genes. The diseases which occur only because of genetic defects could be prevented but, it is said, anyone going so far as to correct such defects might start cloning human beings."

His voice made it clear that this was not a rhetorical question. It was a statement to be accepted or rejected.

Chairman Epworth exhaled a smoke ring which on a pro rata basis must have cost at least an inflated *pazor*. "God might be displeased, which would be bad. Cloning raises questions such as, would first and successive clones have souls which could be saved or be punished in an everlasting hell? But for that last named, religionists, and I stipulate a significant number of exceptions, would perish of frustration. The bliss of being saved would be diluted if there were no damned to make the former appreciate salvation."

"The Stompers and the Testifiers," Doc reminded him, "are getting to be influential. Any views on their political clout?"

"God has not talked to me," Epworth confessed. "And if he had, I'd not be bright enough to understand."

"We're both in the same fix, then?" Brandon eyed Epworth. Their faces were brightened by an almost fraternal smile of understanding. Then, like the smack of an assault carbine, "Come clean, damn it! Now that the manure is brushed aside, why a sneak inspection? And moonlight prowls to promote good digestion?"

"There are curious blanks," the Chairman admitted with mock dreaminess. "The illusion of facing *Smilodon californicus*. Before the creature could slash me in half, I blacked out. Divine intervention, no doubt?"

Doc smiled, wagged his head. "To demonstrate gratitude for intervention, you're going to level with me?"

"I know you've been harassed by bureaucrats!" Epworth rang true, wholly genuine in that response. "I don't blame you for being defensive and suspicious."

There were times when Doc felt that his enemy was not wholly wrong; it did not surprise him, and he was glad that he did have something in common with Epworth. "If you think that I turned that tiger loose, you give me far too much credit! And since we're at it, I'll add that I did not arrange for someone else to turn the beast loose."

"Doc, I owe you a forthright statement. Now we are out in the open. Your God-damned tiger did it for us! Your having lived twice as long as the average North American is proof, by every law of probability, that you have benefited by something which has been kept secret almost two centuries. Serums, vitamins, hormones, genetic engineering, therapeutic radiation, whatever it's been, the nation needs the answer.

"This isn't fun and games. We have traced you. We have brushed aside a barricade of nonsense such as your having fraternized with Taoist masters who live a couple of hundred years, and some of them are said to carry on and on. Chinese talk about 'immortals.' We have not gulped that rubbish. But there are records which can't be ignored.

Fingerprints. Signatures. Physical examination papers for life insurance."

"For an *immortal!* Don't be funny! That blows your notions."

"But it doesn't. No one suggests that you are or ever could be accident- or violence-proof. I, we, *they* have in mind the fact that your existence as an adult has been traced to 1917, when you enlisted in the army for what they called the Kaiser War. That was one hundred sixty-nine years ago. Atfer that war, you faded out. You changed your name and served in later wars. We found records of you in China and in Chinese Turkistan. With phony papers, amazing scientific talents, you made a name for yourself. It took years to uncover your history, your background."

"First you fit me with a synthetic past, now you ask me to live up to it."

Epworth shook his head. "You are far from the standard human. We found you in a stupor when we arrived. Your secretary's bedroom reeked of Nuance, Aphrodisia, and distilled spirits. No wonder neither of you had been smoking. The air was an explosive mixture."

Doc grinned. "I did hang one on!"

"And, sobered up miraculously, drank four of us to the verge of catalepsy. Staged a magnificent show of being fall-down drunk, with your girl dragging you home."

"About that time," Brandon reminded him, "you must have set out for the Burmese village. Sober and reckless enough to intrude when the natives are chanting the devils into line."

Epworth shrugged. His squarish face brightened in a whimsical smile. "The music fascinated me. So did the total paralysis of four men and five women. Folk dancing at full moon. The idea was inviting, and for reasons of your own, you did not have me doped." He paused more for effect than for breath. "Don't tell me that your girl's mattress therapy sobered you up so you could beat off a custom-built tiger."

Doc sighed. "I used to be somewhat of an athlete," he conceded modestly. "Once on an Olympic duelling sword team. *Epée*, you know. One of the runners-up. Good, but not good enough."

Epworth pushed back his chair, got to his feet. "What happened last night was not staged. Everlasting youth? Immortal practically, if not absolutely so? Do not tell me you are an accidental mutant. Your father was a pioneer in genetic engineering. You were planned before you were conceived, if you ever were, in the usual sense of the word."

"Immaculate conception was hackneyed in the days of Gautama the Buddha, born some six centuries Bee-Cee. Long before him, Sri Krishna was born of *two* virgin mothers, and that unusual feat is logically explained."

"God damn it, you can be entertaining!" Epworth's ruddy, heavy face crinkled amiably. "You suggest that being a world savior is out these days and you'd not want to be one, whether manufactured, cloned, or whatever the method might have been. I heard of the two virgin mothers of Krishna from a Unitarian minister in a debunking mood. Here is negative evidence, but it is hard to reject. We have not found a birth certificate, public school record, or census record of your existence. You appeared, full grown, about nineteen years old and accepted for enlistment in the United States Army—a God-damned warmonger, the draft age those days was twenty-one and you went because you wanted to."

The final clause was spoken with good-humored mockery. So was Doc's retort: "Bureaucracy had not been perfected to today's level. Many of my generation did not have birth certificates or any record of birth. And census takers at times missed families living in isolated rural areas. You're out a foot and dragging in the dust, Wilson."

"You've made it clear that you are not going to tell us anything. Let me clarify something: You are going to give convincing answers to our questions. Answers that are plausible to other scientists."

"And if I cannot?"

"The Government's highest level will put you out of business till the end of your endless life. If you think Government cannot find a flaw in your title to Nameless Island, you're demented."

"Granted. Eminent Domain. Retirement home for fruit and nut peddlers."

"Don't bother telling me what Alexander Heflin will do to protect you. He tried to squelch Rod Garvin, and Garvin tore a planned election to shreds. What gave Garvin the clout to shake the Consortium will give Government what it needs to settle you."

Doc chuckled. "Looks as if you're going to make a contest of this. Isaiah will jeep you to my airport. Gentlemen, I have enjoyed this more than you have. Next time you're out this way, give me a few days' notice and we'll have fun."

Chapter 9

Doc Brandon's analysis of the contents of the bottle from the parcel which Wilson Epworth had dropped when the tiger confronted him was no great project. His sample was so small that Epworth would never suspect anyone had tapped the bottle. The solution evaporated quickly, leaving a thin, pliable, and transparent film which was not soluble in water or alcohol. It did not irritate the skin. Neither shaving nor bathing would remove it, though in time it would wear away. Finally, and this was what set Doc thinking, the film emitted a red glow when exposed to a beam of infrared of a wavelength between 0.00129 and 0.00173 centimeters. This was longer than any solar radiation and it was not visible to the eye.

According to U Po Mya, Epworth had marked every white infant in the village nursery with a daub from a bottle, presumably the one which Doc had picked up. The village headman suspected that dirty work was in progress: magic, very likely. For the Burmese to question the Master's guest or to interfere with his doings would be a gross breach of etiquette. However, U Po Mya was as resourceful as he was tactful and courteous. He released the tiger, who would not be bound by social tabus. Intent on his work, he had not been aware of Doc's presence until it was too late. Presumably he had taken a hatchet with him, in case he ran afoul of Epworth and had to defend himself.

U Po Mya, in telling his story, stated that he had followed Epworth and just happened to be at hand when the tiger got to work. The headman had always admired Doc Brandon's instinctive response to the Asiatic mind and ever abstaining from rude questionings. Doc had reached the ultimate pinnacle when he blamed the tiger's escape on the doings of *nats*. For U Po Mya to have confessed would have put Doc into an awkward position; whereas as long as he did not know other than that night-prowling devils were responsible, all was well.

Doc had later watched a Malay and two Burmese nursemaids using a solvent to remove the film from the branded infants, leaving no trace. A question remained, and there were no convenient *nats* to answer it: Aside from marking infants, what could one do with such a solution? And another query: Was that solution's response to infrared rays of a certain wavelength purely a matter of coincidence?

Doc realized that rejecting the obvious was unwise, but he did not dally with such possibilities as marking bills set out as bait for embezzlement suspects or offered to narcotics peddlers or as a blackmail payoff.

In the course of a cozy midnight snack, Doc gave Mona a sketch of why he had been so preoccupied ever since the visitors' departure.

"What's the stuff good for?" And then, "Oswald barely came back to work when he's on the road again. Doc, you and I are never going to have that honeymoon."

Doc sighed. "I know, and I've been promising you ever since we were busy getting used to each other. And I said that when Oswald learned the routine, we'd get away. And I've never got you that broadtail coat I promised you, that freakish cold winter."

"I've always been sorry about the way I slapped you. When you said *broadtail*, I didn't know you were talking about a sheep from Asia. That's what you get for seducing a country girl!" A pensive moment, and then, "He didn't have to hustle away so soon after he got back."

"To convoy that batch of infants. The Adoptive Parents League is screaming like eagles. This batch has to come from Atlanta. I can't have too many coming from any small place, and there is a limit to how often I send to even a large place."

"You don't need the money! I know they're paying twenty-thousand *pazors* for each one, but you're loaded."

"I might as well tell you the rest. Those white infants are Simianoid clones. Because adoption is in and there is a howling demand, by the time the bureaucrats are done processing an infant, he is a draft dodger or she is applying for her Pleasure, Vice, & Recreation license, hence the demand for under-the-table adoptions."

Mona frowned. "Don't tell me you've become a dedicated idealistic humanitarian?"

"Madame Broadtail, I am getting Simianoid clones into a wide range of homes. With enough of them to constitute fair sampling, I could—anyone could—arrive at a valid judgment as to whether environment overwhelms heredity or whether innate nature will prevail.

"No matter what the facts, sociologists in an egalitarian society will stick to their doctrines and strive for a level of mediocrity which everyone can achieve. Now that my thoughts are well off the track, let's have another round of fizzes."

Doc's infrared projector device could save universities millions of *pazors* by reducing, perhaps eliminating, vandalism and arson and indemnities awarded to police seriously injured by hurled bottles, bricks, scrap iron, homemade grenades, and other improvisations not considered to be weapons. The time was at hand. There was much indignation when a frustrated educator declared, in response to his regents' demand for a curriculum which would not discourage engineering, mathematics, and the rugged sciences, *"Ninety percent of our student body has no place even in high school. We can't give them intelligence. All we can do is confer degrees."*

The music of cracked ice in the shaker deflected Brandon's speculations. He looked up and about. Having got his attention from science, Mona confessed that something had been puzzling her. "It's this life-everlasting business. It shows up in lookee-squawkee programs; they work it into gags. And one of the waitresses overheard a few things some of the Board of Visitors yakked about. She had to go back to the farm before she had a chance to tell me much."

"You mean Eloise?" At Mona's nod, Doc continued. "I thought so. Her Number Three husband still borrows books from me. Are you going spiritual?"

"Well, no, but I get curious at times."

"You mean the resurrection theory versus reincarnation? Or dying and going to Kwan Yin's Paradise of the West? Staying right on this Earth by practicing Taoist magic or yoga to live on and on, as I am rumored to be doing—unless I'm using modern science—or dying and going to heaven, the way the Stompers and Testifiers believe? Life everlasting covers quite a field and the funny thing is, nobody who's died has ever come back to tell all about it."

"I never imagined there were so many options. The Alleluia Stompers said there was only one answer, the one that some god or other told someone or other, and if you didn't believe it, you went to hell instead of heaven when you died. You have neglected my religious education."

"I figured the Stompers gave you enough for a lifetime. Getting back to your first question, the Board of Visitors told me that I'd either share the secret or they'd put me out of business."

"Oh, they couldn't do that."

"A majority-rules outfit can and will do anything that'll get votes. I remember right after the Kaiser War, this country made liquor unconstitutional. The men that won the war for democracy had to sneak their liquor illegally. The Kaiser never dared try any such silliness with his people."

"This life-everlasting business," she persisted, and poured the fizzes. "If the Stompers and the like believe what they claim they do, about going to heaven, how come they hang on, year after year, suffering all kinds of miseries, when all they'd have to do is laugh at the doctor, drink good liquor for painkiller, and go to heaven instead of sobering up?"

"Doll, that's always puzzled me. You better ask the Stompers."

Meanwhile, using plastic tape, wire, epoxy cement, Maung Gauk's carbine, plus odds and ends from the shop and laboratory stores, Doc improvised a working model of a device to exterminate alien enemies who stirred up trouble on every university campus in the Republic. The rifle was fitted with an optical system which combined an infrared projector and a telescopic sight. The projector activated the patch of telltale spray on an agitator who had infiltrated himself into the student body. When a sharpshooter spotted one thus identified, he got his man. It would be simple to set security operators to work on the campus. Identifying agitators would be no problem: In their zeal to circulate their propoganda they would skip no one. On the contrary, security men would find it difficult to avoid being approached. He would be a good fellow, always having a bottle at hand and funds for more.

Spraying an agitator with telltale solution would be easy.

Doc sent blueprints and the model to Alexander Heflin, Chairman of the Consortium. The group had no legal status, so it worked off stage, manipulating the paper cutouts whose shadows appeared on-screen: shadows elected by the Plastic Populace, the most highly educated and most ignorant electorate known to history.

The next time Mona brought up the matter of a couple of weeks in New Orleans, Doc said, "Right now, I'm likely to get a call from Alexander Heflin. He has to get the computers programed and convince hell knows how many bureaucrats that no robots need be built. We're not equipping an army! Until my invention's in production I ought to be here by the hotline to Alexander's headquarters.

"Simianoids or Coolies could tend to anything I'd be asked to do, but every bumbling bastard in the hierarchy who fancies he is a scientist is unable to imagine that anyone without a bunch of degrees could settle a production bug."

"Doc, darling, while they are trying to decide when they get their thumbs out and start looking at the specs and blueprints, you and I could go to New Orleans and that Dixie Delta fishing club and paddle our pirogue around the private lake. I'll paddle and you fish. I can mock the moccasins getting the sun on their lily pads, and when you have caught no fish, the steward will dip beautiful bass out of the kitchen pond and we'll have a swamp-and-bayou dinner. I've heard about it so often, I remember everything.

We'll have Peychaud bitters with gin, and I'll hate it but I'll drink every drop.

"Here's where you ought to delegate authority. Look at Genghis Khan: He never even could write his own name, but he got to be Emperor of all Mankind. He had a Chinaman to do his writing. Doc, I just can't understand—"

And then he had armful of woman-in-tears.

"You've always been so awfully good to me. It's been won-wonderful, being away from the Holy Stompers and drinking and whoring around with you. All these years hearing about New Orleans, the Valley of Mexico, looking at travelogues of Khatmandu, Cuzco, Kh-khartoom. We never go *anywhere!*"

"Dream Girl—"

"I won't mix us a drink! I know you always mean what you say. That's why I've told you, over and over, your science crap is more important than I ever was!"

"It won't be more than two weeks."

"Ever since I convinced you I was old enough and big enough, it's always been only two weeks. You've been saying we ought to have a real honeymoon in the only fun city left in North America."

Doc's face solidified into stern angles. "I'll phone Alexander right God damn now!"

Mona drew a deep breath and held it until she was near bursting. Finally she exhaled, slowly sank back into the depths of her chair, and sat looking at him.

"I mean it!" Catching Mona's hand, Doc had her on her feet before she could believe things were taking shape. "Get a load of this, and you might as well learn how to use the hotline."

He fumbled for a key he rarely used, unlocked a small panel in the side of the lookee-squawkee. "Don't write the code numbers, learn them later."

He punched buttons and activated the instrument as for standard communication. The screen came to life. No face confronted him. "This is a recording. Doc, I'm sorry I am not here. Tell me what is going on. That riot inhibitor looks good. Wait for the beep."

"Alex, get someone to work coordinating the riot inhibitor with audiovisual recording. Film the damage, the broken bottles, and the razor-blade potatoes and get sound of a punk saying '*Well, that's not really a weapon, and the pigs are brutal.*' Have someone tend to that routine. I'm taking a couple weeks out, well away from the Island. Mona and I are leaving in the morning. And we will not, repeat *not* be wishing you were with us. Over and out!"

As Doc locked the scrambler keyboard, Mona wondered whether to eat first or start packing.

"Isaiah will boat us to the mainland. We'll make the plane that'll get us there in time to buy you whatever you need. But don't forget your handbag. *Whatever* includes that broadtail jacket."

He dug into the freezer and got black-eye peas, sow belly, hominy grits, turnip greens, hushpuppies.

"Doc, you're making me homesick! I'll be an Alleluia Stomper the minute I eat that stuff. Do they wear revolutionary costumes in New Orleans?"

"It's a showplace; doesn't need masquerading. They've not dared touch a thing in the *Vieux Carré* the past century and a half. The people think in French and their English has a local, special flavor. They still say *banquette* when they mean sidewalk."

"Never saw a sidewalk. This'll be fun."

"*Gallery* means balcony. *Lagniappe* is the extra dividend the grocer gives you when you buy your day's victuals. And at the French Market Coffee stand, what foreigners call doughnuts are really *beignets*. But I've said it all before."

"I love it! Tell me more. I'll not sleep a wink all night."

The bell which signaled a scrambled message did not interrupt rural food. It broke only into half sleep. Instantly Mona was wide awake and tense. She pounced after Doc and stood by as Alexander Heflin said, "Doc, cancel that honeymoon. I mean, postpone it a bit. This is critical."

"No can do, Alex."

"Things are simmering in Megapolis."

"Things are blazing in Nameless Island."

"Bring her along! I'll have the universal passport ready."

"Universal?"

"Well, no farther than Mars."

"Tough shit, Alex! I've been promising her a honeymoon. See you in two weeks!" He cut the switch.

Mona stood beside him, and there was something in her greenish eyes that he had never before seen. The feline expression about which he had so often teased her had vanished, and in them there was only beauty and wonder. "You old devil, I could love you from now till judgment day."

Chapter 10

Doc Brandon's decision took shape in a private dining room of a two-and-a-half-century-old restaurant a few doors off Royal Street. He said to his half-dozen guests, "I'd hoped to sit with you a couple more hours tonight, and I had plans for tomorrow and the day after, but something tells me"—he gave Mona a long, steady look— "that we ought to get out, and now."

Doc beckoned to the waiter in charge of the serving. "Numa, take care of my guests as long as they can sit up and drink. Then get them into cabs and on their way home."

Quitting their hotel, Doc and Mona made the plane with half an hour to spare. From Savannah, a helicopter set them down at Nameless Island's mainland port. A slow launch brought them to the dock. There Isaiah waited to cart them to headquarters.

Once the door of headquarters closed behind Doc and Mona, he said, "The way you did *not* squawk when I pulled the switch on our honeymoon, not even silent sulking—one of these days, I'll make up for it. Help me listen to what's been recorded since we left."

Once in the office, Doc unlocked the scrambler and the inbound message controller. Negative. Doc frowned. "I still stick to my hunch. Before I call Alex, I'll show you again how to put a call through, straight or scrambled. This is the signal keyboard, and the other one programs the computer that works the system."

The buttons were marked ADMINISTRATION CENTER, SUBURBAN LODGE MINOR, THE CLUB, and then a column giving Megapolitan Beta, Megapolitan Gamma, and a few rural spots which Doc did not explain. Mona asked no questions, primarily because she suspected that they were ultraconfidential hideouts.

"These take messages for him. It has to be clear, no scrambling, or I'd not be relayed. See what you can do. If you get him, stand back enough for him to see us both in the pilot screen. Time he's meeting you."

Mona punched buttons. Over her shoulder she said, "If you get the Sultan of Zanzibar, don't blame me!"

When the screen came to life, Doc and Mona faced the Chairman of the Consortium. His usually sleek black hair was rumpled and his angular face deeply lined. "So, you're back!" Penetrating dark eyes shifted to Mona, and the stern mouth became amiable. "No, it wasn't disaster, taking your trip, but I am glad you cut it short."

"Break the news. Mona's reliable."

"She'd have to be, and pretty durable, keeping up with you! Mona, welcome home! Now get this. Your friend Wilson Epworth has cooked up a Parliamentary Commission investigation: selling infants to the Adoptive Parents League. He's trying to get a felony indictment. And there's a limit to what I can do for you."

"Alex, he told me there was nothing you could do. Get me a good attorney and maybe we can surprise Epworth."

Alexander continued, "There've been student demonstrations, pacifistic stuff, the kind that invites war. Promise of not even token resistance. Border incidents in Turkistan. First of all, I want you to go to Mars for a look-see. Among other things, find out how the Simianoids working in the Rehabilitation project feel.

"And the Consortium wants to talk to you."

"Before or after I'm exiled to Mars?"

"As soon as you can get here." Alexander Heflin was not even trying to keep from looking harassed—but then he had a flash of his standard self. "Mona, Doc, soon as things shake down, you get a dictator-size honeymoon at government expense!"

Alexander waved good-bye, and the screen went blank.

Then Mona asked, "How much do you suppose he held out because I was standing by?"

"I'll digest it in my sleep and give you the guess for an eye opener."

Breakfast smells and sounds awakened Brandon. He had slept through Mona's long shower and makeup routine. When they got from grits, eggs, sausages, to fried apples, biscuits, and peach preserves, she said, "Tell me before it gives you indigestion. I couldn't make sense of what you were saying in your sleep."

"It's not the package Alex handed me, though the risks I'm facing—referring to prowling Mars—do bring it to the surface. Every so often, the past couple of years, I've told about that romance, maybe a hundred and sixty years ago, when I met a girl about your age."

"You've always shied away from it before you said enough to count. I got the idea that if you two had aged together, it would have been nice and cozy. But her getting out of step with you got you both started with science and nonscience to keep her from aging."

"That's about it. When she died, I gave up. My father's papers and my work with him gave me a big start in gene splicing, but I dropped the longevity business. I still don't know whether I am a freak or one of the Old Man's experiments that worked."

Mona had a long moment of silence, then said, very slowly, "Maybe he made it and found out it was a lousy idea and killed the records." And then, all pointed and present, "Why'd you dummy up when Epworth tried to blackmail you into giving the scientific world an experimenter's chance?"

For a moment she was sure that Doc was poised on that bridge, narrow as a hair, between heaven and hell, as the Moslems, many of them, visualize. And then she knew better.

He said, "That'll keep. What has troubled me is you and me.

"Our honeymoon was fun in a way that was different from our first getting to know each other, but it wasn't meeting the world, people, and their ways of living. Before Oswald and I signed that permanent contract, I sent him back to spend time with his friends, with women he'd been interested in. To find out if there was one who thought she would see Nameless Island as congenial instead of an ordeal.

"Whatever happened during that leave of absence, he came back and settled for Amina. Or Mei-ling. Or a Burmese girl.

"I've known from the beginning that you had more than just a *right* to meet the outside world. You *ought* to meet it, and it was my obligation to give you a chance. Whether you wanted it or not.

"Getting you out of that Stomper's town-colony was important, but spending time there with those really good people—fanatics, yes, but also good. The big test was in finding out whether you were one of the ninety-nine percent of gullibles who believe the first thing they hear and can't ever admit a new viewpoint much less accept one. Or one of the few real skeptics."

"Which am I?"

"Life will tell you that. Sure, I could say things, but Life does more than talk. My guess is, you're a natural skeptic, and you've gained by living with Stomper fundamentalists, without being poisoned for life by their superstitions. Somewhere I have *The Book of Thoth—An Essay on the Tarot of the Egyptians*. It was published, fifth edition, 1978, but if you can't find mine in the library, you could probably get a copy from a dealer in Megapolis Alpha or Beta, or a later printing."

"I should be a fortune teller?"

"Turn to the '*Prince of Discs*,' page one sixty-eight. '*The fifty-third hexagram, Kien, symbolizes liberation from oppression.*' And about the middle of the page, you get to the deadliest oppression that has ever soul-sickened the Western world. *You were born free.* Not even the Stompers could warp you with their well-meant teachings.

"But here I go, rambling, wandering again."

"That's always fun, Doc. Carry on."

"Back to my point. I knew my duty to you from the start, but I kept putting it off. I hated the idea of ever letting you get out of reach, sight, smell. I still hate the idea—worse than ever. I've become addicted to you. If it got any worse, I'd never live up to my duty.

"So, here I am. The mess that has Alex talking to himself became possible because of science and scientists. A society supported by Simianoids and Coolies, a masquerade ball, the Lard Ass Luxury Life, the Ferocious Pursuit of Gracious Living! So when the Consortium thinks it is time to turn out Damage Control, I cannot back down. Having lived more than two standard lifetimes, I have done twice as much damage as my colleagues.

"Being separated by this local headache which may blossom out into a full-dress war gives you a chance to meet the bitched-up world. Oswald is one of the better specimens. Maybe he'd not be congenial, but he'd do as a basis of comparison when you meet someone you think you fancy.

"In case I am a casualty, there's a fund for you at the Megapolitan Alpha Trust & Savings, and life interest in the Island."

"Doc, you do not like this one tiny bit more than I do. If I met someone awfully fascinating, maybe I'd not come back, and you'd not blame me, but I'd always be sorry."

Doc nodded. "You and I would always miss each other. That's why I dallied, never telling you what was ahead of us."

"I might hurry home, soon as you come back from Mars. I'd know you'd always stay young, and I'd finally wear out and fold." She straightened, brushed back strands of ruddy bronze hair. "I'd not fight it or expect you to keep me young. You can shove science. I've got an answer, right now!"

"Sound off, Doll!"

"I'd read books on necrophilia and buy a nice shroud and we'd both stay young. If that didn't work, you'd learn to get used to outliving women, and I'd settle for having had a good life. Enough is enough and too much is for slobs.

"And now that I have the floor, I'll confess. I did a lot

of snooping and I found old logbooks and stuff. I found out I am a Simianoid, a great improvement on the standard humans.

"So if they are too slobbish, I'll be the odd woman in a Simianoid colony and everyone will welcome me. I'd be taking the place of some girl who has a chance of meeting a Board of Visitors, or going to a convention, or fill in for a girl who is writing a book or thinking of a career or is overdosed with maternal urges and gets pregnant too often."

Each had taken a stride in discovering the other. Revelation gave each a fresh glow until the cloud of whimsy thinned and they parachuted to floor level.

Doc sighed. "I feel better, now that I finally got around to this. Oswald fell for you at first sight."

"He's nice, but he can be dull, juvenile. The standard American horse's arse, to put it bluntly. I'll be sitting at the lookee-squawkee. You're bound to make the news. I've simply got to see a student riot. If the silly bastards don't stage one, see what you can do to stir them up. That infrared gadget ought to be fun—I mean, seeing it working."

"I've survived two lifetimes of grief and trouble." Doc was beginning to feel sad and lonesome, knowing that it would become much worse before it got better. "What'll I bring back for you? From Megapolis, I mean. Mars has nothing but tremendous vistas and some good-looking Gook girls, and you'd have damn little use for either."

Mona got to her feet. She flipped her negligee aside and gave her backside a curved palm slap. Though not with Doc's skill, she did well enough to get that ripe-melon sound.

"Now that I've got my broadtail jacket, there's nothing to bring back except yourself."

Whereby she settled everything except delaying that good cry until Doc was off the Island.

Chapter 11

From the jet which circled for landing, Doc Brandon looked down on the compound domes which housed Megapolis Alpha. The Thought Control Center, the Composite North American Brain of the Plastic Society, was near the central dome; well beyond the Megapolitan limits, the buildings and landing fields of Lunar & Martian Spaceport brought him up to date, with memories of the ill-fated *Saturnienne* and Flora Garvin, Queen of Space Widows, as an extra dividend.

Helitaxiflight from spaceport to Central Mall showed Doc as three-dee could not how Megapolis Alpha had spread. From low elevation he could no longer see the perimeter. And then he was afoot, squinting at plaques and pavement to learn which colored stripe led to areas enclosed by domes that excluded the weather but transmitted ultraviolet, infrared, and all intermediate wavelengths in salutary proportion.

Outliving the colleagues who had designed the heart of that ever-expanding monster of crime, opulence, and futility, he remembered them and recalled the vision which had brightened all their eyes when they had been as young as he still looked. Doc missed those long-departed friends and was glad that they were not able to see how he and they had so far overestimated theory, doctrine, and ignored the immutability of human nature.

He was glad, and he was sad: And he summed it up by

murmuring, "Shit plus two equals seven."

At least one in ten Megapolitan folk wore traditional dress. Another tenth, such as Doc, wore felt-soled shoes, floppy pants, tunic-shirt worn outside, reaching halfway to the knees. The women who flaunted such unisex garb proclaimed that they balked at being "sex objects." Devoid of hairdo and of complexion natural or artificial, they not only could report "*Mission Accomplished*" but also illustrate the meaning of overkill.

The remainder of the population reached extremes of color and elegance and pretense.

Megapolis Alpha, *the* Megapolis, matched her denizens. The malls were peppered with minarets, domes, pagodas, Styrofoam replicas of the mighty columns of Karnak. However little the chance of war with the Egypt of Ramses II, whenever the Islamic Coalition leveled an unkind look at *any* non-Moslem state, protesters set to work with graffiti and explicit anatomical paint jobs, *yoni* and *lingam*, on Egyptianesque temples.

Doc's universal Identification and Kredit Kard got him instant admission to the Administration Building, past three inner offices and three screening secretaries, into the room where Alexander Heflin habitually pondered and abstractedly worked at solitaire or chess problems while the Consortium and its subordinates coped with ulcers, angina, high blood pressure, and died circa age fifty-five. The difference between Alexander and those men was not so much a matter of natural gifts as it was the ability to make a decision, launch a project, and pull the switch instead of fretting and pacing the poop deck. When something fouled up, as things often did, Alexander Heflin was fresh, relaxed, and ready to tackle the tigers of the mental, the intangible world.

The Alexander who greeted Doc was renewed, refreshed, and quite different from the man who had confronted him from the screen of the lookee-squawkee. There was no pause for drinks and chitchat. They went at once to the Consortium's conference room, where the group sat at the table. Two chairs at its head were unoccupied.

Ambridge, beetle browed, swarthy, was sounding off:

". . . sergeant at arms hollered, '*Who called the Prime*

Minister a son of a bitch?' and someone in the spectator's gallery shouted, *'Who called that son of a bitch a Prime Minister?'* and then—"

"Now that the Prime Minister has been disposed of," Heflin cut in, "I know your time's been well spent. I'll not apologize for showing up late.

"Whether or not you've had the pleasure of meeting him face to face, I'm sure you've seen him on Three Dee. Gentlemen, our consultant on Simianoids, the inventor of the Simianoid, Dr. Avery Jarvis Brandon." Then, turning to Doc, "Now you know that the Consortium exists. But for them, our Parliament and Prime Minister would be cracking their skulls trying to cope with national problems and worrying because they do not have sufficient time and energy to dedicate to their paramount concern, the art of being reelected."

Heflin named the half dozen, of whom two were absent, and then, to the Consortium, "Ambridge, lead off, and the rest of you, ad lib when your contributions are relevant. When Doc Brandon has an outline of the situation, he'll know better what can be done, what might be done, and what cannot be done.

"And that last is what usually has to be done."

Ambridge went into orbit: "Alex, when you came in, I was generalizing. Getting down to specifics, Parliament urged our Prime Minister to invite the Marxist Federation to send a division of its soldiers to be our *guests*, join us in our war games on the Gulf Coast, Cherokee Parish, Louisiana. Landing and assault operations.

"It, the idea, I mean, of inviting the Marxist troops is part of the *One World, One Government, One Language League* that started the protests against the war games. Having lost that round, they are urging this substitute effort toward world peace."

Gaylord, a wiry and grim veteran of three wars, cut in. "I thought I'd heard every horse's ass idea, but a man can always learn something new! One division of troops that mean business could take this country over and the peace-at-any-price group would be dancing in the street."

"We're not here to diddle around with our druthers," Ambridge said. "I'm telling you what we are stuck with—

fraternizing with nations that have always competed in teaching each nation to cooperate! Everyone knows that regimental fellowships are the closest bonds in every social order. God damn it, I am not being funny, they mean this! Having a couple of divisions joining in war games would make for international friendship. Twenty thousand Slivovitz troops, seeing what nice people we are, would go home and three hundred fifty million Marxists would spread the word that we are not imperialistic warmonger assassins. They'd all become democratic, honoring human rights, they'd become just like us."

Ambridge glared down the line of faces. "Parliament is committed to it. Can't cancel it. That'd be an international snub. We got nowhere opposing it. Our thought-control routine is a dead loss: Legislators and electorate have become such psychic sponges that anyone can influence them. Our routine isn't working as it used to."

"Who is included in 'we'?" Alexander asked.

"Gilson surveyed the volunteer army. Larry, you report; you did most of the work there."

Gilson, slouching comfortably, brushed back a shock of hair, a species of sandy-mouse-gray. "I heard something you would not believe." He dug into the side pocket of his tweed jacket and brought out a microrecorder. "I took this gadget with me. Hear what the Chairman—Oops! Pardon *me*—Chair*person* of the Parliamentary Armed Forces Committee was telling the Joint Chiefs of Staff."

He nudged the switch. The tiny instrument sounded off: "I am aware that we cannot immediately eradicate the urge to war. For quite too many millennia, the human psyche has succumbed to the thought that violence is the only solution to controversial questions. Accordingly, we do not propose to abolish armies. Such an attempt could not help but fail.

"However, after the usual deploying of forces by each adversary, there would be a conference. A truce before hostilities, instead of waiting until many thousands on each side had been killed. Each army of course would be duty bound to sustain the views of the government it serves."

A new voice came from the instrument: "You mean army commanders stage a debate? The cause of every war is the failure of debate, discussion by civilians, the power-crazed megalomaniacs who stir up an insoluble mess and then call on the 'warmonger' so-called to resolve the problem."

Then the reply: "General, your point is well raised. However, no vocal dialectic is contemplated. The modern way, the proposed enlightened way is that each commander of the entirety of the army groups of his government will feed into an appropriately programed computer the data: that is to say, a tabulation of manpower, supply potential, available armament, and, of course, an assessment of terrain. Thus far psychologists and sociologists have not agreed on the *Kappa* Factor, an evaluation of morale.

"However, omitting that factor will give a valid result, at least one far superior to the arbitration of war. The computer will give a printout in duplicate, stating which army would have won, had war been waged.

"Thus, without bloodshed or the dreadful material waste of war, the issue would be decided. There would be an additional benefit. The loser, so called, would actually be gaining: Representative regiments would be the guest-prisoners of the victor. They would learn the positive aspects of the victor's society, an understanding of his social order, of his life style. At the termination of this stage, the duration of which would be computer-determined, the guest-prisoners would be paroled to their native homes, to disseminate what they had gained."

The recorder cut off.

Irvin, nearly as Doc could remember the name, was the first to break the impressive silence. He seemed dazed, more so than the others, though he proved to be picking his words deliberately, which the others were not yet able to do. ". . . Am I to . . . infer . . . that any . . . human uttered—is that silly bastard a fugitive from an insane asylum? Larry, you sure that is not a gag?"

"I *knew* someone would say that. No, this is straight! And when General Dargan, commandant of the Marine Corps, sounded off, I forgot to flip in a fresh reel."

"Give us the gist of it," Binkley demanded.

"Dargan said he'd heard of a madman shouting down a deep well, but God damn if he'd ever heard one puking before he found a well. Loving your enemy is grand work in Sunday school, but on the battlefield, the North American Parliamentary Republic's Corps of Marines has only one object: destroy the enemy before the sons of bitches escape or surrender.

"So the Chairperson demanded General Dargan's retirement from active duty. The Parliament of North America would have no warmongers in its armed forces."

Alexander nudged Doc. "Begin to see why I wanted you to sit in with us?"

"While the recorder is recuperating from shock, would Mr. Gilson or one of his associates report on the Army and Navy?" Doc said.

Another of the Consortium took over. "The Parliamentary Republic's Volunteer Army is paid well enough to compete with industrial wages. It is packed with conscientious objectors, pacifists, One Worlders, and the like. Great emphasis on Democracy, Egalitarianism. Morale is good. Very little *AWOL*, though about twenty percent of the soldierettes, the Amazons, do not stand reveille. Morning sickness, you know. About that number are on maternity leave. The union is demanding total permanent disability compensation for stretch marks incurred in the line of duty."

"Hold it!" Doc demanded. "No doubt about *in the line of duty,* but how come the *total disability*?"

"If an Amazon goes out for a career as a stripteaser, a model, or a PVR Girl, well, she'd not have the American dream-girl virginal appearance and she couldn't get good assignments."

"Par for the course," Doc conceded. "How about the Navy?"

"The Admirals Club threatened to resign, en masse, unless all the social reforms were annulled, and the service went back to all-male and Men of Iron. Lot of men and seagoing Amazons didn't even protest. They didn't want to enlist, or reenlist. So there's the isolated and untainted Navy. Submariners are top importance."

Gaylord, a veteran of several wars of liberation, reported on the border incidents along the extreme western frontier of the People's Republic of China. "Always 'deplorable errors' and apologies. The incidents are feelers to keep in touch. One side is scared and the other is damn glad of it.

"China has a three-thousand-year tradition of revolution. The Marxist flavor this time was an expedient, and when it served its purpose, it was revised to accord with Chinese common sense, and China did not become a Marxist satellite-vassal-possession. Whereby the Marxist Federation lost reams of face. Particularly because the civilized Chinese with five thousand years of culture of a high order consider the Marxists animals, barbarians, unrealistic oafs even for pretending that you can *ever* get any country going and keep it so when you eliminate individual profit.

"The fat boys know better but they are smart enough to exploit the sucker-mass that snapped at fool's bait. The Chinese revised Marxism, as they have every invasion, and converted it into Chineseishness. Since they consider their country to be the heartland of the world, which it was until the Industrial Revolution, they have no urge to expand. They have all they need, in civilization, culture, and natural richness.

"Which Marxists hate and want to cut in on. So the *Chinaman* People's Republic of China, if courteously approached, might welcome a visitor division of our troops, for an exchange of ideas on desert and mountain war games in extreme western China, which they call 'Sinkiang,' Chinese for 'New Dominion.' They've only occupied it two thousand years. We usually call it Chinese Turkistan, or Eastern Turkistan.

"Parliamentary knotheads would snap at the idea. How wonderful fraternizing with a backward nation! We're going one-world, and since China wears a film of Marxism, we're all the more progressive making this fine gesture of friendliness."

"Nice work," Doc interpolated. "What troops would we send?"

Gaylord, the multiplex war veteran, answered. "Our volunteer troops—they'd go for the cultural experience. The American mind has tagged the Chinese as a mysterious race of dumb plodding coolies—totally backward laundrymen and restaurant operators who are also great artists, philosophers, and, best of all, Marxists!"

"Keno!" Doc exclaimed. "And all Simianoids now in service should be concentrated into solidly Simianoid divisions. Buck up their morale. They'd have no confidence in the typical volunteer crowd. If an outfit has men in whom their comrades can put no trust, it's useless.

"And to welcome the Marxist war games troops to our Gulf Coast landing and assault maneuvers, get an all-Simianoid division."

"Good, but hard to get away with," one of the Consortium objected. "Be discriminatory. You'd have to include women and standard troops."

A more realistic member retorted, "Foul up the paperwork. Order the standard troop division to Arizona for desert training and the Simianoids to Louisiana. By the time you submit forty-two 'explanations,' it'd be too late to unravel the error. Every bureaucrat will go with you. They've never known anything to work as planned."

Doc wagged his head, grinned contentedly. "Alex, it's been nice meeting your associates, but they didn't need me. Thing for me to do is head for Mars and give the Simianoids an inspirational talk."

"You have nothing to do," Alexander countered, as they quit the conference room, "but get out of town before your favorite enemy gets you sewed up in legal proceedings as long as a whore's dream."

Chapter 12

The Forum where Doc Brandon would face the commission which was to investigate his dealings with the Adoptive Parents League was well away from Megapolis Alpha, perhaps two kilometers short of the replica of the Pyramid of the Sun, at San Juan Teótihuacan, a monument to commemorate a declaration of goodwill to Mexico and Latin America in general.

The Commission would convene at a table set at the focal point of an ellipsoid of revolution, a portion of which formed the postscenium of the stage. At the farther extreme of the rectangular field on which the public would assemble was a section of an ellipsoid, a sound reflector. Its curved surface, shaped like a segment of a clamshell, was part of the acoustic system designed to pick up and project voices of investigators and investigated so that the audience could hear the speakers. Since architect or designer had fouled things up slightly, that miracle of acoustical engineering worked perfectly after concealed mikes and speakers were added to the ellipsoidal reflectors. Above the rim of the background of the stage, and supported on cantilevers, was a latticed gallery which overhung and extended the full length of that stage.

In several divisions of that gallery, technicians who monitored the audiovideo operation had their working space. In a room behind the gallery, Doc and Alexander Heflin sat, awaiting their cue.

"Likely to be a student demonstration. Ever since you sent that infrared gear and the formula for the solution Epworth daubed on the infants, we've had Simianoids infiltrate academic circles. Our operators are good-time characters, bringing cargos of liquor, high-proof stuff that's a knockout for normal humans but leaves Simianoids glowing happily. When punks and professors are plastered, the undercover operators mark each foreign agitator. We found that there were so many alien troublemakers that half of them were spying on the other half.

"We picked our operators from the Simianoid strain that has an open face, country-boy expression—the kind that looks as if he could not tell chicken droppings from wild honey if you switched the labels. The agitators are easy to spot. They're self-identifying. They go for the gullible lookers and they lead off with the same dreary clichés they used when you were a boy. They are the *stupidest* bastards. Not a shred of originality. Even a collegian ought to get wise and give them a laugh."

Doc chuckled. "An intellectual with no experience is the most gullible animal on Earth!"

Alexander grimaced. "We have more than students to take into account. Most of the members of Parliament have gulped the social propaganda. The influence goes to the highest levels of government."

"But naturally!" Doc shrugged. "The normal legislator's only talent is the art of getting votes by charm plus taxpayer money spent for social programs— Hey, things are picking up!"

Heflin hitched about. The monitor screen showed the arrival of the commissioners and the gathering of the public. The half-dozen rows of seats right and left of the lane which divided the rectangle were almost filled. Uniformed traffic directors were turning away many who had no passes. These found places on the artificial turf which carpeted the rectangle, from auditors' seats all the way to the acoustical background.

"Not many seats for the public."

"Fewer to replace," Alexander answered. "Students will smash them all within the hour."

Doc's attention shifted to screens on which observers

picked up and magnified the faces of group after group of arrivals. The cameras began to whirr.

"There's one!" Alexander exclaimed. "Third screen, and over there, another."

The infrared device was busy. Here and there Doc saw faces, each marked by a luminous red blob. To the monitors and those sitting in the monitors' compartment the telltales were visible, but not to the people in the forum.

"Who'd think my illegal peddling of infants would draw a crowd!"

Before Heflin could comment, he and Doc were meeting Gregory Panopoulos, Esquire, the attorney on whom Brandon was to rely for making new laws out of old ones. Mr. Panopoulos towered well over two meters, tapering from amazingly broad shoulders to long, narrow feet. His dark eyes, ever questing, probed and recorded the scene. His chin, though solid, suffered by comparison with the majesty of an impressive and somewhat oversize nose.

"Dr. Brandon?" Panopoulos smiled amiably. "I know you'll be an unusual client. I've had no chance to update myself on the situation."

Doc cut in. "This is a blackmail operation."

Panopoulos turned to the elevator. "This is only an investigation. It may not go beyond today's preliminaries."

Heflin gestured toward the monitor screens. "I'll be more helpful here than with you and Gregory."

When attorney and client reached stage level, they saw the commissioners at a crescent-shaped table. Five of the group were the Board of Visitors, Doc's guests at Nameless Island. The others did not count, not as far as Brandon was concerned. Doc whispered, "That blocky, square-faced character wearing the pimp's dream checkered tropical jacket is my favorite one, Wilson Epworth."

There were several unclassifieds at the table. In the wings stood twelve uniformed police, each a Simianoid. The instant identification was not because of erect carriage, placid faces, and apparent disinterest in their surroundings. It came from their being paired, two each of the six basic types.

In addition to truncheons, the cops had gas mask packs, gas projectors, and holstered eleven-millimeter magnums.

"Nerve gas," Panopoulos remarked. "Stops violence before it fairly starts. Leaves them puking-miserable for a couple of days and praying for death. Bad thing about it, prayer is never granted."

A bailiff conducted them to their places at the center of the table, to face the crowd. This made for a cozy conference. Mikes and pedestaled viewers transmitted data to the off-stage monitors and to those on the upper gallery. This was a friendly meeting to be audited by people whose voice was the Voice of God, an idiot god, lowercase *g*.

Donning his most amiable face, Doc greeted Wilson Epworth. "Nice seeing you, Dr. Epworth."

"Your delightful carnival didn't give us enough time to discuss your major enterprise." Epworth's gesture indicated the sandy-haired man whose "peace to all living creatures" expression told Doc that this was his major enemy. "Dr. Brandon, perhaps you have met Mr. Gatewood?"

Doc inclined his head at least two degrees. "We have never had the pleasure."

"Mr. Gatewood has been investigating the Adoptive Parents League of North America."

Panopoulos interposed. "My client is not and never has been a member of that League."

"Counselor, we stipulate that and also that Dr. Brandon did not sell any infant or infants to adoptive parents. However, he did deliver, or cause to be delivered, a parcel of ten infants to the Adoptive Parents League."

"In such case," Panopoulos countered, "an indictment as an accessory before the fact would be in order. I'll waive the question of whether or not you have authority or jurisdiction. I refer to your questioning my client. Since we are here, we'll proceed, but without conceding that you or anyone else has jurisdiction or authority."

"Conceded, and jurisdiction to be established in due course."

Panopoulos resumed, "According to statute, the crime is not completed unless the accused received payment for procuring and delivering the infants. You might well begin with showing that my client had any connection with, any knowledge of the alleged infants, their origin, their destination."

Counselor Gatewood dipped into his briefcase. From a manila envelope he took several twenty-by-twenty-five-centimeter color prints. He dealt the first one face up. "This is not documentation, but these photographs suffice to sustain our investigation. Here we have a readily identifiable Burmese village, with pagoda: Nameless Island, headquarters of the Brandon Foundation. Nursery to the right of the pagoda. Burmese and Malay nursemaids with their young charges."

Doc took a look at the first print. It showed Maung Gauk and U Po Mya somewhat to one side. The former had a bolt-action military rifle and the latter, a double-barrel rifle, a ponderous weapon. To get such a picture with a hovering helicopter as camera station, a picture which looked as though taken from ground level, indicated that good equipment had been at work and that an equally good laboratory technician had made the blowups.

The infants, suntanned youngsters, probably three-year-olds, were white, blue-eyed, and looking up at something: presumably at the whirlybird. Each had on his or her forehead a cross, Maltese, in that peculiar red whose qualities Doc had discovered in the course of his chemical analysis.

"Gregory," he said to his attorney, "take a close look at some remarkably good camerawork."

Epworth, returning from marking the infants, had unexpectedly encountered a tiger. Whatever his plan had been, Doc and U Po Mya had scrambled it. The picture could not have been taken by any of the Board of Visitors except while hovering over the village: the turning out with weapons established that fact. The photo spoke for itself. Why sneak into the village when everyone supposedly would be at the full-moon ceremonies to stencil a Maltese cross on each infant? Absurd, on the face of things, and, accordingly, cogitation was in order.

There were other exhibits. The same youngsters, now in Megapolitan nursery dress, were presented in a Megapolitan interior. Mr. Gatewood and a good-looking young lady who was offering cookies from a brown paper bag were interested in the children but were not ignoring the camera. Each infant had a Maltese cross on the forehead.

"My assistant, Evelyn Watson, went with me."

"If you think I'll waste any more time screwing around," Doc cut in, "you're nuts and fruit. Think up a better charade and I'll play, maybe. Gregory, why not continue this business until there is something to talk about? Meanwhile, see if you can find grounds for a countersuit: invasion of privacy, trespass . . . Burn their tails and hear them squeal! This is blackmail!"

However, Mr. Gatewood was not alarmed. "We are not here to press an advantage which goes against American tradition. We are here to negotiate."

Panopoulos addressed the Commission: "We are not imputing blackmail, but we would like to know what you want. You do not need testimony against the League. The testimony of the purchasers of the infants for adoption suffices. They paid the League, and the League was the dealer. Whatever my client did or did not do has nothing to do with your purpose. What's your racket? What do you really want? If it's reasonable, we'll pay off, *in quantum meruit*,—at your nuisance value, so to speak. Or how would you like a countersuit?"

Wilson Epworth gave Doc a look, a smile, and wagged his head.

"My learned colleague's age has been a matter of increasing interest. There is documentary evidence that he is at least one hundred eighty-six years old. More and more, the public hears speculation on everlasting life. The possibility of universal immortality becomes ever more engrossing." Epworth sighed, shook his head and straightened fully; he became almost majestic, and certainly the man was impressive, more so than ever in Doc's memory. "Frustration compounded has in the past ended in grave public disturbance. The feeling that science is withholding what the public has a right to know, that Government is withholding what it should and could give has in the past stirred up disastrous repercussions. In the interest of the people, we ask Dr. Brandon to share his knowledge instead of hoarding what should be a gift to all mankind."

Epworth paused, then rounded his voice. The public address system made it deep and rich and resonant. "Dr. Brandon, even though by legal artifice you block Government's efforts, you cannot escape safe and harmless. You will live your everlasting life confronted by the hatred of all mankind.

"Avery Jarvis Brandon, we ask Life Everlasting for the American people and for the world."

Applause from the crowded forum made stage, postscenium, and superstructure tremble. Rooting sections competed with each other. Some cursed Brandon, others applauded. Doc got to his feet. Before bottles, bricks, garbage were hurled, one of the rooting groups shouted for silence and identified Brandon. Clearly most of the crowd did not yet know who was who or what. Nevertheless, the automatons began to heed cues and signals; the uproar subsided. Curiosity moved them to hear the public enemy someone had suggested that he was.

Mike in hand, Doc stepped back from the table. He glanced about, picking the most direct line to the nearest exit. Hand over mike, he said to Panopoulos, "Get set to run for it. We can make it before they get the point."

Then Doc sounded off: "Now hear this! This is no drill. I am speaking to the Commission but what I say is for my vast audience—you who face me, and all you between the Pacific and the Atlantic who are listening and seeing. In case anyone still does not know who I am, I'll tell you: This is Avery Jarvis Brandon, also known as Doc Brandon.

"Gentlemen of the Commission! Mr. Gatewood! Members of the League of Adoptive Parents! The infants they say I have delivered for sale are chimpanzee mutants and of a far higher quality than their adoptive parents.

"The secret of Life Everlasting has been a matter of public knowledge for more than two thousand years. Join the Alleluia Stompers, the Testifiers, or any other sect. There is life everlasting in Heaven. There always has been. Go and get it!"

He dropped the mike, shoved Panopoulos: "Get going before those stupid sons of bitches understand what I said."

Doc raced for the exit he had picked.

Chapter 13

Doc had underestimated the reaction time of the Younger Generation. The rooting sections were recovering from the shock and had got the secret of everlasting life somewhat sooner than he had reckoned. The commissioners were on their feet. Wilson Epworth snatched his chair. Two others tipped the table. Though its crescent shape made it a poor barricade, it was better than nothing.

Doc had not allowed for the presence of activists in the front rows of the reserved seats. The advance guard of the student body protesters and the agitators who guided the trained seals moved too rapidly. They were hurdling the stunned and groping dopes who had in good faith attended the open forum. They were scaling the ten-foot face of the stage, and with teamwork which indicated basic exercises in commando operations.

And then Doc realized that he and his attorney had been psychologically handicapped. Doc said, "Suit yourself, but these God damned punks need one more message!"

He smashed a sturdy chair, offered Panopoulos a substantial fragment, and turned to counterattack. Gregory had no more interest in helping the Commission defend itself than had Doc Brandon: Each hoped that the students made a clean sweep, and each had the urge to clobber a couple of troublemaking activist before retreating.

Protesters hurled bottles. Other heaved bricks. Eggs, dried dung, equine and bovine, imported at great expense

from agricultural areas, were symbolic and not intended
for damage.

"Watch the apples with razor blades!"

Panopoulos broke his chair fragment in half across a
skull which would never again be the same, and the
lacerating apples justified him. And bricks were a problem.
Students never used weapons. Bottles just broke and you
couldn't help it.

From the wings, uniformed police flowed out in riot
control formation, plying lead-loaded truncheons. It was
not yet time for nerve or tear gas, but it soon would be.
The protest wave was billowing up and over and to the
stage, blocking the exit wing which Doc had picked. One
smash with his handmade cudgel brought down two rioters.
Panopoulos, with a skimpy scrap of chair still in his big
hand, followed him through.

The defense was better than the activists had expected.
A pampered lot, they were unaccustomed to opposition.
Not whipped up to homicidal mania, they needed assurance. And that they got. From the rear of the forum came
shouts of encouragement. Those who cheered the attackers were passing out more bricks, more bottles to arm the
eager ones who had not yet encountered force. And the
cops began to have a tough time of it. Their primary counterattack was failing. They were driven back, bowled over,
trampled, and booted. The idealists were becoming savage
and determined, carried away by encouragement from the
rear, *always* from the rear.

This ceased when the crisp smack of a 5.56-millimeter
rifle came clear and clean above the gasp, grunt, roar, and
cough of weary slobs who ran out of breath and drive. Ex-
perts were picking targets. There was no volley fire. Only
the wide-spaced whiplash *whacks* of a 5.56 millimeter, one
shot at one rioter, and no second needed. There were no
more bricks or bottles or other *non*weapons. Cops still able
to get to their feet set to work with truncheons.

Far to the rear, a tall student turned against the retreating tide and raised a fist.

A rifle crashed. He folded.

A panel of the gallery slid back, as Doc and Panopoulos
lurched from head of stairs to the compartment where Alex-

ander Heflin stood, surveying the microbattle field. The P.A. made articulated thunder of his voice.

"Now hear this."

A rifle cracked, just once. Heflin carried on. "Go back to school or you will be expelled, and without appeal. Sharpshooters are picking off alien agitators pretending to be students. You have been suckers, hopheads, and nitwits, egged on by foreigners bent on making trouble. We have picked off troublemakers, not students—the ones who would have sneaked away while you boobs faced the guns."

Alexander Heflin stepped into full view. For a moment, tall and stately, he stood. He beckoned, and Doc Brandon and attorney joined him. They watched police clear the plaza. Half the force dripped blood from wounds. Those able to stay on their feet slugged away as though keeping time to music. One, trampled and battered, got to his feet, steadied himself, and resumed his work.

Heflin said, after a moment, "The punks have had it. Even if the agitators were on the job, the suckers would still be knocking each other down to get away while they could. Let's get out of here. The show's over."

Doc and Panopoulos followed him to the underground level and into a passage which led to the Great Pyramid of the Sun. From its complex guts, a government vehicle took them to Suburban Lodge Delta Minor.

"Rougher than I expected," Heflin remarked as he sank back against the cushions of the limousine. "Those gunners were Olympic champions. I don't think they as much as scratched a student."

"And that," Doc suggested, "will teach the agitators a thing or two. And maybe the students too."

Alexander shook his head. "The real Marxist is either a calculating machine using the common slob as a means to an end, or, in the lower levels, he is a religious fanatic who is happy to die as a martyr. Denying religion, damning religion as the opium of the people, the imbecile doesn't realize that he is more of a dope than any of the morons he is trying to convert! The dummies he sells his line to don't even believe in themselves, so they're ready to believe in whatever someone else sells them. Doc, what possessed you to sound off the way you did? Trying to precipitate a riot?"

"No. I gave them the only answer for anyone looking for life everlasting. For twenty or more weary centuries, the Western world has believed in life everlasting. Only very few *really* believed in what they pretended to. If they had even a shred of confidence in what Scriptures and theologians tell them, they'd have to be totally insane to want to stay alive in this fascinating uncertain world. The idiots want eternal security, and they cling to *samsara,* the eternal insecurity of the here and now."

Panopoulos eyed him. "Doc, what *do* you think?"

"Shit plus two equals seven. If you are so unfortunate as to spend one hundred eighty-odd years thinking, I'll bet you the phoniest *pazor* that the Government printing presses have turned out, you'll never rely on thinking or logic."

Heflin took his turn. "Doc, telling the Commission that it could not convict you of a crime because those infants were not human, that they were modified Simians! Your sense of humor is never malicious. How the hell could you give such a boot to the chin? Think of the fond adoptive parents, their horror, their embarrassment."

"The attention span of the Three Dee culture is so short that nobody will remember long enough to be humiliated. The modified Simian is superior to all but the handful of humans at genius level. So the adoptive parents will brag about their youngsters, and who's going to remember what I said, or believe it if he remembers? Let's get down to business. You said something about an inspection tour of Mars and the Simianoid Martian Rehabilitation Colonies?"

"Our public will go wild and assassins will make you the number-one target until they forget you and put someone else on the hit list. Let's have a drink and talk things over."

Chapter 14

In his suite at the Stilton Spaceways, Doc Brandon waited for the *Space Princess* to arrive while contemplating his experiences since leaving Nameless Island, Alexander Heflin's summing up of the state of the nation, and thoughts of Mona. He was divided between relief at having honored a long-neglected obligation and resisting the urge to phone Mona.

He wanted to assure her that he had not been injured in the rioting. He realized that when she appeared on the visiphone screen it would occur to him that it was his duty to give her a tour of Mars before she encountered the Megapolitan and the rural areas of the Republic. However, hardwon honesty checked him.

They had had their honeymoon and their leavetaking. They might meet again—but only if she sought him. As a matter of honor, Doc knew that he must not seek Mona.

Mona did not need assurance. She could see through the slantings and deceptions of the news media. She would be amused, not depressed, by commentator screamings about the fiendish killing of thirty-seven idealistic students; about Barbarous Brandon's exile to Mars for hard labor in the mines, with the length of sentence depending on the measure of remorse and response to rehabilitation.

No mention was made of the Simianoid infants which had been palmed off as human. This the media ignored.

The buzz of the intercom interrupted Doc's cogitations.

The man at the desk said, "Dr. Brandon, a lady wishes to speak to you. She prefers not to give her name."

"I'll speak to her."

The clerk's face faded. The woman who appeared was not Mona. Whoever she was, she wore a most attractive mask, a slick job, and but for his built-in critical faculties, Doc might not have suspected that she was a masquerade-ess.

"Madame, what's on your mind?"

"Dr. Brandon, I have a problem I want to discuss. Well, ah, it is confidential. I hope you understand."

She ended on a suspense inflection. The voice was appealing, inviting, exciting. There was something about it which evoked memories of Mona's playful teasings, bitchi-nesses which he knew she did not mean.

"You've talked me into something. Come on up."

Indeed, there was something tantalizingly familiar in that seductive voice. Misogynists, hearing it, would begin wondering what jewels, perfumes, or broadtail jackets she would like. When the annunciator *brrrr*ed, he still was groping, guessing, and on a delightfully foolish level of Cloud Number Nine. He touched the *admit* key.

The door opened, revealing a woman wearing a pearl-embroidered hood. Her headgear had a trailing of pen-dants, a *coif* which made her throat even more alluring than had Nature's good start. A fine head, carried proudly. Though the dress was of no nation, it suggested T'ang Dynasty, modified for the slightly more luxurious Occidental figure, though, come to think of it, a T'ang Emperor, circa 900 A.D., had a favorite concubine who was a good twelve–fifteen kilograms overweight for her height. Her tunic was slit exactly the distance above the knee to make her legs the most elegant between Terra and Mars.

Doc stood for a moment, admiring and surmising. Then he grabbed her luggage, a massive suitcase from the right, a weekender from the left.

"Come in."

Being a damned fool was exhilarating. Whatever she had behind that mask would be a surprise. The mummy-face of Queen Nefertiti? He recalled Mona's quip about necrophilia.

"Come in," he repeated, and stepped aside.

The door closed behind her. He let the luggage plop to the carpet. "Sit down, Madame! What're you drinking?"

"Whatever you are, and I'm perishing for one."

That voice! Another moment and he'd be purring like a kitten.

He mixed Islay malt and mineral water.

"Dr. Brandon, I am in a desperate situation. I heard you'd been released on your own recognizance and would go into exile without guards. I can't get a permit. I've got to go to Mars. I want to go with you. Anyone of your status would have papers for a companion and her maid. I'd take the maid's place. I'd not be in your way. If you ever gave her time out, I'd be her maid." She sank to her knees, caught Doc's hand, and kissed it. "I *must* go to Mars. You've got to help me."

Doc sank to one knee, took her hands. "This is damned nonsense." He rose, and she, with him. They regarded each other, eye to eye. Despite the mask, her eyes did their duty, and Doc knew that the mystery woman knew that she had prevailed. "You are right, as far as my papers go," he said. "And you are more than welcome. I do not have a companion. . . . If what's behind the mask is as attractive as the mask . . . if it turns out that you and I are congenial, you could literally write your own ticket, and I'd happily be your maid."

She almost stepped back. He let go her hands. Doc could hear the whir of mental wheels.

"Madame!" He waggled *Uighur While You Fly*. "It's only twenty-four hours till take-off. Still time for a selection parade of PVR girls."

"Oh, how marvelous! Then you could let me go as her maid?"

"Of course I could. But a polygamous ménage would hardly be indicated."

"*Polygamous?*" The mask-eyebrows rose. "I don't quite understand."

"You, me, and my not-yet-selected PVR girl."

"Oh."

Doc nodded. "Not surprised that you agree with me! You know, I'll be inspecting Simianoid colonies. The Simianoids are polyandrous. Sounds awfully technical. Really simple—one female Simianoid and four quasi-husbands.

"Just occurred to me that instead of you and me and my not-yet-selected PVR girl, there's just you and me and the First Officer and the Second Officer. It'd help me enormously, getting into the spirit of Simianoid culture. I'd feel more at home when we disembarked at Maritania Spaceport."

Prolonged silence.

"Dr. Brandon, you mean you'll take me to Mars with you but it'll either be polygamous or polyandrous?"

"If you weren't so insistent on going to such a loathesome planet, I'd say, much simpler you took leave of me, and I'll phone for a selection of PVR girls."

"But I *have* to go to Mars! It's awfully urgent."

"No problems, Madame, no problems whatever! Take off your mask and if you're still congenial, it won't be polygamous, it won't be polyandrous. It'd be you and me."

"But you insist on my unmasking?"

"Even for a short engagement with an important client, a PVR girl would undress. An *uncover* charge of twenty *pazors*, if the color scheme is not totally appealing. But you are special. You have the most enchanting voice, and with lights out, well, you would wear your mask only by day."

A silence even more prolonged. Then, "Before we go on with negotiations, I'd like a bit of privacy and a bit of time facing a mirror."

"The bath is all yours."

He gestured. She picked up her glass and her weekend case and headed for privacy. "Mind bringing the big case?"

He did not mind.

Although the suspense was bearable, Doc sat there, fiddling with his refilled glass and wondering whether his masked visitor was as fluttery as he was. Her voice and her silences had told him each step of the buildup had left her shaken and in need of time to develop fresh resolve. He was convinced that she had intended in the beginning to pay her way as maid for a "traveling concubine," as the old time Chinese phrased the solution when none of the household ladies cared to make a long and rugged trip.

"Whatever she is, she's no trifler," he told himself, and began drinking instead of swirling his glass.

When she came from the bathroom, she was not wearing the PVR girl's working dress. She was still masked, and more than ever dressed: tall and stately seeming because of the towering tiara, a spaceship, with exhaust jet portrayed by sequins, a spray of them, blending into what should have been a train for her gown, if it had had one.

"Ever see this?"

"I rarely get away from Nameless Island, two thousand kilometers from here. But give me a longer look, or take off that mask."

She raised her arms. She lowered them and when her hands came down to her cervical vertebrae, as though trying to unsnap a necklace, the space gown parted. It settled about her ankles, finally coming to rest, a frothy heap halfway to her knees. The masked visitor wore bra, pink panties, with a triangular patch of forget-me-nots. An inverted triangle.

"If you want to see more, you'll have to take me to Mars with you."

"And you'd be wearing your mask by lights-on?"

"Dr. Brandon, I'm surprised! A man your age, acting as though a woman's face was her fortune!"

"Madame Anonymous, you want to go to Mars. I do not. I am stuck with it. Science would do a flipflop if logic got you to Maritania Spaceport."

"Male chauvinism: *machísimo!*"

"Whenever you were in command, female chauvinism prevailed and don't tell me it didn't!"

"No matter how homely I am, you'd not be turned off in darkness. Don't be totally chicken!"

"Young lady, I don't accept challenges because someone tells me I ought to. One hundred thousand PVR girls and other licensed whores have fitted themselves with pink panties with forget-me-nots, and another hundred thousand wear blue ones with rosebuds. You're offering no bait at all."

"Doc, darling, can't we make a deal?"

"Take off that mask."

"Instead of the forget-me-nots?"

"Never mind the instead of."

"You are a thorough old stinker! I am glad I am not married to anyone like you."

"So are two hundred million other North American women."

She reached ceilingward and back, and finger twitched something a little above the cervical vertebrae. From the spaceship tiara, filmy fabric descended, veiling all, from bra to ankles.

"Promise me, or I dress and go home."

Doc drew a deep breath. "Very well, female chauviniste! I promise you. Unless armed force, act of God, space catastrophe prevent me, you're riding my ticket to Mars. No matter what is behind that mask, it is a deal."

Unmasking, she revealed Flora Garvin, Queen of Space Widows and Detergent Dream Girl of two hemispheres. She laughed softly. "If you're let down, I'll release you from your promise."

"You do wear forget-me-nots, sometimes anyway. Two hundred million women and as many men are wondering, just in the Republic."

"Doc, being famous has let you in for much grief. I've learned that in just five years. I had to know whether I could talk you into line without depending on Three Dee." She pounced, caught him with both arms, and while the kiss was not the open-mouth, tongue-tangling, saliva-blending kind, it was not a silver anniversary marital peck. "Now that the suspense is over." She stepped daintily clear of the garment clutter and this included the temporary veil from bra to ankles. "Let's have a get-acquainted drink."

"You were so heroic-brazen-hussy! You're a lot more convincing when you face a camera. Sit down, you need a drink. So do I."

Flora choked, clung to him for a moment. "You did see through me! Trying to be a woman of the world." She looked up, blinked. "Trying to be nice to a coddled school-girl. We made a deal, and I won't back down."

He nudged her toward the big red leather chair. It swallowed her comfortably. Doc patted her fingers closed about the Islay and mineral.

"Of course you'd not back down. You'd be the perfect

little stowaway working her way across space, and if I were your age or twice as old, I'd be too happy to have good sense. I'd fall in love with you and we'd marry, and two more silly Americans would be settling for ignorance-is-not-bliss."

"Doc, you're awfully sweet. You're not one of the million who chew lead pencils and scrawl fan letters that need nothing but reptile binding and pictures to make page one of a five meter shelf of North American pornography."

"Sweet, hell! Even before you took off your mask, I knew, more and more, minute after minute, that you'd never made a deal like this—a trading proposition, I mean. A professional who loves her work would be good company. You would not."

"Oh!"

"Settle back in your chair, don't spill your drink. You, trying to be what you are not, you'd be frustration and letdown. When we're aboard ship, pick your corner and I'll pick mine. Keep scenic areas reasonably covered. Too much peepshow." Then, with mock ferocity, "Risk of being raped in space. I'll settle for your telling me why the hell you want a second trip to Mars, after what the first one did for you. You don't need to strip your soul to bare essentials. A level account, and you've paid your way."

"I'd been practicing my act, intending to . . . ah . . . influence my cousin Alexander. But when I heard you were going—"

"So, make a deal with me and save him for something important, a caper I couldn't handle."

Her eyes remained level and unwavering. "Except for details, you've sketched it nicely. Which is what's making me feel like a little bitch."

Doc nodded, pondered. "Flora darling, don't answer what is a purely rhetorical question. You'd quit feeling guilty if I plied you with liquor until you could convince yourself that you were too drunk to know what you were doing."

"I'd kick and scream till I got in the mood and then you'd be a coward and a deserter if you quit."

Chapter 15

Doc and Flora sat in the after salon, watching a freighter change her course as she circled for landing on the flat bottom of a lunar sea long dead. The exhaust of the *Space Princess* made it seem that the freighter's hull was rippling. After a long silence, Flora said, "Do I have to wear this damned mask?"

"Penalty of being the most famous space widow of Terra, Luna, or Mars. You'd not have got cabin fever if you'd stayed in our stateroom but you'd have had red ants crawling all over you, wondering when the Nasty Old Man would start feeling you up."

He backed into an angle of the salon, drew a chair facing him, and beckoned. "Go ahead and unmask. We've got the place to ourselves. The forward salon is attracting most of the passengers to bar and casino."

"I've monopolized the talk! Why not tell me about the Simianoids, while I'm resting my voice? Oh, I've read a lot, and know they have infiltrated our entire system. You invented them. No, don't try to tell me all about *clones* and basic types. I've often wondered—I mean, when I gave them any thought at all—if their polyandry doesn't make for a lot of jealousy and wrangling."

"Meaning, each husband hates the other three?"

Flora nodded.

Doc shrugged. "I know what you mean. Any human female is supposed to be a sort of property, but that kicks back, and the male slave owner finds he has become a special chattel, whence our word *cattle*. So polyandry is something only anthropologists ever notice—in primitive societies not spoiled by Western morals and religions.

"Far as I can find out, each Simianoid is more content with his twenty-five-percent wife than the standard man is with his exclusive female property or she with her hundred-percent proprietary title to him. Whether this is a matter of genes or simply the human acceptance of custom, what difference does it make? If you ever have time to read Montaigne's essay on the force of custom, you'd not be a bit surprised.

"The real point is, they are ideal for developing Mars and keeping Terra going by checking overpopulation. Medical science has become the great enemy: not enough infant mortality, too many aged living far too long, the life-greedy decrepit wrecks— This lecture is a demonstration of overkill! You look sad!"

A tear trickled down each cheek. "It's not your fault. I knew I'd feel low, but I didn't think it'd start so soon."

She blinked, dabbed her eyes, renewed her makeup.

"Rod and I had a wrangle. He hated the Plastic Society and wanted us to move to the Andes or Himalayas where there was a lot of elevation and not many people. After I'd smashed glassware, he walked out, rounded up a handful of buddies and their girls, and got the computer expert of the group to bug the Central Control of Thought to order the party to Khatmandu. Something fouled up, and they were ordered to Mars. From there, you know the rest. With his usual luck, he escaped, embarrassed the administration. Part of the computer foulup upset a fixed election, and he got so much fame that he was put in command of a spaceship that was intended to fail short of Saturn, the impossible goal.

"Naturally, his take-off from Mars was a big fiesta, and my fifth cousin, Alexander, ordered me to fly to Maritania to wish Rod bon voyage. For the first time in our marriage, Rod and I met as civilized people. We had our night of truth and, too late, realized each had been an imbecile.

"I didn't know it at the time, but Lani, the redheaded Pleasure, Vice, & Recreation girl who had been herded to

Mars with him was stowed away aboard his ship, the *Satur-* *nienne*. He or she or both had killed an inspector who had been harassing her.

"So they never found Lani, or the inspector's body.

"Rod outwitted the plan to have the cruiser destroyed in space. She was made of a fissionable alloy. But he circled Saturn, landed on an asteroid for minor repairs. And was finally reported *lost in space*. I think his Martian girl, Aza-deh, knows what actually happened. More and more I'm convinced that he was not lost. That is why I am going to see her."

"Mmmm . . . he knew that the deck was stacked against him, yet he accepted the risk?"

"That was Rod all over. He could have jumped ship in Maritania, hid out with Azadeh and the rest of the Gooks. He went on, to show Alexander a thing or two. Take-off hour, I got a good look at Azadeh. Though she didn't show, she had that smug, happy look. I knew she was pregnant, and a couple of weeks later, I knew I was not. When Floyd's declared the *Saturnienne* lost in space, Azadeh did not look like a widow."

"Meaning, you do look like one? First detergent show, you looked like a passionate virgin itching to lose her vir-tue."

"You help me find Azadeh. I'm betting she has Rod's child, about six years old by now, and I'm going to find out what really happened to the *Saturnienne*."

Doc frowned. "I'd take you along just for the trip. There is something: Maybe you are not a widow. Tell you later. You have paid your way with the Rod Garvin story. I've done a lot of wondering."

Flora put on her mask. "You haven't made a pass at me so far, and I'm a tear-dripping, makeup-smudged mess and I'm so sad that if I invited you, you'd say, *I'll take a cigar instead*."

And she quietly wept her way to their stateroom.

Not long after Flora's emotions were smoothed out and her makeup retouched, automation brought hot meal pack-ages: imitation broiled squash; mock duck soup; natural potatoes, whipped, with synthetic brown gravy; genuine pastry crust with simulated apple filling; reconstituted

Ethiopian coffee; genuine Cognac, a bottle of which substantially eased the French national debt; Virginia-filled Balkan Type Sobranie cigarettes, Turkish flavored; and *Space Princess Gazette,* published daily aboard ship.

When Flora pushed aside her half-eaten meal, she said, "Last time or first time Marsward, I wished they had gulls and fish in space, so food like this wouldn't be wasted." She glanced at the lower bunk. "Doc, I'm tired and, for a change, relaxed. A good listener and a good cry did it. You won't think I'm rude?"

"Except for the ultimate holy of holies, I've seen everything you have. I told you that night before last. I'm not peevish. I'll read the *Gazette,* and no peeping, but you might wear a robe over that see-more sleeping gown, just in case."

Doc read the story of the student riot, and the editorial: *"Rather be killed by sane people instead of animals, but life never was à la carte . . . the punks are sincere activists, sure, idealists, but so were the cops who killed thirty-seven troublemaking Marxists posing as exchange students. . . ."* "Good night, darling."

The ship was weaving and pitching. The deck shuddered as though a meteorite had whacked her hull. No danger. Just routine. Flora wasn't screaming or racing to the head to puke.

He poured another snifter of Cognac. Doc could very well understand why Flora was comfortably falling apart: She'd been dream girl of one and three-tenths hemispheres for quite too long. Good girl . . . had not draped her million *pazors* worth of female goodies all over him, all the while ready to protest if he absentmindedly copped a feel. This she had not done. Not once an accidental display of fascinating areas. . . .

Doc snapped off the ceiling light, and the *Gazette* be damned. That left only the little blue bulb that marked *exit-entry* in case general quarters sounded. Night and day were meaningless in space.

". . . damn if I am climbing to that upper bunk. If I slipped and fell and pawed on my way to the deck, she'd think it was somnambulistic rape and like a nice decent

*stowaway make things easy . . . and never believe it was
an accident. . . ."*

He found the Cognac, took another hefty nip, and made
for the little lounge. *"Space be damned. The human race
doesn't even know how to live on Terra. Got no business in
space. What the country needs is universal compulsory
abortion."* At times he wondered whether he would live
forever or die of old age a couple of centuries hence.

Doc didn't know whether he was awake or asleep. He
hoped he had not been talking in his half sleep and disturbing Flora. And presently, still uncertain, he heard a voice.
Every prophet who deluded mankind heard voices, blamed
it on God, with an uppercase *G*, and lo! a new religion.
But this was a woman's voice. Not even a dime-a-dozen
god would speak with a female voice.

What she said made sense, and high time. "Move over,
Doc. If you don't want a teary widow, imagine I'm some-
body you like. You're the nastiest old man I ever met but
you remind me of Rod."

The hip was female. Other features were female. The
snuggling creature smelled like a lifetime of lovely women
all in one package. Groping and fumbling and fearing he
might wake up, whatever he touched was luscious and finally:

"Damn high time to wake up!"

Then he didn't know who was fondling whom. When she
said, "A good listener and a good cry wasn't enough, but
it was a grand start," Doc got a new insight into male
and female relationships.

"I listen, you weep, and finally, something we can do
together."

Chapter 16

Towering peaks cast long shadows. The low sun coaxed a ruddy glow from the central domes of Maritania and from the spherical segments, rings within rings, which girdled the center. As he pointed, Doc said to Flora, "That smaller bubble, well away from the big group, that's the spaceport. Change much since your visit?"

Flora shook her head. "I was twitchy arriving and awfully low leaving, no mood to notice anything." She caught his hand. "Even if I'd been able to arrange to travel by myself, it would have been dreary, making the cruise alone. You never gave me a moment's chance to hate space. All of it was good, everything. If I'd known how badly I needed a good listener, I'd have come to Nameless Island and told Mona that Mondays, Wednesdays, and Fridays were mine until I'd talked all the miseries out of my soul."

"If you'd made it soon enough, you could have had a seven-day week. Mona would've been big enough but not old enough." He sighed. "I'll miss you."

"Even if we can't make the homebound trip together, we'll have some time in Maritania." She looked well beyond the spaceport. "Those little bubbles you told me about, every twenty kay-ems along a meridian: There's solid green reaching all around the first few. Deepest green I ever saw."

"The ruddy light makes it that way, but the green is saturated. That big dome way out, that's Martian Gardens, where the development was just beginning when Rod's caper brought him here."

"Those little observation posts out in that awful desert! Nothing growing. I hate to think of it! Now, over there, those tall towers?"

Doc's glance followed her gesture. "M.M.M.! Martian Mining & Minerals. Stamp mills. Hoists. Crushers. Solar power for the machinery and the smelters."

The *Space Princess* swung in a long, slow curve. In the thin atmosphere, little heat was developed by friction. The Sun's edge was below the horizon, and as long shadows raced across the rocky waste spaces, the purple, green, cerise glare of the spaceport and the lights of Maritania became ever brighter. From afar they could see the sullen glow of a volcano's crater: It reddened the snowcap of a towering peak.

And then they were settling, with landing struts out.

Doc and Flora were near the end of the airlocked passage which reached from the cruiser's exit port to the spaceport dome. An agile Gook stowed their luggage in an electric car. While Flora and Doc waited their turn through the airlocked tube to the city, Simianoids walked past in a column of fives: The center of each quintet was the most important person, the wife.

"They'll go by bus convoy to Martian Gardens," Doc remarked. "No, that's not a military formation. Look some more; this light is tricky."

"They are chatting, looking about," she admitted, "but it did seem to be."

"I know what you mean. They may be psychically linked. Sometimes it does seem that they are moving by the numbers, but they are individuals, not robots, not dummies. Mix them up in a group of standard humans and you'd not get the impression you had." And then, to the driver, "The Bristol."

"I was hoping you wouldn't be going to that hotel where the bon voyage doings were staged! But once I'd persuaded you to take me to Mars, I was not making any suggestions!"

And presently Flora had her first uninhibited, unsupervised look at Maritania's main street, with vapor lamps and neon signs so bright that the columns and girders which supported the semidomes and spherical segments led up and up and into darkness as though to a firmament without stars.

Doc had often wondered why they had not arranged for constellations. ". . . and make a little heaven," he concluded, sharing his whimsy with Flora.

There had to be English businessmen, wearing the London uniform, except for the umbrella. Not enough mist or rain, you know. The paper in each coat pocket had to be the Martian edition of the *London Times*.

And, the East Indians, Chinese, Japanese, but for whom the scene would be unconvincing; the others, their presence was as meaningless as their absence would have been.

At the Bristol—Hindu operated, of course—Doc got a directory of government employees. He'd barely opened the booklet when he exclaimed, "Damn it! What'd her Gook surname be? I mean, in a Scandinavian country, someone-*datter*, and in Russian, Gubja-or-what-not's daughter, as in Ivan-*ovna* or the like."

"Look in your phrase book, Doc, the Uighur one, or get a Gook-book at the desk."

Doc remained oblivious, or as Flora reckoned it, stubbornly *no-damn-woman-can-tell-me-anything*. A long ago girl in Turkistan, Djénane Khanoum had told Rod Garvin a lot, and this puzzled Flora. Rod's explanation never was really comprehensible: *"She waited till I asked her something instead of running off at the mouth when I didn't want answers, I wanted silence."*

"Which was why those meek Asiatic females led Garvin around by the ear," Flora thought to herself.

"No problem," Doc finally announced. "Garvin, Azadeh."

Flora pulled a long face. "He can't be here, hiding in Gook caves."

"You're downright absurd! If I had a chance, I'd happily hide with you in Gookland, and Azadeh is a first-chop doll too. Right here and now, I am getting you a room for your lovely little self."

"You're sweet, protecting my honor. But it'd do him a world of good, finding us shacking up."

Doc snorted. "With you pretending you like polyandry the way he goes for polygyny!"

"I know he isn't dead, but legally I am a bona fide widow and so of course I seduced a world-famous scholar-scientist to show that woman-crazed devil a thing or two. Two–three–four more lovers, and be tired of trying to even up with his tricontinental score."

"What continents did he skip?"

She slapped him, one-two. "You darling old devil, how many continents are there? Your travelogs all the way from Megapolis were fascinating, and you never mentioned exotic women except in the bazaars, marketplaces, temples. Anyway, I'll put my luggage in the spare bedroom and I am going to be dissolute and immoral. Then I'll seduce Alexander."

"You'll waggle the pink panties that'll launch a thousand spaceship to find the asteroid."

Once Doc had arranged for the adjoining room with connecting bath, there was nothing to do but decide whether to eat at Hesni's Syrian Loqanda, Hong Li Mandarin and Szechwan Cuisine, or Le Papillon, Etienne Prima, Café Français.

"Anything'll be okay," Flora said. "That official banquet Rod and I attended was awful."

"Official banquets always are. Only an American with a union card can produce baked potatoes that are a peculiar slate-gray-blue, a pound and a half of prime rib roast, hors d'oeuvres for the lion at the zoo. Carrots and peas, of course. A tossed salad with cottonseed oil and *distilled* vinegar. Yes, and a Baked Alaska."

"Will those foreign spots be much better?"

"Etienne Prima sounds like an Italian ancestor. Catherine de Medici smuggled Italian cooks into France to introduce real cuisine to '*la Belle*.' He'd be good . . . on Terra. But for Mars, it takes a Chinaman!"

As they headed for the street, Flora remarked, "No one but that Hindu heard you. Still, you shouldn't've said *Chinaman*, that's racist."

"*Merde!* That is universal. First native word I learned in France. Small boys chalked it on every wall. They were literate in those days. *Merde*, even before *voulez vous jig-jig, mademoiselle?*"

"Why the delay, you womanizer?"

"The small boys weren't literate enough to write all that. Anyway, when I was a boy, "*the Chinaman*" had arrived. After barbarity, wanton cruelty the like of which no Black in the South ever imagined, the five-thousand-year-old culture of "*the Chinaman*" prevailed, even among barbarians.

"When my parents spoke of "*the Chinaman*," it was with affection. When two bits bought a lottery ticket and you caught eight or nine spots, I forget, you won two hundred twenty-five dollars, you '*beat the Chinaman,*' you knew he was honest in a way no other lottery in this country ever was. When you cheated enough at solitaire, you '*beat the Chinaman.*' " Doc sighed, and said wistfully, "And once they skipped "*Chinaman.*" They had to, when they spoke of Chinese girls. They said something that was not true, but it was not derogatory, and the girl was always nice. More than her white competitors could claim."

"Why didn't you have a harem of Chinese girls on your island?"

"They are domestic tyrants! A Chinese cook, yes. A Chinese wife, hell, no!"

"Getting away from Rod's favorite subject," Flora interposed, "there's the sign up ahead. Why the Chinaman, because we're on Mars?"

"Let me order and I'll show you."

"I did a lot of gourmet cooking."

"You're not cooking this one."

In due course the pigeon-toed waiter, cigarette tucked carefully behind his ear so no ash would fall on the food, set out shark fin soup, sea slugs sauteed with black mushrooms, tea-smoked duck, and a bottle of hot *shao-hsing*.

Later Doc said, "You ate every morsel."

"You knew I would?"

"Everything I ordered ships perfectly. Everything except the soup and the wine was dried. The stock for the dried shark fin was canned, and the rice wine was bottled."

Flora sighed. "These Chinese are clever people, but my husband had to have a female Martian aborigine. Why'd he skip the oldest culture on today's Earth?"

"In the first place, seeing Azadeh Khanoum on Three Dee is not the same as meeting her. In the second place, with Mars populated largely by Terrestrial thieves, pimps, cutthroats, and scum of the Earth, no Chinaman would bring daughter or wife or mother to this hell hole of desolation which we're trying to snatch from the Gooks who have outwitted Mars for many thousands of years."

"You could've had a sabbatical on Mars and found you a female Gook good enough for Nameless Island!"

"Nothing wrong with Terrestrial women, and you and I got along so nicely on our space honeymoon that I'll miss you for a long time after you write *'Dear Diary, Mission Accomplished.'* "

Chapter 17

When they went to rent spacesuits and an open-country car, Flora had questions. According to the directory, Azadeh, Honorary or Courtesy Mrs. Roderick David Garvin Number Two, worked at spaceport headquarters. ". . . a sort of technician?"

"I'll answer all that as soon as you're into the harness of your emergency air supply and have the hang of snapping your mask into place."

"Oh, these masks!"

"In case a pipsqueak meteorite the size of a Thompson seedless grape drills the capsule dome and we lose air too fast, these kits will keep us going till one of us uses the citizen's band." He took the instrument off the cowling, waggled it, showed her the switch and replaced the handset. "Emergency comes to get us, if the puncture is too big for us to fix."

"If they ever find us! Doc, is this trip necessary?"

"No, I'm trying to scare you!"

"Save that trick until I'm too tired or have a headache."

"Only wives pull that line! First step toward liberation and the really interesting man she met. Now listen: See the miniscreen on the cowling? I put a map of our route into the slot, and I oriented it. Compass, altimeter, and all the rest, including steering and odometer are hooked up to the computer. The little scribe thing traces our course on the screen. No matter where we are, all we have to do is read the coordinates to Emergency service and the rescue car has us pinpointed. Simple, isn't it?"

They were out of the line of traffic, and after dodging a dozen insane cyclists and an apparently drunk prospector, Flora followed the moving scriber and read coordinates perfectly.

"See what I told you? Simple."

"I don't want a tour. I hate Mars, I came to see Azadeh."

Distracted, Doc narrowly missed another cyclist, and before his luck failed, they were in the exit chamber with several other cars. While the evacuator pumped air back into the domes, Flora said, "I'd go mad in a day of this. More things to think of and remember."

Exit gate opened. Doc glanced at the panel. "Both doors tight," he said, reading the pressure gauge. Then, on the paved road which beelined toward a far-off sky-grazing peak capped with a white dome, he said, "That's where we are going. Notice how our graphomat needle scribes a straight line? And watch, there's a meridian-offset just ahead."

The needle scribed a right angle, a short straight streak, another right angle, and straight, dead ahead again. "It's working, and we can rely on it."

"Now I understand everything," she said, laying the irony on with a trowel, "and I'm not one hundred eighty-six years old and I do not have ninety-seven degrees."

"I do not have degrees in Home Economics, Child Psychology, Creative Writing, Wine Appreciation, Advanced Cycling, or that special course for busy housewives."

"Busy housewives?"

"Do-it-yourself abortions, following Home Economics. And now that we're on a straight course and no traffic, I'm going to let you in on a secret. You are busting yourself, living up to that Dizzy Bitch pose that Eve wore to a frazzle." He clobbered the brakes. She nearly bashed her forehead against the windshield. "That was to get your attention. You couldn't possibly be as dumb as you've been pretending. In one lunar month, any halfwitted Greek girl of three hundred Bee-Cee could have set Plato and Socra-

tes to taking turns buggering each other. Just by asking
idiotic questions.

"I said a halfwitted Greek girl. What could a bright
North American wench do? For driving a man nuts and
fruit, the contemporary *Woman americanus* can work wonders. Thirty days after end of honeymoon, she has him fitted with a ring in the nose and he never argues."

"You sound exactly like Rod—"

"If he's ever back with you, you'll tell him he's exactly
like Doc Brandon."

"You're trying to make me weird and incomprehensible.
I'm not complicated, I'm awfully unmysterious, not a bit
obscure, and if you had the brains that God gave a duck,
you'd know that."

"You've devoted your entire life to being a woman," he
retorted, "which makes it natural for you."

"In my awfully short life! Doc, if you'd ever spent one
hour using your imagination, you'd know I'm not cryptic
and complicated. Be a darling and tell me why we are
going to that mountain. I hate mountains and narrow roads
and blind curves and drops a couple thousand meters
straight down to ragged rocks without one little bump to
break the final jolt."

"I am going to talk to an astronomer and if he dummies
up, you can take off your Gook mask. Be a seductive siren, an insidious, calculating wench working behind a
saucer-eyed pose of dumbness."

"You're devious! I know you know exactly what you're
doing."

"I wish I did."

"Before this game is over, I'll know all about being inscrutable, subtle, deceptive."

He began to suspect she was mocking him. He pulled
up, but without clobbering the brakes. "If there weren't so
little room, I'd turn you over my knee and spank your
derrière till your nose bled. Suppose we have a drink instead?"

"Well, you could have said you'd take a cigar instead."

"Didn't bring any cigars. Did bring liquor for the astronomers. And a bit of brandy in case you felt faint, when we
get into those hellish curves the final eighty kilometers."

"Why do you want to ply astronomers with liquor? Wouldn't it be more fun plying Azadeh?"

Doc regarded her critically. "I've never met Roderick Garvin, but I admire and respect him, and Azadeh is his special girl." He twisted about, snatched a small traveling case, whisked it to the front seat. And then, "What the hell are you laughing about?"

"Doc, oh, darling, you're so *funny!*" Time out for laughter that doubled her up. "That indignant look you gave me! And you called *me* incomprehensible!"

He snatched her shoulder, yanked her to sitting straight up.

"What is so God damn funny? Let me in on it!"

"The idea of plying Azadeh with liquor is *outrageous!* But you and me!"

"All the difference in the world! In the first place, she was not married to him, she still loved him. And in the second place, she never crawled into bed with me when I was half asleep. And in the third place, it's none of your business." He chuckled, fought the screw top from a bottle of brandy. "Now that you're as baffled and perplexed as I've been ever since we took off from Megapolis, let's toss one off to better understanding."

He poured dollops of brandy.

"The incomprehensible to the nonunderstandable! It's been fun, from the start, but if we were married?"

"It wouldn't wear out."

"No?"

"Not time enough."

"Clarify, Inscrutable Female?"

"If blunt instrument didn't finish me, arsenic would settle you."

"I'll explain a few things. Everyone knows Rod set her down on an asteroid with unusually great mass for its apparent size. A solid chunk of rare minerals and what-not. Routine repairs, routine upkeep, but he never returned. A very quick decision, *lost in space.* For some reason, the data Rod phoned or radioed to Mars didn't have spatial coordinates. Ship's log pages were televised to Mars, but many images were not clear. Damn odd no spatial coordinates ever came through."

"Azadeh was and is a technician."

"She knows a lot nobody else knows," Doc agreed, "and she could have bitched up the videoimages of log pages. Parliament had appropriated a ream of funny money, billions of *pazors,* to set up three observatories. Equatorial East, Equatorial West, and North Polar. That was before the country was nudging bankruptcy, and the 'interests of science' line sounded good.

"With the distances between the three Martian observatories, and astronomers studying the asteroids, they could determine the position in space, and with three angles on one asteroid, or one nova . . ." Doc paused. Flora did not ask "What's a nova?"

He resumed, "A nova was reported, late one night." And he told her how his phone inquiry had been squelched. He concluded, "It is just possible, it is even probable, that what three observatories spotted and photographed was the detonation of a space cruiser."

Flora nodded. "He said something like that might happen, that Night of Truth. He said he'd outwit them, he'd come back, and he'd um—ah—"

"Make Alex eat shit with a wooden spoon."

"You and Rod must have learned English at the same school."

"Azadeh doesn't look like a widow. Took you a long time to act like one, that night we had the Moon well behind us. Anyway, the Asteroid Folk, nice people, a lot of glamour about them. And suddenly, zero. Rod may have blown up the *Saturnienne* to keep North American culture and exploitation from ruining a happy little vest-pocket-size planet, or maybe the natives beat him to it and blasted the ship to metallic vapor. The asteroid was lousy with fissionable material. There was a wrecked, corroded space cruiser, remember, eaten up by the gases from a fumarole. Those natives had savvy."

"Oh, Doc!" Flora shuddered, clung to him.

He patted her shoulder. "If Rod had been one of the crew of a sailing ship, back in the middle 1500s, cruising the Indies in search of gold and booty, and the galleon was wrecked off a cannibal island, everyone but Rod would have been eaten, and he would preach to the natives, become chief medicine man."

"And keep six native girls busy! But right now?"

"I am going to see what I can do about getting at the confidential files of the observatory, if not the near one, then at one of the other two."

They drove on and whisked along the gentle curves of the approach to the mountain.

"The more we know, the better our chance to get Azadeh talking. Woman to woman, you might make it with her. But ever since that late show and the squelched story of the nova, I've been wondering why the switch was pulled."

The final thirty kay-ems of hairpin switchbacks were brutal. The only cause for happiness was that there was no downgrade traffic. Flora was learning to read gauges, which kept her mind off the three-thousand-meter drop into a rocky ravine. The battery's percentage of charge indicator held her attention.

"If she conks," Doc said reassuringly, "I'll back down to the first turnout and you take the wheel and I'll manhandle her for the U-turn and we'll coast down, in gear, and recharge the battery."

She didn't answer.

Doc was bubbling happy when they made it to the summit and that leveled parking area with a coping a good fifty centimeters high and solid forty centimeters thick. He sighed gustily, gave her a slap on the thigh. She knew all he wanted was a handful of reality.

"God damn it, we made it! You were wonderful. When things got me tense and feeling sticky, you never let out a yeep! Never a fool question. No backseat driving. I could love you till judgment day! A strong silent woman is God's gift to mankind."

"Doc, I was too scared to make a sound, but thanks."

From afar, they saw the enormous dome-cluster of Maritania, the full expanse of roofed meadows and fields. Lakes with ceilings mirrored sunlight and bounced it back through panes of mica. For the first time in a number of years, Doc Brandon forgot to curse science and all the ruin it had worked on Terra. The Martian Rehabilitation Project was working: Seeing it was other than reading statistics. Those tiny domes, twenty kay-ems apart—Doc could visualize Garvin alone in Number Six, devising tricks to recharge cycle batteries for night rides to Number Five, the dome of Lani the deluxe call girl.

Doc was thinking, ". . . *Piecee Inspector, no have got . . . did the missing inspector catch them in bed—or did Rod catch her and the inspector . . . Only facts . . . Lani stowed away aboard the* Saturnienne, *the skipper married her and Admiral Josiah Ambrose Courtney,*" and then he saw verdant hectares where once there had been only sterile desert. "*. . . science isn't so awfully wrong. It's the God damn people. Scientists are people; . . . maybe Simianoids would be better.*"

"Mars went dry before humans fouled and looted it," Doc said. "Dream Girl, don't ask me if Gooks are human." The sun was well past the meridian. "Astronomers sleep late, but they ought to be through with breakfast by now."

Flora grabbed his arm and pointed. "Look! That arrow, ASTRONOMERS' QUARTERS. I won't seduce one until you nudge me."

"You were strong and silent when I needed silence. I'm digging for confidential data, and I trust you."

"You won't hate me if I ad lib?"

"You'll bitch up your own game, not mine, if you talk out of turn."

Chapter 18

At the entrance of ASTRONOMERS' QUARTERS, a good hundred meters from the dome of the main observatory, Doc poked the intercom button and announced himself. The answering voice expressed not the least interest in identity or purpose. A visitor was welcome, two were four times as good as one, and "If y'all done et, there's a drink awaiting you," the man said, in "southern" English which he clearly enjoyed burlesqueing.

There was a buzz, and the airlock door slid open. From that chamber they stepped into a comfortable twenty-two degrees Celsius, with humidity about fifty percent.

Unhelmed, Doc had a chance to whisper into Flora's ear, "If you were a male, I bet there'd be two girls for him and me! This is real hospitality."

She had no chance to reply, though as he drew away from her, he noted her dubious expression, and he wondered what fault feminine intuition had detected. Mona was the only female he knew who did not borrow trouble in advance of immediate need.

And then they encountered the official host, a ruddy, solid young man who glowed with welcome. "Awfully glad to see you, Dr. Brandon! My grandfather used to talk about you a lot! We tend to cabin fever. Loathe the sight of each other." He chuckled, squinted his pale-blue eyes, brushed back his cowlick. "Can't even get along with the women—"

As he opened a small traveling case, Doc cut in, "I brought a few antidotes. Didn't know the folkways of astronomers. Wasn't sure whether or not you"—Doc grinned—"ingested spiritous liquors. If you don't like my selection, I'll drink it myself."

Doc dug out three bottles, and the astronomer's eyes widened. "Good God, Doctor, you can't waste stuff like this on us, we're inured to Gook gin. We always have to get used to good liquor, and by that time, there's none left. Just hang your helmets on the peg." The blocky astronomer was busy, cuddling three bottles: The Glenlivet Scotch, Mr. Avery's selection of Irish, and a sure-enough sour mash from Tennessee. "I'll have places set for breakfast or call it brunch."

* * *

Odors greeted Doc and Flora: broiled meat, peppers, bread that smelled like bread, and coffee that was most un-American.

Doc got all this as Selim Saleeby, First Assistant Astronomer, and Herron, Second Assistant, were presented to the Grand Old Man. But the Head, Leonard Hardwick, was not introduced to Doc, nor Doc to him: They met, by slick protocol, on a rank-to-rank basis. Astronomical Aides handled it so nicely that Doc missed the niceties.

Grandfathers, great-grandfathers, had told these young men all about Avery Jarvis Brandon, the Dean of Scientists, and they marveled that Brandon looked younger than Leonard Hardwick, a tall, square-rigged, square-faced man-among-men: so self-assured that it was easy for him to be whimsical and humorous in welcoming Brandon, the man with ninety-seven doctoral degrees, all of them earned. No one seemed to wonder why Doc never got honorary degrees. Doc could have explained that one handily, but he saw no need.

He was thinking, *"I'd kiss anyone's arse for the first doctoral, but I've got so many already, I don't know what I'd do with any more . . ."* And he was thinking of long-ago Dr. Jay McCollough's lecture: *"We of the West add degree upon degree, as stucco troweled on chicken netting tacked to shoddy wooden framing. Real education . . . it is not laying on another layer, it is the opposite, it is attri-*

tion, peeling away, wearing away superfluities, as an artist in jade wears away the rubbish, until the goddess, the flower, the stallion from the beginning in the heart of the jade is revealed. Education is not adding. It is scraping away garbage, trash, revealing hidden reality."

Doc realized that he had missed a point or two. Hardwick was gesturing, saying something: ". . . they do all the slave labor . . ." Gook girl stepped from the kitchen to take charge of the gift bottles. "We're all slave labor. You'll want to shed your gear." Beckoning to one of the women setting the table, he spoke a blend of English and aboriginal Gook. Then, to Flora, "Alma will take care of you." And Hardwick interposed, blocking Doc's move to follow: "I'm sorry, this is awkward. I hope you'll not misunderstand. What I mean is, your lady won't be eating with us. She'll join the women."

An indefinite gesture indicating everywhere other than the refectory. Doc said affably, "No offense whatsoever. But she is not a 'native.' Flora is Terrestrian, incognito, for reasons not worth going into."

Dr. Hardwick looked off balance and unhappy. "You must be an old Martian hand, coming up here without a guide. What I mean is, it's highly improper for female humans to eat with men. If your companion protégée—"

"Either word is appropriate, though you could consider her my native guide."

"Dr. Brandon, I'm glad you understand without a chart! Our women would be resentful if a strange woman tore etiquette to shreds. They'll explain the matter to her. A kind of pidgin-English-with-Gook for your *convoyée*." His eyes twinkled. He felt better now that he had blatted it out. "It's quite proper to eat with one's own woman, in private. The custom is only for general assembly. As now."

Doc grinned happily. "Once a day, a meal with no interruptions, questions, corrections, or changings to a subject she or they consider more interesting."

"We'll drink to that! One of the women is opening your bottled gifts. Let me help you out of your gear."

And then, in the dining room, the smell of broiling meat and of onions: and a glimpse of discs of bread, about thirty centimeters in diameter, golden brown and fragrant.

"Khubz!" Doc exclaimed. "The original, the only bread!"

The dark, angular-faced astronomer or aide, though it made no difference, came to life and showed a mouthful of fine teeth which brightened the smile. "Well, Dr. Brandon, I'm glad you like it. You'll have no trouble with my name. I'm Selim Saleeby, born in Syria."

"Peaceful Smith. Dr. Saleeby, my Arabic is limited to ordering half a dozen dishes of your delightful Syrian cuisine. But that meat, that *lahhm mishwi,* I can't believe it's mutton! When it was 'in,' the *shashlik,* I mean, we Terrestrians had to have beef, couldn't eat anything but beef, and always got the toughest cuts! And in a Martian observatory!"

"The vegetables," Selim Saleeby explained, "come from the agricultural development. So for that matter, the mutton."

The young lady supervising table service poured clear liquor from a jug. Peaceful Smith said, "Sorry, Dr. Brandon, but we're international. It's not *raki,* it's *akvavit.* From the agricultural project."

Hardwick picked up the talk: "We're saving your treat for the coffee. When it's brewed. What you smell is the roasting. We've been hearing about you all our lives, but never imagined you'd be with us. I understand you're inspecting the Simianoids' colonies." And, inevitably, "When are you going to send one to take charge of the observatory?"

Instead of a quip to parry a quip, Doc pondered, and after a moment of cogitation, he said, "Not until Martian atmosphere is sufficiently dense to sustain life at this elevation, and sufficiently polluted to offset the reason for Martian observatories. And Simianoids will have to improve their abstract thinking, mathematical talents. I'll see if I can get a few assigned as trainees: Your reports on their progress would be interesting."

There were questions about the influential Peace At Any Price group which felt that by building civilian bomb shelters the Republic would antagonize North America's rivals.

"And what are your views, Dr. Brandon?"

"The *PAAP* group," he began, "picked a most interesting designation. The initials are a palindrome. Whether you spell it backward or forward, you still get *PAAP*. And you're wondering how the no bomb shelter plan would work? For one thing, if there were hostilities, they'd be of far shorter duration."

"Most interesting, indeed, sir! Please explain."

"I may be oversimplifying, but essentially, it's this way: There'd be nothing and no one to continue hostilities, and naturally, there'd be peace. May I ask, how many of you have read western novels, or seen westerns on Three Dee?"

Raised hands indicated that at least fifty percent of the staff had followed the Old American Tradition as screened or published. Everyone had heard of Hayes, or Dodge City. Everyone knew that in the Old West, the toughest of the tough never shot an unarmed man.

Doc carried on, "No play on your name, Dr. Saleeby, but there was a law enforcement officer by the name of Smith. He was going to maintain order without gunfire. Look, Mommie, no guns! For a week, barehanded, he arrested and subdued brawlers. And then he was shot dead by gunfighter who didn't notice the marshal was unarmed, or simply didn't give a damn.

"A sincere, idealistic fool! His successor showed up with a double barrel, sawed-off twelve-gauge shotgun. After he cut three-four tough characters off, hip-high, the town became the most peaceful in the West. The new marshal finally died of old age, while I was still a teenager.

"And now I'd like to pose a question, if you please." He frowned, counted on his fingers. "I've been puzzled ever since that report of a nova a good five years ago."

Looking up abruptly, Doc saw facial twitchings and glances exchanged. He went on, "Don't know what possessed me to sit up so late for *Midnight Misinformation*—might've been out of sorts—but a nova was reported by Martian Observatories. There'd been a lot of ballyhoo about a triangulation network, three observatories feeding spatial coordinates, observation time, spectroscopic image, and all the rest into central computer. For all manner of research, of course, but with emphasis on the flare when a meteorite hit an asteroid. Be simple to deduce asteroidal mineral content from the flare."

He glanced from eye to eye. Each face showed just the interest required by deference to a famous scientist. There was something undercover. All that Brandon needed was dirt-moving equipment and a skilled cat-skinner.

"Anyway, the man had scarcely mentioned the flare of a nova at impossibly close range, when someone pulled the switch and the screen went dead. When I phoned from my Island, everyone switched me to someone else's extension, after assuring me that I must have been hearing voices.

"So I pretended to be a damned fool. After appropriate resistance to persuasion, I testified, signed a statement, and conceded I might have smoked, chewed, sipped, or injected—inadvertently of course—enough hallucinogen to confuse me."

Doc assumed a boyish, open-faced look, the gape-mouthed expression which was becoming ever more common among the mass of career Three Dee watchers. Universal innocence made brothers of all men, and the expression was a protective mask for the undeluded.

Breakfast would be followed by tennis, handball, jogging in the gymnasium by the glow of artificial sunlamps. As the group dispersed, Doc intercepted Dr. Leonard Hardwick. He had either cracked the solid front, or he had blown the deal: He might even have hampered Flora.

Chapter 19

"Dr. Hardwick, I'd appreciate it if you gave me information about that interrupted new item. I am not here to embarrass anyone, certainly not interested in a correction of anything. What I have in mind is correlating an observational system such as you have with what might be a practical mode of asteroidal prospecting. The theory is too simple to discuss. Explanation would be an insult to your intelligence."

The Head Astronomer chuckled. "My intelligence isn't as touchy as you imagine."

"I think I know what you mean," Doc conceded. "Mine has become so used to insults that it ignores them. I'll try to make it terse and minimize the affront. It's this way: A cruiser fired a nuclear projectile at a selected planetoid, of which the observatory system has the spatial coordinates.

"When the missile struck its mark, spectroscopic records would be made of the detonation. The spectroscopic characteristics of the missile warhead being known, the minerals of the target could be determined. Elementary, on paper!"

Hardwick nodded. "Simplicities do the damndest things to theory!"

"Even in your field? You should get into biology!"

"Offhand, Dr. Brandon, what bitch-ups would you expect? In the practicalities of the thing."

"No cruiser could fire a nonnuclear shell of sufficient to

volatilize enough of the asteroidal shell to give an unequivocal record."

Hardwick frowned. "Why exclude fissionable material?"

"Sir, the environmentalists have not yet tackled Mars, but the mention of a nuclear missile would stir up more hell on Terra than the actual impact would on an asteroid. First, pollution of the cosmos. Second, there might be sentient life—the Garvin reports, you remember! Third, blasting asteroids on the pretext of prospecting without elaborate facilities for the prospectors would have the PAAP palindrome crowd roaring."

"Practical and political problems," Hardwick conceded. "When you addressed us at brunch, I was sure that more than curiosity moved you. I didn't suspect you had anything immediate and potentially useful." He paused, glanced toward the exit leading to the recreation area and to guest quarters. "You've never before visited this station?"

"Quite right, I have not."

"Spend a couple of days with us. Your survey of Martian ecology, the farm, is bound to take a substantial bit of time anyway."

"Mmmm . . . You're most hospitable, but I'm not familiar with your routine. I'd be a pest and a time waster."

"Many biologists would be time wasters, except for the matter of sociability and staff morale. And mine. Assistants and aides handle the routine. There's more to your question than you may realize. I might enjoy picking details from your enormous experience-mass."

"You've talked me into something. My experience-mass is an erratic mess. You should have seen capers such as my gene splicing tour de force, beginning with a leopard and ending with *Smilodon californicus*."

"And what the hell might that be?"

"A saber-toothed tiger, the creature which bogged down in the La Breatar pits."

"It really lived?"

"Until I had to kill it. Before it killed the Chairman of the Board of Visitors."

The astronomer caught Brandon's arm. "Doctor, let me

show you and your *convoyée* to guest quarters. I'll have an aide bring your luggage."

"She didn't anticipate this detour. And least of all your hospitality. We set out to meet one of the better aboriginal families."

"That's a beautifully fitted Gook mask she wears."

Doc eyed him sharply. "If it'd been so well made, you'd not have suspected it was artificial! Come clean, Doctor."

Hardwick smiled amiably, brushed back his natural waves. "It was her voice. She does not sound like a Gook. It's frightfully interesting, you and your *convoyée* being on such friendly terms with Martian natives. Are they an endangered species?"

"Social Conscience is saving them instead of killing them off mercifully before our culture does it slowly."

"You don't take the usual Terrestrian attitude toward Gooks?"

"My *convoyée* briefed me. I met her aboard the *Space Princess*. Told me much I'd never suspected."

Hardwick's eyes narrowed. The twinkle faded. "The native Martian Woman is not as oppressed or secluded as you may have inferred from our social customs at the observatory. The few visitors we've had—well, their attitude . . ."

Doc broke into the fumbling. "I keep my Burmese and Malay teak forest villagers away from Alleluia Stompers, Testifiers, and other North American primitives."

"So you do understand!"

Doc grinned. "She wore a Gook mask that might endear her to the native family we're going to visit."

Host and guest turned and stepped into a hallway. At its deadend, was a small lobby.

"Almost like one of the better clubs, in miniature."

"Thank you. But let me show you to your rooms."

Hardwick stepped into a passageway that deadended some four meters from the clubroom which opened from the lobby. He opened a door. "Your room, sir. Please step in. I'll invite your *convoyée*. I hope that sharing a connecting bath won't be a nuisance."

"I'm sure she'd not mind."

When the door closed behind the Head Astronomer, Doc plopped himself into a chair upholstered in synthetic leather. He cocked his feet on a matching ottoman, drew a deep breath. Two beds. Three chairs. A bath, fed no doubt by the melting icecap of the adjoining peak which would make Cotopaxi an anthill.

"Soul of tact. Separate room for my *convoyée*. If he'd got one glimpse of Flora-minus mask, one room would have been enough."

Thought of Mona left him wondering how his experiment in being humanitarian and a gentleman was working out on Nameless Island.

". . . I'll be a sad son of a bitch if she develops a passion for Oswald . . . Well, maybe a Simianoidess doesn't fall for stuffed shirts the way most hundred-percent human females do."

His pensive mood was broken by a knock at the door. Doc pounced for the doorknob.

Dr. Hardwick was in the passageway, standing aside for Flora, unmasked. She stepped in. A Gook woman followed, no beauty, but well shaped, with royal carriage. She had style, that quality which Flora had but found so difficult to describe. Perhaps, Doc surmised, this was because, with so few exceptions, everyone looked to someone else for guidance in what to wear, what to do, what to say, how to decorate the kennel and how to furnish it: The other-guided could not have style, being imitations of individuals.

Leaving Flora and the Head Astronomer's lady, Brandon and Hardwick set out for a tour of the observatory.

"Getting funds for bombing asteroids," Doc resumed, "is pretty far out."

"Getting funds for anything," his host countered, "is grim business, unless you can tie it to a Social Program that will cage millions of votes."

"As I get into the spirit of the observatory," Doc resumed, "notions bubble to the surface. It's near the Cosmic Garbage circuit, and the air's thin. I'd speculated on concentration of short wavelength beams on asteroids of unusual density. Fluorescence could indicate substantial deposits of thorium or uranium.

"And there'd have to be a good deal of groundwork done in determining what ores are responsive to what wavelengths. Getting to specifics, our fanatical idealists have antagonized some of our few remaining friends by buying chromite from ill-wishers and paying a higher price for the stuff than our friends were asking—punishing a friend for racism or for what we call violations of human rights, when we don't know the facts.

"Chromite's just a '*for instance.*' There's molybdenum, vanadium. And another approach. Quite useless things fluoresce under ultraviolet, but those no-account minerals are often in company with masses of what is desired.

"Those low-albedo asteroids. Sure, I'm apparently changing the subject," Doc conceded, "but bear with me. It'd help if I knew the masses, densities. The only way you could see them would be when they transit Sun or Moon."

"So far, so good, but I'm left groping."

"I'm what's muddling things!" Doc readily admitted. "Their orbits could be calculated. They couldn't transit Sun or Moon unless they came within the Martian or Terrestrian orbit. With extreme obliquity, a few do just that.

"What I mean is, they could be blasted, bombed, rayed, because being so near to home, the knotheads would figure the enterprise would be a bargain and no one would eat them out for taking bread from the mouths of the tee-bone munching poor! If I knew more of the scope of your spectroscopic work, I might think up a talking point. All I need is something that'll tie to a critical shortage of strategic or industrially important ore."

"This is interesting. Be my guest! My curiosity is getting stirred up."

As he went with his host to the record and computer station, Doc noted the route. He might want to return later and alone.

Chapter 20

But for Flora's urgent mission, Doc would have relished the spectroscopic records. Some were in black and white. A trained observer could read the Fraunhofer lines and name each of the elements in a blend. Others were in color, still others in infrared and in ultraviolet . . . and there was a nova.

"No great event," Hardwick said, as he projected a series of shots of the nova, variously filtered and screened. "Another statistic. And the public gives not a damn."

"Of course not. You can't eat it, drink it, or lay it."

"Your summary of North American values is perfect."

"Sir, that was Marine Corps, and *they* still fight . . . mmmm . . . when did this nova flare up?"

"Let's feed the computer," Hardwick proposed. "May be things of minor interest."

Doc gulped, steadied himself. *"If this is it. I'll get religion, I'll donate a hundred thousand* pazors *to the Alleluia Stompers and the Jubilee Testifiers."* He said, "Hell's bells, don't go to all that trouble."

"It's not every day I have visitors from Terra. What do you mean, trouble?"

He watched Hardwick feed the computer. "Data from North Polar Station. South Polar and this one noted it after brief delay. Integrated observations. Here she is!"

He handed Brandon the printout.

"Nova, January 27, 2062 A.D., *conversion to Terrestrial*

from Martian prime meridian time, integrated angular reading fixed the position in Star Cluster Hercules."

For Doc the calcium, cadmium, strontium, helium, and all the other lines were a dreariness, but he exclaimed, blinked. "Imagine an analysis like that!"

"I'll show you color shots, long-exposure stuff."

Hardwick did so.

Novae are not everyday occurences in the life of an astronomer.

Brandon wondered whether to blat it out, then and there, about the nova of five years ago or play dumb and do a prowl, some time after dark?

The astronomer pulled the switch.

It was not a workroom. This was purely reference, to supply adjuncts to computation and inference. On the other hand, Doc realized that he had taken a dive into the depths of assumption. No telling what might make the compartment, or one adjacent, as busy as a college campus with students primed for protest. Better save the prowl as a final resort, or until he knew more of terrain and conditions.

As they emerged from the compartment, Hardwick paused.

"How about a spot of coffee?" Without waiting for answer, he stepped into a room with four small tables and automatic dispensing gear. "Even handles the empties," he remarked as he set cups on a tray and fingered controls. "Coffee's not mandatory. Darjeeling or Ooolong available. It was cruel and unconstitutional, in the old days, having to stuff empties down the chute."

"Fifteen thousand meters and the air at sealevel is mighty thin, if there were a sea," Doc remarked, as he stirred his ready-mix. "When the agricultural project goes into orbit, there'll be a lake and a datum level. What do geologists say? I mean, peaks half as high again as Everest, on a planet so much smaller than Terra. What's been going on?"

Hardwick shrugged. "Old Moorish proverb, designed for intellectuals. Astronomers find it peculiarly apt."

"Arabic is bad enough, and Moorish is Arabic with the vowels omitted. Me no speakee, you savvee plentee?"

"Sinologist, are you? My Moorish is wobbly. Roughly, *'Head in the clouds, arse in the mud.'* "

"Well bowled, sir!" Doc said. "And before I forget it, that volcano? Quakes? Vibration?"

"Thin atmosphere fools you. Quite a distance away."

On impulse, Brandon wheeled imaginary Uzbek lancers into line, commanded *fours right*, and sounded the charge.

"That nova reported December eleven, 2080, Terrestial time, circa midnight, Eastern Standard. I mentioned that at brunch. Let's hear the off-the-record, no attribution—you know—not even any quoting."

"The nova was someone's mistake. Quicker canceled, the better. We'd be pulled apart, finest Charles Fort style."

"That unnova, then. Could you give me the coordinates?"

"Wish I could, but coordinates of the nonexistent?"

"What's so confidential about all this?"

"Call it a matter of policy."

Doc chuckled. "That's the ultimate incantation. Well, thanks anyway, and I'll grapple with asteroids as best I can. Dr. Hardwick, the details vary."

"Len, as in Leonard."

"Doc, as in doctor."

They shrugged, grimaced wryly, and each knew that the other understood the basics. The younger man thrust out his hand. "Doc, I'm glad you get the point. We're not stinkers by nature, except for occasional exceptions, the sacred cows of science."

"Len, you must have been hiding in the bamboo when the Board of Visitors made a surprise inspection of Nameless Island." Doc thrust back his chair. "I know I'm keeping you from your routine. And I'm sure I can find my way back to guest quarters."

"By no means! Now that we've discussed the no-no-nos, let's warm the cushions of the cocktail lounge. Self-serve, not automated."

And then they entered the cocktail lounge, where Hardwick said, "I've been negligent, though it's somewhat your fault, Doc! I'll phone your *convoyée* and the girl who stayed to show her the women's quarters."

He stepped to the intercom and got a quick reply to his

ring. "Selma? Len speaking. Why don't you and Doctor Brandon's guest come to the lounge and brighten things a bit?" After listening a moment, he cradled the instrument, then said to Doc, "She's feeling below par, and begs leave to be excused. But, thanks. Selma's doing all the speaking. It'd be quite all right if she brings one of the Observatory ladies?"

"Make it so, Len! Social life, Equatorial Ninety West!"

No time was lost. Renée, green eyes, tawny hair, and shaped like Mona, was certainly a Simianoid. Devilish twinkle in the eyes. No, *impish* was the word, and that included a generous mouth. No reflections on Flora, but the sight of Renée's long-legged, luxurious frame made him miss Mona.

Len Hardwick's girl required no surmises, and she evoked no memories: dark hair, dainty imperious nose, and a facial structure accented by piquante cheek bones left no doubt: a Gook, one of the aristocratic strain. She was such by birth; and what Férideh had was beyond what could be conferred by social fiat.

Gracious, stately, more than a nod, not quite a bow, and the smile offset the hint of remoteness. Brandon had qualified, at least for the duration of the cocktail hour, perhaps even for the entire visit.

"Quite right, Dr. Brandon, I am a Gook," she said.

"You're psychic! No doubt you got my other thoughts, *proud as a queen?*"

Férideh was pleased to be amused. "Hardly be proper for me to speak the lines, but since you did, thank you, sir." And by this she meant: not every North American was a barbarian.

"I'd better quit while I'm winning!"

Férideh warmed up perceptibly. "Most thoughts I'm not able to read. Some, I can't help but catch."

His glance included Renée. Doc said. "I have a degree in Girl Watching, and no doubt the qualification tests leave marks."

The impish hazel eyes sharpened, brightened: a quick survey, and she said, "The subjects didn't scratch you."

"Of course not! My degree was awarded during my early years when I had unusually short reaction time."

"Girl Watching . . ." Renée savored the term. "Dr. Brandon, you are famous for science and . . . ah . . . Seniority." She gave him time to acknowledge the compliment. His bow was just right and so was resumption of badinage: "Sad if your vision ever failed."

She was having fun, hamming it: facial mobility was somewhat ahead of the standard Simianoid.

"I'm learning Braille," Doc assured her.

"Renée's vacationing with us," Hardwick interpolated, as he busied himself, mixing Islay and water, and also, Sour Mash with a terrestrian carbonated horror. "Doc, can't I tempt you?"

"Hail, satan, and be damned to you! With the distance and the company, I'll have Gook gin, straight, and don't taint it with *Nine Down*." Then, to Renée, "You were telling us about your vacation?"

The Aboriginal Imperatrix cut in, "Good for you, Dr. Brandon! It's rarely fatal. At the worst, drives the drinker only temporarily insane."

Doc laughed. "I was the prototype Mad Scientist long before the space age ruined Mars for the original owners." He picked up his slug of Gook Sub-One, raised it. "*Ave Imperatrix*, and don't mention farewell! It'll be here all too soon."

And then Renée got back to her vacation: "Dr. Brandon, you're a biologist or anthropologist. My husbands were brawling in Maritania. All four, drunk and disorderly, three in jail and one in the hospital."

"Which makes you the Red Menace?"

"Not while I'm a guest! But when you're a guest while you carry on your Ecology Project survey, be sure to see us."

Doc had never suspected that Martian Observatory, Equatorial Ninety West, could be so much fun.

When dinner was announced, Doc said, "These cocktail snacks, the agricultural project lamb sausages in particular, so amazingly good I overate." He got to his feet. Steady as an adjutant on parade, although his enunciation was a shade too precise, he gave Férideh, the Imperatrix, a lances-at-dawn look. "I did underestimate Gook Sub-One and Gook Sub-Two." He bowed a precise ninety degrees, as at the coffin of a Chinese dignitary. "Correction! I over-estimated myself. Leonard, please offer to your colleagues my respects and my regrets.

"If you have a security patrol, suggest that they challenge three times before firing. I rarely walk in my sleep, but, in case"—Doc addressed an imaginary footman—"Giles, Dr. Brandon's hat, his stick, and his gloves. He is leaving at once."

He bowed to the trio. Twirling an imaginary cane, he strode stately and steadily into the corridor and to the guest rooms, without ever missing a colored guide line. At his destination, he opened the door soundlessly, closed it softly. Carrying shoes tucked under his arm, he picked his way to bed, but with a certainty which would have amazed Dr. Hardwick, and which would not have surprised the Aboriginal Imperatrix, although he may have underestimated her psychic sensings. This possibility did not disturb him: a Terrestrian gulping Gook Gin, Sub-One and Sub-Two, could not be entirely bad.

Imperial haughtiness had tapered off. All Terrestrians were on the defecation-list until they proved themselves worthy of a less unsavory station. And Doc felt that he had not antagonized her. She would not share whatever suspicions she might have.

The Impish Simianoidess, Renée, the Red Headed Menace, he could count on not to air her queries even if she suspected that Doc was not as drunk as he appeared to be.

The computer was one of a widely distributed and esteemed make, with an indexing system which Doc recognized from old times. The Head Astronomer's retrieval of a real nova's history had left Doc with no problem except back-tracking, and, taking cover in the event that some dummy needed data at an absurd hour.

Flora was tired, but no reason why he shouldn't tiptoe through the bath to the adjoining room. The honeymoon was not over, and they were not even married. And then he remembered that the sensible thing would be to fall asleep, and awaken when all proper astronomers had their eyes glued to their instruments.

Chapter 21

Doc awakened within thirteen minutes of the hour he had set for his prowl. He put on socks and slipped into a dark robe. Poised on the balls of his feet, he devoted a few minutes to body-flexion to tune up for *kung fu* if there was an unexpected encounter. Finally, he put on the swarthiest of his emergency masks. A surprise meeting, cut short by an unarmed-combat whack, would leave the victim too bemuddled to have a meaningful account of the event.

There were too many overilluminated passages and corridors. He wished he were in the cozy jungle of Nameless Island. During uncertain moments, he stepped into the shadow of a buttress or column, closed his eyes and relaxed, the better to pick up vibrations normally imperceptible.

No thrills occurred on the way to the record retrieval room. Once he reached his destination, he played his flashlight beam about and located points of concealment, then turned to the computer keyboards. During his earlier years, an equivalent system would have filled the city hall of Megapolis, whereas now, Flora's suitcase could have contained the essentials, leaving space sufficient for blue ones with rosebuds.

Now that he knew where he would work, and how he would operate, he allowed himself a moment for thinking how pleased Flora would be if he handed her significant information. "Like dynamiting fish in a medium-size barrel," he told himself, and closed his eyes to sharpen other senses. Should have come barefoot: better to catch floor vibrations.

Someone was approaching. Someone wearing shoes, and without regard to sound. *"God damned sleep walkers!"* Doc cut the flash beam, pounced for the nearby bank of filing cabinets. When the lights blazed, Doc was in deep shadow.

Leonard Hardwick, Head Astronomer, was heading for the rig from which he had finger-poked a printout of a nova in Hercules. Hardwick knew what he was retrieving: Doc could make too many bad guesses. Worst of all, the afterthought and return might be to wipe out the entire record.

Doc cursed his own glib chatter.

Hard-copy snapped into view. Whatever the subject, it would at least give a glimpse of what had baited the astronomer back to the record retrieval.

Hardwick, the gracious chief, sensed that he was not alone. Being up to some caper, he was as supersensitive as Doc, but by no means as quick. He had scarcely begun to respond to the awareness that all was not right when Doc Brandon landed. He folded. Brandon eased him to the deck.

Doc grabbed the printout. It was not until he read the first line that he realized his prize was the not-*Nova* print out! On the point of racing to his room, he checked himself. There was time.

Doc stepped to the computer and set to work. And when the printout was ejected, he saw that he had a duplicate of the one which the Head Astronomer had retrieved.

Brandon made tracks for guest quarters.

Chapter 22

After her briefing at the females-only brunch, Flora shaped her thoughts and declined the invitation to cocktails. She did not know what Brandon had planned.

"Why that old devil never, repeat, never tells me anything I do not know. I'll play it my way, he'll play it his, and between us, we'll get that printout."

So, Flora had pleaded indisposition.

It summed up in this manner: a *mélange* of women-only brunch, one human terrestrian woman, one Simianoidess, and half a dozen upper-bracket aboriginal women recognized a unique opportunity—that of learning all they could of each other's life styles. Despite her Gook mask, none of the Observatory ladies fancied for a moment that Flora, the companion of a notable scientist, could be anything other than human, and probably, someone's wife romancing with a V.I.P. The local ladies knew a good deal about each other's life styles. They'd find out all about Flora and she would do as much for them. They might find each other most congenial.

She knew that she was among friends. Flora got along marvelously well, face to face, with other women, knowing that most tagged her as a fancy bitch purely as a matter of principle, and only for the time it took to buy a stock of blue ones and pink ones. There was no professional jealousy. Being among friends, Flora whisked off her mask.

"These things can be an awful nuisance!"

Férideh, the Aboriginal Aristocrat shacking up with Dr.
Hardwick, recognized the world's most famous Space
Widow, the dream girl of one-and-one-half hemispheres:
the one woman whose existence had for the past few years
irked, annoyed, infuriated, and humiliated her.

"The one and only Flora, *the* Mrs. Roderick David Garvin?"

"Quite right, and make of it whatever you can!"

With a glad cry, Férideh caught Flora with both arms
before Flora had time to wonder. "Madame Garvin!" The
Gook lady stepped back, still holding the Terrestrian
dreamboat by the shoulders. "This is too good to believe!"

"You leave me happy and puzzled! No one likes me as
much as all this, not in private."

"Oh, but there is so much you do not know!"

"Really?"

"Yes, really. Do you mind a personal question?"

Flora's brows rose. "Ask me and let me decide."

"Do you always wear either pink with forget-me-nots, or
else blue with rose-buds?"

Flora laughed heartily. "From all I can gather from the
grapevine there's not a woman in North America who
doesn't wear either one or the other. I hate to say it, but
our sex includes some of the dizziest wenches!"

"Our sex does not have a monopoly on dizziness!"
Férideh drew a deep breath. "I might as well explain a few
things."

"Wouldn't hurt, would it?"

After a final reappraisal, each of the other, they recognized their kinship: they smiled, as affectionately as sisters
not actively quarreling.

"My sort-of husband has, well, no, not fallen in love with
your Three-Dee image, but it has done things to him. You
might not believe it."

"If you'd lived with Rod Garvin, nothing would surprise
you."

"Oh, I don't doubt that space captains have their quirks,
but . . ."

"What is the problem? Dr. Hardwick is the most darling
man!—charming and brilliant and talented and awfully
good looking!"

"So is your two-hundred-year-old convoyer!"

"Now we've agreed, point by point. My Three-Dee image has done things to Dr. Hardwick. I can't help what my Sudzo show does to two hundred million males! You ought to read my fan letters." She gave the bra area a lift. "*A bite for each*. They have hopes and they're plain in describing them."

"*That*," Férideh said, "is a matter of taste, and after all it's natural. But Leonard Hardwick can't live up to his name unless I wear panties like the ones you traipse around in Sudzo."

Flora drew a deep breath. "Now I've heard everything. Trouble is, I've not staged a new show the past three years. They repeat the old ones, though I do get a nice royalty. I don't know what I could do!"

"Are you thinking of marrying Doc Brandon?"

"Heaven help us, no! He has the loveliest girl, back on Terra. She couldn't take the trip with him, and he's going to be around Maritania for quite a while. This isn't just a caper, but it can't be anything permanent."

"Oh, wonderful!" Férideh's inner light blazed through. "Then you'd not mind!"

"Mind what?"

"Going to bed with Leonard to convince him that whether you're wearing blue, pink, or none at all, the only difference is that none at all is nicer."

"Ah, you mean?"

"It's a fetish with him and it's a nuisance and if you'd try it, it might cure him. The *real* Sudzo girl, with and without. Life could get back to normal for me."

Flora did some fast thinking. It was the first time she'd met a committed wife-or-something who wanted her sort-of spouse to tumble into bed with another attractive woman.

"*. . . he's nice, and it could be fun, thrilling even, making up for lost time . . . loved every minute with Doc . . . Rod's marooned on a not-so-desert asteroid . . .*" And she said, "Férideh, let's figure things out. I'd *love* to help you!"

Chapter 23

As Brandon evaluated the situation, the Head Astronomer would regain consciousness shortly after his assailant was back in guest quarters. With no bruises, and with the printout lying at hand, Hardwick could blame the blackout on something he ate or on what the doctor had mentioned during the semiannual physical that every member of the Pliable Society demanded from cradle to grave. The longer they lived, the more death horrified them.

Flora, indisposed: a chance to study the prize which had seemed unobtainable. A complete analysis of the spectrum of the nova that was not a nova would require instrument evaluation. However, neither Doc nor Flora needed completeness. The major issue became apparent after a few minutes of squinting through a 20-X glass:

The so-called nova, according to its spectrum, had been composed of CX-41, the alloy of which the hull of the *Saturnienne* had been shaped—but vaporized, ionized atoms had made the lines of the printout.

"No wonder the broadcaster said there had never been a report of a nova. If Flora's story is true, Alexander Heflin would have the head of anyone who suggested that the Saturnienne had quit the asteroid where she landed. And she had vanished in a tremendous flare of atomic fission."

Three jumps of a calculator would give the coordinates of the "nova," to within a hundred kilometers.

* * *

Doc, happy and already half asleep, crawled into bed. He began his countings with Iris, dead more than a century ago, and was sound asleep before he got past Mona. Eventually Doc wondered whether he was dreaming, or whether he was cuddling with Flora on a space cruiser. Rememberings and statistics had apparently solidified into a study of higher curves rotated about the X-axis . . . too bad Flora hadn't slid between the sheets from the other side.

"For hell's sweet sake, turn over," a Guardian Angel whispered, and Doc answered, "God damn it, I might wake up and she'd be gone. . . . She smells like Flora, and if you wake up she won't be gone. . . . Get a handful of the stuff that dreams are not made of. . . ."

Not much you can do when a Guardian Angel is supervising an encounter, except go along with it.

She was not Mona. Flora never smelled like Mona, who had slipped a flask of cologne into his luggage, so he'd be thinking of her.

Slender shapeliness on the fringe of opulence . . . Mmm . . . opulence not the word: Understated luxury was better. She did not shave her legs. Sleek smooth. Depilatory job, mmm . . . Syrian or Egyptian. A bit tall for Malay or Japanese . . .

"Oh, don't stop!"

He didn't.

When at last they relaxed to enjoy the infinite depths of nine million massed featherbeds in intergalactic space, she murmured, "You were not being whimsical when you told us about Braille for a Girl Watcher with failing vision. Who am I, which am I?"

"You're not that long-legged, green-eyed redhead."

"I didn't ask who I was *not*!"

"There was one of that one's cousins, but it'd take a tapeline to figure which has the mostest and where. No, you're not that one."

"You're still telling me who I am not."

"Don't ask me which Gook lady you are. I do have my limits."

She sat up, stretched luxuriously. "If I were a lady, I'd slip out the way I sneaked in."

"Madame—I should say, *khanoum!*—I rely on Braille.

Finally I'd identify you. But I won't be able to stay. Not long enough."

"Your guessings were fun. You may snap on the lights, long enough for a split-second look, and resume Braille."

Backing to the wall switch, Doc snapped it, and he got a look: His visitor was Férideh, the Head Astronomer's lady. Doc blinked, gulped. "This is not a breach of hospitality. I did not seduce you. Fact is, your being here accords with ancient Turkistan tradition, the khan's ultimate hospitality. I never suspected I was in that distinguished-visitor category."

"Eve in your silly Garden of Eden legend didn't have to wait half as long as I did. And I did not introduce a custom from Turkistan, I mean, I didn't sell Leonard the idea." Férideh kicked-flipped the sheet back. "See if you can keep your mind on mixing that drink. If you can, you're not a real Girl Watcher!"

Férideh, glowing and being herself, relished the way things had worked out. "Doc, darling, so many North Americans are the lousiest lovers! How long did it take you to learn the answers?"

"I met the right woman, she told me about plowboys, and I listened to her without getting indignant."

There was a tap on the bathroom door. Odd business, Flora tapping. Also, awkward. He did not know what to say.

But Férideh knew. "Oh, it's you. Come on in, darling, you're not embarrassing us."

Doc was choking and gulping. He wondered whether to try *kung fu* or grab that very handy chair.

The woman who opened the door was Mrs. Roderick David Garvin. Flora had a piece of paper in her hand. She did not look as amazed as she might have. "I got it!" She waggled the paper. And then, "You weren't shortchanged. She's lovely!"

"Madame, what the hell is that card?"

"That's the printout you were going to get and I didn't see how you'd manage it." Flora flashed a look at Férideh. "Oh, all *right*! She isn't married to the Head Astronomer, and you and I aren't married, and it was a deal."

Doc began to have suspicions, but he groped for words to

express them. Férideh, however, was not at loss. "Darling, of course it was a deal, and Doc's a sweetheart, but what's so awfully exciting about a printout? It'd take your dreamboat and me a long time to get down to that level! Did you wear blue or pink? Or did you fascinate and inspire so you didn't have to wear either color?"

That final question bugged Brandon. "Will you two young ladies brief me?"

"This," Flora declared, again waggling the printout, "is what you've been wanting these past five years, the nova business, do you remember?"

"Flora, darling, in the dark this lovely person smelled almost exactly like you, as if she'd borrowed your cologne, and before I suspected it was a mistake, I was happy it'd happened. And now that you remind me—"

Doc reached for the nightstand. He grabbed a bit of paper. "Take a look. Here's the printout I got for you, at *eee*normous risk. Not having any pussy-bait to offer, I used my wits."

"So did I, you nasty old man!"

Doc believed her, and he felt guilty about his success, with Férideh as a bonus. Flora laughed out loud, and merrily.

"Doc, he had nothing of me, and when I saw how well you'd done for yourself, yes, I was provoked for a second."

Férideh, out of bed, was slipping into her robe.

Doc said, "I argued, reasoned, but not a chance. All right, seductive siren, you did a slick job, and if there wasn't any pussy-bait, you get my applause and my apologies."

"He didn't say so," Flora resumed, "but I know you played a nasty trick and knocked him unconscious."

"For your female equivalent, he didn't have to be unconscious."

"Oh, all right! We made a bet. He lost. He paid off, being a gentleman. You are guilty of a gross breach of hospitality. Len had been watching my Sudzo shows ever since they went on the air, and we got to talking about them when I took off my mask, and he recognized me, of course. I begged and pleaded for the printout. I explained

why, but he balked. Finally I got a flash of inspiration. I
made it a gambling proposition.

" 'Tell me if I am wearing blue ones or pink ones. If you
are wrong, you give me a printout and I'll go back to my
room, alone, I mean, not with you. If you are right, I'll stay
here with you and I'll be all yours and deal fairly by you.
And skip the printout.'

"I forget the exact words, but I did ask him to make a
clear statement. He said, 'You're wearing pink ones with
forget-me-nots.' He was wrong."

Férideh had edged nearer. Despite congenital poise, curiosity made her sway, lean forward, take a tiny pace to
correct her balance.

"If he'd been right, you'd still be there with him?"

"Doc, your voice almost accuses me. You are right, and
a bet is a bet. Yes, I had my jealous instant, when I stepped
in. But I had a sure thing when I made my bet."

"You didn't know that I'd made it so!"

"Right. I didn't know, not until you told me. But I had a
sure thing from the start." Before Doc could protest that
by every law of probability, there had been a fifty-fifty
chance of her losing, she added, "Only you and an intimate
female friend present! Watch."

Catching skirt at knee level, Flora whisked it to her
chin.

"Be a son of a bitch! He lost, no matter what color he
said!"

Flora turned toward the door.

"What's the play now? Where?"

"I'm going back to him. I was nasty, playing a trick like
that. And he won't be leaving me to come searching for
your prize package! Doc, she's awfully nice!"

Chapter 24

As Doc followed Azadeh's car out of the northern airlock of Maritania, Flora continued talking out her qualms. Again he offered assurance: "Listing herself as Azadeh Garvin means nothing more than accepting our custom of squelching a woman's name when she marries. Nearly as I can figure Azadeh and her people, she did not expect him to dump you in the fine old American way, the way when spouses no longer thrill each other . . ."

After ten kilometers the road skirted a curve of sterile hills past which it led, as Doc put it, "Straight into nowhere." Presently they swung from the way to the mines, where solar-heated smelters spewed arsenic-flavored fumes which smelled like garlic.

After another handful of kilometers, the road dipped until the car tops were below desert level. Not far ahead was a curved surface as though an enormous saucer had been inverted to cover subsurface depths.

Creeping toward the barrier, the deadend of the sunken road, Azadeh stopped a meter short of a gate. Doc followed her through an airlock. Once clear, she pulled up and beckoned. He got out and when he came alongside her vehicle, she took off her helmet. Instead of wondering how many points Azadeh would rate on the Girl Watcher's scale, Doc had an overwhelming awareness which forced him to brush all else aside. He was facing a female expression of what Lao Tzu had had in mind when he spoke of the Superior Person.

The Chinese sage, addressing a mature people, had not bothered to elaborate on the question which arose frequently in the Occidental mind: *"Superior to whom, or to what?"*

That question was suitable for arranging commonplaces in order of merit. It applied to the mass produced. Flora imitated no one. Brandon, himself an individual, knew that Azadeh was not a copy of anyone else.

That she was pleasingly shaped and facially attractive were irrelevancies during that moment of close encounter. Those facts he would recall later. From his childhood, which had perhaps terminated around age six, he had had a high opinion of himself, and for the previous 180 years there had not been much to shatter his estimate. Nor did this eye-to-eye meeting diminish his self-appreciation. During his earlier years, he had several times faced a Superior Person; and of these, one had been female. Here was another.

He would not want her as a partner in anything. Doc Brandon was not wired up to be a subordinate, no more than was this woman, who was in her early or middle twenties. He knew that Azadeh could no more look up to any other human, male or female, than could she look down on any. That was the ultimate simplicity, and in an instant he made an invisible kowtow.

As the moment of recognition lengthened, he noted that Azadeh's eyes, very dark, were perceptibly slanted, little more than to harmonize with cheekbones sufficiently prominent to be interesting. Doc could not decide whether her nose was almost aquiline or almost straight.

Once she knew that he would not kowtow, Azadeh's mouth blossomed in a smile: And he knew then that each had accepted the other.

"It's time you and I met. I was in the news a little while and you've always been. When I turn into a courtyard, park outside. It'll be handier that way."

Resuming the wheel, Doc said to Flora, "You'll do better than you expect. She is genuine."

The sun reached through the mica ceiling of the colony, lighting an expanse of gardens, pools, shrubbery. Although the curvature was gentler, the air-spaced layers of mica rested on vine-masked pillars such as those which supported the domes of Maritania. As Doc summed it up, "These people built their settlements bit by bit, over thousands of years, and developed solar power and ways of replacing air and water that escape from their primitive colonies. We've been working a crash program, borrowing and modernizing some of their ancient tricks."

Ahead was a stretch of trees dwarfed to suit a world whose sky was of mica panes. Scattered at random were cube-shaped dwellings enclosed by walls.

Azadeh turned right and into the entrance which pierced the pink brick wall. When Doc overtook Flora on the patio, Azadeh was saying, "How silly-formal, welcoming 'Mrs. Garvin'! Here's where I live. I hope you'll feel at home."

And then Doc interposed, "This reminds me of a settlement east of El Paso. Little whitewashed houses, like dice cast in the desert by drunken giants. There's friendliness. This is good!"

"I did feel uneasy, coming here," Flora said. "I was expecting the American Indian dislike of my people."

A good start, but it left Doc wondering how long it would last.

They followed Azadeh among stunted trees, remote cousins of Terrestrial yucca and tamarisk, and finally into the flat-roofed house. Passageways led from reception room to living quarters. Rammed earth benches skirted the two walls not pierced by doorways.

Benches and tiled floor were covered by rugs of dark blue, patterned with old gold, apricot, and persimmon colors. The patterns reminded Doc of the ancient Turkestani weaves, though those were of vegetable fiber instead of wool or silk.

Wall niches like little shrines housed jugs, pitchers, small goblets, mugs, cups, and bowls. Some were of metal, others of glazed pottery. In one corner, at the left, was a hearth, the focal point of the room. The wicker basket nearby was packed with wood. Combustion, releasing carbon dioxide, would feed younger growth which exhaled oxygen to replace what fire had borrowed from the atmosphere.

Azadeh stepped to a niche from which she picked a long-necked bulbous jug. This she set on a tray with four cups little larger than the size traditional for rice wine, and put the tray on a tabouret near the wall bench.

"I'll not offer you refreshments until the head of the house has welcomed you. I'll be leaving you for a few moments."

After watching Azadeh cross the room and step into the dusky passageway, Doc said, "Our people look down on these 'natives.' They don't love and admire us as we expect everyone to do, world's end to world's end. Some of them don't care for our social and political notions.

"Azadeh has 'presence.' So has your cousin Alexander and those other once-in-a-whiles who could never swallow the notion of egalitarianism! The end product is mediocrity, the only possible universal equality."

Flora made a wry grimace. "If our positions were exchanged, I'd not be able to carry it off as she does."

"She's not even aware of carrying anything off."

"Head of the house." Flora pondered. "Well, now, I wonder: When we phoned her from the hotel, she made it clear that her father had died a couple of years ago. Are we going to meet Rod's successor?"

Doc did not answer. Flora had been thinking aloud. After a moment of silence, he nodded, gestured. "They're on the way."

Flora's glance shifted to the hallway whose shadows had swallowed Azadeh. Doc, however, was watching Flora.

A boy about six years old stepped from the passageway. He wore an embroidered skullcap, gilt on maroon, and a blue tunic which reached well below the knee. That squarish-faced youngster carried himself as though he owned the place. Azadeh followed, three paces behind him.

The lad's gray-green eyes remained level as he advanced toward the visitors. He moved deliberately until, three paces short of Doc and Flora, he halted. After regarding each, eye to eye, he addressed the space between them: "I am Toghrul, son of Roderick David Garvin, grandson of Samgan Manioglu."

Brandon got to his feet. "A grown man does not rise in the presence of a boy. I am Avery Jarvis Brandon. I stand out of respect to your father, your grandfather, and the house of Mani."

He bowed a precise ninety degrees. Toghrul bowed, and then he said, "My father, my grandfather, and his grandfathers offer respects."

The exchange had been more than Toghrul's briefing could have included. Doc knew this, having spoken on impulse.

Azadeh filled four cups.

Toghrul continued, "Dr. Brandon, they beg you to be seated." At the boy's gesture, Doc moved to the place of honor, nearest the hearth. "Dr. Brandon, you are welcome. Flora Khanoum, you are welcome." After catching Azadeh's eye, he said, "Mother, if you please."

She offered the tray to her son, clearly head of the house. After he had taken a cup, she served the guests. Toghrul said, "The Ancestors drink to your well-being."

Flora glanced to catch Doc's eye. He held his tiny cup with the fingertips of two hands. He raised the cup. The women followed suit. Doc said, "We drink to the Unseen Ones."

Bottoms up.

Toghrul said, "With your permission, the Ancestors take leave."

He bowed, and when Doc returned the courtesy, the boy backed off three short steps and turned, stately as an adjutant at parade, to stride deliberately to the passageway.

Flora got up. She smiled through a blinking of tears. "Very much his father's son. Very much your son, Azadeh Khanoum. Rod was always extravagant. Leaving two widows was in keeping. Though I'm sure by now that you and I are not widows."

Azadeh smiled. "I've not had the benefit of your Western religions. My people regard reincarnation as quite plausible. You seem to suggest resurrection. However incredible another's beliefs, we don't mock and we do not debate.

"Let's leave Dr. Brandon to his ponderings while you and I discuss the interesting idea that we're not widows." She caught Flora's arm. "Dr. Brandon, the book niche might interest you, and don't ignore the gin."

Chapter 25

Halfway down the dusky hall, Flora followed Azadeh into a sitting room which was a relief from the stark reception hall. Two tall candelabra, one on each side, stood at the head of a *chaise longue* fashioned of wicker. This, like the wall bench, was upholstered in Turkestani colors somewhat warmer than those of the runners which framed instead of covered the floor.

Sun filtered through skylights illuminated the room and was reflected from the brass binding of a tall Chinese-style armoire of dark wood inlaid with woods of lighter color. Small tapestry panels hung between wall niches.

Flora almost said, *"Rod had it nice, commuting from here to the* Saturnienne *while she was getting her shakedown."* She checked this in time, and instead, "One little jug, two cups, and all those books."

Her gesture made a sweep of the niches.

Azadeh nodded. "Wasn't that way during Rod's little while." A sigh, and then, "I needed books from the start. The office English is barbarous. I had to improve my style, once I transferred from the office to communications."

"Oh . . . so you could censor messages from the *Saturnienne*?"

"Not really! And when she landed on the asteroid, I was glad I'd studied. Converting Asteroidal talk into idiomatic English took . . . well—agility at times!"

Flora's glance roved. She noted the dressing table and

the curtained bed which peeped from between the drapes of the alcove. Somewhere there'd be a bath compartment.

An air current brought a cosmetic scent.

Before Flora could remark on what a cozy little apartment this was, Azadeh resumed, ". . . And I'm tying Gook talk to the Uighur Rod learned."

"From our predecessor in Turkistan?"

"It would have been a disaster if he hadn't learned a little of her language," Azadeh carried on. "I wonder whether Djénane Khanoum still misses him."

"She must. First time Rod told me about Djénane, he said she was going to marry!"

Azadeh laughed softly. "The Garvin women are a sorority. All we need is a charter. Do sit down! The way we've been standing here! You and I did have a lot of getting-used-to in a short time!"

Azadeh took a jug and two tiny cups from a wall niche.

Flora, still groping, made a grimace. "That sorority: Would we have to include Lani?"

"I don't see why not! If it hadn't been for Lani, he'd never have fouled up the computer system, he'd never have been sent on a one-way cruise, and I'd never have met him. And he was awfully important in her life, much more important than husbands are in the lives of most wives."

"Important? A redheaded whore he was going to shack up with in Khatmandu? Suspected of killing an inspector and stowing away on the *Saturnienne*!"

"Protecting her virtue," Azadeh interposed solemnly. "And don't forget that but for Rod, she'd never have married a retired Space Admiral. Never have become an honest woman. Rod was a lot more important in her life than he ever was in yours!" She raised a hand, checking a flare of rebuttal. "You said that you weren't a widow and that I wouldn't be if we'd been married. Well, now, I've had more fun getting the church broadcasts and learning what North Americans believe. Have they resurrected Rod, demonstrated life everlasting, on some program I missed? I mean the Testifiers and the Alleluia Stompers, and the others that are trying to convert Gooks into believing the weirdest things! What makes you think Rod is living?"

"You're the most unconvincing widow I've met in all my

life! Aside from social and such formalities, you're as much a widow as I am; or would be, if he were dead. I knew you were pregnant long before anyone but you yourself knew. It was that look in your eyes, your expression whenever you were on the air. I know Rod had not been lost in space. I was sure you knew and weren't just hoping."

"So you came to bring me good news?"

"To ask what really happened. You know!"

"You mean, that he might have landed the *Saturnienne* on the unexplored hemisphere of Mars? That he might have worked him way from a secret landing and from one colony of Gooks to another until he's somewhere close to me and our son?"

Flora knew that this was neither mockery nor irony. Still groping, she kept her fifth ace concealed in her sleeve. "Why," she demanded, "are you holding out? Do you think I could come between you and Rod and your son? For a couple of weeks after take-off for Saturn, I hoped I could be offering competition, and then I knew the honeymoon hadn't been long enough. Would I want to force myself where I was not wanted, where I no longer had a *natural* right?"

Azadeh regarded her guest, considered for a moment. "I am sure you'd not want to. No more than I'd want to separate you from him. Not even if I could. During our Gooktown honeymoon, I made it clear to him that if he came back, I'd be Number Two Lady. That people are not property like cattle, except in your North American culture. That I no more owned him than he owned me or owned you. But if you could understand people as he did and I did, there would be no problem."

"He told me something like that," Flora admitted. "During our final hours of the first serious talking we'd ever had. If it had not been for the things he said about you, I'd never have returned to Mars!"

Azadeh smiled amiably. "My turn now, isn't it? Suppose I had the answers you want, what could you do with them? Why would Rod stay undercover? What I mean is, what could you do with information Rod himself would not or could not make use of?"

Flora mustered her remaining scraps of patience and

contrived a smile which was not convincing. "You're fishing! A terrestrian idiom."

"It's true that Martians don't fish for sport, but I have heard those words in the Maritanian information offices. And *you* are fishing! Rod told me how you had always hated space, yet here you are, looking for something that is not. I've never even tried."

"Of course you haven't! You know everything." She dipped into her jacket pocket and produced the printout. "Except this! The day the *Saturnienne* was to take off for home, the astronomers on Mars saw a flare that they thought was a nova. When they studied the spectroscope record, they learned that they'd seen a nuclear blast. Something had touched off a lot of an alloy known as CX-41. The stuff the shell of the *Saturnienne* was made of. If you drilled holes in the alloy and stuffed each with pieces of reactor rods used to power the crusier's drive, you'd have a nuclear bomb.

"The astronomers realized that no nova would have a CX-41 spectrum, so they squelched the report. Doc Brandon was watching the broadcast when they pulled the switch. This printout is what he finally got."

"What's *your* answer?" Azadeh countered. "You tell me. There's nothing I can tell you!"

"Rod told me that he'd be fighting sabotage all the way. But by the time of the explosion, he was homebound. Not even a crew of Plastic Society slobs would have been so dumb as to sabotage the *Saturnienne* then. Alexander is puzzled, so is the Consortium, so is everyone else. Excepting you!"

"Of course I am interested," Azadeh retorted, "but not badly enough to fly to Terra to talk to the well-known Sudzo girl. What are *you* holding out?"

"By the time the *Saturnienne* landed on the asteroid for routine servicing that could have been done in flight, the crew got worried."

"About what?"

Flora answered, "They might have figured that a tough skipper would demand an investigation of their actions. Coming back with a Space Admiral and bride Rod could have written his own ticket—have ringleaders shot or disintegrated, or all the guilty ones exiled to some slow death spot. Rather than risk that, the crew blew the cruiser. The asteroid was better than going home."

"Mutiny on the asteroid. A Garvin scenario!"

Flora nodded. "If you had not known that there was likely to be trouble, you'd have looked the way I felt, month after month after month following Floyd's report, *lost in space.* Doc told me that the coordinates, whatever they are, show that the blast came off in the asteroid belt, not somewhere far beyond the solar system. Azadeh Khanoum, you got a lot of Three Dee publicity, acting as interpreter when the Prince, the Khan, was talking to Maritania. You held out a lot.

"Either mutineers blew the cruiser, or Rod did it."

Azadeh smiled quizzically. "You have more than the looks, shape, and charm to sell Sudzo to barbarians. Smart enough to sleep your way to Mars with Doc Brandon, which is two to one against me."

"Let's quit haggling. I'll tell you something, and then you try it for size. Aside from being very congenial company, Doc told me about things such as exploring the asteroids—not hopping from one to the other, not with a couple thousand of the little blobs to account for. There's a simpler approach: Send out a cruiser with nuclear shells. Fire one at a sizable asteroid. One with high density, like the one Rod picked because of density. The observatories are watching for the aiming point, and they record the big flash.

"And if that asteroid has strategic metals or whatever might be valuable, the spectroscopic analysis would pick the facts. The one that Rod found was the very kind they'd be looking for: big for a planetoid, great density to have enough g to hold water and atmosphere. The type with very low visibility. Low albedo. That is the jargon Doc uses. You or I would call it a dark star.

"The data you're holding out: You'd be holding it out only because Rod briefed you. Give the astronomers the orbit of that little paradise. Save it from a prospector's bombing."

"You do make it clear," Azadeh admitted. "And whether they are blue with rosebuds, or pink with forget-me-nots, they are attractive packaging for the persuader that'll convince Alexander the Great that national survival depends on exploration bombing of the solar system's garbage dump!"

"I hadn't thought of *that*."

"I'm sure you have, or I'd never have been so silly as to mention an infallible approach."

"You Martians do not like us, and I don't blame you. Rod made that clear to me. North American cultural invasion would be less messy than exploratory bombing."

"Your people say, *I'd rather be red than dead*. That's what Rod used to tell me. He was not speaking for himself. When I said that we'd rather be dead than North American, he understood what I meant, and he understood how we aborigines of Mars had been taken over, bit by bit."

"That's how North America has been taken over," Flora answered. "Doc made that clear."

"But with his everlasting life which he can't or won't risk, he's joined the *better red than dead* majority?"

"Let's leave Doc Brandon out of this. My answer is, bomb the asteroid, wipe my people out; my people would rather be dead than North American. I'll tell you nothing." She stretched her arms in an embracing gesture. "Flora, you're awfully nice. I like you! But there can't be peace between us. You're a menace, and I hope you quit Mars before your guest-sanctuary right has expired."

Chapter 26

Doc and Flora sat in the cocktail lounge of Maritania Spaceport, waiting out the hour before her solo take-off. They were saying the things which they had been saying ever since taking leave of Azadeh. Honeymoon's end had left Brandon in a mood at once happy for what had been and sad that it was the grave of all but memories.

Flora was not the starry-eyed girl she had been ever since that night the *Space Princess* had put the moon behind her, heading Marsward. She laid a hand on his arm. "I'll not live long enough to quit being sorry about my caper at the observatory. I'm not blaming that girl. I snapped at her offer. My nasty sense of humor got the best of me. I mean, the bet I made with Len Hardwick."

Doc patted the hand that closed on his wrist. "Can't I ever convince you that *that* isn't what's left me feeling old and weary?" Doc sighed, looked into his past. "You've got to feel guilty about something! I wasn't despising that Gook princess, was I?"

"I bet you didn't ask her to put on blue with rosebuds before you could get aroused. Well, I do feel better because I went back. He was nice, even if I had to put on her pink with forget-me-nots."

"Bet you didn't wear them long."

"How innocent can you be! I had to wear them all the while."

"Confession's over. I'm sad because the honeymoon's

over. And I hope I can make you believe that it ended the way it did because Azadeh made it so clear that you were not a widow. I could not carry on with the wife of a man I admire. If he'd been one of those slimy conscientious objectors, it would have been entirely different. Or a God damn draft dodger!"

"You do have a talent for despising! A match for Azadeh."

"Conscientious objectors," Doc retorted, "have a dirty record. Quite a few years before my time, they began to farm the rich lands out west, the middle west, after the Army killed the Indians or herded them to reservations.

"And in the far west, California, Arizona, Nevada, New Mexico, and Texas, the fighting Army took the Mexicans' lands. Conscientious objectors sit on their lard bottoms, enjoying the wealth of all that territory. The phony bastards! As long as someone else does the killing, it's grand to wallow in the loot!"

"Doc." She blinked, gulped. "I never heard the truth put that way, but you're right."

"High time, and someone ought to inform the punks. But I got myself off the track. Our honeymoon had hardly more than started when it became a lot more than fun and games. So I am sad."

"If you think I am happy, you're demented. How long will you stay here?"

"The survey of the Ecological Project is a front. My job is to size up the Simianoid morale. How they feel about military service."

"You're not hiding out because you are on the student blacklist?"

"They forgot me within the hour. But Wilson Epworth will turn them on again. He's an expert. He understands idealists: a creature which is juvenile, regardless of age. And conceited, thinking he is the first specimen of *Homo* so-called *sapiens* to suspect that conditions are short of optimum. And so ignorant as to believe that he has the answer which the centuries have been waiting for."

The talkee-squawkee bawled unintelligibly. Digits changed on bulletin boards. The exhoneymooners clinched, blended tears, and brushed them aside. Flora won the exchange by a fanny-pat. "If you ever really are a widow . . ." Doc said.

He did not understand her half-choked words as they turned from each other. Doc did not quit the spaceport until the thunder of exhaust stacks told him that Flora had moved the first meter earthward. When the blast was no longer audible, he phoned Azadeh.

Two hours later, Doc was following Azadeh toward Gook Town Number One. One of the tough things about a long life, he mused. Like a damned old fool, he'd be coddling another sadness.

Once the airlock closed behind him, Doc felt at home as he drove into the helter-skelter colony, peopled by aborigines cunning in the ways of survival. They had a life style more natural than that of the masquerade society of the Parliamentary Republic. Azadeh's neighbors were puttering around in gardens. Others netted fish from pools. And then he was following her across the patio and into the reception room.

She set out a jug and wine cups. "Since you met the head of the house," Azadeh said, "we'll dispense with his company."

He raised his drink. "Your health, Azadeh Khanoum! You're not as stately remote as you were the other day."

"I'm not dealing with a woman wondering whether she is meeting Number One Concubine or Number Two Wife."

"Flora gave me a rundown on the proceedings and she did her best to be fair."

"I know she was. There were a few differences of opinion."

"I'm surprised there were so few. If there is anything you think I have a right to know, I'll be listening. Meanwhile, she thinks that having that printout will help her persuade Alexander to set the astronomers to work plotting the orbit of the asteroid. From what I get from your story and the newscasts of some years back, there's a good chance."

Azadeh regarded him intently. "What do you call a good chance?"

"Not mentioning names, but someone destroyed a lot of log sheets written while the *Saturnienne* was on the asteroid. Or maybe they were simply held out and not destroyed. The bigger the gaps, the more guesswork in calculating the orbit.

"I might run into mathematical problems I couldn't handle without a full-dress astronomer to program a computer."

"You're not as omniscient as most scientists?"

Doc chuckled. "I've seen too many make monkeys of themselves and then cover with explanations that do not explain, except to the layman, few of whom give a damn.

"What gags Flora is that Rod blew the *Saturnienne* to protect the asteroidians against North American culture, even though that cut him off from one wife, one concubine, and one son." Doc smiled sadly. "The female North American! Almost every one of them would rate Rod a monster for making such a choice, and you even worse, encouraging him when he phoned you his decision."

"You don't agree with her?"

"No. In our culture, a man is a personal property, and devil take his country. But no chance of telling those spoiled wenches that if their country had ever been held by an army of occupation, they'd not feel so indignant when the Army took a son or husband into the service."

"Dr. Brandon—"

"Doc to you, Azadeh. Give me your rebuttal."

Azadeh's smile was a benediction. "You sound like Rod! Doc, you came to tell me something—or have you already said it? Or ask me something?"

"Both. The Republic is rotting with pacifists who declare we will not fight—the best way to invite a war. Over the years, I've heard rumors about prehistoric space cruisers grounded right here on Mars, and in Turkistan, in the great desert. I've wondered whether there are Gooks who could navigate a cruiser."

"You don't sound a bit scientific!"

"Most of my colleagues are convinced that they are the most advanced creatures in the cosmos. That's theory. All I am interested in is fact.

"It's this way: A homemade take-over usually comes to a badly disorganized nation which has a native clique looking for total power. The clique invites Marxist army to sustain a coup. All that is destroyed is the nation's sovereignty, and it's valueless when it's disorganized. War destroys too much of the prize. Take-over yields far more loot.

"Once Mars is sufficiently neglected and out of touch, Gooks, friendly astronauts, astronomers, technicians could take off for that asteroid, if there are space cruisers— prehistoric ones—that can be operated."

"But how could you work a thing that's been sitting a hundred thousand years, or longer?"

"The kind of engines invented a bit more than two centuries ago couldn't. But nuclear propulsion probably could. It'd be nice for you and Rod."

After a speculative eyeing, Azadeh countered, "And for you, too?"

"If there is a take-over, some of us would want escape from Marxism. If there was all-out nuclear war to a finish, the surviving handful, here and there, would want to escape to Mars, to your asteroid, or to other asteroids. A shuttle from Mars to Terra, when the shooting is over.

"And when the Earth cools off, we could return and start over."

"Doc"—she got to her feet—"interesting talk, good as far as it goes."

"Azadeh Khanoum, how much further do you want to go?"

"Let's take a drive in my car."

They set out across open country, following a rutted dirt track which snaked among boulders and rock outcrop. After somewhat more than ten kilometers, the trail descended into a large sandy bowl hemmed in by jagged hills ruddy in the slanting rays of a low sun. Iron-purple shadows lurked in the sterile crags and reached across the bowl. They were mirrored by the curved gleaming metal of a long shell which extended horizontally, supported on many struts: short, massive pedestals.

"She's got as many legs as a centipede!" Doc said, as Azadeh pulled up at the foot of an incline of rammed earth. Following her example, he put on his helmet and oxygen tank. "And looks brand-new."

Azadeh led the way upgrade to a sealed door, beyond

which was an airlock. The interior was lighted by glow-tubes. After glancing at an instrument panel, Azadeh took off her helmet.

"Much of this is ancient," she said. "Some of the furnishings are made of salvage from spaceways shops, some from the stores of Maritania. What we can't buy or steal, we make."

"And what you can't make, you buy or steal?"

"Of course." She gestured, and he half turned to the shrine set well back in what had been the officers salon. "The Lady of Star Faring."

Doc stood beside Azadeh and, with her, bowed three times to the goddess. She wore a tall miter. She sat, erect, stately, her hands clasped and holding a scepter. Her face reminded him of images of Tien Hou, the Queen of Heaven, she who was the patron of seafarers, fishermen, acrobats, dancers, actors, whores, and all others who led dangerous lives.

"When Rod saw her, he told me of Tien Hou. She might be goddess of spacefarers again."

And then Doc made a tour of the cruiser which had for many a century served as a temple.

Finally, Azadeh said, in amiable mockery, "Aside from being frightfully old-fashioned, she's not bad?"

"Quit ribbing me! I snitched a few samples of lathe shavings in the machine shop and a chunk of ore from the bunker. We have not yet caught up with what's been sitting here for however long it's been. Whatever the alloy, it's tarnish-proof, at least in the Martian atmosphere."

"Doc, you've given me something to think about."

"You're another, which makes us even!"

Chapter 27

Doc's survey of the Simianoid colonies of Mars was intensely interesting, and one of the most gratifying experiences of his career: Like the Nameless Island folk, they were people who made sense. "Simianoids," he would sum up, after a day's tour of a dome devoted to animal husbandry or agriculture, horticulture or scriculture, "don't worry about rights other than their own. The Three Dee programs from Terra, newscasts on riots and demonstrations, strike them as hilariously slapstick."

The only sad feature was the Sudzo commercial: Whether in a cozy Simianoid household of four husbands and their sparkling wife—who was not a bit interested in a career, or in a recreation center—there was always a reminder of Flora and that Martian honeymoon: her voice, her laundry routine, and when there was no Sudzo program, there were Simianoid clotheslines, with colorful floral triangles.

And, despite the many variants of the six basic types, the permutations and combinations of four husbands and one wife, there were reminders of Mona. No one duplicated her, but her type was widely distributed.

Doc was glad when he got the radiogram from Alexander Heflin: *"Come back we need you Stop New phone number Stop Scramble only Stop Call Megapolis Alpha Stop Will relay End."*

The message spelled trouble.

The *Excelsior* made a fast hop to a spaceport on the Gulf of Mexico. Doc bypassed New Orleans: Without Mona and a second honeymoon, his favorite city would be flat as beer on a platter.

As of old, the local helicopter brought him to the Island, and Isaiah picked him up at the Nameless landing field. Before Doc got himself and luggage into the estate wagon, he knew that something was wrong at home as well as in Megapolis Alpha. Instead of comfortable silences broken by occasional comment on the teak forest, the farm, the fishing, or the menagerie, Isaiah kept up a steady flow of words as though rendering an account of the entire establishment. When they reached the guest house, Isaiah pulled into its driveway instead of going on some forty meters to let Doc off at headquarters and proprietors' residence.

Of several guesses, the most likely was that Oswald had moved in with Mona and that Doc had been tactless in failing to radio in time. Sleeping with Mona would be entirely *de rigueur*, but moving in was a gross breach of etiquette.

Doc followed Isaiah into the billiard room.

Isaiah brought him the absinthe drip which had been in the freezer, but not yet assembled. When he set the drink at hand, the first cubic milimeter of the ninety-cubic centimeters of green goddess was flirting with finely cracked ice.

"Isaiah, there is something about this that makes it the emotional and aesthetic equivalent of the Japanese tea ceremony—somewhat simplified, of course. It's been a long time, and it'll take awhile for me to tell you about Mars and escape from Mars. Why don't you mix yourself a drink and sit down. We have a lot to talk about."

Isaiah returned with a second drip, like the first, waiting to be assembled.

"Welcome home, Dr. Brandon."

"It is good to be back, Dr. Winthrop."

At last Doc tasted the drink. "You made this yourself."

"Whenever I let one of the staff mix one, you know it at once."

Another sip, and then, "You add something not mentioned in the book. Some day I'll guess. Meanwhile, I've been smelling trouble ever since you picked me up."

Isaiah dipped into his white jacket, took out an envelope which he handed to Doc. "When something speaks for itself, there is no need to speak for it."

Isaiah bowed slightly, picked up his drink, and turned well away, to go to a corner of the room. It was as though he had entered another dimension. In a sense, he had. Doc sat there, alone and desolate.

The envelope smelled of Mona, as did everything long stored in her suite of rooms. She had not sealed it. Naturally not. The master of the Island read:

Doc, Darling,
That son of a bitch sold you out. He started the trouble you shot your way out of. I mean, really, about the infants that went to the League of Adoptive Parents. Oswald furnished information to the Board of Visitors. Wilson Epworth is still trying to get an indictment or get a grand jury to work. If you go to Megapolis, go undercover.

How I found out is too long for writing down. Oswald got silly in love with me and forgot that fun is fun, so he figured that if he got you locked up, he would have me for keeps.

He is not as dumb as I thought he was. Maybe he got wary when I developed a passion for him and me to go fishing off Jambo Island with nasty currents and sharks. Maybe suspected if I didn't kill him, accidentally-like, Amina would and no taking pains to fake an accident.

While I am looking for him, I'll be getting acquainted with that outside world you thought I ought to know. Before he got suspicious of me, he told me about friends of his I simply had to meet when we got to the big city. He left in a hurry, and forgot to take his résumé and application and references and stuff from the file, so I took them.
Lots of love,
Mona

P.S. If you're leaving because of trouble, or if you're going to stay, don't forget Amina. She's nice and she likes you.

Doc drained his glass. "Isaiah?" When the steward returned to the three-dimensional world, Doc continued, "Mind mixing me another? I'll be phoning Alexander Heflin. You get word to U Po Mya and his number-one man. Ask them to invite their friends to come to dinner at the guest house. Might as well tell him to bring along some of the village cooks. That way, you can eat with us.

"I'm likely to be leaving early in the morning and I don't know when I'll be back."

Doc phoned Alexander Heflin. He sketched the Nameless Island situation. "I can't guess how much trouble Oswald Fenton and Wilson Epworth are stirring up," Heflin answered. "Take your time getting here, and don't get picked up. The Forty-Seventh Marxist Slivovitz Division is now on the Gulf Coast, by invitation of Parliament. For the war games we talked about. It looks like a *coup d'état* without firing a shot.

"On the way up here, see if you can dream up some trick for preventing a negotiated surrender disguised as an 'alliance.' "

"Where on the Gulf Coast are our guests?"

"Cherokee Parish, Louisiana. Bayou country. Mosquitos, water moccasins. All the narcotics smugglers, the big-time pimping and alien smuggling outfits are moving out. War games with live ammunition make it dangerous."

Doc chuckled. "Hell, Alec, they're bailing out because they don't like the kind of guests we've invited."

Billiard room, card room, library, and *lanai* offered space enough for all the villagers. Doc and Isaiah sat in the dining room with U Po Mya and Maung Gauk, who had showed up in formal dress, which included, respectively, a .600 Jeffries and a 5.56-millimeter assault rifle. There was Sang Chung Li, the accountant, who wore Italian silk jacket and trousers. Two Malays, each with a *barong* hilt peeping from his sash. The elephant driver, called Habeeb for short, sat alone at a table a meter distant from the host's table: Although his caste scruples did not prevent him from serving food to the sort of people Doc invited, he could not eat with such outcasts. Nor would he touch Burmese food. He ate what his wife had prepared. She was at home, where she belonged.

Amina was not at home. She was where she had decided to belong: standing behind Doc's chair, to serve his food, which she had with her own hands prepared. Amina contrived to be present without the social horror of having a woman sitting with men when the meal was a formal occasion.

Broiled meat dipped into the most peppery of sauces. Tiny fish, fermented with herbs for many a day under a blazing sun. Larger fish, fresh caught and not reeking to the shuddering stars. Much rice. And many not readily identifiables, and bits which Doc recognized as duck and as chicken.

When the Burmese cheroots were served, Doc, who loathed smoking, accepted one. When Doc broke out New Hoyo de Monterrey cigars, pallid things which the guests found uninteresting, each guest accepted and fired up.

Doc said to the group, "In teak forestry, follow old custom. In everything else, Dr. Winthrop will rule until I come back. If I do not come back, you all, and your families, inherit this Island.

"As long as there is income, you will live according to what the Elders decide. When comes the day of working all day to earn taxes that Government gouges, you can go to your native countries where the Government is equally a looter and a spoiler.

"This Island offers food and what we need to make clothes."

Each filed past, paying his respects. When only Isaiah remained, Doc said, "I have a good many things to tell you. Let us sit in the billiard room. You have a power of attorney to act for me, in all Island business. Once I'm on my way, you might find out where you could get one hundred fifty-one proof rum, perhaps forty or more barrels of it . . . and before I forget, didn't you tell me that you had a lot of military experience, quite a few years ago?"

"I did."

"Mmmm . . . that may come in handy. A lot of us are

going to need military experience, whether we like the idea or not."

"I am to be going with you?"

"Not at all. As far as I know, you'll be busy taking care of the Island. Now we'd better discuss communication. I am going northwesterly, and incognito. I'll be driving, and I'll keep in touch with you by radio.

"We have time enough, but none to waste. Is the Island's utility truck, the panel delivery job, in good shape?"

"Reliable, but battered looking."

"All the better! Let's get the microwave fitted."

Isaiah said, "I can attend to that, no problem at all. I'll see if U Po Mya can rig a raft so we can tow the panel delivery to the mainland, and meanwhile, you can be digging into papers, records, and whatever you'll need."

"Just right!"

Doc got up to go to headquarters, but Isaiah detained him.

"I think that Amina will be standing by to help you pack."

Chapter 28

Amina's tawny complexion, Asiatic eyes and facial structure disguised Doc by association; and the panel truck did its bit. A wealthy scientist who owned an island which should have been given to the poor would not be driving a noisy crate which reeked of synthetic fuel. The grimy vehicle was emblazoned EAGAN WILL FIX IT. Though Doc had made no attempt at gypsy coloring, Amina was a reasonable facsimile, with her striped skirt, scarlet blouse, and green scarf drawn snugly about her lustrous black hair. Finally, the fugitives were following rural roads, far from airports and freeways.

The self-styled Eagan was a tinker. He could fix anything mechanical, electrical, or electronic, and he spot-welded farm or kitchen equipment. Things of metal were treasured from the days before plastic was the king and the accursed. He also filed saws and sharpened cutting implements.

In the clutter of travel gear and tools, Doc had what appeared to be a citizen's band radio. It had started out as such, but its inner workings had been modified for microwave transmission.

By shifting the workbench and doing things with lockers, the junkyard on wheels handily converted into kitchenette and bedroom.

Except for grocery shopping, they avoided villages and parked of a night in wooded areas. There, while Amina cooked rice and broiled the *satay* of meat, onions, peppers, and whatever else was available, Doc was calling Nameless Island.

One night when she was done pinching bits of meat into a blistering-spicy sauce, Doc said, "Bet you don't know what you are this time."

"Every evening, you are so flattering. Yesterday, it was good cook, other time, most elegant when swimming by moonlight. Now what is it I am so good for?"

"Isaiah says you are a fugitive from the law. So am I." Amina frowned. "What law?"

He explained that the snoopers noted the day after his departure had proved to be marshals of the Republic, looking for Doc Brandon and one female companion, known as Amina: hair, black; eyes, brown; height, one meter fifty-five centimeters; weight, fifty kilograms; ace of clubs birthmark on left hip.

"The specs," he concluded, "are quite accurate."

Born in Johore Bahru, Amina had grown up linguistically in Surabaja, Banjarmassin, and Sarawak, with a finishing course in Luzon, where she learned English at a mission school and picked up Spanish and Tagalog, all of which blended to make a complex of pejoratives and obscenities spiced with Chinese, Urdu, and Gujarati.

"That *chingado!* That *bugao! Puta-ng-na-mo!* Nobody but Oswald could say all that, and with the birthmark too. That *cabrón!* I'll kill him!"

When she paused for breath, Doc had a chance to say, "I don't have a degree in cosmetology, but I can take care of that birthmark, though it *is* attractively placed. Do you *have* to kill that *bugao?*"

"As a matter of honor, of course."

"That," he conceded, "does make it necessary. But couldn't you postpone it? Those pig-loving police don't know what honor means. They know that you're traveling with me, and they'd claim I told you to do it. And if they put me in the pokey for killing that *borrego*, I couldn't do the work that Alexander—Alejandro, you know—wants me to do."

"Lord Doc." Amina drew a deep breath. "You are taking me to the big city. You are always so nice to me. I'll wait until it does not embarrass you."

"You are a sweet girl. This would be a miserable lonely trip without you. Thank you."

Recalling Mona's farewell letter, Doc decided that her information as to Oswald's associates would make it easier for her to hunt him down than for proud and impulsive Amina. Taking into account his generation and background, Oswald was far from a bad specimen.

"Ought to have his damned arse kicked till his nose bleeds," Doc silently summed it up. *"But capital punishment, that's a bit too much. Well, for a first offense."*

Alexander Heflin's administrative center was about two hundred kilometers southwest of Megapolis Alpha, skillfully lost in a wooded area which had security traps every sixty or seventy meters, random spaced. Before Doc came to the masonry and rustic building which looked like a hunting lodge, he said to Amina, "I bet this dirt road is mined to blow an XM-5 tank to bits too small to make spare parts for a watch."

"This," Amina said, "is far from the big city."

Waiting for each go-ahead signal apparently had been a preliminary screening. Doc was interested but not surprised when the ground-level door of the lodge slid aside and two armed guards beckoned him to drive into a parking garage large enough for vehicles the size of truck and trailer. A third, apparently not armed, stepped up.

"I'll drive your rig to guest parking." He pointed. "You take the elevator, get off at fourth level. I'll meet you there and show you to your quarters."

Taking their hand luggage, Doc and Amina stepped to the elevator. They had only a short wait until the guard came from the parking area and showed them to their quarters.

"Compact, but everything you'll need. Bar supplies in the kitchenette. Mr. Heflin is expecting you, but you'll have time to rest and freshen up." The aide indicated a panel with half a dozen push buttons and transmitter-speaker. "This connects you with inside circuits. Nothing outbound."

Two hours after Doc and Amina had made acquaintance with the comforts they had been missing during their leisurely flight, Doc was sitting with the Chairman of the Consortium. Alexander's conference room had none of the amusing automation which made his Megapolitan office as entertaining as a carnival.

Alexander poured Islay malt and slid a bottle of spring water toward Doc, who picked up his drink and said, "Here's to crime! I'm sure you know you're harboring a fugitive from justice?"

"Welcome aboard." He raised his glass. "I'd begun to worry. Figured you might have been unlawfully detained along the way."

"Avoiding the lawful and the unlawful made the trip slow. No speeding tickets, no traffic hassles. We went through ox-cart country, where my Malay girl would be mistaken for a gypsy. Isaiah, my steward, briefed me every day by radio. That's how we knew we were fugitives from justice."

Doc opened his briefcase and dug out some papers.

"Here's the history of my absconded assistant, Oswald Fenton. Security could check on his references and his résumé. You could locate him easily."

Alexander shrugged. "A bit too late to do any good."

"I think not. In the first place, his frigging around trying to get me locked up delayed my arrival here. He's wary of Mona—bailed out in a hurry suspecting that she was on the war path. So he'll try to keep me in trouble. And ever since you told me that there is a Marxist guest division on the Gulf Coast, I've been thinking that if you got a Simianoid outfit to maneuver with the Marxists, I could be helpful."

"How?"

"If General Kerwin—I understand he's in charge of the war games—had a staff officer who knows Simianoids, he'd get amazing results. Otherwise, the visitors are going to be invited to Megapolis Alpha for a friendship parade or review. Some such caper, but regardless of the detail, it'll turn into a take over. Just as you said when I phoned you, a *coup d'état* is around the corner, but I have figured out a surefire trick to handle it."

"What's the play?"

Doc shook his head. "It is not a detail. It is a principle, knowing Simianoids. I invented them. I understand their wiring diagram."

"That's exactly why I want to hear your idea."

"God damn it, no! It depends on my being on the scene, getting the feel of the situation. No matter what I tell you now, it doesn't mean a thing. Before General Kerwin will get in line, he is bound to want details."

"That's exactly why I want details! Now."

"Shit plus two equals seven! Use the psychologists, the sociologists, their patter. The Army has got used to submitting to all that crap, they have automatic responses, complying and in a way as harmless as they can make it. I'd be a liaison officer, to promote goodwill between the Simianoid and the Slivovitz Marxists."

Alexander brightened perceptibly. "I begin to catch on."

"If you shovel on the social-psychological manure heavily enough, any Parliamentary Committee will gulp it without choking on hooks or sinker. You don't know what I have in mind, so you can't make any slips. Get one of your staff to compose bona fide peace-to-all-living-things, one-world, international amity muck, and get me the job. Liaison officer. Once I size things up, I'll deal with whoever the general is when I get there.

"Contrary to mob opinion, notions circulated by dopes who know nothing about the subject, generals are highly individualistic. They are not a standardized product, like bureaucrats or intellectuals.

"But from here on, it is your business. Get in touch with someone on the Armed Forces Committee, talk social programs crap. We've only just begun drafting Simianoids. Their military history is nil. And we do not want any clashes between our troops and the visitors. Okay, now you know why I don't want to be harassed by this adoptive-parent business."

"Sounds good! I'll get it going."

"Before I forget it, I ought to be a brigadier general."

Heflin sat back and blinked. "For Christ's sweet sake, a *general*?"

"They have a three-star general who never did squads right. He's the head of all the chaplains. And they have another one who heads the medical corps. Why the hell shouldn't the inventor of all the Simianoids for six generations rate one star?

"I rate three stars, really, but that's all that Kerwin has, and that'd not be tactful. Fact, two stars, he'd still rank me, but not enough. So I settle for B.G. No God damn colonels talking out of turn to me."

Doc hitched forward in his chair, tossed off the remainder of his drink. He hunched over the table and said, "Furthermore, as a general, I rate an aide-de-camp. Usually, a B.G. settles for a lieutenant. My aide-de-camp has to be a captain at least."

"Be nicer if I got you Julius Caesar or Genghis Khan, wouldn't it?"

"My steward, Isaiah Jackson Winthrop, Litt.D., is a scholar, and he is not going to be any white-haired lieutenant. Is that clear?

"Since there's no argument left, you might tell me, is this underground a bombproof?"

"It does reach six levels down, but it hasn't been bombed and so I don't know if the contractor skimped on material."

"Before I forget some more—" Doc dug into the briefcase. "Here's the report on Simianoid morale. Better induct a division of them and bring them from Mars, in case the conscientious objectors mutiny or the pacifists revolt."

Alexander nodded. "They'd kill anyone but a foreign enemy. And by the way—I'll have Security check up on Oswald Fenton. If they tangle with Mona, they'll invite her to have a talk with me, be persuaded to abandon her plan for liquidating Oswald. It might kick back and involve you.

"That reminds me! My girl, Amina: I noticed a Malay *creese* in the panel truck. She has a grudge against Oswald. He hurt her feelings."

"Another nice girl you don't want to get into trouble?"

Chapter 29

Doc Brandon's favorite enemy, Wilson Epworth, had digested the report of the Parliamentary Marshals who had failed to catch Doc and Amina, and now Epworth and his close associate, Harry Offendorf, Member of Parliament, were listening to the tape recording made at Nameless Island with the knowledge of the steward. Each auditor had read the typed report. The playback of the tape dramatized the fiasco and raised their fury to a new high.

" . . . *Naw-suh, white folks, Ah jest don't rightly know wheah Doctah B'andon done went. He don't nevah tell me nothing, 'cepting what he want done—*"

"Maybe you heard things? His secretary, Miss Dabney, she was giving you orders and asking you questions for a couple of months before she left. I mean, ever since Dr. Brandon went to Megapolis Alpha and then went to Mars."

"*Yassuh, Miz Mona she sure done give me orders, plenty to do, she kick about de housekeeping like Doctah B'andon never thought of.*"

"That is what I mean, Isaiah." (The words were persuasively spoken, and what followed had a flattering intonation.) "The Government has an important assignment for Dr. Brandon. He'd be gone a long time, and how long did you say you've been steward?"

"*Twenty-two years, boss, and six–seven months.*"

"Then you'd know a lot more than Dr. Fenton. That's the Administrative Assistant's name? Oswald Fenton."

"Yas-suh, that is the name. He sure a brilliant young white gentleman. I do everything, but I don't know nothing. Doctah Fenton, he don't do nothing, but he know everything."

They questioned U Po Mya. They quickly agreed that Isaiah had been right in warning them before they set out for the Burmese village that "They is high yellows that is too dumb to speak English."

Despite its length, the totality of the tape was *"Boss, if'n y'all wants someone to run the plantation till Doctah B'andon come back, you needs a white gentleman. Ah jest don't know nothing."*

One bit, whenever played back, came out clear and crisp:

"No, suh, he don't leave here all alone, he done left wit a tall long-legged white lady wit red hair. No, suh, I ain't never seen her befo', ain't never seen her since, I jest don't know. I took 'em to de mainland in de launch and I got a rental cah and druv 'm to de aihpot wheah de helicopter takes 'em to de plane."

This repeat performance was for the benefit of Oswald Fenton, who was renewing old acquaintance with Epworth and Offendorf. He heard it out before he flared up.

"That black son of a bitch has been shitting you all the way to your eyebrows! Doc left with a Malay girl."

"Interesting, Oswald, very interesting." The automatic stop had cut the recorder. "You left, and when we followed up on your report, we learned that Mona had quit the Island, and so we got this delightful Old Plantation Darky dialogue of two centuries ago."

"That old devil speaks better English than any of us. The dopes you sent to check up fell for vaudeville dialect that was out of date so that you learn it only in Afro-English courses, where I bet he learned it, to get his degree—Doctor of Literature, in case those asshole Parliamentary Marshals would like to learn it!"

"That is exactly what we are getting at, Oswald," Epworth said patiently. "Perhaps you can cast light on the matter? This Malay girl—what do you know about her?"

"Doc was sleeping with her whenever Mona wasn't in a demanding mood. Doc is a sort of satyr, you know."

"That is quite probable, but how'd you learn of the elopement?"

"I'd forgot something relating to the pictures I took for you and the League of Adoptive Parents. I phoned the Island. Isaiah told me that he deeply regretted to state that Miss Amina had departed. He did not say *she done left*.

"What he told others is beyond me, but when one of your team asked me about Amina, I was good and fed up. I told them she was a little brown sister from Singapore, and recited from memory of her office record a description which seems not to have been helpful.

"If you'd not sent such a pack of dummies, you might have learned something."

Epworth's eyes narrowed. "Your description of Amina is more detailed than an employment application or group insurance or anything else of the sort would be. How did you ever learn about the mole on her left hip?"

Oswald straightened up. He wagged his head, chuckled. "I am a Girl Watcher. With twelve-power binoculars one does nicely. In case you master anthropologists do not know it, the Malay is as fussily clean as any Japanese. Female Malays change garments, once or twice a day, while bathing in a stream or a pool.

"There is a pool near the Burmese village. A change of garments has never offered a look at an intimate area. Nevertheless an experienced Girl Watcher can get a bare hip in profile, for a split second, if he is sufficiently far away. So she is unaware of being watched."

"Oswald," the member of Parliament said, "if you never had a Malay girl, you have missed one of life's major experiences. Meanwhile, I know you've never offended one."

"Quite right, but how would you know?"

"If you had, she'd have sliced you so quickly that half of you would be smiling at the other half."

Oswald gulped, blinked, and looked disturbed.

Epworth picked up the ball. "Now that we know Brandon and a green-skinned girl from Venus eloped in an ox cart heading for Arizona, I shall risk outguessing a Black gentleman who has a better knowledge of human nature than most of those now present. Brandon may be almost anywhere, but he is probably conferring with Alexander Heflin. About the Martian situation. We know he made for Mars, and we know he came back. He boarded the *Excelsior*. She docked in the Houston area. It's almost certain he'd stop for a look at his Island. Where would he hide out except with Heflin?"

"Nothing to do but nuke Heflin's headquarters, sift Brandon from the crater, and ask him about everlasting life?" Oswald quipped.

"My dear sir," Harry Offendorf, M.P., retorted, "the Marxist Forty-Seventh Slivovitz Division is on the Gulf Coast for war games with one of our Simianoid Divisions. An international goodwill gesture.

"And it'll give the Simianoids the feeling that they are wanted and necessary. There'd be no resistance to the draft, and many of them would enlist. And the way Simianoid police performed during the student riot which contributed to Brandon's being sent to Mars makes it clear they are not conscientious objectors. Demonstrations still occur, but they're very sedate ever since the thirty-seven who were killed proved to be foreign agents."

"Sure, it's a good idea," Fenton retorted. "But what has that to do with getting Brandon into the open?"

"I was getting to that," Offendorf answered. "Brandon knows Simianoids and their psychology. General Kerwin needs him as a liaison officer, specializing on promoting fraternity with guest division, and advising the General on how to make the optimum showing with his war games.

"It's no secret that our regular troops are a sorry mess— except for the Marines and the Navy. If we can get a Simianoid component, gradually get an all-Simianoid armed force—"

"But what the hell's that got to do with Brandon and our project?"

"Snatch him and sequester him and have a calm talk with him. Keep him from his Simianoid protégés. The thought that they might not prove as superlative as he wants them to be would get him talking, anything to be released so he can get back to the war games.

"Stake out all the likely spots he'd be hiding in and keep an eye on his secretary, if we can find her. He might be shacking up with her. And grabbing him from the war games would not be a tough job."

Chapter 30

That the airport nearest Alexander Heflin's bomb-proof was forty kilometers from the fringe of the wooded area which concealed headquarters had an obvious explanation: The ground was sterile, spattered with massive granite outcroppings. Not being worth the cost of divesting it of rock, it had not been cleared. Beyond the waste, arable land reached out to Irvington, a rural community which had an airport.

There had been a show of logging at the fringe of the wooded country. Sufficient rock had been blasted out to make a rugged roadway along which occasional trucks brought timber to Irvington's new sawmill. It made sense to Doc that by night, two thirds of each load was hauled back to the forest fringe. Although the mill made much noise, it had little output. However, this fooled satellite observation, offering a logical explanation of the road from Irvington.

The government sedan which carried Doc Brandon and two Security men moved by night: first, because Doc and his companions were to get a plane leaving Irvington somewhat past midnight, and second, because it was undesirable to have other than freighting hauls recorded by alien observers.

Everything made sense, most of all the security agents to make sure that judicial maneuverings did not interfere with Doc's reporting to General Kerwin, in Cherokee Parish, Louisiana. With Amina temporarily pacified and enjoying, at least for a while, the novelty of subterranean living, Doc could relax: Security would trace Mona and perhaps have her waiting at the bombproof when he returned from the war games.

Once the car had put the forest behind it, the driver switched on the parking lights. When the vehicle crossed the east–west freeway, the headlights went on. There was little talk, and that the few exchanges were dull and impersonal made it all the better. Doc was debating whether, in the event of his staying with the Army until the crisis was settled, Isaiah would want to go with him. In such case, it would be a good idea for the steward to travel with him to Nameless Island to destroy all the gene-splicing records.

Doc was thinking in terms of crisis, and more than ever since his talks with Alexander Heflin. With Isaiah as aide-de-camp, Doc was sure that they could prevent the negotiated surrender that was certain to take place if ever a Marxist division marched on its goodwill tour to Megapolis Alpha. There would be no resistance: The one world, one government, one language force of idealists had become ever more powerful.

The idealistic simpletons had not paused to realize that the one language would not be Esperanto or any of its variants: It would be Slivovitz; there would be one government composed of those who spoke that language, and armies of occupation would be distributed, to prevent war or civil disorder. Armies of the sort which the guest division represented.

Why bomb and destroy a rich prize when you can negotiate a surrender by invitation? Marxist instructors had monopolized the colleges for several generations. Skeptics in the student body were exceedingly few, and they were undercover. They had to be.

Doc was comparing alternate solutions when Hansen, the lanky red-haired Scandinavian, sat up straight. "Be good-God damned," he grumbled. "CAUTION, it says, ROAD WORK."

Doc and the other security man, Craig, saw that a dark mass loomed beyond the blinkers which flashed their red warning. Denby, the driver, slacked off on the throttle. "Grader parked crosswise of the road. What the hell!"

To ride the shoulder and pass the obstacle was not possible. Side rails indicated a culvert. A caterpillar could cross the dry watercourse but not a truck or car.

Denby got out to have a look.

Axel Hansen fumbled and found a flashlight.

Craig opened the door on the left, which switched on the dome light.

Each security man wore a holstered nine-millimeter automatic. As Craig swung the door out, Doc noticed a dim glint of blued metal in a shoulder holster.

"Spare gun?"

Craig answered, "For emergencies, you can't ever tell."

"Divvy up while you go sightseeing."

Craig chuckled. "You're right, Doc. Hey, Axel, our job is right here, remember?"

"Seeing where we're going is part of the job."

Hansen went with the driver.

Craig drew the derringer. "You don't miss much."

Doc hefted the weapon. "Heavy little package."

Craig chuckled. "It has to be. Double barrel .41 magnum."

The driver returned. "Nothing but a cat could make it. And we have a traffic jam. Northbound car stranded, other side."

A headlight beam from the far side of the grader verified his words. Trailing after Denby and Hansen a man stepped into the light of Doc's vehicle. He raised his hat, mopped his forehead.

"I figured I'd be waiting all night for someone to turn from the crossroads to Irvington." He was towheaded, boyish looking, pug nosed, and whimsical. "Well, that rental car"—he jerked a thumb to indicate his vehicle—"charges by the mile, so it's not costing me a penny to be stranded." Waggling a raised arm, he said, over his shoulder, "Hell with it, I'll get a snooze." He glanced at his watch. "Road crew will be on the job in six–seven hours. Southbound can U-turn and go north. Northbound can U-turn and go south. Nobody's going anywhere."

With this summary, he squeezed past the roadblock. A moment later his headlights blinked out. Doc's party could barely distinguish the parking lights. After long silence, Hansen muttered, "These God damned optimists!"

Craig's complaint: "Nowhere to go and all night to get there."

Denby, the chauffeur, had an idea. "With this front-wheel drive, I can back right to the rim, U-turning, and head back to headquarters."

Doc said, *"Merde, alors!"* and translated for Hansen.

Three fired up cigarettes. Doc declined offers of smokes. Denby presently said, "Too bad this isn't a rental car."

"What good'd that do us?"

Craig answered, "A rental's a rental. We could take that joker's on the other side, he could take ours, and no problem. Hell, I'm going to have a snooze myself."

"I've missed planes before," Doc said, and made for the car. Denby cut the headlights and turned on the emergency flasher.

Hansen contributed a bit: "What's all the yakking about? We can take his car, it's a rental. He can take ours: It's government property, he couldn't go far, stealing it."

"That happy joker's going nowhere. How about paying him to drive us to the airport and getting himself a room?"

Hansen skirted the grader and hailed the other car's driver.

"Hey, you!"

No answer.

He repeated the hail.

"Happy bastard's asleep."

"Throw some pebbles."

They did so and finally aroused the carefree traveler.

When the bargaining reached forty *pazors*, it was a deal.

"Okay, Doc, you make your plane. Our driver is on his own. We'll get a rental in Irvington in the morning."

Doc was neither annoyed nor out of sorts. This was a novelty: a bitch-up and no bureaucracy to blame.

The driver of the rental car made his U-turn without getting the rear wheels too far down the embankment.

Hansen got in from the right. Doc led, with Craig following from the left. The dome light was not working. The emergency light was neither ticking nor flashing. The driver muttered something about the God damned fuses always blowing. And then Doc caught a peculiar odor.

He came near shouting a warning but checked himself. Narcotic gas. One inhalation and out. The slight leakage became a hissing. His security men choked, coughed, cursed, tried to say something but could not make it. They collapsed, pinning Doc down.

Though he was holding his breath, his thoughts were stuttering and blinking. He heard voices outside the car.

Someone said, "They out yet?"

There was an answer which he could not understand. He was about to lose his fight against sneeze or cough. Though twitchy, puking sick, he got Craig's derringer before an involuntary gulp of gas left him helpless, but not totally out.

Double-barrel derringer and two men to kill.

And on that thought, Doc Brandon blacked out.

Chapter 31

When Doc Brandon's consciousness shifted from confusion to awareness, he was in a room about the size of that allotted to a sergeant in barracks. The chair, the table, and the metal frame bed on which he lay suggested barracks, as did the clothes closet. The bath was a refinement beyond a noncom's life style.

The place was airconditioned. He got to his feet and did not have to feign unsteadiness for the benefit of possible observers. However, he was not as groggy as his muttering and cursing indicated. Doc twisted and fumbled the switch, dimming, brightening, and at last cutting the vapor tube which lighted the room. He wove his way to the bath. Beyond the door, slightly ajar, light guided him.

Doc studied his watch. He had been out about two hours. He dipped into his side pocket. He still had the derringer. Since Hansen and Craig had belt guns, his captors had not bothered to search the man they were protecting. But if they noticed that one of the security men had a small empty holster, they might start thinking.

The weapon was loaded.

Doc made choking sounds and flushed the toilet. He staggered to the wall switch, turned the control to low. He went back and closed the bathroom door to block all but a thread of light, and lurched back to bed. Once flopped to the mattress with much spring creaking, he got his pocket knife into action and made a small slit in the bottom of the mattress, near the edge.

Making a nest for the weapon, he stowed it, working it well into the mattress filling.

Counting his rhythmic abdominal breathing did finally get him into a twitchy half sleep in which he did not know whether he was awake, alone, or asking visitors questions. This went on until at last a sharp knocking at the door made him realize that he had been asleep.

"Don't be so formal! Come in if you've got the combination."

Lock and deadbolt slid clear. A man in gray uniform opened the door. One similarly dressed stepped in with a tray of breakfast. The smell of coffee and of bacon reminded Doc that he was hungry. The long-faced man at the door had a holstered gun. The butler was not armed. Each wore a private security badge.

After setting breakfast on the nightstand, the butler, or perhaps he was only a footman, said, "If you've got a spare suit in your case, we'll take the one you're wearing to the cleaner."

Dead pan, Doc asked, "How much extra will that be?"

The answer was in the same tone: "All service is free."

Doc got to his feet, swayed, steadied himself by grabbing the bedstead. When he no longer swayed, he peeled out of his coat, flipped it to the bed, kicked off his shoes. He got out of his pants without falling on his face, fumbled his belt free, and said, "Don't know if I got a spare."

Tossing the trousers to the bed, he set to work grappling with his tie, and then, "Mind looking to see if my wallet's in my coat?"

The man did so. "Maybe it's in your pants pocket."

Doc brightened. "Hell, I bet it's under the pillow."

It was.

"How about taking my shirt?"

The footman turned valet took a plastic bag from his pocket and stuffed Doc's things into it.

"Cold as a witch's teat," he grumbled, and got a robe from his suitcase. Finally comfortable, he unrolled the *Alpha Gazette* lying on the tray and tackled his meal.

The plastic coffee container and the paper napkins came

from Hank's Diner, 7233 Bridge Boulevard, Lindenville. The worst thing about take-out food was the plastic knife, fork, spoon.

The security guards might be from an armored truck outfit, doing some moonlighting. Or industrial plant patrol men. Having asked no questions, Doc had given his captors no idea of what his thoughts were.

By the time Doc's clothes came back from cleaner and laundry he felt quite at home. Hansen and Craig, he reasoned, had probably been released to tell their stories. The daily paper contained no reference to Doc's disappearance or to his security men.

When his attendants brought Doc's fourth breakfast, the one who always remained at the door said, "Some people want to talk to you."

The footman-valet-butler led. The man with the pistol followed. Doc heard no street sounds. It was as though the building were unoccupied. Airconditioning, artificial light round the clock, no hall windows: Brandon surmised that he was underground. Three colored lines ran down the center of the linoleum-covered hallway. For one who knew the code, they were guides to destination.

Doc still had the derringer. It was compact, hammerless, and no more than seventy-five millimeters long; a nasty package with no front sight to snag.

Doc was not a precision marksman: To him, target practice was an expensive way of perforating paper. At short range, he could fire from the hip, and the slug would land where his eye was looking: that is, at an area where a bullet would be fatal.

In Brandon's arithmetic, a gun was not to intimidate, to threaten, or to warn: It was to kill, and you never drew a gun for any other purpose.

Since Doc did not know the butler's name, he decided that "Giles" gave a touch of class which would otherwise be lacking. Following the red line, Giles quit the green and the blue when they continued, straight ahead. The red line was notably scuffed, the others bright and clean.

Giles halted, knocked at a door, then stood, listening. When he knocked again, a voice answered. Doc followed his guide into a conference room. He was facing a group of five conservatively dressed men who sat at a table. It was crescent shaped, so that the confreres could better address each other. Wilson Epworth was at the extreme left.

"Son of a bitch! If I could only have a playback of that Burmese village charade, with U Po Mya on stage!" was Doc's thought. He said, "Funny thing, Wilson, I was thinking of you. I'm not sure I've ever met your playmates."

The central man of the quintet got up, pushing back his chair. He was tall, broad, ruddy, with a plump face and a fine head of wavy black hair. "I'm Harry Offendorf, Chairman of the Parliamentary Committee on Public Welfare and Education. At my left, Alvin Benson, of California. To his left, Harley Scrimshaw, of Arkansas. At my right, Alan Carson, of California." He chuckled amiably. "And I've heard that you and Wilson Epworth meet frequently."

He gestured to indicate the chair which was at the center of the circle whose arc was the curved table. "Please be seated, Dr. Brandon."

The security man had closed the door. He took his post at Epworth's right, hitched his gunbelt, and relaxed. Giles found a chair in a corner.

The Honorable Harry Offendorf fingered the recorder sitting on the table. "Dr. Brandon, this is not going on the air. I am taping our discussion to avoid the inevitable errors a reporter introduces. I trust that you do not object?"

"Not at all. But one thing I'd like: a lapel mike, or one I could hold in my hand. That way I could sit where I am and answer each of you instead of addressing the built-in mike of the recorder."

They did have an accessory microphone. It was attached.

Doc hitched his chair back a meter, glanced along the cresent of faces.

Having gained one slight advantage, Doc played for a second.

"Outnumbered five to one, I may develop strained vocal cords. In such event, I'll ask for a coffee break. I'm sure Giles wouldn't mind hustling it for the group?"

"Giles?"

"Of course." Doc gestured. "The club steward. Or butler?"

The Chairman chuckled. "I'm glad you are so much at home!"

When the Honorable Mr. Offendorf caught Epworth's eye, the latter said, "Very well, Harry, I'll open the session. Dr. Brandon, this is not related to the Adoptive Parents League. We are interested in longevity, as you no doubt have anticipated.

"We have researched your history, and since it is a matter of record from a previous meeting, we need not repeat now. We did not mention your experiments in genetic engineering, which have been valuable in combating sickle-cell anemia and hepatitis. I doubt that we need reiterate your achievements.

"Your menagerie is evidence of your having used genetic engineering to reproduce creatures extinct for a million years.

"The Simianoids—some might call them Humanoids —they are a tremendous contribution to social and economic advances. Is this an acceptable outline of your career?"

"In pattern, yes. But I must interpolate this—that I served an apprenticeship with my late father. It would be impossible to separate the latter stages of his work from the more mature phases of mine."

"With your interpolation included, the résumé is correct?"

"Yes."

Epworth resumed, "We have convened in private to avoid student riots or other intrusion."

"One detail, if you please!" Doc cut in. "I do not admit that I had a chance to decline or to accept your invitation. I am here only because of surprise, chemical warfare and armed force. Nothing that I say may be construed as prejudicial to my seeking legal remedy, whether in actions criminal, civil, or in equity.

"Do you severally and as a group, so stipulate?"

"So stipulated," the Chairman said, and each individually so affirmed.

"Explicitly, then, what the hell do you want?"

Epworth said, "Harry, you take over. Dr. Brandon and I have enjoyed a running feud."

Harry Offendorf said, "As Chairman of the Parliamentary Committee on Public Welfare and Education, I am—admittedly in an extracurricular sense—acting within the scope of my office. To put it another way: However unofficially, I speak for and I represent the Parliamentary Republic of North America. The Parliament of which I am a member considers it in the national interest for you to reveal your knowledge of prolonging human life far beyond its normal expectancy. I avoid using the term *live everlasting*, not only because of the religious connotation, but because neither you nor we know that your life is or ever will be everlasting. The facts relating to your approximate age of one hundred eighty-six years suffice."

"The Spanish Inquisition had a package of ways to encourage candor when questioned."

"You are too valuable to be harmed. Moreover, we are humanitarians, not religious fanatics. Scientists already know the theories. We need your cooperation. We need the benefit of your vast experience. We ask only that you join us so that we may be with you as benefactors of mankind."

Doc glanced at his watch. "Let's relax, while Giles gets us coffee and doughnuts. Sugar-dusted for me, if you please."

Doc had got them to agree to his request for an accessory microphone. They were now acceding to his request for coffee. He was getting them accustomed to accepting suggestions. However far this was from brainwashing, they were establishing a habit of accepting his trivial notions and acting on them.

"Don't forget the sugar-dusted on the doughnuts, Giles."

Giles muttered something. It made little difference what.

Chapter 32

Giles had done picking up the cups and plates, brushing crumbs and powdered sugar from the table. The Chairman resumed, once Doc took his station, facing the quintet:

"Dr. Brandon, you protest our detaining you from military service you have been appointed to undertake. I refer to your acting as consultant to the Commanding General, International Goodwill War Games, Gulf Coast. Your participating in such maneuvers subjects you to risk of injury, serious injuries. You are far more valuable as a scientist than as a military man."

"That's flattering! The fact is that I am anxious to see that General Kerwin does everything possible for the Simianoids to show up favorably in comparison with a crack division, as the saying goes, of our allies. The outstanding Forty-Seventh Slivovitz is world famous. If our well-trained but inexperienced Simianoids were to fall short, foreign methods might be applied in an attempt to improve them, and I assure you that such would not succeed."

Having no argument other than repetition, the Chairman changed his line of attack. "I won't try to undermine your firm belief in your having unique qualification for ensuring that the Simianoids will derive the utmost benefit from the proposed maneuvers. I appreciate your zeal in their behalf. But you have other advantages at your disposal."

"Such as?"

"Your financial resources are impressive. Nevertheless,

if you cooperate with other scientists, domestic and foreign, you would have at your command not only the unlimited funding of our Government, but also be the spearhead of a worldwide effort."

Doc shook his head. "With world population now exceeding ten billion, lives even as short as mine would soon cause disastrous food and space shortage."

Epworth interposed: "If you accepted the leadership of such a tremendous project, bringing together the outstanding sociologists, psychologists, demographers, anthropologists, and whatever other scientists might become relevant, a dangerous population explosion could be avoided.

"Instead of the present helter-skelter uncontrolled reproduction, acceptable restraints could be imposed, a fair exchange in terms of evolution, individual and racial. The individual could perfect himself, herself, in arts, sciences, or for that matter in the most self-centering of self-improvement, and avoid today's idiotic greedy scramble. Your life and your achievements testify to the validity of my assertion."

Epworth raised his arms, flung back his head, and for a moment, Brandon's enemy became an Old Testament prophet.

"Dr. Brandon, you have watched seven generations come into existence. The talent you have marshaled and the potential you have realized during your more than one hundred eighty-six years indicate the cumulative effect of continuity: carrying on, instead of having lapsed a century ago into comfortable old age and extinction!"

When the upraised arms dropped to the man's thighs, Doc said, "Wilson, you've never, I've never——" His voice faltered. He steadied himself. "I've never heard the arguments presented as impressively. Your conviction and the impact of it—the statement itself is nothing novel, but the *feeling* of it! If I had not lived as long as I have, I'd be sold! Here and now.

"You almost persuade me to concede the doubtful proposition that science and law combined can ever curb the egocentric passion for reproduction. Short of universal ligation, universal vasectomy—supplemented of course by mandatory abortion for those who eluded the regulations—eternal life couldn't work."

Wrath choked Epworth, who with good reason had believed himself to have prevailed. "You're pessimistic, insanely so! You—"

"You are asking for selective or haphazard cannibalism," Doc countered. "Infanticide, and rationing years at the adult level!"

"I repeat, your pessimism is intolerable, insane!"

Doc pounced to his feet. From the corner of an eye, he caught the twinkle of blued metal. The guard's gun was sinking toward its holster.

"Insane!" Brandon echoed. "Welcome to the club! We all are!"

Then all the fire subsided. He felt his age and wondered whether he looked it. He drew a deep breath, and his shoulders slumped. He was mortally weary. Responding to Epworth's vision, even momentarily, had been disastrous. Doc saw the five faces change. He had left his marks as they had theirs.

"Play it all back, digest it!" he said. And then, to the gun guard, "Get off your pratt! You, Giles! Take me back to my cell. Get me the evening paper, my chow, and some doughnuts."

He turned his back to guard and to the Commission. He followed Giles, who was obeying.

Chapter 33

"I'm sending a staff car and a light pickup," Alexander Heflin said to Flora's image on the screen. "Get out of town right away, and take your valuables and wardrobe."

The peremptory tone and stern face left her groping for words. Alexander continued, "Do not mention this to anyone. Do not cancel appointments. Get going and I'll tell you why when I see you. Too much has happened since I told you about golf in Khatmandu."

"Ah—Alex, let me call you back!"

"You can't. Not where I am. Transportation will be at your street entrance. This is no drill!"

He cut the connection.

Flora was perplexed when the black limousine circled Selfridge, a small town more than a hundred kilometers west of Megapolis Alpha, for the third time. But an hour later, when darkness masked its route, the limousine peeled off the freeway, followed a paved road, and then, headlights off, took a wagon track. Despite darkness, she was sure that the car was crawling among tall trees.

She asked no more questions. Something had happened, or was about to happen. And then Flora settled down to remembering her Martian escapade and her plans for Alexander.

"No, this isn't his plan for me," she told herself. *"Something bigger is planning for us. . . ."*

Flora's Martian adventures had shot down in flames all accepted notions. She had not long returned from Maritania when she was nagged by fantasies centering on what she and the astronomer could have done, if they had had a few nights for complete acquaintance.

And suddenly there she was: in a bombproof, half a dozen levels below the surface, with Alexander looking over her shoulder as she put on the after-breakfast makeup. Finishing touches—a dainty dab of lipstick, a hint of pencil, one tiny bit more on the left eyebrow . . . mmmm . . . well, a barely perceptible pat of rouge to add—add what?

"That's it!" he exclaimed. "The way it was yesterday and the morning before. I mean it—Transfiguration! No other word. The mystery of it!"

"This isn't illusion. The miracle is what has happened to us," Flora declared.

He caught her by the shoulders, held her at arm's length. "You're not the only one who left this world for a while." His hands slowly slid to her waist, came to rest at her hips. "Whatever has happened to us, we're up to our eyebrows! The thought of wanting you, fifteen–sixteen years ago. Whatever your wants did to you—"

"The other night," she cut in, "I knew why I'd admired and hated and despised your decency. You could have had me in the first dark corner when we were kids—no, *I* didn't hate you—it was twitchy femaleness with no sense, no judgment, bottomless pit of cravings."

He followed her to the galley dinette. Flora rounded up glasses, gave them a quick rinse and reached for the half bottle of Oloroso. As they slid to the alcove bench, she said, "We're both crazy! But it's wonderful."

Alexander poured, and they drank to truth and discovery.

"We've wanted each other ever since I was twelve, and now I'm nearly twenty-eight. And too busy even to think of baiting you and bargaining until you explored the asteroids. Now that war's about to start, it's too late."

"Alex, it was easy to hate you when Rod told me about the one-way cruise to Saturn, until I realized that since he knew all about it and went to make you and the Consortium feel foolish, nobody could blame you. And when I learned from his Martian girl that he had blown a billion-*pazor* cruiser to keep American culture from ruining a lovely little asteroid, I began hating him for thinking more of her tribesfolk than of me." She laughed happily. "And it didn't take a psychiatrist to make me realize that I'd hated you because you didn't relieve me of tantalizing virginity."

"Flora, since we're confessing, I'll take my turn. Rod was a menace; he blew an election and the enlightened dopes voted for the wrong man!

"I was responsible for sending him on what turned out not to be a one-way trip. Yet I liked him, I admired him, and wished he had been for us instead of against us. Becoming a hero made him a menace to a social order not worth saving.

"I did my duty. He did his. He and I were in the same fix. Imagine a military commander receiving his orders. No matter the personal ties, no matter the friends he has in the outfit that's about to face the overdose of hell that *someone* has to soak up: He cannot change his orders.

"Since we're talking shop, I'll give you an example. We, the Consortium, advised Parliament to move to a bomb-proof spot that was waiting for it. The members balked. They said that the Marxist Federation would consider such a move as evidence of hostility."

"War that near?"

Alexander shrugged. "Consult an astrologer or the *I Ching*. The Consortium did not tell Parliament that the chance of being bombed out was greater every day. We would have been mocked as warmongers playing for bigger defense budgets."

Long silence.

"How long am I to stay here?"

"Until I know that we should be somewhere else."

"You've practically invited me to go with you."

"What you do from now on," he answered, "is up to you. As long our being together does not interfere with my duty, you'll not leave unless you wish to."

"If things are awfully bad, we may end in Khatmandu?"

"Khatmandu, Cuzco, or hell."

"We're in a confessing mood, so I'll make a clean sweep."

"Whatever you're going to say, it'll be because you want to say it."

"I slept my way to Mars with Dr. Brandon."

"Damn few women can say that truthfully."

"Well, Doc never did go to Mars except occasionally."

She told him about her caper with the astronomer, how it began and why. Flora concluded the minisaga by saying, "There was no one else before you phoned. I was reckless this time on Mars. I've begun to wonder whether I could ever be pregnant."

"Confession complete?"

"Awfully good for the soul too."

Chapter 34

Brandon and the Committee became an amicable debating group; a two-way contest in persuasion, except that Doc's approach was indirect and unsuspected. Coffee breaks with sugar-dusted doughnuts started them in their acceptance of reasonable requests. Doc knew what he was doing, and the Committee did not. And then he had Giles and the sour-faced gun guard escorting him for exercise, always within the building.

Whenever he exercised, he noted the ants gleaning minute bits of powdered sugar. Neither Doc's nor any other human eye could perceive the microscopic granules. The busy gleaners however were clearly visible, if anyone cared to look and see.

Until ant traffic became well established, Doc had to mark time. Finally he could make an educated guess as to which of the colored stripes on the linoleum led to the exit not far from Hank's Diner. Doc had learned early in life that there was no use leaving until you knew where you were going and how you would get there.

Meanwhile, there were invariables. Whenever he exercised, Doc had Sour Face and the hand gun behind him, with Giles leading the way. Giles knew the way to Hank's. Sour Face apparently knew little or nothing except quick response when there was cause to go for his gun.

Meanwhile, General Dennis Kerwin, on the Gulf Coast, might begin to wonder when Brigadier General Avery Jarvis Brandon would appear for duty as expert on the care and feeding of Simianoids and as liaison officer between him and the commander of the guest division.

Doc, however, was not unduly worried. His aide-de-camp, Isaiah, knew soldiers, he knew liquor, and he had the gift of instantaneously appraising a situation. When he had reason to play the Stupid Nigger, he ran shoulder to shoulder with the Chinese scholar pretending to be a fool.

When Giles led the way back to the conference room, Doc was careful to avoid trampling the ants. And he always stepped to his appointed spot as though to a leather-upholstered chair reserved for him in one of the better clubs in London.

On this morning, he was notably amiable. "Good morning, gentlemen. Thank you, but I simply could not accept yesterday's suggestion that my ration come from otherwhere than Hank's. So my breakfast came from there again. I like Hank's. He's entitled to a bronze plaque on the door: *Doc Brandon ate here, and none of your business where he slept or with whom.* Where did we leave off yesterday? Never can keep track."

The frowning Chairman responded to Doc's bonhomie. Another amiable session: but Doc was under increasing pressure. He could rely on Isaiah; but he had to see that Security got Mona out of Megapolis Alpha. According to the newspaper, the 47th Slivovitz Division would parade in the capital when the war games were concluded. He hoped that Flora would have sense enough to get well out of town.

"I've been facing you so long that you are beginning to enjoy my company and look forward to each session."

Chuckles of appreciation all around.

"We have enjoyed each other's company." He eyed Dr. Epworth. "Yes, damn it! Wilson, after years of hating your guts, I've come to see you as a comrade in a tough predicament."

Doc was convincing. He meant what he said. However much he remained opposed to his favorite enemy, he had begun to see him as one sincerely, if mistakenly, desiring immortality for all mankind. Doc no longer regretted saving him from the tiger. He was actually glad.

"You and I are polar opposites," Doc continued. "Each

has been the other's . . . no, not opponent, but partner in despair and confusion. We have met as opponents. Each of you would have burned me at the stake if that could have got you my supposed secret process."

Doc snapped to his feet. The gun guard reached for his holster, then relaxed. He was getting used to the prisoner's impulsive but meaningless moves.

"Here we are, you five, under pressure from pitting your will against mine. I have faced your fivefold force. I wonder which is the rider and which is the saddle. Let's quit squirming and pretending. What are you going to do when I cut all this verbiage and tell you I won't deal? How would Gestapo rough stuff make me a worthwhile genetic engineer?"

He eyed each, and each face silently answered.

Then quick-witted Offendorf said, "Injunctions, income tax investigations, every known routine—and we'll invent new ones. The government has a century and a half of supreme court decisions based on the totally unconstitutional but invariably enforced theory that where Government is concerned, the defendant is guilty until he proves himself innocent, which he rarely is able to do."

"Unless he is poor or one of a minority, or both. I'll sweat out those legal tricks and when every man of you is ashes or worm bait, I'll be here with new answers, maybe new courts, and going strong.

"Gentlemen!"—Doc made a two-hand spread, a sharp gesture which he checked before more than half a meter apart. The derringer he had secured in his coat sleeve using a strip torn from a shirttail almost slid into sight.

"Gentlemen," he repeated, "you can screw yourselves! How you likee?"

Sour Face was moving his hand away from the holstered gun he had become accustomed not to need. But Doc quarter-pivoted, perhaps one third of a left turn, and the gambler's fatal "deuce" appeared in his hand.

"Five men, a gun guard, Giles the Butler, and only two shots in this deuce. You don't know which two I'll kill. I know. Two dead men. Take farewell looks at each other."

Doc had reached the level of omniscience: *Know all,*

hear all, see all, past and present and future. But, being human, Doc could not outwit destiny.

Epworth screamed, "Don't, you dizzy bastard!"

The guard's gun was moving into line. Epworth lunged as Doc's derringer spat a .41 caliber magnum. The guard's automatic chewed plaster from the wall, the derringer bullet drilled Epworth. Doc cut loose with his final cartridge. The guard folded, and Doc scooped up his weapon before it hit the deck.

"Only five left. Giles, get over with them."

Giles lined up.

Doc did not warn the Commission against following him. He did not even back out of the room. He walked out, and he wasted no time looking for ants. The blue line led to Hank's.

There he saw a cab pulling up. "Coffee can wait," Doc said. "You have a passenger."

Chapter 35

When Rod Garvin, skipper of the *Asteroidienne*, had the asteroid belt well astern, he said to his First Officer, "Caspar, I don't know whether it was luck or clean living, but the whirling garbage dump hasn't done more than bounce a lot of gravel off her plates."

Tall, stooped Caspar Tweed brushed back his cowlick. "It wasn't all that bad. Taking it at a narrower angle than we took on our way out and going with the garbage instead of cutting squarely through: Sure, we're losing time, but why bust your tail hurrying?"

Bland and grinning Mr. Tweed eyed the skipper, and resumed, "Rod, strictly off the record, and asking a question is not mutiny, what's been giving you the shakes? The general outlook?"

Garvin frowned. "What outlook?"

"Aljai and Azadeh, meeting Mrs. Garvin eventually."

Garvin sighed. "I should have accepted the concubine Aljai thought would be a good idea."

Tweed nodded, tucked a chew of *snuus* substitute under his tongue. Though the base was not tobacco, when it was ground fine and soaked in mulberry brandy, it wasn't bad, especially if you mixed in some pulverized asteroidal spices. "Aljai fitted out with an assistant concubine, and then Azadeh and Mrs. Garvin, there'd be four ladies, and with two teaming up to hate the other two, each group would keep on their dainty toes."

"That's what the Gur Khan told me," Garvin admitted. "But look how it worked out with him!"

"That was a special case," Tweed pointed out.

"Balls and death! Every time women are concerned, all rules automatically screw up. The exceptions and special cases—you cannot win!"

"If women are such a complicating headache, how come you don't spend more time and effort avoiding the wenches?"

"God damn you, Caspar, that quip is pretty nearly mutiny!"

"Well, Lani is redheaded, pregnant, and a special case. How's she standing the cruise?"

"Nothing bothers her. She seems to be one of that rare type that doesn't even look pregnant until a week before she gives birth."

"Good girl. Skipper, count your blessings! Too bad the old Admiral had that heart attack. Rod, why don't you marry Lani? She'd be the fourth of the set."

Garvin shook his head. "As the Admiral's widow, she gets a juicy pension. I wonder if she got the wedding papers off the *Saturnienne*? Hell's fire, I entered it in the log when I married her and him. I can testify, make an affidavit, or some God damn thing, that she married the Admiral and that he died the night of the mutiny."

Tweed frowned. "You think of everything. Hey, wait a *minute!* She hadn't been a widow more than twenty minutes by the clock when she married the Gur Khan. That screws up her pension!"

"For Christ's sake, Caspar! No wonder you never got your skipper's ticket. Under Parliamentary American law, it was polygamous, bigamous, illegal, null, and void, and not a marriage at all. Anyway, the Gur Khan doesn't exist officially, and if he did, he rates like a Gook and nothing counts. Not unless Gooks ever got the status of a minority race, in which case he could get a juicy Parliamentary pension and vote twice in each election. Nuh-uh, I am not marrying Lani. I have done a lot for her, and I am still stuck."

"Skipper, I got to stand my watch."

Garvin made for the companionway to the shop where

Hamlin Daly, the artificer, was fabricating helmets, air tanks, and space jackets for landing on Mars. The *Asteroidienne* had no radio equipment, and despite his knowledge of electronics, Daly could not rig up gear to communicate with modern systems: Materials were not available.

Already the compartment was approaching the appearance of the Terrestrian workshop in which Garvin had discovered the pop-eyed, blocky operator. After a few years of space cruising, Daly turned to computer servicing and making special-purpose ID cards which could not be distinguished from the genuine and legal. Like Garvin and Tweed, Daly was one of the Coolies who had worked for a living instead of putting up with the other-guided Megapolitan citizens who lived on taxpayers bounty.

The accumulation of metal scraps, lathe turnings, bits of sheepskin, insulation, and unclassified rubbish was impressive. Daly was so busy with the milling machine that he neglected the mulberry brandy he had cooked off for the cruise to Mars.

Glancing up from his work, Daly pulled the switch. "Skipper, what are you looking so constipated about?"

"I've got to help Lani get her future whipped into shape. If you hadn't buggered up that black box, the computer wouldn't't've sent the pack of us to Mars instead of Khatmandu where I promised her we'd go."

"For Christ's sweet sake! If you'd gone to Khatmandu, you'd not have met Azadeh, Lani'd not have got the first wedding in space, she'd not have a Space Admiral's widow's pension when she gets back, and she'd not be a princess rating a gold-plated parasol."

"Those landing jackets: How're you getting along?"

Daly spat a jet of tobacco substitute. "That tubing I got out of the supplies compartment cuts clean but it's tough to work. Shaping valves is slow. Lucky I got to work on the air compressor before we took off. This sheepskin leather for jackets is working out and native mica isn't half bad for helmet faceplates."

"Being an artificer must be a tough life. I've got nothing to think about but setting this crate down nice in a flat space. No instruments. And if I set her down on a flat lake bottom, the cushion jets will blast up a cloud of sand and potash that'll leave me blind."

"You're making it a challenge. Let me set her down. Come to think of it, we've got no radio and no chance of improvising anything that'd communicate with current gear, Mars or elsewhere."

"Want to take a trick on the bridge?"

"I've neglected my drinking, and until I catch up, I'm not navigating. Give the Asteroid-Gook trainees a chance."

Garvin moved out and toward his next stop.

Mars loomed ever larger. From space the red disk remained untainted by the slowly extending vegetation and surface water, even when viewed with the binoculars Garvin had rescued from the *Saturnienne.*

He planned to fly low and follow ravines, thus avoiding observation by Terrestrian cruisers or by the astronomical stations. The repulsion jets along the *Asteroidienne's* cylindrically contoured bottom permitted hovering as low as fifty meters; with propulsion power operating, she could advance horizontally: quite maneuverable. To settle lower than fifty–sixty meters was entirely feasible, except that the jets would kick up blinding clouds of dust or their heat would release fumes and smoke from the ground.

Tweed, Daly, Barrett, and Ames, survivors of the *Saturnienne's* crew, were bound Marsward with wives, concubines, and the start of families. Natives of the asteroid had crowded aboard with their families, for fun and to meet their Gook kinsmen of Mars.

To avoid having small fry cluttering the passageways and making a madhouse of the *Asteroidienne*, Garvin had set aside a compartment for them to infest. A proper decision in principle, but it offended Garvin's sense of spacemanship.

He stepped into the chamber of horrors and winced—as usual. The bulkheads were decorated with pink elephants, woolly blue lambs, Chicken Little, and the Bad Wolf before the woodsman got busy with his double-bitted axe. Lani, a prospective mother, had insisted, and so she had with her own hands painted the darlingest stuff.

Before the compartment engulfed him, a woman said, "Wait till you see what's ahead of you in Gook Land."

"Azadeh would never pull a truck like this!" He turned, faced Aljai, regarded her appreciatively: thin, elegant nose, with a suggestion of the aquiline, and longer than what would be right for a Chinese girl. The barely slanted eyes were dark pools of amiable mockery. He couldn't help but chuckle and grin in response. After all, she was wearing her formal makeup. "You're getting better looking year after year."

"You're getting used to me. Since we're on the subject, wait till the honeymoon is over before you call *her* Aljai in absentmindedness."

"I used to call you Azadeh often enough. Too often."

"You still do."

"It'll be sticky, if I call Flora by your name and then correct myself and say *Azadeh*."

"You men are so thickwitted! Call us *darling*. All of us. But there may not be any problem."

"How come?"

"Maybe you've been reported or declared lost, dead, and Flora has married someone else."

And now they were at Lani's suite.

The long-legged redhead wore a sedate gray tunic, silver lamé sandals with green heels. The tunic, Shanghai style, was slit only three-fingers' breadth above the knee. And she wore a dove-gray hood embroidered with silver.

"Except for the dress, you look like old times in Megapolis. Nothing missing but low Sun and see-more skirt."

Lani clapped her hands. "No use asking what you'll have." When her maid stepped in, the redhead said, "The usual."

Garvin's glance shifted to the corner of the sitting room. "Bring your parasol?"

"Of course I did! You might know Alub would never let me give it back."

"Princess, Your Royal Highness, you can't have a title of nobility. It's unconstitutional."

"You're off base! I'm an asteroidal citizen by marriage."

"You've forgotten your native country. Someone's going to call you Mrs. Khan, or maybe, Mrs. *Kahn*."

"Touché! Anyway, why not brief me about Azadeh's people and their protocol?"

"Mmmm . . . you've been wondering whether to have your parasol bearer attend you, and if so, whether to go ahead, alongside, or follow you?"

"Rod, I don't know what I'd do without you. Yes, I was."

Garvin frowned. "You sound as if you intend to stay in Gook Town for more than greeting and welcome."

"Naturally, I do. Mars is international. I want my son born there so he'll be a prince and no constitution to kick about his rating a three-deck parasol."

"Only one-and-a-half decks."

"Rod, you old bastard! You never change."

"How can I? Once a bastard, always a bastard. Dad died years ago, too late to legitimate me—if he felt like it, I mean."

But all this was wasted speculation: Lani's son was born before the *Asteroidienne* was set down in a box canyon not far from the temple where Garvin and Azadeh had decided it'd be better to go home and there discover each other.

And that was when Roderick David Garvin got confirmation of his notion that where woman was concerned, he lost every argument. When Lani entered Gook Town, there were two parasol bearers, one for the Princess, and a second, with three decks, for her son.

Chapter 36

When he heard Doc Brandon's account of his escape, Alexander said, "You're still one jump ahead of the shock-wave. Right now you are reported as having been seen in Memphis, Rochester, and Albuquerque. With two killings, one of them important, chalked up against you, it is time to haul out: That is easier and has far fewer fishhooks than my fighting to keep you in the clear and trying to keep you as General Kerwin's special staff member."

"Mmm . . . military affairs and the Prime Minister sure as hell wouldn't okay me as a brigadier general, though generals are all supposed to be assassins. Any chance of my having no rank at all?"

Alexander shook his head. "God damn it, I have my limits. I don't want to waste my reserve clout. I might need it when the last chip is on the line."

Doc nodded. "Tell you what: While I was wondering whether I'd escape alive, I'd been thinking about Isaiah. Maybe I've never told how I discovered him, ages ago. I was in a Detroit liquor store, in a rather tough area. Here was this Black man sitting out of the flow of customer traffic. He had a 5.45 millimeter carbine, some army's war surplus, with a magazine of twenty cartridges. I was asking him if they had many holdups. He started telling me, and then he said, 'Excuse me, just a second, please.'

"Things had got quiet in the store. Three men with hand guns. One said, 'Quiet, and everybody lie on the floor.

This is a holdup.' His last words. Isaiah stitched each man with four–five slugs. He'd carefully avoided a customer too scared to lie on the floor. Then Isaiah said to me, 'This doesn't happen often. These persons must be strangers in town.'

"When cops and meat wagon got through, I offered Isaiah a job at Nameless Island. He was a Doctor of English Literature and working on another Ph.D., but he dumped that when I made him an offer.

"If you can get Isaiah on the phone, wherever he is, I'll tell him a thing or two. Did he get his captain's commission?"

"He did." Alexander punched a few buttons, spoke a few words, and continued, "When they find him, you can tell him anything you want: last-minute thoughts or whatever."

And then Doc remembered. He dipped the .41 derringer from his pocket. "Give this to Craig, the security man. And thanks. I don't blame him or Hansen." Doc grimaced ruefully. "Life is weird. I killed a tiger by hand to save Epworth's life, when I hated his God damned guts. But he and I finally came to realize we were polar opposites, partners in a very tough, very grim game, and we quit hating each other. No, he didn't lay down his life to save *me*—it was just idiot impulse. He was afraid I'd be killed and a great secret would be lost. Poor bastard fooled himself; I don't have the secret."

They settled down to outline Doc's leaving the country before the Parliamentary Commission had done explaining Brandon's and their own presence in the basement of an untennanted meat-packing plant.

"They're likely," Doc suggested, "to deny that I was there and have the media claim that a gun was accidentally discharged by someone who was cleaning it and didn't know it was loaded."

"That'll come later. Someone panicked and a scrambled version got on the air," Alexander conceded.

Doc chuckled. "Like that report of the nova, but not scrubbed as quickly."

"Government could never carry on without God damned liars. Particularly in our type. An autocrat does not have to explain his or its boners. Our people demand answers, even though they could rarely understand one, not even when it's true.

"But speaking of nova and reports—that reminds me! You're concerned about getting Mona out of Alpha before it's taken over by the Forty-Seventh Slivovitz Marxist troops. In case you've been wondering about your assistant—your secretary, I think she was—on that Martian survey . . ." Alexander hunched forward, regarded Doc intently, shook his head. "Don't ask me 'what secretary?' As a gentleman, you are required to be a God damned liar. She did not sleep her way to Mars with me, and I do not have to be a gentleman.

"Flora Elaine Garvin was browbeaten and hypnotized out of Megapolis Alpha and into protective custody. I am not saying where she is. It is most unlikely that you would meet her, but if the almost impossible did happen, you will not, repeat, not give her the facts that you and I have."

"Understood," Doc agreed, "that my nonexistent secretary with whom I did not, with whom I am not, and with whom I shall or will not sleep whether en route to Mars or Khatmandu, is not to get even the faintest hint as to the stinking situation in the capital and otherwhere in this great nation."

"And furthermore, I am going to tell Flora Elaine that your first question when you arrived was to inquire concerning her, since you phoned and phoned and got no answer from her apartment. You were rapidly going nuts and fruit, pure anxiety and distress at the prospect."

"Of a nonexistent danger, of course?"

"Doc, Flora not only admires you, but she is genuinely fond of you, despite the hundred-sixty-year more or less age gap, and she is grateful for your assistance when I was a thorough son of a bitch and would not help her.

"If by any freak you were to have words with her, you will tell her of your anxiety, even when imprisoned by the Commission."

"Me savvee plentee! I really was thinking of her, in spite of the news I got when I read Mona's note and driving with Amina through ox-cart country.

"If I were a hundred fifty years younger, were not an

unfortunate immortal, and not involved with Mona, and if Flora Elaine were not married to Roderick David Garvin, a man I greatly admire, she is the girl I'd want to marry. I'm awfully fond of her."

"In spite of the liar a gentleman has to be, you've told a lot of truth. Anyway, back to your role as fugitive from justice!

"We have guest troops in China. Yes, war games. Our American deserts are different from the deserts of Turkistan." Alexander's wink was a burlesque. "The Dzungarian Basin, north of Urumchi. And the Takla Makan, between the middle and the south fork of the old Silk Road. As a trick of nature, a critically important pass—leading through mountains from five to seven thousand meters elevation—is located there.

"Urumchi is an industrial city. Kashgar, on the southern route, manufactures but is largely agricultural.

"As a fugitive, you'll have custom-built identities and documents to sustain them. Size things up and present appropriate papers, and you'll be in the military service where you can learn the most about things I should know—*off the record*, you understand."

"I begin to catch your meaning."

"Your orders will read so that the officer under whom you serve will release you for other duties whenever you believe you should be elsewhere doing something else. Memorize numbers that will get you directly or indirectly in touch with me. Military or civilian channels. You have been in Turkistan—Sinkiang Province—a couple of times."

Doc frowned. "Last time, sixty–seventy years ago. Know the country, but no people."

"All the better. No people know you anymore. You will have orders for Urumchi and for Kashgar. A contact in Turfan and one in Kashgar."

Doc pondered. "I have a feeling that I ought to be in Kashgar—no logic to the notion. Now, just in case Mona or Amina or both enlisted in one of the Amazon outfits in the Kashgar area, have Mona's orders written so she can readily get a leave unless there is actual combat in the area. Same for Amina."

Doc chuckled. "Be funny if Oswald Fenton was drafted

and sent on a 'cultural' quasi-military war-games assignment in Turkistan and a border incident precipitated a sure-enough battle!"

Alexander responded to Doc's whimsy. "If Mona or Amina assassinated Oswald, there'd be damn little comment, and it'd save me the trouble of keeping one of your girls out of trouble here at home. While you were gone, Security reported having sighted Mona but it may take a few weeks for a pickup. You should not wait. I'll have no trouble helping her enlist as an Amazon assigned to Kashgar."

"Neither of those girls is a draft dodger or conscientious objector—pardon me, *objectrix*."

Alexander poured more Islay. "Doc, you and Mona may have a chance for completing the honeymoon I interrupted."

Doc reached for a refill. "Speaking of Oswald, I've often wondered how much he contributed to that hassle about illegal sale of infants who turned out to be Simianoids. I know it's a dead issue, stage-one blackmail that failed."

"Doc, since you've raised the point, Security was working on everyone remotely associated with the Adoptive Parents business. They got all sorts of irrelevant data before the case fell apart.

"Here is the way it looks: Epworth scheduled his surprise visit to tie in with full moon, the Burmese tribal ceremonies at the pagoda. He brought that telltale solution along to identify infants as individuals. To make a tight job against you, he was going to spy out the village. He would be a first-class witness who could not be tripped up on local color, details. When he got through with you, you would talk or face an indictment, a trial, a conviction on a felony count. However, he did not suspect the infants were Simianoids whose *legal* status had never been adjudicated.

"You would tell all about immortality, life everlasting! Or so Epworth thought."

"I'm with you so far," Doc cut in. "But after all that neat work, he had it made. Including U Po Mya with a .600 Jeffries, and Maung Gauk with his assault carbine. Why a moonlight painting?"

"Doc, it's this way: He figured that small fry look pretty

much alike, same as Asiatics are supposed to. So he used
the telltale dope, each cherub branded so he could say 'Yes,
I marked each one while the Gooks were chanting at the
pagoda.' "

"Mmmm . . . I begin to get it," Doc conceded.

Alexander resumed, "Your nursemaids washed the film
off the infants. In rehearsing the act before the Commission convened, Epworth or one of the League folks failed
to find the brand mark when they tried infrared rays.
Someone corrected the error and as usual when too many
great minds collaborate, things were screwed up. A zealous
expert used a neat stencil, like Security used to tag alien
agitators on the campus."

"It all does tie together," Doc agreed. "And even if he
had done everything right, the blackmail would have
flopped. The courts would have taken years to adjudicate
whether a Simianoid is a human being in the contemplation
of North American law. You do have a grand Security department."

Alexander chuckled. "We have to. Well, getting back to
you and Mona—you're likely to resume your interrupted
honeymoon. But those routine border incidents in Chinese
Turkistan, the gnawing, nibbling away, always staying
short of war—the Chinese People's Republic and the
Marxist Federation have hated each other centuries before
either group got its present-day name.

"The heart of the Marxist Slivovitz country is packed
with people who never forgot Genghis Khan and the really
great Turks—Suleiman the Magnificent, for instance—and
smaller operators: Arpad, who led his armies out of Turkistan around 956 A.D. and took a chunk of territory they
liked. And no one has been man enough to this day to send
them home."

"What you are telling me," Doc said, as he reached for
his glass, "makes me think of King Arthur's last battle."
And Brandon recited, " '. . . *Then he drew his sword to
slay the adder and thought of none other harm. And when
the host on both parties saw that sword drawn, then they
blew beams, trumpets, and shouted grimly. And so both
hosts dressed them together.*' Malory says it better, but one
'party' was wiped out to the last man, and King Arthur was

mortally wounded, with two knights left, one badly wounded."

"Doc, do you see something I don't?"

"Don't crap me! You see plenty." He sighed, looked far into space, and then they picked up their glasses. "I can't leave till Captain Dr. Isaiah Jackson Winthrop calls me. Now I want a few words with Amina. She needs rest from honing that kris—"

Alexander said, as they got to their feet, "Seems to me that Po Chu-i said something about many more going to war than ever come back from it. But you've come back from quite a few."

"In some wars, going is safer than staying home, and you've come back from a couple of tough ones," Doc said.

They drank. They gripped hands. And each went to tell a woman of that day's end and of tomorrow's prospects.

Chapter 37

Alexander Heflin's staff screened all but immediately urgent communications: The remaining ninety-nine and sixty-eight hundreths percent of the demands on his attention were taped and boiled down by assistants who gave him the few which rated a quick glance. The day's summary of the situation did not demand much time: It required even less to supply the remainder of the Consortium's ulcer and headache ration. Finally, there were sufficient of those who felt important because of devoting sixteen hours a day doing their devil's dance in a ballet of waltzing buzz-saws.

With no fear of death, destiny, God or what "they" thought, Alexander's health was good. Like Doc Brandon, he knew that poor health was self-inflicted.

All in all, Alexander's on-the-job honeymoon with Flora Elaine was not as fragmented as most of those which were conventional.

When Security, watching Oswald Fenton, nabbed Mona and brought her to the bombproof, Alexander made room for her. She was happy since he had suggested that once the draft board located Oswald, she'd have him right where she wanted him.

"Wait till Oswald is in foreign territory," Alexander counseled. "Whatever happens then can be blamed as an act of war if you are the least bit sensible about the details. Furthermore, there is a Malay girl with a better claim than yours. Why don't you two young ladies draw straws for first whack?"

Two vengeful women got more of Alexander's time than did swarms of draft dodgers and student rioters.

Then there was that breakfast: the unofficial empress of North America persisted in gourmet cooking. She had shaken up an omelette of straw mushrooms from Taiwan, a crabmeat custard, and crêpes suzette. A calendar with a week-old date was marked out with an X.

"I've spent more than half my life," she began, "hearing women discuss the thousand reasons that could make this turn out to be a false alarm . . ."

"Darling, one thing puzzles me—who congratulates whom, and when are condolences in order or, even, mandatory? If I'd had any sense, I'd have written Susie Saunders for advice. You look so damned pleased with yourself, you look like your description of that Azadeh lady."

"And you," she cut in, "after hearing all my confessions about my married and my dissolute life, look so insufferably conceited about scoring a first—I mean, in my life! The only first left for you!"

So they congratulated each other.

Then, "Madame, there are discussions I will not hear! None of the standard business about stretch marks, and will you ever really get your shape back, and how much permanent weight gain, and a *double* no-no, do not ask me whether you should go through with it."

"Mustn't ask you, not even *once*?"

"The grim fact is that no one else on Earth can feel labor pains. Nobody on Earth, neither this world, the next world, or the Third World rates one tiny fraction of a word on whether you go through with it or call the twenty-seven finest abortionists in North America. It is your business. Only a presumptuous ass would suggest that it is his or her concern."

"You're a darling. Oh, I know this isn't going to be fun, and I'll curse the day, from time to time, but I'm glad too, and for more than just learning that none of my equipment is missing." A long silence, and then, "With so many silly bitches flashing their Sudzo panties and taking them off at the wrong time, I'm going to endow a home for unwed mothers."

"Why all the sound effects? *I'm* asking you. I'd have asked you sooner but I was afraid of crowding you."

"That's the most romantic proposal I ever had."

None of the billions of Sudzo viewers had ever seen her as glowing as she was savoring that proposal.

Alexander sat blinking. "The most romantic! You were still a teenager when you and Rod—"

"The future space hero said, 'Well, if you're knocked up, it'll be easier for me to talk you into marrying, and your family won't squawk so much about me being a half-ass space tramp.' " Flora caught Heflin with both arms and then calmed down enough to say, "Alec, let's wait till the next *X*—I mean, to be sure we want to. This could be a false alarm. If it *is*, and we still want to . . ."

"If this is a false alarm, you'd always feel awkward about it, even if you were sure you'd not herded me into a marriage."

"I'm glad you understand the idiotic business. So we'll wait."

And then, before the *X* day they anticipated with interest, the most secret and confidential of the three private phones sounded off. The line was video. The input was scrambled. The output was screened by Alexander himself, while the caller waited, hearing only *"The party you are calling will be available presently. Please wait for him to answer."*

The ready light glowed. Alexander jabbed a button. The screen became a glowing blank. The speaker made meaningless noises, and then a code number blazed from one corner of the screen. Heflin consulted an index. He frowned, shook his head. "Flora Elaine, this is a miracle of science or some joker is showing himself a temporary good time.

"That is Roderick David Garvin's code card number."

"Rod—"

"Let's hear him."

"Roderick David Garvin calling Alexander Heflin. None of your God damned business what my mother's maiden name is, I gave you my card number."

The speaker was addressing the recorded voice, a very good female voice. Alexander twisted about, caught Flora's hand, snatched her to her feet. Her color changed; of a sudden, her makeup was a mockery. She licked her lips and gaped unbeautifully.

"That *is* Rod."

"How the hell can it be?"

"Maybe he invented—good God, how could he call from the asteroid!"

Alexander's breathing ceased for a moment. "Get over to one side, stay out of sight. I'll check this for size."

The dark blobs on the screen pulled together, brightened, shaped Roderick David Garvin. A few more lines. A deeper tan. An embroidered black skullcap concealed his hair. He wore a red tunic with gilt floral patterns. A bit gaudy, ever the conspicuous Garvin. "Oh, all *right*! Mother's maiden name was McTavish, the Black McTavish . . . I do not mean African, you stupid bitch."

The image blinked out. Alexander said, "He's calling from Maritania."

Flora and Alexander were shouting each other down, their guesses none the worse for confusion and incoherence.

A switch click. The screen blacked out and brightened again. Through the miracle of science there was now instantaneous two-way transmission.

"Alex, you old bastard! For years I'd forgot the code card you gave me when the *Saturnienne* was refitted."

"So did I! What are you doing on Mars? How'd you get away from the asteroid?"

"Long story. Right now I want you to do me a favor. Remember that long-legged redhead, Lani—the doll who married Admiral Courtney? The Admiral died. No, it wasn't too much Lani. I told you it is a long story. Are they still wondering who killed Inspector Philip Morgan?"

"What's the problem?"

"I got her into that Martian mess. Once I get her back to Terra, I am in the clear. No more obligation. Problem is, getting transportation for Lani and her infant son. After the Admiral died, she married a prince on the asteroid."

"I'll put the staff to work. Feed your Martian address to the tape and they can work from it. Give all facts you recall."

"Will do. And I want to get in touch with Flora. Can't get an answer or trace of her, not anywhere."

"Leave your number for a call-back. I'll find her. She's as beautiful as ever. What's detaining you on Mars?"

"Too early for details."

Garvin edged off scene. A dark-haired woman with skin the color of magnolia blossom moved into the picture. "I am Azadeh. Rod is waiting for some of my fellow Gooks to learn how to navigate one of our own cruisers back home. The one Rod flew from the asteroid."

"The asteroid people built a cruiser?"

"I mean that the cruiser had sat there a hundred thousand or more years. Rod got it going."

Rod took the scene again. "The asteroidians and the Martian aborigines are kinfolk and they want to fraternize a bit, compare notes on their homes, and get some ideas on Terra. And don't lose too much time locating Flora. Azadeh wants to have a talk with her and arrive at a sort of understanding."

Alexander demanded, "Who's that girl crowding in with you? She doesn't look like Azadeh."

"Nobody looks like Azadeh. This is Aljai. She interpreted for me from the asteroid when we landed. She's learned quite a bit of English."

"I imagine she would have! But then, talk to Azadeh and brief her about the situation. If you gave Aljai a chance, she could demonstrate her English."

All Aljai had to say was that she and Azadeh would be most happy to be Number Two and Number Three, with Flora as Number One Wife, no matter where Garvin settled down.

Alexander again promised to expedite Lani's getting to Terra and to lose no time in getting Flora in touch with her co-wives. And then, over and out.

Flora said, "I'm glad I got the uncensored dialogue. I'm an eavesdropper who heard nothing but good about herself."

Each regarded the other. Finally Flora said, "You and I

have a few things to sort out. Ever since I moved in with you, I've been so fluttery getting my preteenage cravings taken care of that I forgot that regardless of how the X on the calendar falls, I am still Mrs. Roderick David Garvin."

"Meaning we can't marry until you get a divorce."

She nodded.

Chapter 38

Doc Brandon arrived in Urumchi, Sinkiang Province, in the extreme northwest corner of the People's Republic of China, wearing Identity Number One. He had become Captain David Harper, Army Intelligence, although to all but the Commanding General, North American War Games Division, he was a staff officer with a special assignment.

When not observing maneuvers, Doc was busy in S-2, Plans and Training. Only General Whitfield knew that Captain Harper was Army Intelligence. To put it explicitly, Tamara Sinclair, of Three Dee fame, hostess of the Allied Services Association, which staged dances and entertainment for military personnel, did not know that Captain Harper and Intelligence were in any way related. Tamara mistook Doc for an idealist like her lovely self.

Because of her mistake, Tamara wasted opportunities to sleep with field-grade officers—majors and the various colonels—by spending a cozy weekend with a mere captain. And, thanks to Tamara's error, a new dervish followed a camel train headed for Kashgar.

Doc, having been posted as a deserter, devised for himself an identity which served his immediate purposes and permitted him to keep in reserve his Identity Number Two, which he would need after he and Mona met for their number-two honeymoon. Unless war broke out before Alexander's Security caught and brought her to the bombproof for an updating on the possibilities of duty in Sinkiang.

211

Doc wore a sheepskin cap, a knee-length *khalat* which was so grimy that its color was unidentifiable. His trousers were dirt brown and patched. He carried a knapsack stuffed with road necessities and rations such as parched barley, tea, and butter to add to the mush of tea and barley which was the caravan man's standard ration. In addition, there were raisins, dried melon slices, and a flask of distilled spirits, *raki*, aged for at least a week.

His shoes were sturdy, and so was the quarter staff he carried for armament. It was of dark, exceptionally heavy hardwood.

There are dervishes who live in monasteries and devote their lives to chanting and whirling. Others make a living eating live snakes, scorpions, or fire coals. A dervish may be a magician, fortune teller, juggler, con man; he may be a "guest of Allah," begging his meals; a poet, saint, scholar, exiled prince retiring from the world. Thus anyone of quick wit can make his way as a dervish, and if he is—or pretends to be—half insane, all the better.

As Doc inhaled dust and the stench of camels and licked dust from sun-parched lips, he enjoyed freedom for the first time in many a year: Much as he loved Nameless Island and its people, escape was good for the soul. Nothing missing but Mona.

". . . Having a glorious time. Wish you were here. . . . Never heard of a female dervish . . . discrimination—no, Madame Sudzo is not rugged enough . . ."

Uighur While You Fly had updated Doc, but not enough, and the phrase book apparently had been compiled by a native scholar who had learned most of his English from an American truck driver, cat-skinner, and freighting flier in Sinkiang. It was entertaining, but if the compiler had gone to a missionary's school, the book would have been more helpful. At least he would not have used a four-letter word as a generic term for all female humans.

The Uighur equivalent, however, was entirely nice. Doc had no linguistic problems. His eyes and hair and complexion and his mangling of the language made it obvious that he was a Tadjik or some other foreigner from Iran, but civilized enough to wash his hands with sand, when water was lacking, before he prayed.

"*. . . el hamd ul lilahi . . . rabb'il alamayn . . . malik i yaum i deen . . .* praise be to Allah . . . no God-damn scientists . . ."

Never long enough with one caravan for his trailmates to see through his imposture, he'd stop at a village and rest, then plod alone to the next. Again he would walk by night. But when a motor convoy of troops came thundering along the caravan trail with lights out, Doc began to wonder whether that might not be one of the by-products of the phony information he had given idealistic Tamara to feed to the Marxist agents.

That ended Doc's hiking and sizing up the country, col-lecting native gossip. Thereafter he paid for rides with truckers. At Aksu, he phoned Alexander. "I gave Tamara obsolete plans and training stuff that I doctored, changing figures—particularly dates—to make it current. The doc-toring does not show in the microfilm strip I gave you. I'm a deserter now, Kashgar bound. A copy of the filmstrip is going to you. Movements of our troops from Urumchi to Kashgar might be our answer to what the Marxists are doing because of the misinformation I fed her. Where's Mona?"

"In Kashgar by now," Alexander said.

And for Doc, nothing to say but "Over and out."

The truck finally brought Doc to the fringe of the great oasis where yellow loess, deep and fertile, was windblown to make the sky a gray murk, dimming the verdure of fields and gardens. Irrigation canals, fed by the Kashgar River, watered orchards, vineyards, and cotton. The truck barreled through suburbs, haphazard scatterings of flat-roofed houses made of sun-dried brick. Poplars shaded the houses, and willows lined the canals which watered gardens in and about the walled city.

At last the vehicle pulled up at what once had been the Consulate General of Great Britain. It had become a trucker's haven, where drivers ate and slept before going eastward to Khotan, City of Jade.

Doc set out afoot, picking his way through the Old City which lurked behind massive walls and iron-faced gates. Where once fly-infested bazaars had been, he passed

Western-style department stores. So much new, but as he skirted the canals which picked their way among gardens, he found landmarks until he emerged in the no-man's land between Old City and New Kashgar.

The tiled dome and façade, the towers at the corners of Apak Hodja's mausoleum got him back on his course. After picking his way among walled gardens for more than a kilometer, he came to the home of Ahmad Abdurrahman, who would be expecting him.

The gatekeeper listened to Doc's recital, in Uighur, of the substance of Identity Two and accepted the papers which sustained it. He closed and locked the gate before reporting to the master.

Ahmad lost no time in coming to greet his visitor. His lean face and dark eyes seconded words of welcome. Far back on his head he wore a maroon skullcap, apparently kept in place by prayer and fasting. The skimpy headgear exaggerated the height of his forehead. Ahmad was nearing seventy, Doc judged from the weathered throat exposed by the open collar of a velvet *khalat*. A black moustache and the white tuft of beard which jutted from the pointed chin, counterbalanced a nose full fledged and lordly.

"You are tired, thirsty. Who would not be! And most welcome."

"The friend who sends me to you," Doc said, "will be happy to know I am here. Happy as I am to be here."

He followed his host across a shaded garden ablaze with roses, peonies, tawny golden lilies, and into the house. The reception room was the usual barren expanse, relieved by the blue borders, the red ground, and the four multicolored medallions which ran the length of the narrow Yarkand rug that covered the rammed earth wall bench from beyond its midpoint to the ceremonial hearth. The walls had niches for whatsoever might need stowing: smoking gear, coffee or tea service, or flowers from the garden.

"Dump your pack! You are the Guest of Allah." Ahmad gestured. "Sit by the hearth. The ghost of fires is enough for this day."

An Uighur girl came in with a bowl of mulburries, a flat cake of bread, of that day's baking. From the tray she also set out a dish of pounded sesame butter blended with crushed garlic, lemon juice, and eggplant puree. When all had been set on the *kang*, she took from a wall niche a small gooseneck ewer and a basin of matching size. Setting the latter on the *kang*, she poured water over Doc's grimy hands. Once she had poured water over the master's slender, well-kept hands, he offered the golden-brown cake of leavened wheat bread to his guest.

"Fadl!" and then, "In the name of Allah."

"Thanks to Allah and your presence," Doc replied.

Doc tore a small piece from the bread and dipped it into the sauce. Ahmad did likewise, and they ate: the old Moslem sacrament, the sharing of bread.

The girl set out tiny Chinese wine cups and a decanter.

"Although the Prophet, upon whom be the blessing of Allah and on his pious companions, advised most vigorously against wine, the accursed," Ahmad said, "he never forbade spirits."

"It would be irreverent and disrespectful," Doc added, "to suggest that the Prophet of Allah was forgetful. It seems rather that the Prophet, on whom be peace and blessing, remembered that the Uighur people would be unhappy without distilled spirits."

Having agreed theologically, guest and host hoisted a few tots of *raki*.

Once Doc bathed and ate a staggering meal, he would be briefed on the local situation and how it related to whatever messages Alexander had sent to await his arrival.

Doc followed the Uighur girl to the bath. Felt boots, white trousers, a hip-length jacket, and a skullcap awaited him. A shave and a cleanup would be a novelty.

When Doc stepped out of the bath, the girl was waiting to tell him that the master would speak to him when he had eaten and rested. He followed her across a backyard garden and to a small house faced with blue Persian tiles.

Once in the reception room she set his knapsack—minus dirty laundry—on the *kang*. Bowing, she nodded as though in approval of bathhouse transformation and new garments. Then, "The Lady will cook your meal. I beg leave to depart."

The door closed behind her, and there was a click as though a lock had operated. After a moment Doc felt a breath of breeze from a hallway: It was spicy sweet, cosmetic.

For a guest to sleep alone would be a breach of hospitality as gross as withholding food. And then Uighur hospitality, long-haired, emerged from the hall. She wore an ankle-length Turki tunic secured Chinese style. Of all the women in Turkestan, Ahmad could not have chosen better: Mona.

"Surprise! Thought you'd be sleeping with Najeeba, didn't you?"

"Madame Broadtail!"

And when the clinch eased up, Mona said, "After all the traveling you've been doing, you won't want a tour of the house."

Between tapping a flask of *raki* and pumping the bellows to get a charcoal fire going for broiling skewers of mutton while Mona got rice started, Doc was kept busy. And presently the spicy bouquet of sauce for *pilau* blended with the savor of broiling meat and onion chunks.

"The apricots, grapes, and the rest of the stuff, all of it good for you," she announced later, as she whisked the napkin from a plate of diamond-shaped pastries, each a hundred or more paper-thin leaves, thin from many foldings and rollings, and with honey and butter and ground nuts sprinkled on the mass between foldings and flattenings back to size. "Now let's lose our figures before we go where figures don't count."

It was not until Mona poured tea that Doc got the message from Alexander Heflin. "He positively forbids you to take part in the war games. The pretense of maneuvers and drill is wearing thinner than a flake of *baklavat*."

"So I am supposed to be an Immortal who won't risk the precious life that mortals are putting on the line? Shit plus two equals seven, and double it for Alexander! Am I going to be hiding out somewhere, incognito, so I'll not be a horrible example to a pack of punks who don't need any such precedents rubbed under their noses?"

"Before you and I do anything else, we're going to have another honeymoon. In Kashgar, or in the foothills, a couple thousand meters above oasis level."

Mona took two miniature towels from a bowl of steaming water, squeezed them dry, and handed one to Doc.

"Before you get absentminded and put honey and butter prints all over me."

"I never did like Mona-flavor contaminated with anything but Nuance, or Attar of Roses."

They mopped their faces, degreased and dehoneyed their fingers. As she poured more *raki*, Mona resumed. "Yes. I am to talk you out of the danger zone. By the time you get back to North America, the dearest friends of the two men you killed will pay Parliament to pass a law permitting you to commit rape, murder, and arson every Monday, Wednesday, and Friday, providing you work on your eternal life project.

"What Alec actually said is, '*If there is a nuclear exchange, we'll need every scientist in the world to help rebuild what is left—if any, and there's bound to be something.*' "

She boiled down Alexander's essence of what an anthropologist or maybe a sociologist had stated in more precise language: "If an astrologer or good operator with the *I Ching* or Tarot could pick out the several thousand genius-potential infants right at birth and strangle them, the entire culture—civilization, or whatever you like to call it—would fall apart. No advances in industry or art or science or anything else. Nothing could be kept the way it is, such as seems worth keeping. Mere maintenance would be impossible. In a couple or three generations, we'd be living in caves or the trees, and one day someone would invent the bow and arrow, or the wheelbarrow."

"Alexander said that, or words to that effect?"

"That's right. He did."

"He was speaking bare truth. Now, this culture we have is too crazy to exist.

"For instance, in one of the Western states rape is a young man's idle-hour timekiller. Repeat offenders are heroes in their crowd. There was a woman who had conscientious objections to rape, and before the party was over, she was lucky enough to grab a knife and get in a couple of good slashes. The female judge agreed with the prosecuting attorney that rape was not a crime of such violence as to justify the woman's use of a deadly weapon. The resisting woman was lucky to get off with a suspended sentence.

"Now that you've got that standard piece of North American culture, try this one: Among the Navajo and Hopi and Apache savages of the old Southwest, the rapist was staked out over an anthill, and the busy little ants rehabilitated him. There were no repeaters, and rape was seldom heard of. Relapse to primitive viewpoints would do the country a lot of good."

"Doc, darling," she mocked, "don't be sticky! You're acting like one of those silly people you despise."

"I despise so many. Do be specific, Madame Broadtail."

"You sound like an *idealist*."

"You were smiling when you said that, so it's okay."

"Please do get some common sense, Doc. You really are more valuable to whatever is going to be left of North America than the million slobs that may be exterminated in the war that the idealists are inviting with their we-won't-fight yakking. The survivors are going to need your help when they invent the wheelbarrow."

Doc shook his head. "What they need is the idea of fighting. If I happen to be killed in action, it'd prove either that an Immortal doesn't find immortality such a prize, or else that I was a faker and there's no immortality except in Heaven."

"Doc, darling, let's compromise. Just stay out of this, and they'll forget all about you. Three Dee gives them the attention span of infants. We can find a quiet little oasis settlement or something high in the Andes where nobody ever heard of you. Risking your valuable hide as an example to the kind of clods spewed out by the millions every year! You have the experience now, how science screwed things up first time around: Let it blow things all to scraps and then give the survivors the right start."

"That is downright good sense. Your practical mind is sustained by the way our intellectuals buy Marxist doctrine."

He told her of Tamara Sinclair, a true idealist compelled to serve her country by selling it to the enemy. ". . . and is sincere! And she's not the first one. In one of the liberation wars I fought in, a century or so ago, they had a few like her. Movie and such like stars, going over to the enemy, causing the deaths of thousands of servicemen and coming home, welcomed instead of being backed up against an adobe wall to face a firing squad.

"There was a petition out around then to pardon Tokyo Rose, and I signed it. When someone asked me how come, I said, 'She was an unheard of nobody till the enemy made her get in line. And look at that bitch who went over to the enemy because she was against her country and proud of it. And she still lives.

"No compromise!"

"You win, Doc. You win." She fumbled at the fastenings of her tunic, disengaged the top three. "This is just symbolic, and I don't have new fittings. You've seen everything. And if I threatened to move out unless you listened to reason, you'd remind me that what's her name, Najeeba, would be sleeping with you if I hadn't been here. Old Uighur hospitality."

"Uighur hospitality, yes. So you're not threatening?"

"No, you crazy old bastard! I know how stubborn you can be. So I am compromising again."

He had known from the start that Mona was going to be decisive, but now she had him guessing.

"Let's hear it."

"This is going to be the nastiest war on record. The world has owed you and me a honeymoon and we're going to have it. And then, when things begin popping, I am enlisting in an Amazon regiment. If those lard-bottom dolls do nothing but punch typewriters and sleep with generals, I will desert and sneak into your outfit once things get fouled up by battle and everyone and everything look alike.

"And if I am shot up, or if I am a prisoner of war and get gang-raped by those silly asses, it'll be your fault."

"Madame Broadtail, before your start threatening me, wait till you've survived the honeymoon."

"Dr. Brandon, this is going to be your first honeymoon with a starved and desperate Simianoidess. Let's talk about survival later."

Chapter 39

Cherokee Parish, the most unpleasant area on the Gulf Coast of Louisiana, had been losing population ever since the Coast Guard set up helicopter patrols sufficient to make piracy and the smuggling of aliens, girls, and narcotics unprofitable. However, landing operations and assault training maneuvers had for several weeks filled the space vacated by farmers, fishers, and the criminal element.

Major General Dennis Kerwin, commanding a division of Simianoid troops, was observing the amphibious maneuvers. Half his outfit and half the Marxist division had combined to act as defenders. The ships standing offshore—the attackers—were manned by the remainder of the Simianoid Division and the rest of the Marxists. When one of the phases was completed, another was staged, except that details were different and the former landing party became the defenders, and former defenders were now assaulting the nastiest of the Gulf Coast's many nasty spots.

The General's staff was on its own, dictating notes to minirecorders. Coordinated, and collated, with inevitable duplications deleted, their observations would be the basis of the evening's critique.

General Kerwin's sharp eye and squarish, grim-jawed face made him look like a sculptor's preliminary sketch of a bulldog. He was dividing his words between a lapel mike and Captain Isaiah Winthrop, technical advisor on Simianoids. "Tide's nearly right."

They were waiting, as were twenty thousand Simianoids and a like number of Marxist guest troops, for the bomb blast and red-star signal that would start the final day's game, the summing up of ebb tide, flood tide, neap tide.

"Isaiah, if we took out our earplugs we could hear each other. Let's get away from here before things fire up. With my staff over half the God damned parish, there's nothing you and I can see that they won't be recording into the ground. Nothing you have said thus far has been dumber than my staff has recorded."

"Thank you, sir. I'd been wondering whether I'd been impersonating an officer at all convincingly. There she goes!"

A rocket rose from the signal tower well eastward: A red flare tinted the afternoon sunlight, and then the rumbling blast from the heart of the red splash. Twenty thousand meters offshore, a four-hundred-millimeter gun boomed. The shell passing overhead sounded like four subway express trains roaring by at once. Landing craft, tank, and landing craft personnel were rolling off ships between the battle fleet and the shore. Planes soared, circled over their carriers, then raced landward. Antiaircraft miniguns spat red and green trails, diving and spiraling crazily yet showing the general trajectory of the otherwise invisible bullets.

Bombs dropped, well clear of ships and landing craft.

Umpires swooped about in light copters. Several landing craft went home: An umpire had declared them totaled. Troops hip-deep in the cypress swamp learned happily that they had been annihilated by the laws of probability: Their exposure, their grouping, the amount of explosives the bombers and the naval guns pelted at them, far over but in theory right on them, should have caused a statistically probable number of casualties.

Getting out of the mosquito-thickened air would have been worth real casualties.

The General shouted and gestured. The Black Captain got the idea. There was not a silent spot for miles around. Sign language was the only mode of communication until Kerwin and Winthrop reached a spot where a swale, cypress trees, shoulder-high reeds and the lee side of headquarters building offered comparative silence.

"What I wanted to ask you—" Kerwin roared like a lion, and then grimaced, repeated himself many decibels lower. "Isaiah, I've wondered why you turned down a major's commission."

"General, your hints did tempt me. I appreciated the compliment. Captain is respectable, but not as impressive as major or colonel. I had read the scope of the operation and I didn't even understand the language that described it, and a field officer should have."

"God damn it! You were not supposed to. You are a specialist."

"Sir, that is not the essence of the matter."

"Let me hear the essence while there is no audience handy."

"To avoid rivalry, visitor versus home team, the assault is half of one, half of the other, and so for the defense. Being an inconspicuous captain, I had nothing to do but say 'Sergeant, keep this going,' and he would keep it going.

"Nobody knows I speak Slivovitz. Nobody but rabid socialists or one of the literati or a philologist would ever bother with it."

"More of us God damn well ought to! Your approach is interesting." Kerwin dug a cigar case out of his tunic pocket, offered it to Isaiah, and took one himself. "Fire up, and carry on."

Isaiah selected one, pinched the tip, lit it, whiffed the smoke.

"Sir, this reminds me of one of Dr. Brandon's choicest."

"He sent me five hundred along with regrets that having killed two men kept him from military service for a while. Otherwise I'd not have suggested your being commissioned with the grade of colonel or at least major. Carry on, please."

"I fraternized with Slivovitz troops—company grades, of course—and complimented them on their English, which was quite intelligible. Naturally, I said I wished I could speak even a few words of Slivovitz. Later I heard someone say to a comrade, 'You think that Black fellow can't understand a word of what we say?' and comrade answered, 'Americans are the world's worst linguists, and anyone white-haired and only a captain, the old bastard is too dumb to speak his own language.' "

And then Isaiah spelled it out: When the war games were over, the famous 47th Division would go to Megapolis Alpha for a Fraternity Parade. By invitation of the North American Parliament. To declare a Marxist Democracy, lawfully approved by that Parliament.

The General's squarish face lengthened. The lines became deep; the eyes, flinty bitter as his mouth. Wholly ignoring Isaiah's presence, Kerwin said as though talking to himself, or to an invisible ghost staff, ". . . if our only reliable troops, the Simianoid divisions, hustled these bastards to a homebound troop transport or, better yet, surrounded their camp in Alpha and declared them prisoners of war and machine-gunned them by mistake, it would be civil war: armed resistance to the lawful act of the supreme legislative body of the Republic."

He jerked as though startled. Perhaps he was. "You heard me muttering to myself?"

"I did, sir. Not having been dismissed, I could not avoid eavesdropping."

"Captain Winthrop, you know far more about Simianoids than do my staff officers. I am not disparaging them. They are soldiers, and God damn good ones too. But the only effective response to this situation that my staff could make would be armed force, civil war, and however insane our Parliament is, it is unhappily the ruling body of this country."

A long pause. Isaiah still looked far into space. Finally the General said, "For hell's sweet sake, Captain, say something!

"What are your constructive thoughts? Do not tell me you need time to think. You've been at it ever since this farce was dumped on us. Right?"

"Substantially, yes, and I did orient myself."

"I want your thoughts. They can't be as crazy as Parliament's."

"Sir, a properly selected civilian, clearly not a member of the military service, could handle this situation nicely, and in a way that would avoid civil war. If Dr. Brandon were not a fugitive from justice, he would immediately get things moving."

"What would he do?"

"He would suggest to the Commanding General that to further the intent of the Parliament, the Simianoid Division should make a gesture of goodwill and fraternity before comrades in war games parted company.

"For instance, marching with the Guest Division to a more salubrious area for rest and cleaning up. Then, preparation for the Forty-Seventh Slivovitz's march or motorcade to Megapolis Alpha. And before setting out, some truly American festive expression would be most appropriate."

"Such as?"

"Such as a California-Mexican style barbecue. To avoid procurement problems, all supplies would be donated by the Brandon Foundation."

General Kerwin raised his cap, scratched his head. "Just what the hell do you have in mind?"

"Sir, Dr. Brandon would refuse to answer that question. In such case, you would demand his immediate resignation. Is my assumption correct?"

"In principle, yes. Or convene a general court-martial to try him for insubordination. In practice, perhaps neither. Right now, *God damn it!* quit crapping around and give me facts. You are cooking up some kind of caper."

"Correction, sir. This is an Avery Jarvis Brandon caper. May I suggest that you let it go at that? Between now and barbecue time, I can arrange for cattle on the hoof, dig pits, line them with stones, get suitable fuel, and serving equipment.

"Meanwhile, this could allow the Commanding General time to get in touch with the Chairman of the Consortium and suggest that your division be transported by fastest available transportation to China, for the final phase of the Sinkiang Desert War Games."

"Captain Winthrop, now that you have practically taken command of this division, I want to know what the plan is."

"Sir, to spare you the embarrassment of demanding my immediate resignation, I am tendering it at once." Isaiah dug into his tunic pocket and took from it a paper; he un-

pinned his captain's bars. "I shall be happy to carry on as a
civilian. You will note that my resignation is dated as of
today.

"If I were to appear just before barbecue day, in uniform
and wearing insignia of rank, it would probably be your
duty to file a complaint with civilian authorities, charging
me with impersonating an officer."

The General pondered for a long moment. "Parliamentary Committees will gulp the fraternity and goodwill
muck," he finally said. "And I begin to suspect that I'd
better not know what you fellows have cooked up. As long
as I have orders to get my division out of the country after
the barbecue, the Chairman of the Consortium can be sure
I'll not be starting a civil war."

Isaiah waggled the papers. "General Kerwin, my resignation."

"Isaiah—Dr. Winthrop—" He thrust out his hand. "If
you and I do not end facing a firing squad because of this
caper, I'll thank you publicly for what I suspect will be a
God damn good job!"

INTERLUDE

Ahmad's villa, and the honeymoon spot where Doc and Mona had renewed old acquaintance, were 160 kilometers east of Doc Brandon's outfit, which he had joined as a private in the 114th War Games Casual Company. There he was learning that he had little to learn about war games. On the other hand, he knew all that there was to learn about Mona, which in his war-games musings he summed up to this effect: *"When she began agreeing with everything I said, I knew she was going to do as she God damn well pleased."* He wasted no musings on not knowing what Mona would do, when she would do it, and least of all, how. . . .

Most Amazons, being superior intellectual types and largely career women, knew nothing about office work. Many wondered why a dizzy bitch without a degree started with Staff Sergeant rating. Mona did not inform them. She was busily attending to her duties and observing the Old Man's habits until she knew how far he would work his way through a stack of papers before he quit bothering to read what he was signing.

One day he learned that he had signed an order promoting a noncareer Amazon to a job which until retreat, previous day, had been filled by Mona. When the Old Man recognized his signature and lower-echelon endorsements, he saw little reason to question anyone. When, after a surreptitious and furtive personal search, he realized that Mona had never appeared on a payroll and that not a paper in the files indicated that she had ever been at Headquarters, he saw no reason whatsoever to inquire further. As far as paperwork went, Mona had never existed. The New Amazon, though she did not rate a broadtail jacket, was in all other respects fully equal to her predecessor.

The Old Man had no cause for moping or pining, all the more so since he never realized that he had signed a number of orders which Mona could use to further her own purposes, as required . . .

Chapter 40

Doc's breakfast was a cooked meal, but hasty. Contradictory rumors built up tension such as fact could not have. Out of the mumble of voices came scraps which reminded Doc Brandon of long past places, people, and wars. The scene was old stuff for him, but for most of the lineup, it was a first.

". . . this is no war . . . it's the real McCoy . . . Christ, they can't make us fight . . . They told us this is just maneuvers . . . swim home and protest . . ."

Other voices: ". . . they lied to us . . . I won't fight . . . They can't make me . . ."

"Balls! When those fuckers start shooting at you, your conscience goes AWOL . . ."

". . . Kee-rist, this's just another God damn drill . . ."

"Drill . . . what'd they issue cartridges and live grenades for?"

"So you can pull the pin and shove 'em up your ass!"

A wide range of opinions was voiced concerning extremely early reveille. The whiner, the weeper, the defiant idealist resolved to die before he would kill another human being might become an exultant man-slayer, glorying in having exterminated a platoon of the enemy. Loud, bold talkers might run, they might stand and fight to the end or die of battle diarrhea. Silent ones might set off a *banzai* charge. They might settle down methodically killing, being part of that ten percent which does the man-slaying, while the rest of the force wastes ammunition or crouches helpless, too scared to move. Doc had seen all these: Kwang Chau Fu, Banjarmassin, and at Khartoum. If battle and soldiers were predictable, a general armed with a computer could compare notes with the enemy commander and settle the matter without firing a shot.

The troops set out as for day-after-day maneuvers. Engines purred, grumbled, muttered, or rattled: the same old stuff, but made different by darkness, by bandoliers of real cartridges, grenades which were not cardboard noisemakers. As for the plastic charges to slam against a tank, there would be no camera this day, within or without, to help umpires decide which of the crew was dead or captured.

Instead junk and vultures would decide the score.

It began as had every war-game formation: troops at route step, except that this time, no smoking. Although silence was not yet mandatory, there was less and less vocalizing as the columns advanced ten kilometers to prepared positions.

The west was no longer black as Doc neared the long ridge which began not far from the old Silk Road and reached northward. It was still too early for any eastern brightening to light the snowcaps that towered seven thousand meters skyward when he wondered how come a stranger had joined the platoon.

"Thought they'd skipped our outfit," he was thinking, as he got a stronger whiff of cosmetic scent. *"But that'd be discrimination, no fruit ration."*

A dark blur moved nearer and the scent became unmistakable. It wasn't the fruit ration: It was a real woman, to wit, Mona.

"God damn you, I told you!"

"You old bastard, I told *you.*"

"So you're AWOL."

"A soldier, so-called male, reported sick and I wasn't. So I took its place."

"I smelled you three meters away. You've got no sense."

The troops took their war-games posts near the crestline. Doc's unit had nothing to do but stay ready. Enemy tanks would lead. Defending tanks would counterattack; the enemy infantry would follow through to fight it out with the defenders. Now that the troops were in their familiar games position, everyone was serene, wondering who had started that latrine rumor about combat. But to make the most of the initial apprehension, veterans explained that the chance of being blasted to tatters by your own air or your own artillery was better than the chance of being clobbered by enemy fire.

"Never let the enemy worry you," an instructor advised. "Get at the bastards quick as you can, and stay safe from your own troops—once you're well away from them and you've got nothing but the enemy in front of you, you've got it made."

A Marine officer who supervised boot camp instruction had given those words, to offset another instructor's declaration that being surrounded by the enemy was the great triumph of any war: "No matter which way you go, you've got them at your mercy. Nothing to do but bayonet the sons of bitches when you run out of ammunition! It's just a matter of being able to overtake them."

Finally Doc got his mind on the drill that was neither war nor battle. Glancing eastward, he saw the beginning of sunrise in Kansu Province; and then, looking westward again, he saw what was coming up out of the pass beyond which lay Golden Samarkand, Khiva, and Bukhara: or were they from Naryn?

It was no drill. The tanks coming out of the gap fanned out at two-hundred-meter intervals and swooped into broad flatlands and sands: a real, not a drill-ground enemy. This was invasion from the Marxist Federation, west of China's uttermost west.

Doc shouted to Mona, "Broadtail, flatten down! Or you'll get it shot away!"

She hunched up on her elbow, twisted, patted that *derrière*.

"I'm handicapped fore and aft. Take a last look, Doc."

"You silly bitch, this is no drill!"

He got up.

"You better get down yourself!"

Abashed, Doc Brandon bellied against the hard rocks. The tanks, iron gray and with no insignia, spread farther and farther abreast. Armored troop carriers followed, and after them, a second wave of tanks. Thus far no air support, and no Chinese air attack.

Engines roaring, treads clanking, the invaders were a good twenty kilometers into Sinkiang and thus far without opposition. Moment by moment, the light became better.

Turret guns shelled the crest behind which Mona and Doc and a division of war-games troops lurked. Behind the tanks, personnel carriers halted to discharge their passengers. Infantry advanced, veterans to whom this was no more than another unpleasant routine.

Decibel by decibel, the sound level rose. Tanks fanned out on Doc's left, as though to flank the southern end of the long ridge and enfilade it.

Doc remembered reading of Thomas at Chickamauga, more than two centuries previous: all out of ammunition, and the enemy at the foot of a long ridge, preparing to charge again. Thomas was not retreating. The bugles sounded, *Fix Bayonets!*

But that was history. Doc and Mona looked about and learned that they were very much alone.

She said, "We are not with our outfit. Does that make us deserters?"

"I don't think everybody has bailed out," Doc said, after a glance to each flank. "But here and there folks are taking cover, really getting flat to the ground. As long as they stay put, I'm staying put."

"So am I. Let's stay here."

Tanks had deeply penetrated the basin into which Doc and Mona looked. There was no return fire along the entire crest. No tanks came from the rear to meet the invaders. Doc said, "I'm looking at what I helped make: the American way of living."

"Maybe this is the best spot! Looks like some of the tanks are swerving toward the Silk Road. If they're going to make for Kashgar, they'll machine-gun the cross-country runners and when all's clear we can head for the hills."

Doc caught her by the arm. "Let go of that carbine, and get your mind off those hills. Not even a nymphomaniac would like that area! Those woods are no fun spot!"

He pointed. "Look! Get it! Over yonder!"

Tanks were coming out of the wooded area.

The nearest enemy tank was enveloped in a red flare and a billow of black smoke. Before the sound of gunnery, shell blast, and explosion reached the ridge, another erupted in flame. Advancing infantry, moving to form columns on the Silk Road, had expected no opposition. They began crumpling, cut down by machine-gun fire and the chattering assault carbines of defenders not yet visible.

The many who made dives for cover were stitched to the ground by small-arms fire from upper slopes.

"Chinese intelligence," Doc said, "or maybe ours had a hand in it, used war games to bait a trap. We've got a grandstand seat, and no rooting section to scream us deaf. The visiting team is going to be wiped out."

Mona unhitched her canteen. "I knew I'd be scared witless, so I filled it with *raki*." She waved to a distant diehard and brandished the canteen. "Come over and have a snort with us!"

Whether shock, curiosity, or discipline had detained them, a handful of troops remained at their posts until recall sounded. The party which marched down from the ridge consisted of a few from every unit, and included officers, noncoms, and enlisted men in almost the proportions prescribed by a table of organization.

Not long after evening mess, the outdoor screens which showed filmings of each day's war games offered an explanation of the day's surprises.

Chinese Intelligence had learned of war games west of the pass. American satellites had observed unusual concentrations in that area. Accordingly, Chinese troops had taken stations to warn the Marxist forces in the event that any of their units crossed the border by mistake.

Doc was fascinated but not surprised by the Chinese definition of warning.

Not wishing that overseas guests be forced into the awkwardness of defending the territory of their host, the People's Republic of China interposed. As a matter of honor, guests had to be kept safe and harmless. Finally, however deeply it was regretted that the night problem had been interrupted, the People's Republic hoped that the unscheduled demonstration had been interesting and instructive.

Doc said to Mona, "You have just heard an example of Asiatic *politesse*."

Another speaker took over: "We have received an expression of profound regret and a tender of sincere apology from the Marxist Federation whose troops crossed our border in error. You will now see a newscast of the general court-martial of the officer responsible for a gross error which might have compromised the goodwill always existing between the Marxist Federation and the People's Republic of China."

Another flash: the General responsible for the error was facing a firing squad.

"Let me translate," Doc began.

"His English," Mona declared, "is better than mine. I got it."

"Sure you got the words. I'll give you the meaning. The Marxist General was shot for doing exactly what he had been ordered to do. He was not within two thousand kilometers of the action, but the outfit to which he gave orders blundered into a trap and his government lost face. The People's Republic pretend to believe the yarn. The Marxist Federation pretend to believe what the People's Republic puts out. No one fools anyone. Maneuvers will be resumed as soon as the dead and the wreckage are taken away.

"Our troops will stay put, but they'll be backed by a Simianoid Division, like the seasoned one that fought in Ethiopia. And there's going to be another 'mistake,' another border incident, one that will be better planned."

"Our new troops will be backed?"

"If they retreat, they'll be shot by veterans who do not waver under fire. Once they learn that advancing is not as dangerous as retreating, they'll fight like tigers. That was the way General Gouraud saved Paris, during the Kaiser War: Any soldier retreating without being ordered to do so was to be shot at once."

"Isn't there any other way?"

Doc grimaced sourly. "Yes, when it works."

"Do you suppose the enemy knows our troops panicked?"

"When the leading tanks got knocked off like ducks in a shooting gallery, there was too much smoke for anyone to see what was happening. But you can bet spies got the facts to the Marxists."

Chapter 41

General Kerwin's staff pretended to be as ignorant as the General pretended to be. Former Captain Isaiah Winthrop's hints, however, had made a deep impression, and as a result, the Defense Language Institute had sent to the Simianoid Division staff every student proficient in Slivovitz and kindred languages.

The Consortium cooperated as Isaiah Winthrop had predicted. Things were working out as though Doc Brandon were on the job. Thus the 47th Slivovitz Guest Division and Kerwin's Simianoid Division would set out from the Gulf Coast to open country, well north of the swamps and bayous. This was to be a comradeship march which would terminate with a classical California-Mexican barbecue, after which the Simianoids would depart for war games in the vast Mojave Desert and the 47th Slivovitz would move onward, in personnel carriers, to parade in Megapolis Alpha.

A division of pacifist volunteers would be the guard of honor to parade in the capital with the Marxist troops.

Relieved of duty, Isaiah became quartermaster—purchasing agent—of the Brandon Foundation, in behalf of the Comradeship Barbecue Authority. He chartered refrigerated trucks to load up with quarters of prime beef. Speedboats raced across the water to Jamaica, Guyana, and other spots where rum worthy of the occasion was available.

"Rum," Isaiah explained to the General, his staff, and to the press, "is an international drink. The former enslaved colonies of imperialistic empires, now independent nations, will supply it, and there are great rums produced in South American republics and in the Philippines and in Indonesia. But Bourbon, rye, Scotch, Cognac, and all the others, each is nationalistic in its associations. This we are avoiding in offering rum."

The Parliament accorded Isaiah Winthrop a vote of thanks for such zealous attention to international amity.

The California-Mexican Barbecue was unrelated to the well-known American barbecue of sandwich fame; it antedated the imperialism which had robbed Mexico of Texas, Arizona, New Mexico, California, and other territories. That a Black scholar had taken charge was an additional point.

As warmonger and mass butcher, Kerwin got no credit. The General did not complain of discrimination. It was Brandon Foundation's job, not the Army's.

The Comradeship March was routine once the troops emerged from the land of mosquitoes, water moccasins, and bottomless mud. Pitching camp, cleaning up, resting—those had top priority. The comrade-troops had to be groomed to the ultimate smartness. War games, field duty, had introduced sloppiness, slackness: And so there would be tightening up, parades, and exhibition drills, with each unit composed of Simianoid and Slivovitz troops alternating in the ranks, shoulder to shoulder, one of the home team, one of the visiting team.

That pleased the Parliamentary Board of Visitors. Straight-faced, General Kerwin said, "We've done our best to avoid competition in our competitive drills. No matter which unit wins, there is no discrimination. But we have failed in one respect."

The Bulldog General was turning on the charm, which he could do, and that touch of humility. He was sure by now that he would not get a decoration, but he saw a prospect of fun.

"General, in what respect have you failed?"

"Our officers and noncoms should give the commands in Esperanto or other international language."

* * *

The battery of linguists from the Army school, combined with the excellent disciplines and military sense of the divisions, kept from being the nightmare foulup that was reasonably anticipated. But it took time and sweat.

The time, however, gave Isaiah's plan its chance to grow into shape.

Civilian labor from farms and rural villages leveled off a parade ground and dug the barbecue pits, each of which was to be lined with smooth stones from creek bottoms, and large enough for several beefs. After forty-eight hours of wood firing had heated the stones, freshly cut saplings and alfalfa would be placed to separate beef from hot stones and one quarter of meat from another, layer upon layer. The entirety, finally, was to be capped with alfalfa, and a foot or two of topsoil after a twenty-four-hour barbecuing.

Until the day before firing the pits, Simianoid noncoms and officers were giving commands in Slivovitz, and their Slivovitz opposite numbers gave commands in English.

"Bugger me blind," Kerwin said, to Brigadier General Appleby, his second in command. "This is not the screwup I expected. They'll have it pretty well coordinated in a couple more days."

Appleby shrugged. "It's this way, Denny. Half an outfit understands the commands, whichever the language, and these Marxist bastards are good soldiers. Only stupid thing about them is their political religion."

"Our ex-Captain Winthrop understands Simianoids. I begin to suspect I was far from wrong in going with him as I did."

"That colored gentleman understands a God damn sight more than a lot of people suspect. I still wonder why he made such a point of our heading for the Mohave and immediately taking off for China."

General Kerwin chuckled. "Just keep wondering patiently."

When the pits were hot and the beef packed according to tradition, the long day of waiting was devoted to the Comradeship Chili Tournament: Row after row of kettles hung over savory fires, incense-smoky scented. Competitors had come from as far as western Texas and from all other areas with pretension to chili con carne expertise. And there were kettles of pinto beans from the pinto bean capital of the world, Portales, New Mexico.

The Board of Visitors and a Parliamentary Committee realized the tremendous propaganda value of unlimited beef: a great boost for American-style democracy, to demonstrate the wonders Marxism can achieve when properly expounded. They speculated, discreetly, as to the number of Slivovitz Division men who would defect.

Trucks rolled down the troop streets of the vast encampment and unloaded kegs of chilled beer. Other trucks brought barrel after barrel of rum, sufficient to provide well over a liter for each soldier.

The Board of Visitors and the Parliamentary Committee did not distinguish between a barrel of beer and a barrel of rum. The latter was kept in Simianoid custody, closely supervised, and properly diluted with water, the classical grog. General Kerwin had published a division order to such effect.

While waiting for the Comradeship feast, and when not busy with linguistics and drill, the visiting troops toured farm villages and saw farmhouses; they learned of the gracious American way of life. The inhabitants of this region, like all other rural and in most industrial areas of the country, were workaholics, Simianoid, Coolies, and a great many Blacks who loathed the Megapoli. These backward areas of so-called slave labor which paid for the gracious life of the Megapoli were inhabited by crusty folk who had for years heard of Slivovitzland and of the blessings of the Marxist gospel.

Droves of military police escorted guests on the sightseeing tours and to small-town dances and other doings. This had been going on from the first day of Comradeship Camp.

The military police, aided by interpreters, expressed it in words to this effect: "These farmers are good-hearted, old-fashioned crackpots, crabby and irritable. We are not here to protect you, we are with you to make sure you do not accidentally break their backwoods tabus."

This was also expressed in Slivovitz language leaflets.

There was an infiltration of linguists who passed as Simianoids and who feigned total ignorance of the language of the visitors.

Properly diluted grog, served at reveille, loosened visitor tongues. There was happy anticipation of what would happen when the visitors paraded in Megapolis Alpha and marched on the Parliamentary Hall and the Prime Minister's palace to add another People's Republic to the Marxist Federation.

Grog, hospitality, splendid prospects, combined to foster high spirits: There were haystack dates with farm or village girls, and there were those who propositioned and tactlessly fondled local women who were not pleased by their sudden popularity. Meanwhile, the Simianoid Military Police were relentlessly running big-town hustlers off and away from the guest area.

By the termination of the Chili Tournament, town folk and rural folk were increasingly irritated. Not because of mass seductions and mass propositioning which got no results, but rather because the visiting division was becoming proprietary and condescending in a crude and flat-footed way which quickly wore thin.

Once General Kerwin, his staff, the Board of Visitors, and the Parliamentary Committee had sounded off on international comradeship, they bailed out, each having had a bowl of chili con carne and a token slice of barbecue on a sourdough bun.

Refreshment dispensers added less and less water when they ladled grog into troop mess-kit cups. And the beer barrels now offered porter and full-bodied ale for Men of Iron, instead of the bland swill which North America, a land of beer haters, guzzled avidly. And as grog was served, the dispensers patted the rum barrels, and winked, and practically skipped the water.

The stuff from the West Indies and the Demerara River Valley was overproof: specifically, 151-proof and, when slightly diluted, so smooth that a drinker with a few shots of normal grog or beer in him could scarcely suspect that he was guzzling straight rum.

After the barbecue there were diverse reports, many of

them conflicting, although on a few matters no one argued. Simianoids, military or civilian, drank the stuff straight and showed no greater effect than did Doc Brandon or Mona. One fact, however, was not known or publicized: that Brandon, like the Simianoids, had an unusual metabolism whereby alcohol was burned as rapidly as it was ingested: a fine, a happy glow and little if any other effect.

The visitors were laughing, good-humored, snotty, arrogant good fellows, stumbling and unsteady, careless. Who clobbered whom and why was uncertain: Maybe someone had felt up the wrong girl, or a linguist, somewhat high, overheard too much about the proposed take-over of Megapolis Alpha and went patriotic. It could have been a blend and cumulative resentment at seeing too many flowers of American Womanhood with grass stains on their rumps. Or it could have been all these and other things.

Attempts to quell what was a four–five–six man affray was like using rocket fuel as fire extinguisher fluid. It is likely that the first shot fired was accidental, a fumble, or perhaps someone had cut loose in boyish glee. Someone did sound *call to arms*, possibly for fun.

The Simianoid soldiers fought with fists, boots, cordwood, and being steady and certain, had no urge to go for long gun or handgun. A barrel of rum, two thirds empty, dribbled enough of its highly combustible contents to the hot rocks of a barbecue pit to start a blue streak of fire, a fuse racing back to the source.

The combination of empty space and alcoholic fumes made an effective bomb. Blasted apart, the keg scattered blazing staves and a flow of blue-flaming rum. Tents caught fire.

The country folk, alarmed, irritated, and most of them owning shotguns, rifles, handguns, decided that if the Slivovitz wanted war, come and get it. Others set to work with cordwood, or with a rifle snatched from a stumbling-drunk visitor.

There were far fewer deaths than the face of things would indicate. The visitors, their feet and their reflexes as muddled as their tongues and their wits, scattered like quail although not as rapidly or in lines either as straight or as effective. Those who fell were unharmed. Those who wove and pitched about were slugged, kicked, beaten.

Many reached neighboring settlements. Garbled telephone talk alerted farmers who did what they considered their duty: Some fired at will; others enjoying the moonlight, grabbed pick-axe handles, chunks of two-by-fours, pitchforks, and set out.

Meanwhile, the camp city was well ablaze. Breeze and straight rum from other blazing barrels kept things going.

The sober Simianoids enjoyed themselves.

Fire call went unheeded.

Call to arms incited many to pursuit of the scattering comrades.

Mess call? Shove it, we've eaten.

Pay call did it.

Order was restored, but only after the 47th Slivovitz Division ceased to exist as an organization. The exploding of small-arms cartridges had contributed to the flight. While the media, including audiovideo operators, were recording the riot, the fire, and panic flight, hospital corpsmen were looking for casualties. Their tasks were light. The ambulant majority of Marxists was far too widely scattered; drunk, unarmed, they were easy game for kilometers around—as far as, eventually, two hundred kilometers from Megapolis Alpha. Country jails were packed to overflowing by visitors happy to find refuge while sobering up. Others were harbored by rural folk far from the riot. These fugitives were delighted to defect and find new homes in a land where, at a single barbecue, they had eaten more meat than in all their previous years.

The Consortium had no difficulty in persuading Parliament to get the Simianoid Division out of North America and claim that it had deserted, en masse, to the Marxist Federation's most bitter enemy, the People's Republic of China.

Chapter 42

The day after a division of Marxist Federation troops ceased to exist as a military organization, the North American war games west of Kashgar terminated. The troops quit their weaponry and joined Chinese labor battalions in digging tank traps, emplacing and camouflaging rocket launchers, antiaircraft guns, and heavy artillery.

Amazons, instead of getting rump callouses from sitting at desks, got blisters on their hands and their feet. Shoveling, picking, passing cases of explosives to troops working with air hammer and star drill gave new meaning to the military term "fatigue detail." Amazonism took a power dive in popularity.

There was happiness among the Chinese, accustomed for five thousand years to manual labor, and not even feeling that such was a crime against nature. This great joy came from watching the screens which presented movies of war games, every evening, with a critique. Now they cackled gleefully as they watched rioting by light of a blazing tent city and heard the idiotic *pop-pop-popping* of cartridges as the blaze spread to another tent. Seasoned combat soldiers set off hundreds of strings of firecrackers to celebrate the traditional enemy's ghastly loss of face; and the troops of the Imperialistic Foreign Devils gained great merit.

A Chinese scholar remarked, "The clowns west of the Tian Shan have lost prestige twice in a row."

There were rumors of another division en route for

China. Far to the north, the Dzungarian Gate was being covered by artillery and tank traps were dug by night. That beautiful idealist, the Three Dee star who had seduced a gullible captain and had got training and plans data phony as a three-*pazor* bill, had done little to help the Marxists she adored.

Mona said, "Doc, you stuck around too long! That caper Isaiah pulled means war."

"You stuck around too long. I told you to haul out while you could. Deserters in time of war face a firing squad, provided it's far enough away for the sob sisters not to hear of it."

"You nasty old bastard! Don't look so constipated, and don't tell me that war is man's work. It used to be, sure, but on that ridge, remember? A frail woman couldn't run: Too many faster men were blocking the way. And if you're going to lead garbage like that, it is something I have to see!"

Doc shrugged. "There is General Gouraud's way, which worked. And then there's the dangerous way, the gamble that may work."

Then came a broadcast in Chinese and English. The speaker deplored the cruel and treacherous murder of hundreds of guests as they slept in their camp, trusting their Simianoid comrades.

Doc, engaged in his talk with Mona, had missed the station identification. He yawned and said, "Typical Slivovitz crap! But they have a real turncoat: pure-strain Americanese speech!"

A bystander cut in. "Soldier, you're out a foot! That is a member of Parliament and he's giving you the straight of things, maybe for the first time in your life."

Doc knew better than to argue. The punk was probably right. The patriotic idealists of the nation would be on the job, and Tamara Sinclair undoubtedly was at it, full bore.

About twenty-three hours, Kashgar time, bomb alert sounded. There were no absentees. Amazons and their lovers were too crippled by the fatigue details for amorous games away from quarters. Lights blazed over the entire cantonment. The public address system blared the news:

". . . is now eleven hours twenty-one minutes Eastern

Standard Time. The North American Parliament was in session until a nuclear bomb at four thousand meters centered on the Hall of Parliament and destroyed most of the nation's capital. Megapolis Beta and Megapolis Gamma are smoking ruins.

"Alexander Heflin, Chairman of the Consortium of Advisors to the Parliament, has declared martial law. The Consortium has declared a provisional dictatorship until the surviving electorate can elect successors to the late Parliament. Repeat, the Parliament was in session and as far as known, only a few absentees survived. The Parliament had convened to condemn and disavow the treacherous assassination of the Forty-seventh Slivovitz Division as it slept in a guest camp. The Dictator is said to be negotiating with the Marxist Federation, after requesting a truce.

"Simianoid regiments patrol the destroyed Megapoli, Alpha, Beta, Gamma. Looters and disorderly persons will be shot without challenge. There will be no arrests as jail facilities are far from adequate for the floating criminal population out on parole.

"There will be universal conscription of all able-bodied males except industrial and agricultural workers, transportation, and distribution employees.

"To restate it—only Coolies and Simianoids not now in the armed forces are exempt. Students and all adults in the four-hour-week work therapy regime will be impressed into service.

"While awaiting induction and training, they will be put to work clearing away wreckage. To restate things: The intellectual, the decorative, the academic, and the leisure class will work under military supervision.

"In bombing the Megapoli and the former Parliamentary Hall, the enemy destroyed his only friend in North America. Surviving intellectuals and academic Marxist Cultists are said to be having second thoughts."

An hour later there was another announcement. All were awake to hear it.

"Alexander Heflin, Imperator of North America, is conferring with selected Moslem governments. He undertakes to supply cooperating powers from our industrial and agricultural resources, provided that they undertake an all-out

Holy War, a *jihad* against the Marxist Federation. During the Imperator's absence, a deputy will administer North American affairs.

"You are not commanded to sleep, but sleep is recommended."

Before lights out sounded, Mona asked Doc, "If I quit the Amazons and join your outfit, do I get shot for desertion?"

"The Regulars will be too busy shooting rookies sneaking from the firing line. I'll put in for a company clerk. I forgot to tell you, I'm promoted to captain. Had the rating all the while, on paper, but this is sure-enough."

Reveille sounded at four in the morning. There had been little sleep, and no one was drowsy. Mess call, thirty minutes later. Those who wondered whether the bouquet of frying ham was hallucination had scarely begun speculating when the first out of the chow line told of a miracle of procurement: eggs, not dehydrated or the Chinese hundred-year-old "preserved" kind, but the sort which Americans associate with ham. And there were pancakes. The cook's crew, agleam with sweat, turned cakes and flipped eggs.

"Took a bombing to do it!" one said, and another quipped, "If they'd bombed Megapolis Delta, we'd've got crêpes suzette."

The troops ranged from sullen darkness to flaming exaltation. The high peaked as the sun came up out of China to brighten westernmost Sinkiang.

And before the first to call for seconds learned that they would have dehydrated egg-scramble, the loudspeakers blared news:

"The North American Imperium's Mediterranean Submarine Strategic Ballistic Nuclear Fleet bombed Slivovitzgrad. Twelve missiles simultaneously launched and detonated at three thousand meters obliterated the city. According to satellite observation, there are no ruins. There is only a hole in the ground. Wood was consumed. Concrete was fused. Metal evaporated. We spared the enemy capital so that a government would survive to answer demand for surrender.

"Out of humanitarian considerations, the Imperium served notice that the next city to be vaporized has been selected but would not be named: This is to prevent panic and injuries caused by attempted evacuation.

"You will now hear Alexander Heflin, the Imperator:

"Marxist Federation," Alexander announced, "is not dealing with the North American Parliamentary Republic whose Socialistic and Democratic Government was bombed out of existence. The new regime is a friend of the Moslem world and sustains the Chinese people. Our subsequent bombings will spare the many Marxist Federated Republics whose right to secede from the most hated and feared regime in recorded history has been repeatedly denied by armed force.

"While we are waiting to evaporate our next target, prudent members of the Marxist Federation will have time to act as seems best for their interests."

The troops forgot their ham and eggs.

Doc said to Mona, "I am more than a hundred and eighty-six years old, but this is the first time I have heard our Government talk unpleasantly to the enemy and not, repeat, not promise to lose a war."

What brightened Doc's morning was that the enemy did not have sufficient navy and airborne divisions to invade North America. Having been invited by the Government to take over, they had not prepared for opposition by a subversive Capitalistic Underground.

Chapter 43

After the first day's work with pick axe, crowbar, with sledge and star drill to sink holes which would be charged with explosive, Captain Avery Jarvis Brandon's company of conscientious objectors and other assorted civilians— among whom lurked a good lieutenant and a half dozen potential soldiers who had only to learn a few answers— was weary. No one griped because the carpet of needles from the tall conifers was too thin to pad the mountain-side's rocks.

Blankets seemed thin as cigarette papers. Bivouac two thousand meters above oasis level chilled them to the bone: and no fire, no smoking, no lights at night. If someone else is keeping your favorite Amazon warm, it means that perhaps it's not your turn with her, or maybe that she's turned her affections elsewhere. Or, *Don't you know there's a war?"* Or monopolizing goodies is antisocial.

In addition to Mona, who was company clerk and demonstrated that Doc Brandon's rank gave him exclusive rights, there were five other Amazons who had nothing and nowhere to write: Hence they had herded the fifty pint-size donkeys which had carried implements, canned rations, and endless cases of explosives which forced rock apart at fissures instead of fragmenting and scattering the pieces. Doc's task was to improve the road five hundred meters below, in the narrow pass through which the Old Silk Road snaked its way.

As a security measure, the Uighur sheepherder and his wife who had guided the company from the oasis to the slopes above the Taoist monastery and into the winding trail had been detained. The thrill, the high which had stimulated the troops had shaken down to aches, blisters, sprains from working with crowbars to pry boulders from their beds. Others they pulled with winch and cable to the rim of the narrow cleft in the Tien Shan range.

As misery eased off and the company became accustomed to all but the boredom of sweating from dawn to dusk, skepticism took command. Generations of Tee-Vee had made entertainment a vital need. At coffee breaks this addiction found expression.

"Whoever said this is war? . . . Captain Brandon, we heard you been in a dozen wars. So far, nobody's been killed here . . ."

"I have," he answered blandly. "But this is what most war is like. Long spells of tiredness, dirt, sweat. Once in a while flare-ups of combat."

"Sir, may I ask a question?"

"This is your coffee break. Sound off."

"Someone said you could have been a colonel only you turned it down."

Several troops approached. The questioner apparently had been primed. Doc nodded and answered, "I told the Commanding General that a captain has a better chance of getting acquainted with a company than a colonel has with a regiment."

"Sir, you ever been a colonel?"

"I have."

"How long before you got to that rank?"

Convinced that this was leading up to something, Doc strung along with it. "Do any of you feel that you're not advancing rapidly enough?"

"No, sir, it's not that. We've been wondering about this man's army. None of it makes any sense."

Doc chuckled. "That's what soldiers have been saying ever since Julius Caesar's day, and earlier."

"Who was that fellow?"

"Evidently your social studies teacher thought history was irrelevant! What's one of the million things that make no sense?"

"Well, they say you got jumped from second looey to colonel in one day. We ain't seen no one get a promotion."

"You've not been in the right place, that's all. It's simple. Colonel, lieutenant colonel, three majors, and a dozen or so captains were killed off and we'd already run out of first lieutenants. It was a busy day. I took command until we ran out of enemies, which was not long." He sighed, shook his head. "And I never felt one bit guilty. I never liked killing people, but the only way I could protest or demonstrate was to knock those bastards off before they did as much to me."

He nodded, and they knew that the coffee break was over.

Doc resumed his study of the map. He taped several of the bungalow-size boulders poised on the rim. He backed off, eyed the growing collection, then stepped to the rim. With an optical range finder, he got the distance to the opposite rim and the distance to the road shoulder. His map proved to be more accurate than he had anticipated.

That night, when he completed his round of inspecting the sentries, Mona was in his tent.

"Fraternizing at coffee breaks?"

"Yes. My notion is that they are edging up to how easy it is to face the risks of war when you're immortal. If everyone had a bulletproof job behind the lines, the way colonels and generals are supposed to have it, there'd not be so many conscientious objectors."

"Mmmmm . . . didn't Shakespeare say *'conscience doth make cowards of us all'?*"

"Something like that, and my footnote is, *merde, alors!* The Bard had it ass-backwards. *Fear makes people conscientious.* Fear of here and of hereafter. Look at the Moslems. If you're killed in a Holy War against the infidel, you go straight to Paradise, so they don't have conscientious objectors.

"Military service was a supreme honor. No Christian or Jew was allowed to serve; only Moslems were eligible for service in the army of Suleiman the Magnificent. And when Suleiman broke wind, Christian Europe defecated."

"Doc, you're history on the hoof! How long do we stay here?"

"The enemy has not told me."

"You think Alexander can make it?"

"With enough Simianoids and Coolies, yes. He's probably ferrying Simianoids from Mars to fill in for those who are getting into the Army."

The buzzer of Doc's scrambler radio awakened him a few evenings after Mona's report on Amazon morale. He listened, he answered; over and out and then called back. Kashgar answered, confirming that Kashgar had just called him.

Doc caught Mona by the shoulder. "Get the pine needles out of your hair! Reveille is now. Make the rounds of the Amazon tents. Lots more tactful, a lady breaking into whatever might be going on."

"This is it?"

"Do you hear it?"

"Hear what?"

"Far-off armor. Very far off."

She listened a moment, then dressed in blackout.

Soundless reveille.

Doc fingered a switch. There was a deep rumbling, earth quiver, a louder mumble, mutter, grumbling. Mona was out of the tent, getting a few odds and ends into shape.

"That was the strangest explosion."

"We used a heave-explosive, pushing the rock piles and a lot of the cliff into the ravine. With their tank noises, they'd not hear it."

Doc picked his way among the conifers, dodging troops who stumbled and fumbled in darkness. They were packing and loading all that was to be cleaned up from the site of the labor camp. This was a matter of discipline.

Cold as a whore's heart . . . cold as a witch's teat . . . Rock dust rose from the road five hundred meters below. No fires. No lights. No smokes. Vacuum jugs furnished coffee.

Cursing the budget cutbacks which kept him and his men from having starlight scopes, Doc grabbed his cup and raced to the rim. The mutter and mumble and clank of armor and engines became louder. No headlights thus far, but grinding, crunching, clanking.

Doc called Kashgar: "They're at the block, running blacked out. They're on it!"

Doc got away from the rim. "Run for cover!"

Forty-two centimeter guns had been trained on the pass; these and 210-millimeter howitzers searched the ravine at two hundred meter intervals. Explosive shells junked the stalled tanks. Flame and smoke gushed up and over the rim. Shells which struck the walls tore great chunks from the cliff.

When Doc ventured back to the rim, he saw that the pass was blocked by the avalanche his company had prepared, and that west of it a second roadblock had been created by invading tanks, now a clutter of flaming junk as far west as he could see.

When he turned to radio Kashgar, he found that a stray rock had totaled his gear. Kashgar would fire until ammunition ran out, or aerial observation reported the pass full to the brim.

"Mission accomplished! Get out before their air spots us!"

He had never seen such zealous response to a command.

Chapter 44

Whether the invaders had cleared the pass or were crawling over debris which blocked it was irrelevant: Battle was developing in the air and at oasis level. The Uighur sheepherder said to Doc, "There is a harder trail but less chance of planes seeing us. Don't want to have bombing and machine-gunners hitting things like the Taoist monastery, the one we passed going up."

A point walked ahead of the company. On each flank was a patrol. Although actual attack was a remote possibility, the patrols, one at a level lower than the trail and the other higher, could observe what the main body could not.

Enemy and friendly planes, higher than the ever vigilant vultures, maneuvered to shoot each other down. The far-off chatter of machine guns was often followed by black smoke, a blob of flame, a comet shooting earthward. Rocket launchers and self-propelled guns blasted tanks and scattered blazing junk all over the rocky expanse of desert between mountains and the distant oasis. The action was glimpsed when there was a line of sight where forest thinned and kept the column aware of what was happening, yet it was quite too remote.

The regulation hourly rest period combined coffee break and discussion of things the patrols reported.

There was the standard bitching: ". . . wouldn't be so God damn dull if you could see more of what's happening . . . those poor bastards out on both flanks! Who's going to attack us from the upgrade side? . . . Captain isn't really a bastard, it is the God damned dumb army . . ."

Lieutenant Halley cut Doc from his approach to the group.

"Captain Brandon, I'd like your opinion. What can you do with these . . . ah . . ."

Doc filled the pause. "Pete, I have been wondering what *we*, you and I, can do about whatever needs doing."

The wiry young lieutenant grimaced. "Sir, correction accepted, but digesting it is my personal job. You are responsible for whatever I do right or screw up."

"Something been eating at you?"

"Plenty, sir. These . . . ah . . . um . . ."

Doc chuckled. "*Or words to that effect, to wit.* But the word we use is *men* or *soldiers*. They might live up to either: two words for the same idea. Any insubordination?"

"No, sir."

"Any so-called silent contempt?"

"Sir, I understood that Parliament abolished that concept. And gestures don't qualify. There have to be spoken words."

"Parliament was abolished by the enemy. Is there any way I can help you?"

They eyed each other, the lean and intense young man, hunched forward, and the Captain whose relaxed posture and expression were convincing because they had to be.

"Captain, anything you say, I'll try to digest it, but in hot weather, a man has to do his own sweating. It is these holy, superior uh . . . ah . . . *men* who would never kill another human being because human life is alleged to be sacred. Not mentioning names, they say that the man who closed the switch and touched off the roadblock and got the artillery firing is a mass murderer."

Doc grinned amiably. "Glad to hear it. I've been blaming General Farnsworth. He'll be happy to know he's not guilty. They tell me that generals are butchers and warmongers. God damn it, you ought to know that by now."

Lieutenant Pete Halley almost laughed. "I've been wondering what would happen if we tangled with *fighting* men. The enemy must have patrols to warn him if some of our troops come up from Kashgar to catch them from the flank."

The young officer stopped short. Although this was not a challenge, it was the Captain's move.

"There are three things which you, I, and the others can do."

Pete frowned. "Three choices, sir?"

"First, trample everyone who blocks your escape route. Second, stand and face it. Third, attack. You alone might kill six of them. And the laugh would be on them. All six could not do more than finish one you. Don't ask what I would do."

"No problem, sir. I'll be watching."

"Quite right, Pete. Everyone will be watching me. And you."

*   *   *

Sound and smell made it plain that there were many casualties on each side. Another way of expressing it was that no one advanced because neither gave the other sufficient ground room. And thus far neither had found a way to catch the other from the flank.

Being company clerk, Mona slept with no one but the Captain.

"Doc," she wondered, after commenting on how luxurious pine or spruce branches were, compared to a thin blanket spread over raw rock, "were you really a colonel in one of those wars?"

After telling Mona what he had told the troops, he learned that by the time the yarn got to the Amazons, a twelve-year-old drummer boy became colonel because all the officers had been killed off in two hours of fighting.

After admitting that she'd suspected a bit of exaggeration, Mona got back on course: "What would happen if we ran into some of the enemy? Or did you tackle this job as a suicide project?"

"Someone must have told you what I said to Lieutenant Halley."

"Someone did, and your answer was watch and see."

"Just about the size of it, yes."

"You're as insidious as Dr. Fu Manchu!"

"If I only were! Maybe I could see my way about under-standing what I am said to be commanding."

"Doc, you must know: You were a colonel a century and a half ago."

"We had men who didn't fear God or Death, so they had no qualms about the sanctity of human life, no conscience to worry them to the chicken stage! They died like men or lived like soldiers."

Chapter 45

The grumbled remark about the uselessness of scouting on the upgrade flank of the company nagged Doc. He said to the Lieutenant, "Pete, I'm going to worm my way along somewhat higher than the topside patrol. Take command till I come back. Sergeant Gilland is in charge on the downhill flank?"

"Right!"

"Send a runner down to tell him you are in command."

Doc clambered his way up to a rocky knob rimmed with junipers little more than a meter high, a meter and a half at the most. Their gnarled trunks were nearly a meter in diameter, with limbs wind-beaten to slant with the slope, leaving no more clearance than he needed for crawling to the summit. Sweat-soaked, chilled by wind which lanced his jacket, he kept his head below the pungent needles and berries while worming his way until he got his first good look far down and into the rocky bowl whose bottom sloped toward the distant oasis. His line of sight followed the long ridge which reached northward from the Silk Road.

Simianoid and Chinese troops held that ridge. A lower and much shorter ridge faced the troops who commanded the road to Kashgar and the ridge which skirted the snow-capped Tien Shan Range. That road reached Aksu, Kucha, and finally Urumchi in the north.

The two ridges were separated by a rock-strewn plain dotted with acacia scrub, tamarisk, and occasional poplar clumps. The area was dotted with burned-out tanks, combat vehicles, gutted planes. Vultures circled, looking for accessible rations. From Doc's observation post the pattern of wreckage and the shell craters in the well-chewed Silk Road indicated repeated attempts to turn the flank of that rocky ridge. On its back slope were the charred ruins of buildings.

Elbows digging into the carpet of dried needles, Doc braced himself, steadied the binoculars. He was looking at the remains of a field hospital. There were infantry combat vehicles, armored and with sides pierced by gun ports. Stretcher-bearers were coming down the back slope. Some went to the dressing stations not far from the ruins. Others made for the combat vehicles. Because of a shortage of ambulances, troop carriers had been disarmed. Infantry would be going nowhere until the stalemate was broken.

Shifting his line of sight, Doc picked up the Taoist monastery which his company had skirted on the outbound march. In the first courtyard he saw stretcher-bearers coming out of the building. They carried something covered with a sheet. Outside the wall, grave diggers were at work.

Now that he had reconnoitered, Doc realized that he had violated the principles of command. His place was with the main body, where he could immediately respond to messages from scouts or flank patrols. Excuses followed him, drove him down the steepest ways he could risk. Doc's work at the pass had cost the Marxist men from beyond the mountains time which they could never regain.

Well done, Brandon! But as company commander, his place was with his troops. Duty demanded that he get at least one honest fight out of 150 impressionable slobs of a culture rotted flabby. Or, at the least, give fifteen or twenty a chance to do their ragged best.

What nagged him was the certainty that if any survived an encounter, it would be the garbage majority.

Much of what Doc had known without awareness now drove him, bounding, landing, poised, swaying, and leaping again. Despite gravity's speeding him, he was out of breath. The elevation was far too high for such exertion. He clung to a cedar trunk and looked again. Although trees and a ridge blocked his view, and he could no longer see the monastery, there was compensation. He saw now what had not been visible while he was with his company.

He now saw a rutted wagon track, a clearing quite close to the Silk Road, and a glimpse of the ridge which Simi-anoids and Chinese were defending. He jammed his binoc-ulars against the tree, clawed the bark, and steadied him-self. Doc had been wondering why the enemy had not made parachute drops: and now he ceased wondering. They had landed troops in a clearing with scarcely a sprin-kling of scrub. A stand of dense growth screened the clear-ing from observation from the long ridge.

There was a Chinese infantry combat vehicle minus guns: an improvised ambulance, well into the clearing, leaving the wagon track unobstructed. All the invaders need do was to capture additional converted personnel car-riers, man them, and at the right moment, emerge, across the Silk Road, and attack from the back slope of the long ridge.

"Neat work!" Doc admitted to himself. "Drive to the pickup spot, and no opposition. With assault rifles, pour out and make for the crest, enfilade the line, half firing north, the other shooting south."

The ambulance Doc had seen in the monastery court-yard would be seized as it returned to pick up more wounded.

Doc bounded, balanced, leaped again, almost fell but re-covered. He finally lurched across the path of the upgrade patrol. Quite too surprised, they neither challenged nor shot him. The Sergeant had more good intentions than experi-ence.

Doc gasped, "Too God damn busy to eat you out for being caught flatfooted. Get your patrol to the main body. We have a job to tend to."

"Very well, sir." And then, "All right, lard asses! You heard the Captain."

When Doc joined the main body, Lieutenant Halley said, "Sir, I got the God damndest report just now. Hig-gins, you tell the Captain."

Private Higgins said, "Captain, the Sergeant sent me to

tell you he heard a couple of shots. He didn't hear nothing more."

"Where was all this?"

"Quite a piece downgrade from the patrol."

"Can you find your way back?"

"Just head downgrade, sir."

"Tell the Sergeant I said stand fast. Hold it! Did you see or hear anything? How many shots?"

"Two shots, nothing more. Well, yes, I forgot, he sneaked up taking cover and come back blinking like a toad in a hailstorm. He tried writing a message but he was too shaky and he said, aw, shit, go tell the Old Man there's a hundred or two of those fuckers waiting for trouble and they got a Chinese armored troop carrier with no God damn guns, sir."

"Higgins, you tell the Sergeant that the company will be down his way soon as we can make it. Come right back. I need a guide to get us to where the patrol is halted.

"Take cover! Your Sergeant will tell you all that."

When Private Higgins was on his way, Doc sat on a rock, drew a deep breath. "Pete, send a runner to tell our sheepherder guide to get the pack train moving and keep going till they get to Kashgar."

The Lieutenant said, "Sir, how about holding out the animals carrying rations?"

"Our emergency rations will last as long as we will. Get the Amazons together and tell them to follow the pack train. Get out before there is trouble."

Lieutenant Halley frowned. "You mean, pack animals, women, the sheepherder, and his wife are to get going immediately?"

"Make it so."

Halley uncoiled his lean length from the rock on which he was sitting. "I understand your order clearly, sir, but it would help if I knew whether our next move is to rescue the downhill patrol or to attack a company of paratroopers."

Doc got to his feet. "Since none of the enlisted personnel are within hearing distance, I'm telling you again: I won't know till we get there.

"I had a glimpse of that scene myself, the one Higgins told us about. My hunch is that the enemy is planning to attack the ridge from the rear. They've taken one of our ambulances to use as a troop carrier. The two shots Higgins heard probably settled a driver and a hospital corpsman going back for more wounded.

"You asked me about attacking a company of paratroopers?"

"I did, sir."

"I did not get around to telling you that there may be a second company or even a third waiting in the woods. One company could enfilade our line, up on the ridge, but it'd be too close to a suicide mission, Two companies, it would be a better operation.

"A surprise party started with troops riding in ambulances would kick up enough of a diversion to cover the assault troops coming out of cover in the woods."

"Captain, you told me that I'd know what you'd do when I saw you doing it. I pretty nearly know without seeing, but it would help if I knew more of your plan."

"We have three tracer bullets in each magazine. And we have grenades. If we can get those commandeered ambulances set afire, the enemy would be disturbed more than by small-arms fire. From that point on we'll have to improvise. So will the enemy."

Lieutenant Halley considered this amusing. "With his tail all ablaze, we can improvise better."

Chapter 46

As shadows lengthened, the sun coaxed fire from snowcaps and glaciers of the Tien Shan, the Mountains of Heaven, whose nearest pass had been the road to hell for defender and invader alike.

During his reconnaissance, Doc had noted landmarks which he had not mentioned to any of his trusted handful. The lightning-blazed tree which he now saw might not be the one he had observed from the heights. Then he got a glimpse of the monastery, well behind him. Maybe it was the area he sought. Doc had never been so lonesome in all the years of his life. He recalled ancient thoughts, words he had uttered, words others had spoken, things he had read: and out of that devil's dance of thought companions, one persisted, never more than a moment obscured by the many he brushed aside.

"If you pick the wrong lawyer, you get a few years in the pokey and a parole to go out and do it again. The wrong doctor gets you, you'll die and nobody worries too long. Accept the wrong preacher, and relax, it's all guesswork, nobody had ever come back to tell you about Heaven or Hell. But the wrong General: You lose the battle that blows the war and an army of occupation rides a nation."

That for Doc had been gospel for the past century and a half: And now it was becoming personal. "He could have said that about Captains. I begin to get what old Colonel Waldron meant when he said never downgrade the rank of

Captain. No army is a bit better than its company or battery or troop commanders."

A quirk of the breeze brought the smell of raw gasoline: faint, very faint, and if he had been a smoker, he could never have noticed it.

The drumming and the rumble and the thunder, the sound of distant fighters trying again what had failed, and failed. Next time might make it.

"With the package I have, how many chances do we have?" His thought echo was the answer: *"One at the most, and maybe you're screwed before you start."*

Gasoline scent, and a whiff of rank tobacco. This must be the spot. And then Brandon learned that there had been insubordination. A woman was saying, "The pack animals are heading for Kashgar. The Amazons are here, except two—three too pregnant ones."

Mona speaking. She held an assault carbine and wore a shoulder pack that bulged with grenades.

"Sweet Jesus! What's this?"

"Mutiny, sir."

"Flatten out! God damn it, I know you're below the rim, but flatten out."

"You can prefer charges after the show."

Responding to Doc's hand signal, the well-spaced troops bellied down short of the grass fringed rim. As he inched forward, he could see that there was a scattering of trees which offered no cover ahead and below. The birds-eye view had fooled him. He could look into the clearing where, just beyond the wagon track, two ambulances were parked. That tied in with Private Higgins's report rendered in American Militarese: two shots, two men dead, and another ambulance converted back to troop carrier.

"Practically everyone followed you. I mean, Lieutenant Halley had no problem sorting them out after you and your party led off."

"You talked those wenches into their caper?"

"Didn't have to. Curiosity made them follow me."

"Too dumb to know any better. You knew what you were doing."

"Still do. You're worrying because I'm here. That's unmilitary."

"I'd be happier if you were with the pack animals. Better yet, if you'd stayed home."

"And miss our honeymoon at Ahmad's villa? I came to tell you why I quit tracking Oswald."

"The Security men watching Oswald grabbed you. I'd briefed them."

"I was trying to find out if he could still do you any damage. I'd dumped the idea of frying his liver with onions."

"Conscientious objector at last?"

She ignored that quip. "Doc, you are waiting for something. Tell me."

"Lieutenant Halley's been having his wonderings?"

"He didn't put me up to asking you."

"He would not. I'm waiting." Doc gestured. "Something is building up. *They* are waiting. The battle has a voice. The voice is changing."

"You've heard battle before. For me it's like Megapolitan music: all the same, a lot of ear-splitting racket. You're wondering how many will follow you over the ridge."

"I used to, but not now. A few will, and the job takes only one. Those bastards killed a driver and hospital corpsman. Two ambulances now, for their next move. Quit the mind picking. Tell me more about Oswald. While we have time."

She knew he had made up his mind about something, and she was almost sure she knew the pattern: a *banzai* charge, and to hell with everything.

"I quit our happy Island to slice that son of a bitch, just for the fun of doing something to suit my mood. But I met so many brainwashed plastics that Oswald began to look like a little hero—I mean, compared with the standard Megapolitan citizen. I dropped the hate and when Security operators nabbed me, I was glad."

"Glad?"

She nodded. "Sociologists, social sciences, intellectuals, all psychology patter, the clichés, round-the-clock parroting! One world, peace at any price, put up with anything rather than end our civilization. *What civilization?* Our Burmese village and the seven hundred million devils from

Tawadeintha every full moon were never as crude and crazy and phony as what I met in Megapolitan Alpha. Millions of parasites playing games, protesting this and that, and so busy buggering each other they forgot what they were demonstrating about."

Mona grimaced. "If I'd lived half as long as you, I'd lead a *banzai* charge and you'd follow me."

"Honey doll—Madame Broadtail—you've been reading my mind."

"I've always loved pornography."

"Our final honeymoon is just ahead of us, and it won't be in bed. Can't kiss you, here's Lieutenant Halley and he is loaded with fire and fury I have to live up to. While you have a chance, tell those fool Amazons to get the hell out of here. I am pulling a trick, a surprise party. Too many people will get in my way. If every man and woman in our party were an experienced battle soldier, trying to fight it out would be suicide.

"If what I want can be done at all, it won't depend on how many, or even on how good. Nothing but hunch and guesswork can make it work. So get those idiots out of here before it is too late."

Mona got well away and Lieutenant Halley pounced for the spot she vacated.

Doc said, "Pete, Higgins was right about those two shots he heard. They killed driver and corpsman. They have another ambulance. They may be waiting for a third one. The enemy is clobbering the ridge, meaning more wounded will be coming in and another ambulance load will go for the monastery.

"Get the tracer cartridges out of your spare clips and I'll load them into my first business clip."

Halley shook his head. "Captain, I scrounged around and found some silly asshole who had been issued a lot of tracers by mistake." He handed Doc a clip of twenty. "All tracers, and here's another. You think the grass is dry enough to start a good fire?"

"I started with that thought, but smelling gasoline fumes gave me a notion. If tracer bullets can't penetrate the shrouding that protects the gas tank of each ambulance, grenades under it, right on the ground, would do the job for sure. And the fuel would run all over, blazing, till the empty tank explodes."

"Meaning they can't sneak up to the back slope to enfilade the ridge!"

"Right! Hot pants and no girls interested. How's the morale of the outfit?"

The Lieutenant made a wry grimace. "They—some of them—are writing their wills. One asked me if I thought there was time. They are either desperate or going chicken. Skipper, I can't guess how those, uh . . . men are going to show up."

Doc chuckled. "Relax, Pete, relax! It'll only take a couple or three of us to start a fire. And you've got a good Sergeant."

"I briefed him. He's to take command if you and I are disabled. He said he'd give the Corporals their orders, according to rank, to be sure to take care of the Amazons."

"There's been enough drill on that subject."

"Sir, he might not have meant it that way."

"If he's any kind of a soldier, he would have. Pete, I bet the Sergeant will be with us. Did anyone figure out who was going to get those wills to the APO?"

"Sir, they'll either head for the nearest Army Post Office or they'll follow us."

"There is still time to check up on details. Such as, some of the troops ought to have ball cartridge clips. More than so much Chinese New Year effects would not be profitable.

"This battle has a voice. I'll hear it, I'll taste it, if that makes sense. There won't be any signal or command. I'll move when the time comes. There is something I want to tell you."

"I hear you, sir."

"Those conscientious pr—ah—those men, a lot of them—have been gulping the story that I am immortal and don't run any risks. I do not give a good God damn if no one follows me. I have lived so long with death dodgers that I am happy to get off the scene. If you have time, tell them to bail out, follow the animals and the pregnant women before the show starts.

"I've had it. So have you and another ten or so. I am fed up with all this muck about peace and fraternity and equality. Nothing is equal to anything or anyone. While I am waiting for my cue, act according to how things add up."

Doc thrust out his hand. "Whatever you do, it'll be correct." A twisted half smile. "None of my business, but have you made your will?"

"Sir, I spent half my pay on women and liquor and the other half I spent foolishly." He thrust out his hand. "I'll be back."

Doc Brandon hitched over, slid toward Mona. She said, "He'll be back. I heard what you were saying. There's a lot you didn't say."

"Could be."

"You're not peeping over the rim. What you're listening for is more than the signal to start a grass and gas fire. That fire is a lot more than just a blaze." She paused, but not for him to comment. "Before I hush up so you'll hear the voice, I'll tell you this: What you're cooking up is going to keep this from being suicide. Some of us are coming through whatever's ahead. In case I'm not one of them, I'll tell you something now. I always loved our life on the Island. I never knew how good it was till I met the Megapolis.

"It's been good, saving my best years for dessert."

And without moving, Doc withdrew to commune with battle.

Chapter 47

The sinking sun drove the shadow of the enemy-held ridge to the foot of the ridge held by the defenders. Artillery pounded the entire line. The low sun had to be blinding the counterbattery gunners who were shelling the enemy. And then Doc heard the roar and thunder from the west: Hell on tracks was pouring out of the pass which he had blocked, a lifetime ago. A regiment, a brigade of tanks, was followed by infantry combat vehicles.

Not enough antitank, not enough rocket launchers, not enough of anything to check the flood of steel which Doc could not see but which he could judge from its voice. And *they*, the enemy, lurked in the woods with the combat vehicles they had snatched. Unlike Doc's company, they had radio; they must have. And they must have been awaiting orders.

The troops defending the long ridge would be squinting into the sun, their attention focused on the threatened envelopment by armor coming down out of the pass. Doc knew that his time had come: His estimate was justified, and here was his chance, a trick which one man could turn, though a handful to back him up would help.

He could not make himself heard. He tossed a pebble to catch Lieutenant Halley's attention, and he gestured. Then Doc scrambled to the crest. He had a shoulder-slung bag of grenades, and at the ready, an assault rifle. At the rim, he paused.

"Get down, you idiot!" Mona screamed.

Doc got down: down the slope and toward the road, the clearing, the enemy. The trees, wide spaced along the road, offered not enough cover to be worth trying. His hunch had been good. Invading paratroopers were standing, but as though leaning against the incessant blast of battle, the concussion of gunnery, the roar of engines. Their attention was westward, northward, away from the low rim which sheltered Doc's company.

They were waiting for a signal. Had they been alert to anything but what they were awaiting, they would have seen Doc despite the long shadows.

Doc did not look back.

Mona screeched something.

Don't look back. Don't hurry.

Then Mona was beside him.

Looking straight ahead, he said quietly, "Don't gang up. We've got to spread out."

One of the enemy, unkinking his neck, looked earthward.

Doc sprayed that man and others with rifle fire. It spewed pyrotechnics, bullets which burst into colored flame, red, blue, green. Combustion altered their weight and their balance, but despite their corkscrewing and swerving, they indicated the general trajectory and gave useful information as to range, a matter which concerned Doc not at all.

Doc raked the ambulance nearest him, firing low. Bullets whined, screeching as they ricocheted. Mona swept the left of the group. At the chatter of her carbine, he began to heave grenades. The first landed beneath the vehicle and a second followed. A prolonged roar sounded; acoustical capers made the explosions merge. There was a surge of flame, a billow of raw gas fumes, a gusty roar, and the blast of grenades Mona had heaved.

Doc snapped home a fresh clip and fired through a curtain of gasoline flame, the smoke of burning rubber and of blazing grass and scrub.

Mona lurched, stumbled, recovered. From the rear came the rattle and chatter of assault rifles. Both ambulances were burning. The enemy was returning the fire from the rim. Doc flung two grenades and emerged from the smoke.

—

He felt the tug of bullets and then the impact of one. And of a second.

He did not know how many men had followed him but they were spraying the clearing with slugs.

A shell dug deep into the clearing. "Down," Doc croaked, and took a dive himself.

The ground shuddered. Earth and leaves geysered skyward. Screaming shards of metal sliced branches from the trees. He did not feel pain, but he knew he'd been drilled twice though he could still move readily. Nothing mattered anymore, now that that first shell, probably a 180-millimeter, had landed. It had come from the ridge. His fire and his musketry had alerted the defenders. Whatever happened, they would not be taken by surprise.

Doc shoved home another clip. Half blinded by dirt and smoke, he fired low, heard the bullets ricochet, reaching upward. The sound told him what his eyes could not.

He got to his knees, gestured. "Get out—get out—"

Nobody could have understood his words. The approach of a heavier shell spoke for him. Of lower velocity, it was behind the sound wave it set up. A 210-millimeter howitzer, a hundred kilos of metal and explosive looking for a spot to land.

The blast knocked him flat. A second one was on the way. Machine guns from the ridge searched the skimpy woods. The artillery plastered the area, each round twenty meters farther west and twenty farther south, then back finally, repeating the pattern.

On his feet again, Doc wove, swayed. "Get away while they're busy!" He staggered north and east. "Get out of everybody's line of fire!"

Machine guns were feeding tracers into the woods to start a brisk blaze.

A dozen or twenty of the company were clearing the rim which Doc had quit. They were shooting at a forest they could not see for the fire and smoke.

". . . forgot their God damned consciences and they're having fun . . . remember all their manure indoctrination and feel guilty . . . or think it beats tennis . . ." And Doc almost laughed out loud when his next thought assailed him. ". . . so gullible, so impressionable, they'll buy

*anything . . . Even this . . . hypnotized . . . suggested
off their lard bottoms . . ."*

The converted man-slayers' wild volley drew disciplined
answering fire, from behind the curtain of dust and smoke.
And then Doc realized again that he had been hit a couple of times. Clawing grass, he knew he could not get
up.

Halley stumbled out of the smoke. A dozen men followed him. Two were keeping Mona on her feet.

The Lieutenant knelt. "Captain, I lost my God damn
first aid kit!"

"Get out of this mess before the artillery works back this
way. Dump the company clerk! Issue ammunition! Take
command, Pete, those bastards'll come out of the woods!"

Between bullets, blasts, fumes and shouting, Doc blacked
out.

He did not know how long he had been out. The sun was
not entirely below the Tien Shan Range. West of the great
mountains, there would be brilliant light. Sky glow bounced
down into darkening desert.

Doc shivered. He was freezing.

"Doc!" Mona was speaking. "The COs are still working.
They're soldiers, well, quite a few of them."

A volley flashed. Muzzle blast kicked up a long line of
loess dust. A junior-grade forest fire was trying to do something important. Doc caught the odor of roasting flesh. He
tried to get up. Mona caught his shoulder.

"It's too late even if you could move. I noticed it a while
ago. I snitched one of those syrette things. I'll give you a
shot."

"No narcotics on duty. Drinking on duty's different."

She unhooked her canteen. "Nothing but water."

He noticed that someone had fixed him up with a tour-
niquet above the knee and a compress on his head.
"What've you been doing?"

She didn't answer. He took a swig of water, grimaced.
"Brandy is what we need."

There was a new sound which alerted Doc: a tremendous roar and rumble, a strange voice, and from the direction of Kashgar. This did not make sense.

The outfit he'd privately tagged as the bug-out company formed about the skipper. "Get out of here, there is something on the way coming from the west! And from Kashgar."

"We saw it." The Lieutenant speaking. "You put me in command. We're getting you and the others back up there behind the rim."

"Something's happening. Get the clerk out of here. I'm staying." He gestured. Dark-red afterglow colored the east. Five long dark shapes, longer and larger than any aircraft anyone except Doc had ever seen.

Lieutenant Halley blinked, licked his dusty lips. "What do you make of that? You can't stay! There's all hell coming out of the west."

"If there's a man in the outfit with a snort of liquor, I'll drink half and not report him for drinking the rest of it on duty. Those up there? I saw one like it. In Gook Town, on Mars. Last time I was out there. A hundred thousand years ago, it was modern. For us, it's the newest thing I've ever seen."

Mona tried to sit up but could not make it until Private Higgins gave her a lift and a supporting arm. "Captain, you done seen them things before?"

"One, yes. But never in flight. A Gook lady said it'd fly if a pilot knew how to handle it."

Halley cut in: "Captain, what're they going to do? Only five of them and the road is bumper to bumper with tanks and combat vehicles. I'm betting infantry is hoofing after them to capture Kashgar."

"Sir, they ain't taken Kashgar yet and I bet the scum won't."

"Higgins," the skipper said, "a hundred *pazors* say you are right."

"Christ a-mighty, they're fixing to land."

Retractable wings edged out as retrojets spewing flame slackened the ships' velocity . . . And then Doc's unspoken question was answered. They had no landing gear exposed.

From what would have been the keel of a vessel designed for water, columns of violet flame reached earthward. As each ship's velocity decreased, stern jets fired up, impelling the strange cruiser to skim fifty–sixty meters above the Silk Road, supported by a hundred or more jets.

"If they shoveled on enough power," the Lieutenant shouted above the roaring, "she'd jump straight up like a helicopter."

Doc croaked loudly enough to make himself heard. "Look what's been coming toward us while we were gaping."

The brigade of tanks was nearing the ridge. The artillery did not respond, nor were rockets launched. The newcomers now skimmed a scant fifty meters above the road, quite too low for the tank guns to attack. Behind the quintet, the road was glowing. Fumes boiled up and blazed: pavement afire, rock melting from the jet blasts which sustained the cruiser.

Altitude jets made the cruisers advance in sinusoidal curves, and made them spiral, flame spraying the gun ports of the tanks. Their weaving was to evade the marksmanship of distant artillery which might score a hit, despite targets' virtually skimming the road.

Tanks veered crazily into the rocky bowl and stalled, burning out. Others exploded, blown apart by their cargo of shells. Infantry vehicles were enveloped in flame.

Like a baleful comet, the alien flotilla whisked over the distant pass. Flame rose behind them from the summit. They incinerated everything which moved or failed to move. Presently, having completed their long sweep, they returned, circled the enemy-held western ridge, mopping up whoever, whatever had survived the first traverse.

Up a loop, a pinwheel, and the flotilla went north and east.

Along the long ridge, artillery roared a salute to the flying tanks from Mars. And as these swept out of sight, ambulances came from the ridge to pick up survivors of the unscheduled attack on the invading paratroopers.

Tank lumbered from the ridge to probe the devastated woods. Parachute flares supplied light for the mop up.

Neither Doc nor any of the others protested when hospital corpsmen and women gave each a shot to ease the miseries of the bumpy trail to the monastery.

Chapter 48

After destroying the column of tanks which was entering the Dzungarian Gate, just beyond Urumchi, Rod Garvin and his squadron soared eastward into Kansu Province where Alexander Heflin awaited him. From his early years of air freighting, Garvin was accustomed to the *yamen* of a provincial governor, or the family dwelling of an important official. He found Heflin in the not so miniature walled village "inherited" from a landlord deceased nearly a century and a half previously. And now, after he knew not how many hours of coma, Garvin sat with Heflin in the Great Book Room of that labyrinth of halls, courtyards, apartments, each the home of one of the four or five generations who lived with the head of a family. There were also quarters for the household staff. All in all, the complex was living, lounging, and working space for several hundred persons.

Leaving the management of the newly founded Imperium of North America to the old Consortium and its Vice-Chairman, Alexander Heflin had come to deal with China and the Moslem world. Much of the last named had risen in hatred of Marxism's heartland and joined the ring of satellite republics in exterminating the enemy.

The vengeance-bent were too numerous to leave room for allies.

Garvin leaned back in a *tsui wang .i*, the "drunken Lord's chair," very much like the *chaise longue* of the Occident. He looked up at red lacquered columns, at the tall screen which made a background for Heflin's massive official chair, beside which was a side table, ends curving upward for the study of a scroll or scroll painting. Like the one beside the drunken lord, it was of dark and heavy *tzu t'an* wood. A tall cupboard harbored as many bottles and bar accessories as it did books.

"With a temporary spot like this, you'd be crazy ever going home!" Garvin hitched himself up and reached for his Islay and soda. "Still don't know whether to take a nip or a yawn. How long have I been sleeping?"

"Sleep, hell! It was catatonia. Not counting sitting up for a bowl of soup and a tot of grog once in a while, I'd say about two days."

"How's Doc Brandon doing? Will he pull through? Either I was all a muddle or the report was."

"Could've been both. Only difference is, you usually are not muddled and the media always are. By the time you swept the Silk Road, Doc's caper had saved the people on the ridge from getting massacred." He glanced at his watch. "News ought to be on any minute."

"Alex, for Christ's sake skip the media crap."

The Imperator chuckled. "To screw things up is human. To give the news a Marxist slant . . . no, not a capital offense, but damn few will risk it a second time."

"Even so, stick to basics. I'm still punchy."

"Fair enough. We, the Mediterranean Submarine Command, dropped every warhead that could take off at once. They were perfectly timed, like the classic shrapnel demonstration trick at proving grounds. No wreckage. What did not burn melted or evaporated. All you could see was where something used to be. I got that straight from a satellite picture."

"Sort of overkill?"

Alexander shook his head. "Scattering the warhead among half a dozen spots would not have had the same effect. There was a hole with fused edges. Glazed earth. Right in the heartland. Not one of the surrounding satellite republics were touched." He paused, leaned forward. "Wreckage they could have taken, they're used to that. Annihilation shook them. So the satellites seceded. They always had the right, but trying to exercise it was suicide. Now they were hustling to prove that they were independent, that they had not had a thing to do with the bombings of our Megapoli, from Alpha through Gamma.

"And to prove their point, they're invading the heartland, and *there* old political grudges are settled by assassination."

Garvin chuckled. "Funny thing, the enemy that blasted Megapolis Alpha killed the Parliament that for half a century had about made North America a Marxist province."

Alexander wagged his head. "Naturally. They expected to take over, and the first ones to exterminate would be the idealists, the dreamers, the emotional idiots who might make trouble for the new regime. The realistic, materialistic son of a bitch is practical; you can depend upon him to watch and protect his own interests. The idealist is fluttery, fuzzy witted, dangerous. Suggestible to the verge of insanity."

"Now the Moslem world is waiting for its whack at power?"

"A lot of people wish there had been lots more waiting. The Moslems have cleaned house in Bukhara, Smarkand, Khiva. The Kirghiz and the Uzbeks butchered every 'infidel' who didn't mount his bicycle and ride like hell. And the puppets who sold out to Marxism."

"So you're waiting for the enemy to be destroyed by his home-grown enemies?"

"Funny thing about it, the real enemy is almost always home grown. The domestic product nearly finished us before we blundered into a chance to get free. We had so much freedom we began to be enslaved by the muddle of activists, criminals, and maniacs who were lousing things up by fighting for their rights and buggering the rights of everyone else. Anyway! Did you hear something about yourself?"

"About me? Piloting that squadron from Mars? Getting briefings from you? Hoping my original *Saturnienne* crew had done a good job of training Gook and Asteroidian crews?"

"So you didn't hear references to you and Doc Brandon?"

"What references? If you're talking about decorations or citations, they can shove them."

"Spoken like a philosopher. You and Doc did a pretty good press, but, well—"

"With a garland of horse turds?"

"Of course! You are a sadistic monster, a fiend, the worst butcher since Genghis Khan. Barbarous warfare."

"The Bleeding Hearts, the Enemy Lovers don't seem to realize that with the jets from my cruisers around five thousand degrees Celsius, there is no time to feel pain. What's Doc being grilled about? Failing to give the enemy fair warning?"

"You've never met Doc?"

"Never have. I don't imagine he's too keen on autographing a shell fragment for me. Probably will break out with profane cursing and swearing when he hears he is on the blacklist."

"Mmmm . . . they do say he is a fraud, a phony, a four flusher who led a labor company in an attack on three companies of paratroopers and got about fifteen percent of his labor company killed off."

"Labor company did that grand job? You mean, conscientious objectors?"

"That's a polite word for them."

"He *led* them?"

Alexander nodded.

Garvin sighed. "The man's a military genius! I bet he can walk on water, raise the dead, and turn Oolong tea into Demerara rum. How come they call him a phony?"

"Having the secret of everlasting life, a secret he refused to share. By his cheap showmanship he baited idealists into that suicide mission. They claim he's malingering, pretending he'd been seriously wounded."

Garvin whipped his legs over the edge of the drunken lord and snapped to his feet. "They couldn't be that crazy!"

"Rod, five–six years on an asteroid has got you out of touch. They are eating me out about martial law that's kept the criminal majority in hand. Every time a looter, mugger, or rapist is shot dead in the act, there is a scream of indignation. Civil liberties outfits demanding due process of law, arrest, and release on bail."

Garvin needed a drink. He poured a stiff hooker of Islay. "I was in a peculiar state when I barged in on you. Didn't know whether I was afoot or in orbit. I had sensings. The kind you get when you're so worn out you function like a zombie or robot. I do not know how I led that sweep from Urumchi to the Dzungarian Gate, or even if I actually did.

"I did not see things, but it was as if someone were telling me you were worried, sweating something out. Something no one else could help you with. I quit thinking you were a stinker for sending for me."

"Rod, I did not send for you. I was wishing I could talk to you. This was right after I got first news of the Dzungarian Basin cleanup. I'd digested the report of the hell you raised in the Kashgar area. You didn't have communications systems in those cruisers that jibed with our systems."

Garvin blinked. "I knew something was worrying you, and when I saw you I knew I'd been right. But I was too burned out to ask, or to listen if you'd told me."

"There is. And since you got so much by extrasensory perception—" Alex drew a deep breath, got a fresh start. "It is such an idiotic mess, I'll have to tell you everything. It was tough enough to begin with, ever since you phoned me, after all those years—but becoming an international hero except in Marxist circles, that threw dung in the fan."

Chapter 49

"Rod this is awkward," Heflin began. "I don't know how to put it." He frowned, eyed the whirlpool of liquor in the glass that he swirled. "It's all such a muddle."

"Blat it out!" Garvin finally demanded. "Is Flora suing me for a divorce? Azadeh and Aljai are two grand reasons."

Heflin drained his drink and flipped a dollop of Islay into each glass. "You must be psychic! Mentioning Flora: that makes it easier for me. She decided she must not marry me."

Garvin sighed. "Excepting me, she could not have rejected a better man. You and Flora had plans? After what I told her about the one-way cruise to Saturn? God damn it, it was the Consortium acting as a group, no matter who dreamed up the idea. A matter of public policy. I mean, she was furious, that night in Maritania—fit to be tied. So, you two having plans! Well, it does make it simpler for me!"

"She talked to Azadeh. Talked to Aljai. Learned things that the public never got. In spite of hating space, Flora went to Mars and came back, demanding I send a cruiser to find your asteroid.

"With the international situation what it was, a search was out. All the meetings did was get us emotionally involved."

Garvin shrugged. "Flora's that kind of a girl. Look what

happened to me when she and I met! But where do I come in now?"

"It's a long story." Alexander snapped out of the dignitary's chair. "She ought to tell it her own way. When you hear it, you'll know why it'd be awkward for me to state the same facts."

"Nice, but where the hell is she? You were going to put me in touch with her, remember? Well, the way hell's popped, I am not blaming you."

"Easier than you realize."

Alexander stepped out of the Great Book Room and went down a passageway, the main thoroughfare leading to every cross-passage of the maze. Garvin did not have long to wait.

The seventy-year-old Number One Boy, who appeared about forty, stepped into the room. He moved aside, holding open a door. He bowed a precise right angle, out of respect to the Master's guest. The woman who entered needed no one to announce her.

She wore a T'ang tunic, the sleeves of which trailed to her ankles. Her hair, elaborately coiffed in a pair of towering swirls, was secured by pins with long, mutton-fat jade heads. Her gown was crimson, with gilt piping, and appliqué of gold embroidery.

"I be God-double damned!" Like a mechanical toy, Garvin got out of his chair. "Lucky Alex warned me. You're more at home here than I am."

Flora Garvin stepped to the chair near Rod's drunken lord.

"There's another visitor. Thanks to Alex, we had a bombproof over our heads."

"In Tun Huang. Of all places to meet!"

And Flora's Chinese makeup came to life with that old familiar charm. "It's been fluttery business, waiting for you to get my messages."

"If I'd not been warned, well, I can't even imagine it!"

"You, too?"

He nodded. "I'm glad you didn't wear that *Saturnienne* space gown. That would have been much too much."

Flora blinked, gulped. "Takes awhile for anesthesia to wear off and get used to our looking at each other."

A gong sounded, somewhere in the mansion. The brazen voice reverberated, surged anew, subsided at last to a vanishing whisper.

"Royalty?" Rod whispered.

"Gets you, even you?"

Shock was wearing off. Flora relaxed.

Then a little drum: at a guess, hand held, with one padded stick tapping a stately rhythm. Presently a man wearing a white kaftan, white trousers, and a black skullcap stepped into view, moving in cadence with the drumbeat. He held the staff of a golden parasol with golden bells, tiny bells, tinkling along its rim.

"What the hell's she doing here!"

"Shhh. She'll tell you."

Though the woman was veiled to her gray-green eyes, the gossamer was transparent. Lani, once wife of Alub Arslan, was living up to her Asteroidian rank.

Flora came so close to Garvin that he got the fullness of her perfume. "Space Bouquet?" he whispered.

"No, Zombie, darling! The Saturnienne Essence I wore that night."

Since the occasion was private, Alexander followed instead of leading.

Seven girls carried Lani's train. The parasol bearer stationed himself according to Asteroidal protocol. Lani seated herself when the attendants had taken care of her train.

Alexander stepped to his tiger-skin chair. Lani and Flora sat on silk brocade.

Garvin said, "The drunken lord is too informal for all this."

Two of the major domo's staff moved an impressive chair, with tiger skin, brocade, and a cushion. To match Alexander's status, they set a screen behind it. The drumbeat stopped. The door closed. The quartet was alone.

Alexander stepped to the antique Chinese ice chest, lifted the cover. He took out four glasses, twisted the gilt-foil from the neck of a magnum of champagne, and set the glasses on a side table. Opening the bottle, he filled and offered glasses to his guests.

"Whatever we talk ourselves into or out of, let us first

drink to old days. No matter how often one speaks of happy returns of the day, no day ever comes back. This is to friends we may again meet, and to those we'll never again see. Except perhaps in the next incarnation."

They drank, and Alexander refilled the glasses.

Flora said to her husband—curious how natural it seemed to think of Rod as such—"When I heard you were expected to lead a war party from Mars, I hitched a ride with Alex."

"So did I," Lani added.

"It took me a long time," Garvin declared, almost defensively, "but I finally did get you back to Megapolis Alpha."

"Flora, it's time you made a few things clear. Rod's still puzzled."

"Puzzled?" Garvin echoed. "I've been punchy ever since this charade started."

"The very first time Alex and I ever met, it was at a family reunion, a good fifteen–sixteen years ago. Each developed a passion for the other. Purely insane, of course, it was. And to keep from getting scandalously involved, we settled down to hating each other in self-defense. And pretending that we didn't.

"And when you and I met, Rod, we fell on our faces in great haste to marry."

Garvin got up, bowed to Alexander. "She closed her eyes and imagined I was you, and got it out of her system."

"Dozen or fifteen years ago." Heflin sighed. "Seems like a couple of lifetimes."

Flora resumed, "By that time I was convinced I was not a widow: but Azadeh told you all about that. Anyway, my pleading with Alex upset our compulsory hating, and we broke down and confessed and decided we'd marry and either kill that passion or let it incinerate us."

Garvin drew a deep breath. "My life has been an open book. Soon as I can hustle Azadeh and Aljai to an enlightened Moslem country where I can marry them, they'll both be virtuous women and you'll have grounds for two divorces."

"But I *can't* marry Alex."

"Who says you can't? After my several burning passions,

it's time you cooled yours. Hell's fire, am I such a stinker that I'd file a countersuit?"

"Rod, you are a national hero, a space hero come back from the dead! Commanding the Asteroidal-Martian Escadrille, incinerating a Marxist task force, winning the battle of Kasghar."

"If I had your shape and looks, I'd make a million with a cigarette program! Madame, I am not scorning you, I need a Number One Wife to keep Azadeh and Aljai in line."

"Rod, I told Alex as soon as you won that battle and he had to make himself Imperator of North America that I simply could not marry him. Look at the horrible press that would give him! Taking the wife of a national hero! Darling, there'd be rioting and street fighting."

"Not with martial law, there wouldn't." He sighed. "But I guess he'd have a lousy image."

"Don't you see, right while Alex is leading the nation out of alien bondage and international disrepute, some moral clown would run for Imperator and win, and we'd be worse off than ever. Being in a Democracy, my Sudzo program wouldn't be a fatal background image for the Imperatrix, but, good God!—shacking up with or marrying the wife of a hero!"

"I figured you'd hate the hell out of me," Garvin countered, "for blowing the *Saturnienne* to keep North American culture from ruining a cozy little asteroid. No right-minded woman could squawk about Azadeh or Aljai, but being rejected, and unwanted—jumping Jehovah! No woman could take that." Garvin smiled ruefully, sadly; then his old-time whimsy took charge, and he was wholly himself. "One of life's little ironies! You and Alex finding out neither was loathsome, and you had your chance to make up for lost time, I have to show up with my record and bitch up the works. That's not irony, it is pure disaster."

Alexander took charge. "With all the bilateral penitence and all the fond recollections on a silver charger, why not get to here and now. Rod's as good as asked you to keep on as his Number One Lady."

Flora smiled, eyes aglow, each through a near-tear. "After going to Mars and talking an astronomer out of space coordinates and getting Azadeh's story, I couldn't back down now, could I? But we were awfully young and awfully hasty about our marrying! Here we are, in another emotional whirlygig!"

Flora's glance shifted from Rod to Alexander and she said to them, "Wherever we'd go, we'd face audiovideo teams. What we need is somewhere that gives a chance to get acquainted with each other, with what we used to be and what we've become."

Garvin agreed. "It makes sense. And it's a must if it gives us a better start. But where can we get away from cameras and mikes?"

"No problem," Alexander answered. "Go to that monastery where Doc Brandon is recuperating. And if that's not secluded enough, the abbot can steer you to a *real* hideout."

Flora went saucer-eyed. "A preliminary honeymoon in a monastery!"

"Coast back to Earth, Madame Sudzo! Buddhist and Taoist spots are not quite what you're thinking of. The monks have room for weary travelers and laymen looking for a retreat and a chance to think things out.

"Alex, she quit kicking and screaming. Have your Number One Boy consolidate my gear and Flora's. We'll have to leave too early to see you at breakfast."

"I'll arrange all that. And before I get to my desk for a while, there is a private announcement I want you to hear. It won't be on the air until the Pan-Islamic Conference in Cuzco."

"Cuzco? What's Moslem about that?"

"It isn't, which is just the point. It's neither Sunni nor Shia' nor any other sect's territory. And aside from the Himalayas, anything in the Andes is a summit that is super-summit*issimo*!

"I am announcing my conversion to Islam, which means that for the time at least, I'll have to eat ham and eggs in private and do my drinking unofficially.

"You've heard the word *Imperium* and *Imperator* in the news. In view of the national universal illiteracy, these terms will be defined by action. Since *democracy* and *agrarian reformer* have been defined by the Marxist confederation and have become unpopular, new words are needed. Meet the *Imperatrix*.

"Lani, pick it up and carry on!"

The thinly veiled lady did so.

"There are five or six million Moslems in North America, and I don't know how many millions in China. And with Alex having to fraternize with Moslem kings, emirs, sultans, he simply could not fool around with the catchwords of democracy. A country the size of ours rates an Imperator, and as long as elections are the vogue, we'll continue having them.

"The Simianoids have too much good sense to swallow the kind of propaganda that pretty nearly finished the country. And with the fifty–sixty hour work week, under a no-work, no-eat regime, the intellectuals will be too worn out to sit all night at their talkee-squawkees. Theories and doctrine will put them to sleep.

"Maybe a couple of centuries of crossbreeding with the Simianoids would improve the breed. Nothing really ever was wrong with our country except too many people got too far away from their simian ancestry."

Garvin caught Flora's hand. "Madame Sudzo, you've just heard a simplification of what I was trying to express with my capers. I didn't have the words."

Alexander applauded. "Both speakers included," he said.

"One more thing, Alex, something I forgot. Mind if I lower my veil, just this once? Something I want to whisper in Rod's ear."

"Why not? There's not a strict Moslem in the house."

Alexander turned toward the ice chest.

Flora released Garvin's arm. "I want to whisper something to Alex. I'll never ask what you and Lani say."

Lani's veil was below her chin.

"Rod, she's grand! I know you two will make it. And with *three* of the right kind of women in your life, you're bound to amount to something."

Garvin regarded her for a moment. "If you and I ever meet again, I may not have a chance to tell you that if it weren't for Doc Brandon's reconverted chimpanzees, you and Alex would never have a chance. Good luck!"

"Thanks, and I'll never forget how you and I beat Mars and the system. You brought me luck."

Flora, a couple of meters distant, was waiting.

Garvin bowed. "*Ave, Imperatrix*. And you too, Emperor of Apes."

Chapter 50

Venerable Zeng Ta-Yu, Abbot of the Taoist monastery which had received wounded soldiers from the battle of the ridge, stepped from the first courtyard. After a glance about, he walked a good fifty meters, his white-soled felt boots raising yellow dust with each stride. Although too stately for haste, the abbot's gait was purposeful. The long yellow robe with Taoist symbols embroidered front and rear, and the tent-shaped green hat, ridge pole right to left instead of fore and aft, was the most formal outfit he had.

The Reverend *Tao Shih* halted when he heard the grinding of gears. A military four-wheel-drive reconnaissance car came up the steep grade, rounded the fishhook bend, and halted.

"Lord and Lady Garvin," the Abbot began, in Uighur.

No ballet star could have surpassed Garvin's soaring leap from the vehicle. In flight he had shaped the first of his proposed three bows. The abbot beat him only by a split second.

"Lord Abbot, coming out to meet us: You're psychic!"

The unwrinkled Chinese face blossomed in a smile. "The North American Imperator notified us, and Kashgar Military District radioed. One of the monks was watching with binoculars."

The four-wheel drive fumed its way, bringing Lady Garvin to the first courtyard. Garvin gave a hand for her alighting, and then he said, "How is Dr. Brandon doing? Are visitors allowed?"

The Abbot said, to Flora, "In time, you will become accustomed to my English. Madame, answering Lord Garvin's question: Yes, visitors are welcome. It was not made clear that he would be arriving with a non-Uighur or non-Chinese lady."

"There's always a first time, Lord Abbot."

"It is my pleasure," Master Zeng resumed, "to tell you that Captain Dr. Avery Jarvis Brandon and Madame Broadtail are still our guests. All other patients are now in the Military District Hospital.

"Dr. Brandon remains here to undertake Taoist studies. He seemed more seriously wounded than Madame Broadtail, but he recuperates rapidly."

The driver and two monks got the Garvins' luggage and made for the second court.

"You are plane and road weary," the Abbot said, as he led the way to a guest apartment. "While you are resting and cleaning up, I'll tell Dr. Brandon and Madame Broadtail that you will receive them in duc course."

"What's this? We came to pay respects to *him*."

"You brought fire from Mars and destroyed the invaders. Now I beg leave to depart."

Garvin groped but found no appropriate words.

Monks came in with tea, trays of *dim sum*, jars of wine. Others brought portable bathtubs, pails of steaming water, pails of melted glacier ice. Flora remained serene and smiling until the doors closed after the hospitality crew. Then she let go in what she later called silent hysteria, and clung to Garvin.

Finally she was able to vocalize and, presently, achieved articulate speech: "Kansu to Kashgar, flying over that horrible desert! Honeymoon in a monastery. My own personal bathtub, carried in by monks. Sergeant Mona Smith, also known as Madame Broadtail. Captain Dr. Brandon will come with her to knock their foreheads on the floor, nine times."

"Darling, you're skipping something. The girl I eloped to Mars with by mistake stowed away on the *Saturnienne*, married the guest-Admiral, got promoted to exwife of an Asteroidan prince, and is Empress-Elect of North America gave you her blessing before we left Kansu." He jerked a thumb toward a sofa upholstered with embroidered stuff. "No use fighting on foot. And for a change, we're not wrangling. I can't believe any of this either. None of it could happen, not even in Turkestan!"

Her eyes widened. "You're as bubbling over as I am!"

"It's as far out of the world as you and I, that night in Maritania, when the security guards had me carry you from the cocktail lounge to our suite in the hotel."

"You remember all that?"

"You think I don't? And that space gown with a train like the one Lani's trying to get used to before she appears at the summit in Cuzco!"

"And you, carrying me and declaring the cameramen draped my skirt so they could film everything up to my navel."

"They didn't miss it by much!"

"And you believed me when I said I'd not planned any of the publicity pageant, and I ripped that gown from neckline to waist and stepped out of the wreckage."

When they finally stretched out in their tubs, Flora complained whimsically, "We're contrary as ever! Sane humans would relax after all that flying and driving."

"The hot *shao hsing* did that for us, and the *satay*'s no good cold."

"You and I are not the only ones who have made the mistakes we've made," Flora said, after a long and thoughtful silence which he had not broken because he had sensed that she was engrossed. "But getting a second chance, a real chance, not a talkee chance—it's too good to foul up. You and I can't ever fool *ourselves* the way we used to."

"Woman, there are so many ways we've not got around to trying! We've never spoken the same language! You doing your Sudzo pitch, a zillion wenches understand and snitch from the grocery budget to buy Flora-panties. But damned if I ever get your meaning of the moment. If I get anything at all, it's what the same words meant day before yesterday, or are going to mean next week!" He raised a peremptory hand and checked a rebuttal. "The Consortium, the various space crews, the people of that Asteroid, and even women got my meaning."

"No problem," she assured him. "We understood each other perfectly, night before take-off from Maritania. Each said things that back home would have touched off a blunt-instrument murder or a lot of Haviland china damage."

"Nothing to do but live as though each day was our last."

"That," she conceded most glowingly, "might take a lot of . . . well . . . practice. Why haven't you told me that you and Aljai didn't misunderstand each other?"

"Jumping Jehovah! I'd not dared. All right! Believe it or not, we just didn't."

"Mmmm . . . you learned Old High Uighur from her."

"And she learned New Low English from me, so we never misunderstood each other."

"Darling, you spent all your time at home with Aljai. Try the same routine and learn my language. And maybe I'll learn your Low—pardon me—*High* Obscure English! Now that we've tended to *that*, let's dispose of other roadblocks."

"You're looking too sweet and beautiful. Here comes trouble!"

"Not really. We've both been too punchy to see the trees of the woods we've been dumped into. I've been thrown at you. No, I wasn't discarded by Alexander. Don't bother saying I did not give him time. I wasn't even squeamish about giving you the news that he and I had plans. Oh, damn it, double damn it, you *had* to become a national hero before you had time to phone Alec and demand he locate me instantly. And don't think he couldn't have; I stood out of range of the screen, first time he phoned you."

"All *right*!" Pantomime of tearing out a handful of his own hair, while pondering taking her scalp. "You didn't throw yourself at me. You were cooling off a lifelong passion and leaving me stranded with only two awfully adequate exotic women. Nothing but a world emergency, anyway and at least national crisis and circumstances left me free to talk you into our getting acquainted again."

"If anything threw you at me, it was world events, and I could have dodged! But I didn't."

"You were too paralyzed."

"I was too God damn happy!"

"Gone six years, come back, and a wonderful little war leaves the Sudzo Dream Girl on the loose! Sixteen hundred of the bumpiest kilometers I ever flew, Tun Huang to Kashgar, plus a shell-cratered road to the monastery, and you serenely flip everything but your ear pendants and don't remember you're supposed to kick and scream till after a long soak in a tub and some wine still warm enough to drink! Christ on a life raft! And I am said to be incomprehensible!"

"Oh, Alex—uh—Rod, darling—why the sound and fury! All I meant was, it has been a long time, and everything, I mean, *every*thing was wonderfully wonderful, but I was looking to our future."

"With such a present, be damned to futures!"

But he remembered that it was a second honeymoon, and he could not reasonably expect her to make sense about anything, so he relaxed and listened to Flora clarify matters:

". . . we do have a lot of things to sort out. There's more than the business of learning each other's language. Our lives have become more complicated than they were during our earlier days."

Garvin set his chopsticks on the hors d'oeuvres platter and took a nip of wine. "You met Azadeh and my son. The way my getting to Mars with Lani was covered by Tee Vee, well, it was embarrassing, but nobody can say it was furtive or sneaky."

"One of your great virtues, too brazen to be sneaky. No, I am not being bitchy."

"File a bill of exceptions, and I'll carry on. Now, Aljai: There was no communication after I blew the *Saturnienne*, and she didn't move in with me till after the blast. I wasn't furtive, not really."

"Rod, once I talked to Azadeh, I got the news and I wasn't amazed or annoyed. If there had not been *any* women on that blessed little asteroid you love so well, your guardian angel would have winged across space with a lovely under each arm and one riding piggy-back, so you'd have a fair assortment."

"All *right*! Then there's nothing to sort out, and nothing

complicated. Officially, being Number One Lady is new to you, but you've had sort of a shake-down cruise, and what the hell *is* there to sort out?"

"Oh, you idiot! You're willfully setting up roadblocks! You know what I mean! Those five–six years we were separated. Well, I *am* human."

"Never mind the confessions. You as good as said you were shacking up with Alex in his bombproof or I'd be a wailing bedraggled widower."

"Wailing and fighting off dissolute and immoral women!"

"Skip the confession stuff! Or I'll tie you to that formal chair and make you listen to a blow by blow of me and Azadeh, and me and Aljai, and—"

"And Lani—is that all you can brag about!" Her mocking tone was affectionate whimsy. And then, earnestly, "We're off to a good start. You've not shouted, and I've not screamed. I mean, since we left Alex. I don't want anything to separate us again. There are things I am going to tell you. My Sudzo career has made me so well known. I wore a mask, and a cab driver recognized my voice."

"Carry on, I am cooperating."

"I mean, even if we moved to Khatmandu or Cuzco, things would get to you, and all warped and horrible. I have to give you facts!"

"I begin to understand." He sighed. "Mind if I get a good book and a snort of that *kao liang*?"

"You are going to *listen*! Out of fairness to yourself and to me. Self-defense, and each other's defense."

Garvin shrugged. "Sound off, Madame, I promise I will stay awake."

"When I tried to buy a ticket to Mars, I found out that space travel was severely restricted. Doc Brandon was going on official business. He had the usual papers for himself and a companion and a maid, and he was alone. He made room for me. He was a sweet character and didn't talk about taking it out in trade. I was in a mood and crawled into bed with him."

"So far, your taste in playmates is almost as good as mine."

"At the Prime Meridian Observatory of Mars, Doc tried

to get the bearings of what looked to be a nova. He suspected that it had been the detonation of your cruiser. He couldn't make it. I seduced the Head Astronomer and got the coordinates. No, it was not a horrible sacrifice. He was rather nice."

Garvin yawned. "Let's not make our honeymoon a historical society convention."

"I'm so happy you did not dump Azadeh or Aljai; that would have been a horrible way of trying to be nice to me. Oh, if I'd only known! The other things, I didn't have to tell, but this—"

She was on the verge of falling into a puddle of tears. Garvin snuggled Flora in the crook of his arm.

"Now what's wrong?" He had his suspicions, but he said, "Sound off, doll, it can't be as bad as all that."

"I'm pregnant. No, I did not tell Alec."

"Number One Wife, would I talk out of turn?"

Flora gulped something inarticulate and relaxed.

"Now you listen to *me*," Garvin resumed. "You'll be a stepmother to my son. I won't ever bother being guilty on account of Azadeh. I'll bust my tail trying to be as good to Alexander's whatever-it-is. If a girl, she and my son can start a dynasty with maybe sense enough to live up to the Simianoids who'll run the world that humans-so-called have screwed up.

"You and I have nothing to do but rest until tomorrow. Doc Brandon is not coming to kowtow. That was Asiatic exaggeration. I'll be seeing him tomorrow.

"I'll see him alone. I want you to have a few words with him. Tell him all while I am having a chat with the Lord Abbot. The driver told me of a spot for our honeymoon, and I'll check with the Abbot himself."

Flora glanced at her watch. "World Savior, shall we have hot wine and a full meal now, or wait till later?"

"I'd say *both*, but you'd not understand."

Chapter 51

The Abbot went with Garvin to the door of Doc Brandon's room.

"One visitor at a time is enough, so I'll not go in with you. When you're back this way in a couple of weeks, he'll be up to a longer visit."

"Thank you, Venerable Master. That lodge looking down on the Kizil Ssu sounded good when the driver told me about it, and with your okay—be so kind as to radio for the driver? With your permission, we'll be taking leave when he gets here."

Doc Brandon sat comfortably back among the cushions of a drunken lord's chair. Garvin said, "Aside from bandages, you look pretty much like the still they had in the news flashes."

Doc extended his hand. "An old picture taken about the time you were making news in Maritania. You've changed. Tired, but more relaxed. As though you'd found what you've been looking for all your life. When are you going on the air about social conditions on the asteroid? About the oppressed underdog?"

"Well, now, I'm far from sure—God damn it! Doctor, for a second I thought you meant that quip! Less I hear of that tripe, the better. After a remark like that, I'll ask you how you ever got conscientious objectors to follow you. If only there'd been an AV team handy!"

"I had a good Lieutenant, a good Sergeant, and that Amazon idiot, not sense enough to get scared. She and I survived because we surprised the enemy. Got a fire started before they got their attention off the ridge they were going to enfilade."

"Dr. Brandon, every survivor has to say it was luck and other people's good work, and probably it's true quite often, but that still does not explain how you got the troops over their moral scruples."

Doc grinned. "Moral scruples, even when genuine, are acquired late in the evolution of humanity. A lot of it is peer pressure, each phony, self-deceived twit building up the others' phoniness. Get them into a tight fix, scare the be-jesus out of them, shoot at them, and those that aren't paralyzed become homicidal maniacs; self-preservation makes killers of them.

"And generations of thought control, of sitting glued to the Tee-Vee, of psychic sponges, hour after hour."

Garvin frowned as Doc paused for breath. "That'd just fix them in their notions!"

"Up to a point, you are right, Rod. That was the doctrine. But when generations get into the receptivity habit, they will gulp suggestions from any source. They crave direction. No matter how disastrous, or what pure nonsense, such as Marxist crap, they'll buy it.

"So they bought the idea of going over the rim. I went over, Mona went over, so did the Lieutenant and a Sergeant, and if you think apes are monkey-see-monkey-do, you've seen nothing! The Plastic Society creatures buy humanitarian ideas, sure! And Marxism. And the percentage of killers for fun, robbing mom-and-pop groceries, and killing to make a day of it. Same for old folks living alone. Beat them to death. No conscience. Raping and killing women.

"But when it comes to facing a trained enemy, well armed, an amazing proportion develop conscience, scruples about the sanctity of human life."

"Your logic worked out, Dr. Brandon, and balls for doctrine!"

"One thing, Rod, now that I've talked myself out of breath. Your flame-throwing escadrille. I hear you piloted one from the asteroid. And I saw one, the one Azadeh showed me."

"Same principle, so we had no trouble firing up those that Azadeh didn't tell you about. Hence the pyramids."

"Hence the pyramids, Rod, and you saved my hide. If those bastards in the woods didn't get us, the deflection errors in what our boys were throwing from the ridge could have totaled my party or what was left of it."

"You and I come out even. I'm a sadistic monster who incinerated helpless humans in tanks. You are an Immoral Immortal who baited Idealists into forgetting their ideals."

Doc thrust out his hand. "As one son of a bitch to another, it's been good meeting the likes of you."

"My pleasure, sir." And then, "Doc, before I leave, there is one thing I have to tell you. I came especially to tell you. Flora's going to Mars for information may look as though it was a wasted effort. She did everything she could, and that was good for her soul. Nothing she did was wasted. Everything, I mean, *everything* did its bit for our better understanding of each other, in a way we never did before."

"We're having a honeymoon. Then Azadeh and Aljai are meeting us and we'll decide where we're going to live."

"Flora, Azadeh, and Aljai."

Garvin grinned. "With two junior wives to supervise, Flora can't find so much fault with me."

"Flora hates space. It was heroic, her going back to Mars. Rod, you and your ladies might like Nameless Island. And once Megapolis Alpha is rebuilt, it'll be a quick flight from my Island, for a change of pace and shopping." Doc pondered, sighed, then said, whimsically, "If that Malay girl ever comes back, you'd like her."

"What's her speciality? Aside from being a sweet, high-tempered, proud-as-a-queen hellion?"

"My clown of an assistant hurt her feelings and escaped with his life. She is out in the great world with a well-honed *kris* to slice him apart. If she finds him before her forgiving nature takes charge again. Amina is a doll."

"Three dolls, Doc, is a package, but thanks anyway. I'll take a cigar instead. Never let Amina know I said that! Now there's one thing more. While I'm taking leave of the

Lord Abbot, I'd like Flora to have a few words with you. It's funny how things turn out. If I'd not returned when I did, she would have married Alexander Heflin. I could not have blamed her, but if she had, it would have been a disaster for me. Everything she did ties together and gives us a better chance, this time. *Everything*, Doc."

A long moment of savoring Garvin's words, and then, "Rod, you'll never know how glad I am that you came to see me. She's a grand girl. Keep her happy."

When Rod rejoined Flora, he said, "I talked with the Abbot. He said that lodge is not far from K'ang Ssu, looking down at the Kizil Ssu. Never been there, but people speak well of it.

"I asked the Abbot to radio for the FWD and the driver who brought us here. He knows the road. You go right now before Doc takes a siesta and give him thanks for everything—understand, *everything*. I told him I wanted you to have a few words with him. We'll be seeing him on our way back, but a thank-you and good-bye. Just in case."

"You're awfully sweet!"

"I'll search the place for scattered belongings, pack my own, and leave yours for you to pack."

And so it was done.

Chapter 52

When Garvin and Flora cleared the outer courtyard, the Abbot got four monks to carry Mona in her reclining chair to Doc Brandon's room. While one adjusted the cushions, another got a tray of tea, with cakes and peaches. The team then set the chair so that Doc and his visitor faced each other, with Mona's back turned to the wall toward which his feet pointed.

"Half crippled, Doc, but nothing essential damaged."

"That goes for me. Time we had a drink together. Maybe you missed that broadcast? Back in the States, the media made me a hero till they learned I'd live and then they remembered their duty and gave me pure hell for baiting fine young men into a glory hunt, half of them killed off as a sacrifice to my vanity. It was less than twenty percent."

"That's par for the course."

"The humanitarians," Doc continued, "called Garvin a fiend and a monster for cremating the enemy. Don't know what they were squawking about. Maybe they never read Matthew thirteen, all about who invented the fiery furnace, weeping, wailing, and gnashing of teeth. Garvin's fire worked so fast they never felt what hit them."

"When's your trial as a war criminal? I mean, by our side."

"Trying to be funny? With North America's bleeding

hearts, nothing would surprise me. Mmm . . . I said something about a drink."

"Come to think of it, Rod and Flora mentioned a bottle of *kao liang* they didn't like any too well, so they stuck to rice wine. These well-meaning monks probably figure that millet spirits or *shao hsing* wouldn't be good for invalids."

"*Kao liang* is okay once you get used to it."

"When the monks start chanting, burning incense, tapping the 'fish head,' I'll slip into the bridal suite and get that bottle."

"You think you can walk?"

"If I can't, I'll crawl! Now that *that* is settled! You were cursing bleeding hearts. Carry on, you're always at your best when you're on that subject."

"Well, thanks, but there's something else." He pointed at the tray. "Those peaches remind me of another gripe."

"*Peaches?*" Mona looked perplexed. "How do they feature?"

"They're a symbol of immortality."

That left Mona groping. "I've been thinking of that subject ever since I got my overdose of war," she ventured uncertainly.

"What I had in mind was the Board of Visitors, student riots, kidnaping. Once the media run out of important stories, they'll remember that I shot my way out of false arrest."

"During that grilling, all you told them was why it'd be disastrous to have immortality—overpopulation and how Nature decontaminates the world when humanity becomes too plentiful. Cataclysms, plagues, famines to wipe out excess human vermin."

"That's a fair sampling."

"But you never said it was impossible. I mean, immortality."

Long silence. "Not to you, and not to them."

"Why not?"

"The Simianoid gene splicing turned out so well that I've been afraid someone might improve on my father's experiments. Maybe I am a mutant, and maybe I am one of Dad's experiments, a one of a kind. And if he had a record, he destroyed it."

"You never said overpopulation could not be prevented."

"I told them that human nature being what it is, it probably would not be avoided. I'll quit hedging. Life indefinitely extended, even when it is as comfortable as mine, with no more decrepitude of old age than I have up to date—"

"Which is nil, minus."

"—everlasting life still would be a disaster. *They* were in no mood to listen. They were too greedy! You rate my answer in full."

The pause to shape words was interrupted by a gentle tapping at the door. Just as gently, Mona murmured, "Damn, oh, double damn!"

"That may be our bottle," Doc suggested. "These monks are sometimes psychic. Come in and welcome."

It was one of the older monks. He had an envelope. "Lord Brandon, the Venerable Lord Abbot got this message from the Emperor of North America. I beg leave to depart."

"Thank you, Venerable *Tao Shih*. And go with blessings."

The envelope contained a sheet of paper which had been laboriously written on in the Swedish Missionary English of the Abbot's boyhood.

"It's been places, relayed between origin, way stations, and finally, Kashgar."

"What's it say?"

"Not readily apparent." He regarded the sheet, frowned. "Seems it's been censored along the way. I'll give you the sense of it. It started from Alexander Heflin. He's in Cuzco. Some kind of summit, conferring with Moslem notables. Imperatrix Lani unveils sufficiently and in private to send love and best wishes to Doc and Mona. Oswald Fenton, who loved you so much that he sold me out to the enemy, is the first hero to be cited for the Imperial Medal of Honor. Valor beyond the call of duty.

"Oswald's outfit was digging tank traps on the Dzungarian-Urumchi Highway. His company was pinned down by paratrooper platoon. The left was returning enemy fire, but just holding its own. Another parachute drop would break the tie and disaster for our side.

"Oswald came up from the far right, where everyone apparently was too scared to do anything. Enemy did not even know anyone was there. Didn't notice Oswald's gallant *banzai* charge till he got close enough to heave a couple of grenades.

"Here it's pretty readable: '. . . *inspired by Private Fenton's gallantry, Amina Esmitt, an Amazon from Headquarters Company, followed him, brandishing a bayonet. Others of the company began firing. One squad charged with assault rifles.*'

"What it amounts to," Doc continued, after pauses to curse and frown, "is that the distraction kicked up by Oswald's grenades and prolonged by the belated covering fire from a supposedly unoccupied stretch of sand and tamarisk scrub gave the left flank of the trap diggers a notion and they closed in."

"Esmitt? Amina?"

"Sure. A lot of languages can't say words that begin with two consonants, so they prefix a vowel to make it pronounceable. Amina Smith."

"That'd be our Amina. She enlisted, gave Smith as surname."

"More I can figure out, sort of. Amina found Oswald. When he heard her she probably screamed *puta-ng-mo*! or even more unladylike words and went for him with a lady's size *kris*. He made a *banzai* charge before Amina could slice him crosswise. She was deadlier than a distant enemy." A pause. *"Oh, God damn it all—"*

"Doc, what's the matter?"

Brandon choked, gulped. "When a couple of bullets broke Oswald's stride, he stumbled. Amina was exposed to enemy fire. It knocked her flat. She got to her feet to finish him before he could get up. She got in one slash and folded. He heaved his second grenade."

Doc swallowed, brushed the back of his hand across his eyes. "The hero is in the base hospital, recovering. A Medal of Honor, pension for life! Whenever he wears the decoration and is on a military post, Number One at the guard house comes to attention, snaps to port arms, sounds off, *'Turn out the guard! Medal of Honor!'* and comes to present arms with the rest of the guard."

"She got in one good slash. Good for her! Alex can't let that phony award get by. She swore she'd kill the punk, but it's mission accomplished anyway."

Doc shook his head, blinked away the tears, and let them trickle as they would. "Heroes are so scarce that you can't debunk Oswald. The *banzai* charge wiped out the enemy, and the tank trap was completed. It was useless, with Garvin on the way with fire from Mars.

"Only good thing about it, Amina got in with one slash before she dropped dead."

"Doc, you must've been awfully fond of Amina."

"When I left our Island, she wouldn't let me pack my gear and she wouldn't let me escape alone. Did the laundry, Malay style, in a pond or creek, and cooked the best curry and *satay*. She was a sweet girl."

Mona contrived twists and wriggles until she could lay a hand on Doc's forearm. "You needn't feel bad because she can't hear you speaking your mind. She always knew how you felt about her people."

Doc nodded. "Proud as a queen. Taken all in all, her people are a noble race. They have a sense of honor, something that my people have lost. The Malays are not practical. Too generous to amount to much in the ways that we reckon things."

"She was at Alexander's bombproof," Mona said, "when Security rounded me up. We became close friends. Her enlisting and getting China duty, just to follow Oswald, well, a lot of people would say it was crazy, but it began to make sense to me.

"Amina loved you."

"Wait a second! In the arithmetic of her sane world, a world that is closer to nature than ours has been the past two thousand years or more, it would have been all wrong, a crime against nature, to let me do the cooking, the laundry, the camp work. It wasn't *me*, it was my being the Old Man of Nameless Island."

"I didn't say she was 'in love' with you. That's something else. You always loved those people, Malays, Burmese, Eurasians, and assorted exotics. Respected them and their ways. You had *everything*! Until I was gone, and you were leaving. Then she had something to offer, and she did."

Doc nodded. "That's gospel. This 'love' and 'in love' business, put it into English and it becomes crazy. And speaking of being crazy, punchy, that telegram: Alex can't debunk the war hero. But he can get a decoration for the Amazon, the woman who inspired Fenton to make a *banzai* charge."

Mona considered the idea. Pensively, seriously, she at last said, "Her courage kept him moving. Even a bastard like Oswald sometimes amounts to something, if he has the right woman behind him."

"Broadtail, one more like that and I'll bust a gut trying to keep from laughing and crying at the same time. I'll write a message for the Abbot to forward to Alexander."

The tremendous voice of the temple bell shook the monastery. Then a gong, and the *tock-tock-tock* of the "fish head," the *tumpa-tumpa-tum-tum-tumpa-tump* of a little drum, the chanting of the monks: exultant, exalting. Doc wondered if that could have been the beginning of a ritual in honor of General Kwan Kung, traditional hero and guardian of shrine or shop.

Mona wormed her way clear of the drunken lord's chair and got to her feet. She swayed a little and stood steady. "I'll get paper and that bottle. Doc, darling, I've never seen you look so God-awful sad."

"And you won't, not until I outlive you."

He watched Mona's resolute progress to the door.

". . . *ran interference till the enemy broke his stride . . . he'll never forget you . . .*" Doc blinked, choked. "*Catching up . . . swish of the kris, and a rump slash.*"

Chapter 53

"Amina! Good-bye and good going, *shireen*!"

"I'll drink to that. Happy landing, Amina Esmitt!"

Doc refilled the tiny cups. "Best *kao liang* I ever tasted."

"Magic in a Taoist monastery." Mona shivered. "That chanting does things, once you get with the spirit of it. You were going to tell me something when we got the bad news."

"Mmm . . . now I remember! Taoist adepts, lots of them, spend many a year studying and experimenting with all the approaches to immortality. Diets and breathing exercises and elixirs and ritual sex like the Tantrists specialize in. But they are not greedy. They are not running scared. Most of them are too wise to crave indefinitely long life."

"Doc, I never heard that one, not the way you put it."

"Simple! *They know that life already is everlasting, always has been, always will be.* Civilized people have always known. No occult tricks necessary. They live their lives and they die easily. *The leaves fall to the foot of the Tree.* In the next life, they're going to pick it up again, after a good rest, and carry on. Right here, in this world. There is no other. Nirvana is only in *samsara*, the always here and now world."

"You've given me so many hints, but you've never carried it through. Going to trust me, finally?"

"What'd happen if I got on Tee Vee and sounded off from the *Bhagavad Gita* something like this: '*Think not that ever there was a day when you and I were not, or ever a day when we shall not be. The reincarnated Spirit goes through infancy, middle age, old age, and death; and it is born again in a new body. Like discarding a worn-out garment and putting on one that is clean and new. The Spirit in all bodies is never born and it does not die with the body. Why fear death, why mourn any creature?*'"

"The Alleluia Stompers would squawk because it's different from what they say. It sounds like good sense to me. Nice work if you can get it! Is this reincarnation thing in their Bible?"

"No, but it belongs there! It would be, except that some seventeen, eighteen centuries ago, they outlawed the idea. They did their damndest to kill those who did accept the idea. Those who managed to escape, they got off with being cursed by remote control. As long as people went for the reincarnation teaching, they could not be scared of everlasting hell-fire like they are today."

"Doc, have you experienced reincarnation?"

"Broadtail, sometimes I think I have. I need more experience. Like everything else, it's another of my tentative acceptances until I know that I know. That it makes sense does not mean that it is true. But look at it this way: Suppose I had everlasting life in the way these half-baked juvenile-adults crave, what would my prospects be?"

"Look at the wisdom you've picked up in less than two hundred years, seeing through what most people believe."

"All those years, I was also bogging down. It's been like doing a hundred-yard dash in quicksand, or wearing lumberjack boots for dancing a ballet. Everything I've experienced has been evolutionary. You said as much, and you are right.

"But nobody stops to think that as you are *evolving*, you are also being *involved*. Evolution and involution cannot be separated. No more than you can saw a magnet in half at the neutral midpoint, and get one piece that has only a north pole, and another piece with just a south pole. Going Taoist, look at *yang* and *yin*. They are polar opposites. Neither can exist without the other.

"Here I am: With my evolving, I got involvement. More and more people, more things, more encounters, more experiences. The generations I have outlived have become part of me, along with my judgments of situations. Sure, you understand me, but that is your mind working. Experiencing is something like eating: Until the food has lost its identity as food and become a part of you, it's of no use at all."

Mona frowned, grappled. "Doc, I almost get it."

"Try this one! I am not tired of anyone or of anything. I am simply tired."

Mona brightened. "Now I begin to get it! One night in New Orleans, while I was half asleep, I said, 'grand, and all I need is a long rest.' "

"*Keno!* That was life-and-death in miniature, two faces of the same principle. Oversimplified, reincarnation is a new body, new emotions, new brain for the essence that animates them: *It* has rested, shaken off involutions, and is ready for a fresh start." He picked up the little cup. "This doesn't look like millet or sorghum or whatever they distill. This *kao liang* is the essence. So is the something distilled from previous lives."

Mona refilled the cups.

Doc continued, "Nature could not be so insane as to give you ninety years of life and then hustle you to so-called 'heaven' to stagnate forever and eternity. It is a gimmick to fool the majority. Don't tell me the cosmos is crazy." He made a wry grimace. "Nothing to do but figure a way to convince those oafs that life in an everlasting body would be a dreary business."

"Sounds like a contract."

"You can come closer to it than any other living person I know of."

"*I* can?"

"Yes. Iris and I shared lots of grief and good, but we'd not lived long enough to share insights. The five–six years since you and I began real sharings, I had a hundred and eighty years behind me. You had a better chance. So much more to rub off, you might say. It works both ways. I can gain much more from you than I could if we'd met a century and a half sooner."

"Doc, I'm groping."

"Welcome to the club, darling."

She sat up very straight. "I get it. Our first real sharing was a breakthrough." She laughed softly, happily as though at her own obtuse gropings for what she had always known. "Almost got it."

"Keep living your life. You've recuperated more than I'd reckoned."

"I've been on the rim of saying something like that to you, but I was wondering."

"We are a bit stove up." He pointed to a bookcase. "You can't read Chinese or Uighur. Maybe if we teamed up, we could hobble over and keep each other from folding while I pick the book. If the right one is there."

"I hobbled back with the jug, didn't I?"

Doc managed by sufficient contortions to get to his knees and finally to put one foot on the floor. "Like getting out of one of those God damn sport cars."

And then they were two towers of Pisa, each leaning against the other. "Doc, anything to be sociable, but how is a book so awfully important?"

"Unless I misread your voice and eyes, a pillow book fits your mood like nothing else."

"*My* mood? You old devil, how about yours? But finding a pillow book in a monastery!"

"If not here, then in the library."

But Doc found one. Back to their drunken lord's, they sat crosswise and shared the leg room of a *chaise longue*.

The pictures made the text needless. Doc explained, "This is for fun for laypersons, and for others, it is Taoist magic. Hsi Wang Mu drew the vital essence from a thousand young lovers and became an Immortal. The Jade Emperor became an Immortal by absorbing the female essence of twelve thousand concubines.

"Those approaches seem a lot better than elixirs of cinnabar, lead, arsenic, and so forth."

Mona grimaced. "You mean they drank poisons like that?"

"Some literal-minded people did. Even emperors, and it killed some of them. Ko Hung's writings must be symbolic. Fatal for the literal minded. And very likely the immortality that fascinated so many sages was spiritual, a stepping out of your body and not returning. Instead, you go back to the Tao, out of which all things came, and back to which all things go."

Mona turned another page. "Doc, darling, I've been listening, but I've been in a mood the past couple of days and this does it."

"Turn more pages till you come to one that'll show us how to outwit our handicaps. I'm going to try walking without leaning on you."

With uncertainty that became an increasing steadiness, Doc skirted the wall. After pausing to rest at a three-leaf screen, he resumed his course until he came to the book closet. Mona's interest in the picture book was stimulating, renewing. He swallowed his triumphant "Haven't folded yet!"

When he reached the sleeping alcove he did not sound off. The click of curtain rings on the rod made her look up. Then he demanded, "Do I carry you, or can you walk?"

"I'll bring the book and the bottle," she retorted. "Just leave room for my other nine hundred ninety-nine lovers."

"My eleven thousand nine hundred ninety-nine concubines are waiting in the hall."

She made a derisive grimace. "The Jade Emperor never had it this good! Even if this doesn't make you immortal."

"Madame Broadtail, it'll be a good start."

Chapter 54

The four-wheel-drive brought Garvin and Flora from the lodge above the Kizil Ssu, down to the timberline, and into the junipers and cedars of the lower slopes. They had packed the lookee-squawkee to brief them during their couple of weeks of becoming accustomed to each other again. On their way to the monastery they preferred their own voices, saying over and over again the things they had been saying to each other, and repeating the new which each had discovered in the other. For each, a blend of savoring, a fresh richness; and, as food for reminiscence, their sharing of long ago.

They had had their fill of hearing Rod and Doc Brandon vivisected, enough of Alexander and his Veiled Imperatrix, Empress of Apedom, preceded by a seven-decked golden parasol and asteroidal drummers.

"Your quip about my being your son's stepmother and your being my his-or-her stepfather stands for everything being balanced. We're through with the past. And the first thing for our future is deciding where we're going to live."

"All I'm deciding is where I am not going to live. Meaning, no Megapolis, not even if I got a golden key to the city. From there, you tell *them* what is what, Number One Lady."

Flora frowned. "Azadeh has a low opinion of Terrestrians, and Aljai might be homesick for her cozy little asteroid. My first move is bound to make me a domestic tyrant!"

"That's a part of being Number One Lady! Anyway, it's not quite the problem you think it is. If the two junior-grade girls disagree, I'll vote with one, you vote with the other. Or if they agree, then you and I will agree with each other, and again, we get a tie, and leave it to Doc Brandon to cast the final vote. Sort of arbitration stuff."

Having an ally made Number One Wife feel more in control of things. "It'll keep! That old Uighur proverb you love to quote, *'don't cross your bridges before they are hatched'* seems to fit."

"Number One Lady, *Tai-tai*, that was Early Garvin, not Old High Uighur."

The way in which they had been rehearsing their act convinced Rod and Flora that however complicated the new ménage was going to be, it would not be as tempestuous as in the old days. Instead of becoming opponents, each needed the other as an ally.

Dismissing trivialities, they settled down to self-congratulation and relishing here and now.

Having been briefed by the driver who had paused on the upgrade run, the Abbot came to the monastery gate to meet his guests. After welcoming the honeymooners, Venerable Zeng Ta-yu added, "Azadeh Khanoum and Aljai Khanoum and your son, Toghrul Khan, will be here tomorrow afternoon."

They followed the Abbot to their former guest room. There he said, "While you relax from your ride, there is one who wishes to offer tea, *shao hsing, kao liang*, and other refreshments."

Garvin flashed a side glance to Flora. Instead of looking properly worn out, she sparkled and nodded her okay. Like the submissive Asiatic female, Flora assured him that he had her permission to be himself.

"Have at it, Lord Abbot."

Garvin was wondering who was to bring refreshments, or rather, who would come with the servers. It could only be Doc Brandon, yet he had no urge to inquire; he was happy that New Flora had no questions. Garvin was thinking, *"Age of miracles! She can endure moments of silence and wait for events to furnish answers. Still doesn't look pregnant . . . bet she could walk the Takla Makan and leave no footprints."*

And then Garvin heard the whisper of felt soles, with an odd drag and hesitancy. Brushing reverie aside, he saw the Lord Abbot, followed by a long-legged woman, not red-headed golden, but of a color akin, a sunkissed tawny copper. *"Two teated luscious and carries herself like a queen! Where's Doc Brandon? Surprise?"*

The good-looking girl with the hazel eyes carried a tray loaded with goodies, solid and fluid. Although she did not limp, her walk was not normal. There were scars, raw-red, which indicated that she had been unbandaged for a big occasion.

Saving Captain Dr. Avery Jarvis Brandon as *pièce de résistance?* He rates a nine-decked golden parasol, nine drummers, and a nine yak-tail standard.

The quasi-redhead set the tray on a side table near the sofa which had invited Garvin and Flora. The Abbot gave her a hand, steadying her toward one of the chairs which faced the visitor.

Garvin got up.

Zeng Ta-yu rose.

Garvin said, "Lord Abbot—"

The Old Master gestured. "Be seated until I say that this is the Lady-Soldier who followed Lord Brandon when he surprised a company of the enemy and caused their destruction. You may pay your respects to Sergeant Mona Esmitt, the survivor."

Garvin was on his feet. "The survivor? How about—where's Doc Brandon?"

The Abbot gestured. When Mona knew that attention centered on her, she said, "When I have filled the glasses—"

Flora got to her feet. "Please sit down! Let me fill them. You mustn't overdo." She poured a very dark *shao hsing,* which was tasty without being heated, and she served the others.

Mona said, "Two-time hero Roderick David Garvin will be saddened to know that Doc Brandon's answer to the excess of surviving pacifists prevents him from being with us. Let us drink to the absent friend."

They drank. Bottoms up.

And then Garvin took the floor. "What happened? What'd they do? I'd counted on seeing him."

Mona sighed. "So did we. But since he cannot be with us, I speak for him."

Garvin seated himself.

Mona began to sum up the media estimates, all derogatory.

Garvin cut in, "Skip that crap! Nobody believes what those bastards say! Let's have some facts."

Mona smiled and she was radiant. "You speak Doc's language. I wish he could hear you! Doc told me he would convince the imbeciles who craved everlasting life in the physical body, a notion that made conscientious objectors of all too many. They could not risk lives which might any day be made everlasting by Doc's or some other scientist's genetic engineering."

"Sweetheart, please do knock it off! What happened?"

"There was only one way," she said, speaking very slowly, "that he could convince the world that he did not have the secret of everlasting life. Because he survived that nasty skirmish, he did the only thing possible to convince idealists that they might as well impersonate men again, face the hazards of war and of peace, of land and of space. There was no immortality of the body which they could protect. He died, willingly, happily."

"Oh, Christ!" Garvin groaned. He choked, bowed his head, muttered. When at last he looked up, Mona was smiling through tears.

"He did not do anything that you imagined. Listen, I'll tell you. We found him sitting, reclining in a drunken lord's chair. Halfway between happy and contented, nothing left to desire. Mission accomplished."

She paused, flung back her head, eyed them each in turn.

"We're friends. Why not tell all I know?"

She summed up Doc's thoughts on living too long, his belief that death was a rest which was followed by rebirth,

fresh body, fresh mind, experience converted into impersonal wisdom. She told of the Taoist experiments and saw
the Abbot's understanding smile.

"I think I've given a fair sketch. If I haven't, there are
lots of books. Well, they carried me in so Doc and I could
have our first talk after we got shot up. I could walk a bit
and I managed to hustle up a bottle. And he found he
could move and get around.

"We got to talking about the Jade Emperor and his
twelve thousand concubines and about Hsi Wang Mu and
her thousand young lovers. It'd been a long time for folks
wired up the way we were. So we studied a pillow book
and found the answer."

"If an overdose was what finished him," Garvin declared, "he couldn't have picked a nicer way!"

Mona sighed. "He'd been telling me how Taoist practices
make it easy to step out of the body. Instead of coming
back, you keep going. To your destination. To be an Immortal, or to be born again, for a fresh start. Guessing is no
crime."

No one asked Mona what her guess was.

She sank back in her chair.

Garvin finally said, "Whatever's the answer, it makes
sense. I wish Azadeh and Aljai could have heard your
story."

"They can. It's been taped."

Still thoroughly shaken, Garvin turned to Flora. "Coming back to me is a lot more of a compliment than I suspected." Then, to all, "Nothing to do but figure where
Number One Lady and two wives are going to settle
down."

"Doc told me," Mona said, "that before you made up
your minds, you might spend a bit of time at Nameless
Island, Doc Brandon's world. Now it's mine. Be my guests.
I'd love it."

Garvin slanted a long glance at Flora. "*Tai-tai* thought
highly of Doc Brandon. Talk to Azadeh and Aljai. I don't
think either would kick and scream, and we all need a long
rest."

ABOUT THE AUTHOR

E. HOFFMANN PRICE (1898–present) soldiered in the Philippines and France during World War I. At war's end he was appointed to the United States Military Academy, where he entered intercollegiate pistol and fencing competition. He was graduated in 1923 and commissioned in the Coast Artillery Corps. His first fiction sale was March 1924, to *Droll Stories*. By 1932, he was writing full time—fantasy, adventure, westerns, detective. When the pulps folded, he earned grog, gasoline, and groceries by holding two jobs and by filming weddings and practicing astrology in his spare time. Thanks to his incessant motoring, he met and made enduring friendships with Farnsworth Wright, Hugh Rankin, Otis Adelbert Kline, Lovecraft, Howard, W. K. Mashburn, Clark Ashton Smith, Edmond Hamilton, Seabury Quinn, Jack Williamson, Robert Spencer Carr, Leigh Brackett, C. L. Moore, and a comparable number in the nonfantasy fields.

During the past sixteen years, Price has been known in San Francisco's Chinatown as Tao Fa, the *dharma* name conferred by Venerable Yen Pei of Singapore, and he is mentioned in prayers every new moon and full moon in two Taoist-Buddhist temples. As a gourmet, he cooks shark fin soup, sautées *bêche-de-mer* with black mushrooms, and steams "tea-smoked" duck. He declares that in addition to silk, gunpowder, and the magnetic compass, beautiful women were invented in China. Doubters are invited to meet him at dawn, on horse or afoot, with sword or pistol.